C000282712

THE EDGE OF THE BLADE

The Falkan castle of Tremellion is visited by the
mysterious Lord Vaulmier, Treasurer of the Crusade,
and his beautiful daughter Christiane de Magnat-
Vaulmier. Seeking finance for the Third Crusade
against Saladin, they negotiate with Sir Geoffrey
Falkan and inveigle all the Falkan fortune, to the
fury of Sir Geoffrey's elder son, Ranulf, who resolves
on patricide and ambushes the baggage train
carrying the treasure. Baynard Falkan, hero, younger
son and knight errant, is sent on his quest – to find
Christiane with whom he has become infatuated, to
avenge the bloody killing of his father, and to rescue
the treasure. Baynard, Guthric the Constable, and
Quillon the poacher travel through the
Mediterranean en route for the Holy Land,
encountering on their way picaresque characters,
pirates and bandits until they reach the Siege of
Jerusalem and the clutches of Ranulf and his men.
With a sensitive and inspired vision of the medieval
world, Graham Shelby weaves a tale of courtly love
and destiny in the great tradition of adventure.

About the author

Graham Shelby is author of several critically acclaimed historical novels. Having travelled widely in Europe and Africa, he now lives in an isolated farmhouse in the south of France. A confirmed medievalist, his previous novels include: THE KNIGHTS OF DARK RENOWN, THE KINGS OF VAIN INTENT, THE VILLAINS OF THE PIECE, THE DEVIL IS LOOSE and THE WOLF AT THE DOOR.

The Edge of
the Blade

Graham Shelby

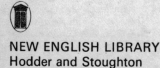

NEW ENGLISH LIBRARY
Hodder and Stoughton

Copyright © 1986 by Graham Shelby

First published in Great Britain in 1986 by New English Library

New English Library Paperback Edition, 1987

The characters and situations in this book are entirely imaginary and bear no relation to any real person or actual happening.

This book is sold subject to the condition that it shall not, by way of trade or otherwise, be lent, re-sold, hired out or otherwise circulated without the publisher's prior consent in any form of binding or cover other than that in which it is published and without a similar condition including this condition being imposed on the subsequent purchaser.

No part of this publication may be reproduced or transmitted in any form or by any means, electronically or mechanically, including photocopying, recording or any information storage or retrieval system, without either the prior permission in writing from the publisher or a licence, permitting restricted copying, issued by the Copyright Licensing Agency, 33–34 Alfred Place, London WC1E 7DP.

British Library C.I.P.

Shelby, Graham
  The edge of the blade.
  I. Title
  823'.914[F]   PR6069.H42

  ISBN 0-450-41733-6

Printed and bound in Great Britain for Hodder and Stoughton Paperbacks, a division of Hodder and Stoughton Ltd., Mill Road, Dunton Green, Sevenoaks, Kent TN13 2YA. (Editorial Office: 47 Bedford Square, London WC1B 3DP) by Richard Clay Ltd., Bungay, Suffolk.

for Bill and Anne,
Voyagers and harbourmasters both

CONTENTS

THE TRAVELS
OF
BAYNARD FALKAN
OF TREMELLION

INGDOM OF
HUNGARY

BYZANTINE

EMPIRE

BRINDISI

ARMENIA

CYPRUS

PAFOS

PALESTINE

CRETE

TYRE

ACRE

MEDITERRANEAN SEA

•JERUSALEM

PART ONE

The House of Tremellion

ONE

THE SITING of the castle had added two hours to his journey; the time it took to skirt around the bleak Cornish ridge. It was his grandfather's fault – well, no, entirely to the old man's credit – that Tremellion stood where it did. Its broad back to the north, the castle dominated the ridge. The base of its outer wall was planted sixty feet up from the Hexel River. The wall itself rose another twenty-two feet, its long northern side further strengthened by four semicircular towers. But only a madman – an army *commanded* by a madman – would attempt to scale that near vertical face.

Indeed, it would be lunacy to choose either route, for the now dead Sir William Falkan had, as was said, chosen his perch with care.

Nevertheless, admiration for Sir William's cunning found no place today in the travel-weary Baynard Falkan. He was soaked to the skin, his hands and face slapped raw by a bitter March wind, the nagging pain of toothache in his lower jaw. The nearest physician was, where? In Launceston? Too far away. No choice then but to submit to the less-than-tender mercies of Constable Guthric. Think of that and maybe the pain itself would cringe and grow quiet . . . .

Tremellion had never housed much by way of a garrison; few castles did. Fifty men was fifty mouths to feed, fifty bodies to be lodged, clothed, armed. It was unnecessary in time of peace, easy enough to recruit from the villages if war or menace loomed. A castle was not, after all, an hospice, and the ashlar blocks of Tremellion were its most daunting show of strength.

So Baynard's escort consisted of no more than five men-at-arms – a quarter of Tremellion's watchguards – and the two servants who occupied themselves with the baggage, the crude leather tents, the purchase and cooking of food. The tents had been pitched on a dozen separate occasions during Baynard's month-long absence, though part of the month had been spent at his destination, an island fortress off Cornwall's north-west coast. A memorable experience, once the choppy crossing had been made, for the castellan of Ardelet Island was an old friend of Baynard's father. They'd been on crusade

3

together, these two grizzled warriors, and the master of Ardelet had welcomed Sir Geoffrey's son. Eager questions were answered with a full and courteous response, and Baynard had been deemed worthy of further introduction to the household. This came in the shape – and the very shapely shape – of Ardelet's two young daughters, each of whom decided the tall, wiry visitor was for her. They set out to charm him, amuse him, impress him with their accomplishments – and all the while speak sweet poison of each other. Delighted to find himself in such fragrant demand, the young Baynard Falkan might have bedded them both, dreamed of it certainly, regretting the fact that the island baron was a friend and ally of Tremellion. He imagined how it might have been if . . . This girl tonight perhaps, that one . . . Or even, well, why not, it was possible, he was lusty enough, God knew, why not the three of them together, churning and writhing on a bed of skins and fur . . .

To hell with honour. Discipline be damned. Would Ranulf have withheld? *Cul de diable*, he would not! Given the chance, the merest whisper of a chance, and Baynard's hulking, self-serving brother took his pleasure wherever, whenever he could.

Wet through and whipped by the wind, the younger Falkan led his escort across the moorland and around the western base of the brutal ridge. He found fault with his grandfather for having positioned Tremellion so. Found fault with Sir Geoffrey for having instilled in him the precepts of knighthood. Felt ashamed of himself, remembering what Ardelet's daughters had asked him as he'd prepared to leave the island. One of them sidling close to inquire, 'These few scant days you've spent with us here, Sir Baynard. Is it truly *all* you've spent?' And then the other, softly edging him aside to murmur, 'You seem so complete in your bearing, Baynard Falkan. What a pity the weakness is so *very* well disguised.'

As for Ranulf, who might by now possess the county's most extensive collection of faults, vices, iniquities, sins and imperfections, it made Baynard grind his teeth – and wince as he enraged the ache – to realise he actually envied his elder brother. Not always. Indeed rarely. But at this moment, setting honour and duty in the scales, then balancing them with the imagined nakedness of the girls, then yes, just for the instant he saw a devilish wisdom in Ranulf's view of life.

By the time the travellers reached the entrance to the ravine, the elements of weather had combined to a harsh spring storm. Rain

4

flooded the southern side of the ridge, splashing up at the riders, buffeting their horses. The early evening sky was shutting up shop. Oddly, there was a mutter of appreciation from the escort, thankful that Baynard had driven them hard, goading them all day, bringing them home to Tremellion before dark.

But if home be thought of as the gateway to the castle, it was still a long way off. Not so far in distance, no more than two hundred yards, yet two hundred yards that exemplified Sir William's cunning, the talents of his architects, the skills of the Cornish masons.

Here, to the south, the ridge was partially severed by a deep, natural ravine. The floor of this gully sloped upward, its sides chipped smooth, offering nothing by way of a foothold to the invader. You would attempt to climb the steep granite ridge, or you would come along the cutting, the choice was yours. But once on the ridge, you would be vulnerable to arrow-shot from the wall, from the gatehouse, from the fists of the southern towers. Your ladders would slip on the escarpment, your flesh seared to the bone by boiling lead, tipped from large hinged cauldrons. Sharp-edged rocks would kill you outright, or smash you, horribly wounded, to the grassless foot of the slope. You would not, unless led by some madman, even attempt the ridge. All you would do – all you *could* do – was battle your way the length of the ravine.

If Tremellion was Sir William Falkan's finest achievement, the southern approach was his *chef d'oeuvre.* He'd found this term appropriate, for the fortifications of this minor Cornish castle had been inspired by one he'd seen in Southern France. A fortress built to withstand the ravages of the Moors, sweeping up through Spain. A frontier fortress, with a similar narrow approach, offering the enemy the same limited choice. Scale the rocks and perish in the attempt, or see how far you could get along the gully.

The problem was simple, the solution yet to be found, for the narrow upward cutting that led to Tremellion incorporated a series of walls. This one jutted from the righthand side, that from the left, forcing the attacker, even the visitor, even the homecoming Baynard and his men, to zig-zag their way around the end of one wall, cross the width of the ravine, then zig-zag again. And again around eight separate high stone hedges.

To make matters worse, an iron-strapped door closed off the entrance to the cutting, with a second door halfway up. Reduce them to splinters and you'd reach the upper end of the ravine – peering at the massive towers of the gatehouse, and trapped in a well of walls.

It had yet to be proved that anyone could enter Tremellion, without first being admitted by the Falkans.

But Baynard was recognised, the door held open, greetings voiced by the guards. Dulled with fatigue, he climbed from his horse, his link-mail hauberk heavy on his body, his linen surcoat drenched to a rag, the quilted undergarment wet and ponderous. He lifted his acorn-shaped helmet from his head, fished inside it for the cord, looped the leather thong around the pommel of his saddle. Pushing back the mail hood, and with it the hood of the gambeson, he let the cold rain drum the sweat of travel from his hair. He turned then to his escort, managed something of a smile and led them through the ascending alleys, guiding his horse, but allowing the palfrey to nudge him up the slopes.

Twenty years of age, the younger son of the Falkans of Tremellion, Baynard let the horse chest him forward, jolting his senses awake . . .

He'd done what he'd been sent to do, delivered a letter to the Lord of Ardelet . . .

Accepted a written reply . . . safe in his saddle-bag . . . addressed to Sir Geoffrey Falkan . . .

Enjoyed his stay on the island . . . Relished the company of the daughters . . . Suffered the ache in his groin . . . Suffered it worse when they'd said what they'd said . . . Not having *spent* himself . . . So *well* disguising his weakness . . .

But that was just a midden of a thing to say . . . What did they expect, those frivolous, flouncing women, that he should seduce the daughters of his father's lifelong friend? See the result of *that* next winter! The two girls, isolated on their island, each with an infant sired by Ardelet's guest! Try explaining *that* to their father! Try explaining it to his *own* father! Where then the precepts of knighthood?

The palfrey continued to chest him up the ramps. Guards signalled a welcome from the second iron-strapped door. It pleased them to see Baynard home again. A decent young fellow, Baynard Falkan. He held honour well. But what a blighted shame he wouldn't inherit Tremellion. It'd go to Ranulf, of course. Had to; had to go to the elder son. Point of law; tradition; the way it always was . . .

Baynard stumbled on the rough-hammered cobbles of the ramp. Pain jarred through his body, found its way upward and set the tooth

6

in his jaw dancing with agony . . . It reminded him of the man he most respected in the world. After the recently crowned King Richard, of course. And the heroes of the Crusades. And the heroes of legend. And Sir William Falkan. And his father, Sir Geoffrey, though admiration was mingled with love, that was the difference . . .

But the man Baynard most respected was the Constable of Tremellion, the more-or-less-forty-year-old chewed and scarred assembly of muscle that was Guthric. Unsure of his age, he possessed less imagination than a backward flea, less knowledge of poetry and music than an ill-tempered brachet hound. His humour swung from the gallows, his opinions of the world as rough and pitted as his own pock-marked skin. There was no profit in trading wit with Constable Guthric; he'd take what was offered and crush it beneath the heel of his dour response.

And yet his values were hard to fault. Foremost among them was his loyalty to Sir Geoffrey, the protection of Tremellion, the hard, unyielding eye he cast upon Ranulf and Baynard. Ranulf had learned to sneer at Guthric, talk of him as a worn-out creature, a remnant who'd outlived his time. But this same sneering Ranulf had never said as much to Guthric's face . . . Wouldn't dare to . . . Who in all of England would be quite as stupid as that?

The gatehouse loomed. A clever gatehouse, since an attacking force would have to follow a turn in the wall, the sudden angle jamming their approach to the eastern bailey. And all the while, above their heads they'd find *meurtrières*, murder-holes through which the defenders would loose their arrows, drip the ghastly, flesh-corroding lead . . .

Baynard led his companions through the arch below the portcullis, around the righthand turn of the tunnel, out into the bailey. The palfrey gave him a final nudge and he caressed the animal, wiping the rain from its muzzle. He didn't expect his father to venture out in such dismal weather; knew for certain his brother wouldn't trouble to do so. As for Guthric, well, Guthric was probably busy –

'You got back all of a piece then. There's visitors here, Sir Baynard, come from Outremer. Pity you wasn't home afore midday, 'stead of dawdling down from the coast. Been nice to have seen the Falkans out to greet 'em. The best food's been eaten, though you might find something set by for you in the kitchen.'

And there he was, the grim, indestructible Guthric. Set like some snouty bear in the entrance to the guardhouse, his massive frame tented in a peaked leather hood that spilled to form a cloak. He gazed unblinking at Tremellion's younger son, ignoring the sag of Baynard's shoulders, his admission of fatigue.

A month away, and the dark-skinned Baynard wanted to tell the constable he was pleased to be home. But Guthric would shrug the sentiment aside – a month away and Baynard was half a day late. Hadn't got back in time to greet the travellers from Palestine. So Baynard let his greeting go unspoken, and asked instead who they were, these overseas callers.

'They hadn't stated their business when I left 'em,' the constable growled. 'But my guess is they're recruiting. Men or money. They're acting so polite with Sir Geoffrey, there's bound to be a begging bowl brought out.'

'Will you see to the horses,' Baynard said. 'I've a letter should be delivered to my father.' He unstrapped the saddle-bag, a protective pouch for Ardelet's reply.

Guthric turned aside, barking a command to someone inside the guardhouse. A man emerged, nodded at Baynard, caught at the bridle of his horse. The weary young Falkan started through the muddy spread of the bailey, halting when he heard the constable add his name. 'There's a young woman with them. Better you should show you're half alive than look half dead.' Then he barked again at the ostler, leaving Baynard Falkan to make of that what he would.

The ravine maze was not the only barrier Sir William had devised against a would-be attacker.

Once through the gatehouse you were in the eastern bailey, the long outer yard of the castle. Swarm across it and all you'd take were the stables, the chapel, one of Tremellion's three wells. You'd kill some of the garrison – those in the gatehouse, the guardhouse – but all the while you would be prey to the shafts loosed from the towers and the curtain wall.

The same height as the outer walls of the fortress, the curtain cut Tremellion neatly in half. Angling a little off-centre from the north wall to the southern gatehouse, it contained its own fortified entrance. Seize the eastern bailey, and you were only halfway home.

Baynard tramped through the entranceway, followed the wide stone path to the lake, crossed the wooden bridge and climbed the final ramp to the solid, rectangular keep. A moment's pause and he was admitted to the damp, unwelcoming structure that was home to the Falkans. Here, beyond the portcullis and double-barred doors of the keep, he was faced with a choice. Climb the spiral stairs on the left to the Great Hall of the castle, or the narrower spiral on the right that led up to his chamber. Grunting a reply to the watchguard's greeting, he gestured to the man to unlock the door to the private stairs. Then he toiled his way upward, clutching at the newel post, feeling the beads of wetness that exuded from the stones. Thirty-six steps – always spiralling right so a defender could use his sword, an attacker forced to switch hands – and he emerged in a narrow passageway, illuminated by a single bracket torch.

The first door on the left admitted to his own bachelor room. Opposite was Ranulf's chamber, the widower Sir Geoffrey's at the end of the passage. This last chamber was extensive, shared until three years ago by Sir Geoffrey and the Lady Elena. But the Greek-born mother of Ranulf and Baynard had died, along with countless thousands of others, in the winter epidemic of 1187, leaving the Lord of Tremellion to prowl the quarters, alone.

Entering his own austere cell, Baynard's sole desire was to drop the saddle-bag, divest himself of the heavy, link-mail hauberk, unlace the quilted gambeson and stretch out on the narrow, leather-braced bed. Surely Ardelet's letter could wait till tomorrow. Surely too, the youngest of the Falkans would not be needed when the begging bowl was passed around by the visitors from distant Outremer.

On the other hand, there was the thing Guthric had told him; the remark that he'd better look half alive than half dead, for a woman was with them, across there in the Hall. Not just any woman. The constable wouldn't send him to meet some thrice-married hag. What the Saxon had meant was that Baynard would do well to summon his energies, perch with the other Falkans – and see for himself if the visitor took his fancy.

He struck a flint, touched a taper to the spark, carried the flame to a squat, ringed candle. By the time he had stripped, sluiced his body from a basin of cold water, raked his hair with an ebony comb and dressed in a plain, belted shift, dry shoes and a mantle pinned at the shoulders, the candle had burned a quarter of its way to the next hour-mark ring.

Very well. So he'd miss what was left of the food. But at least he'd deliver Ardelet's letter to Sir Geoffrey. And meet the foreigners. *And* see the woman Guthric had slyly recommended. Not that some daughter of Palestine would be a match for the girls he'd – only just – resisted on that rocky offshore island. Most likely her skin would be burned to a crust by the sun, the whites of her eyes tinged grey.

9

Her teeth would be good, he'd heard that the women of the East had excellent teeth, but the last thing he needed tonight was a dazzling reminder that his own hurt like the devil.

Yet curiosity drove him and, pinching the candle, he made his way along the passage that skirted his father's quarters, emerging in the high, arched entranceway that led through to the Great Hall of Tremellion.

TWO

It was sheer bad luck that Ranulf saw him first. Seated at the far side of a long refectory table, Baynard's brother was slumped in his chair, his impassive features gelid with boredom. His gaze was turned upward to, what? A cluster of bats in the rafters? The drifting patterns of smoke that rose from the fire-pit? Unfortunately, the object of his indifferent gaze was directly above the archway, so Baynard's arrival caught his attention.

Ranulf rocked forward in his chair, right arm extended, spatulate fingers curled to a pointing fist. 'Surprise guest at the banquet! D'you see him? Come to liven the proceedings, brother? You see him, my lord? The messenger back from Marathon!'

Baynard counted seven of them at the table; grouped at one end of it of course, for the massive oak planks ran for more than twenty feet along the centre of the Hall. Sir Geoffrey was at the head of the table, Ranulf to his right, a skinny, bald-pated cleric farther along from Ranulf. The cleric had pulled himself close to the table, a scrawny bird surrounded by a nest of quills, inkwells, a jar of sand, sheets of parchment, some of them stitched together, others yet to bear his painstaking scrawl.

At the other side of the table, and for the moment with their backs to Baynard Falkan, sat a finely-dressed man, a woman beside him, a second woman, then a scribe who, at first glance, Baynard took for an Arab. It was hard to tell from the vantage point of the archway, but the Moorish scribe seemed content with a single inkwell, a single quill, a single sheet of paper.

But by now heads were turning, Baynard advancing to greet the assembly. He bowed courteously to Sir Geoffrey and stood there as the warlord rose from his chair. The man was fifty years of age, old for his time. His body was scarred by wounds he'd received in the East, his left eye clouded, less alert than his right. His movements were slow now, yet his grasp was still firm and he caught his son in a heavy, bearlike embrace. As for the brothers, their greeting was achieved with the murmur of Ranulf's name and, on Ranulf's part, something less than a nod.

'It went well?' Sir Geoffrey growled. 'No rats to nip you on the way?'

'Felons in ambush, and the like? No, my lord, though we started a boar and its sow up near Marnham. Gave them a chase –'

'And missed them both?'

'And missed them both,' Baynard admitted. 'And went hungry that night, by result.'

Pleased to have Baynard back with him, Sir Geoffrey said, 'They've a damned quick speed to 'em, those tusky pigs.' The man on his left nodded polite accord. Ranulf Falkan shrugged.

Aware that protracted delay would be impolite to the visitors, Baynard said quickly, 'I've a letter from the master of Ardelet, my lord. He did not discuss its contents with me, though I'm to tell you his response is favourable. He instructs me to tell you "Yes".'

'Well, now,' Sir Geoffrey acknowledged, turning to address the others. 'Is that not what I told you before? Worth your time to go up there. I'll read his reply later, and you shall have whatever details he mentions before you leave. But first, I'd present to you my younger son, visibly wearied by his travels.' The implied criticism jerked Baynard to attention. It was true; he was bone-tired and his tooth ached and he wished himself in bed and in dreamless sleep. But Guthric, blast him, had sparked his curiosity, and now that he *was* here he'd best do what the constable suggested – look half alive, rather than demi-dead.

The man who was seated at Sir Geoffrey's left came easily to his feet. He was taller than the warlord, taller than either Ranulf or Baynard, though he matched the younger Falkan in the leanness of his build. Aristocratic in his bearing, he wore a long, pale linen tunic, its hem embroidered with gold and crimson thread. The tunic was loosely gathered at the waist, the supple leather belt knotted in place of a buckle. His surcoat was shorter – part gown, part mantle – the silk-trimmed garment lined with fur. It was held at the left shoulder by an ornate silver brooch and turned back to give freedom to his sword arm. He inclined his head in a bow to Baynard, then identified himself in a calm, clear voice.

'Gilles de Magnat-Vaulmier, Duc de Querinard, Comte d'Almé, on commission from the Christian Lords of Outremer and, *hélas*, the sadly-lost Jerusalem. You may or may not have heard it from the guards, Sir Baynard, but I lead what might be termed a mendicant expedition. My lords of the Christian Kingdom have sent me to beg for funds.' He said it without apology, his tone devoid of arrogance. That was the way it was and Baynard now knew it, take it or leave it be.

Young Falkan thought Magnat-Vaulmier just about perfect for the task he'd been empowered to undertake. His presence commanded respect – by God, he was tall enough for it – and the nobleman was a world away from the stuffed-bellied bishops and weasely officials who traipsed the length and breadth of England, soliciting coin.

Another thing; he had a wry sense of humour, this Magnat-Vaulmier, guessing correctly that word was already around. What was it Guthric had said? 'They're acting so polite with Sir Geoffrey, there's bound to be a begging bowl brought out.' The constable was right, and Magnat-Vaulmier had recognised it, and now he'd pitched his approach correctly. We are beggars, yes, but beggars for the Cause. The Christian Cause in Palestine. The greatest Cause the West has ever known.

'With your permission, Sir Baynard, I'd present these other self-invited guests at your father's table.' He caught Sir Geoffrey's eye, smiled as the warlord said, 'Invited and welcome, my Lord Vaulmier.' Then, with a fine match of courtesy and dismissal, murmured something about the scribe, something about the chaperone, his comments seeming to please them, yet leaving them seated where they were.

After which, there only remained the young woman. The one Guthric had recommended. The one Magnat-Vaulmier now introduced as his daughter. 'As travel-weary as yourself, I daresay, Sir Baynard, though embarked on a somewhat longer journey. Her name is Christiane.'

So much for the stupid mental sketch he'd drawn in his room. So much for the sun-crusted skin, the dull opaqueness of her eyes. So much for all his jaundiced expectations of the foreigner.

This one – this travel-weary daughter of the well-tempered Vaulmier – well, now that he could see her clearly, he felt a surge of pity for the girls on Ardelet's island.

She extended her hand, palm downwards, and he bowed to take it, though not daring to touch her fingers with his lips. He stared at her, heard his inner voice soundlessly query: *Is that how it's done? Seemingly no twitch of the line, yet the fish is hauled in silent shock to the bank?*

His mind attempted to register the myriad aspects of her beauty. But the candlelit colours of the mosaic refused to form. The fineness of her features . . . the unflecked blue of her eyes . . . her fingers, long and elegant . . . pale hair tressed . . . the yellow and silver thread of her bodice fused by the breath beneath it into gold . . .

He managed, 'My Lady Christiane.'

Listened to the low pitch of her voice as she murmured, 'My Lord Falkan.'

Then watched as she turned away, the woman making no attempt at all to conceal her absolute lack of interest in Tremellion, the proceedings, or the wiry young man who'd been hooked ashore, struck by a *coup de foudre*, the thunderbolt that signifies love at first sight.

He forced himself to sit shoulder to shoulder with Ranulf, dragging his chair alongside the brother he despised. He was deeply fatigued, his sense of balance tilted, but when Christiane yawned, her fingers fluttering as a fan toward her mouth, Baynard wanted to bring it to Vaulmier's notice. 'Your daughter is weary, sire! A paragon of beauty and you'd let the clouds of lassitude shadow her brow?'

Thank God the young Falkan didn't give voice to his thoughts, but contented himself with gazing at Christiane. There were more important things to be discussed than the idiotic feelings of a lovelorn knight . . .

With Sir Geoffrey's willing agreement, Magnat-Vaulmier offered to give a brief resumé of his business in England – this for the late-comer's benefit.

Meanwhile, Christiane's chaperone divided her attentions between Baynard and her charge. He wasn't the first to be smitten, this lean young Cornishman, and he wouldn't be the last. Even so, he'd bear watching, for what was it the poet said? 'Lust and love stand hand in glove; yet the sinful serpent far below the dove.' It would mean another sleepless night, this one in damp Tremellion, but the chaperone would see to it that the Lady Christiane slept undisturbed.

The cleric and the scribe stopped writing.

Already bored by what the aristocratic beggar had to say, Ranulf went back to his abstracted study of the smoke that wreathed the rafters.

But Baynard leaned forward, nodding his thanks at Magnat-Vaulmier. It was good of the man to repeat what he'd told the others, though Falkan was forced to conceal a smile of admiration. A true salesman, the Duc de Querinard, Comte d'Almé, on commission

14

from the Lords of Outremer. Tell the story twice, why not, and hammer the message home . . .

'You will know, my lords, of the situation here. King Henry dead, his son Richard crowned seven months ago in London. You will also know the new king has sworn to lead a crusade in God's Holy Land. Less well bruited is the fact that we've lost Jerusalem, that most sacred city, to the brilliant strategist *Salah ed-Din Yusuf, al-Malik un-Nasir* – the name that sits better on our tongue as Saladin. His religion is that of the Devil, but – it has to be admitted – he is himself the devil of a commander. Two years gone, and the Crusader force is pinned to the hem of the coast. He massacred our armies at Hattin, drove us from every frontier castle, and is now set fair to make us swim from the beaches. Germany drives against him, as does France under *their* king, Philip Augustus. Richard vows to lead the English in the mightiest effort yet. But to do so he needs the ships, the *matériel*, everything in short from tents to trebuchets. There are leaders enough – I'm inclined to think *too many* jarring leaders. And, now the Church has eased its rules, opening the gates of heaven to all who take part in the Crusade, we are not short of able-bodied men.

'But money – yes, that *is* in short supply.' Then he broke off, smiled briefly and shook his head. He asked the assembly if word had reached Cornwall of King Richard's recent cry. 'It may not be true,' Lord Vaulmier told them, 'though it sounds like Richard, like him to the life. Supposed to have been counting up the money with his chancellors, aumoniers and the rest, when he fisted the table and yelled to the heavens, "All the things a monarch might sell! By God, I'd sell the city of London itself if I could find a buyer!" Who can say if he meant it? But knowing the man England's taken for its king, I'd hazard this bullish giant would trade your great island itself, if it gained him Jerusalem. Mark me as a critic if you will, my lords, but Richard of England is an oddity among men.'

Magnat-Vaulmier reached for his goblet of dark, Cahors wine, brought it to his lips, eyed the Falkans of Tremellion. He decided he was speaking to one of them, maybe two. Certainly to Sir Geoffrey, who had already seen service overseas. And in part he was speaking to Baynard, though he could sense where the young Falkan's interests truly lay; more with Christiane than Christendom. As for Lord Ranulf, one wouldn't expect so much as a tarnished groat from the man. If money was to be forthcoming from Tremellion it would not be thanks to Sir Geoffrey's elder son.

Hair grey, face lined by life, the Cornish warlord thanked his guest for his reprise of the situation.

'What you tell us is clear enough, Lord Vaulmier. Our armies are in desperate plight. For myself, I'd rather be barred from Heaven than see the Holy Land go to the devil. Mayhap you'll think my views simple, but I've held staunch to them through all the years of my life. The True God belongs to the Christian faith. And that resides in the West. It was, as we know from our teachings, born in Palestine, spread across the Mediterranean, found favour in all of Europe. Well, perhaps not in every corner, but as far as the broom can reach.

'It is *we* who weep for the blood of Christ, treasure the bones of His saints, kneel at His command. Without our firm belief in salvation we are no more than animals – the tusky pigs my son failed to catch near Marnham; fish down there in the Hexel. We are no more than vermin. No more than industrious spiders, knitting for mindless flies.'

Baynard listened, his gaze directed at his father. He could not remember a time when Sir Geoffrey's voice had been so resonant, each word stamped with clarity, measured to a rhythm. It would have suited the younger Falkan if the warlord had spoken till dawn.

But Sir Geoffrey was tiring fast, his clouded eye blinking. He lost his train of thought, repeated what he'd said about the spiders, then rallied to look directly at his visitor.

'So I'll tell you – repeat what my old friend Ardelet's told *me*. Yes, my Lord Vaulmier. Glancing at the letter he sent me, yes, we are both agreed. You shall have what you came for.'

Tremellion's visitor was no fool. He had made his plea, won his case, heard Sir Geoffrey Falkan mould his final strength of the night into a vow. *You shall have what you came for.* There was no need to push for details. Tomorrow would do as well.

Magnat-Vaulmier stood up, assisted his daughter, waited for the chaperone and scribe to leave the table. Then he nodded at Ranulf and Baynard, deepened his nod to a bow at Sir Geoffrey and murmured to the warlord, 'Tremellion was ever high on the Christian list, my Lord Falkan. It might please you to know you were noted down before I even set sail from Tyre. Oh, yes, and Ardelet too.'

It did please the warlord to learn it, for it meant he was still remembered out there; a long-ago Crusader who'd had nothing to offer in those distant days but his faith and honour and courage; universal currency, though it lacked the chink of coin.

*

16

Baynard started to his feet, eager to bid Christiane goodnight. No, not that at all, but to catch her eye, hear her speak to him, earn himself a smile he could stitch into sleep.

But her chaperone was already guiding the woman away, the two of them ignoring Baynard, yet, oh yes, smiling at the warlord.

The youngest of the Falkans called after them, 'Sleep well, my Lord Vaulmier, my Lady Christiane.' Then watched in despair, seeing the words fall short of their target, his call so uncertain it dipped the flight of his voice.

He waited as Tremellion's cleric gathered the nest of his tools. It seemed to take an age before the wizened bird scuttled from the Hall. Then Baynard walked slowly around the head of the table, passed behind his father, settled himself in the chair Lord Vaulmier had vacated. Ranulf sat across from him, his ponderous features hammered to a scowl. Unwilling to look at each other, the sons of Tremellion turned their attention to Sir Geoffrey, the man who must now explain what he'd meant by his promise to the beggars from abroad.

Ranulf jerked a thumb in the direction of the spiral stairs that led to the topmost floor of the keep. 'I can bear it that we house them tonight, and even accept they've been fed three kinds of meat. But I'd hear somewhat more from you, sire – a damn sight more, may it please you – about this money you say you'll drop in Palestine's purse.'

He glared with open animosity at his father. 'Call it Tremellion's money if you will, but let's not leave it at that. It's mine too, remember. Mine by interest and inheritance! So let's hear an explanation, my lord. Let's hear what you mean when you say they'll have what they came for. Have *what*, beyond their food and lodging, and a swollen purse of coins?'

Baynard said, 'Be calm, brother Ranulf. These things are best discussed, not disputed.' Then he flinched and stared hard as Ranulf swung toward him, telling the younger Falkan to hold his tongue, bite off the end of it, shut his ears and nail his blasted lips. It was nothing to Baynard *where* the money went. He was low on the list, and might as well be abed as sitting this out. 'Why not crawl under the coverlet, brother, and work at yourself as you dream of Christiane? You made a sufficient fool of yourself, gawping at her, so why not go and seek your own release?'

Ranulf's evident anger served to infuriate his father, incense the lovelorn Baynard. The Lord of Tremellion drove himself from his chair, Baynard likewise coming erect. There was a moment of confusion, the nobility of Tremellion trading insults and warnings, the brothers drawn close to physical violence, their father growling at them.

'Get you apart, and be seated! God's eyes, but don't you know how sound can travel? You, sir, have a regard for your language! As for you, my jumpy Baynard, reclaim your chair and keep it!' He glared at his sons as they glared at each other, Ranulf by far the stronger in physique, Baynard convinced his brother was nothing but shout.

The fifty-year-old Sir Geoffrey Falkan remained on his feet, wagged a warning hand at Baynard, then turned to deal with Ranulf.

'You say your brother is low on the list – a cruel observation, but true. He stands to gain nothing from Tremellion, a second son, but don't you suppose he knows it?'

With a glance at Baynard, Ranulf said, 'I'm sure he can bear reminding.'

After that, the youngest Falkan was forgotten. He could not be sure if a war was drawing to its close, armies brought into final conflict by the calm requests of a nobleman turned beggar. Or maybe it had to come anyway; the eruptive anger of the elder son; the final, familial swing of the warlord's power.

'I want to know,' Ranulf bored, 'how you plan to pay off Vommier, whatever-his-name-is, and his gypsies. Not to upset you, sweet father, but you'll be gone from here one day. Gone to the scented Heaven you believe in. The great Sir Geoffrey Falkan, Lord of Tremellion, warrior in Palestine, loving husband of the dark-skinned Greek he tumbled across – excuse me, wooed and courted – pleased and brought home from some island in the East. A romantic story, it calls for flowers, what a pity it's not yet the season. But beyond all that –' his voice was as hard as boiled leather – 'I need to know which trinkets you plan to give away for the sake of the Christian Cause. You're an old man now, let me say this to you, and no doubt charmed that your name's remembered away across the seas. But that was then. All that matters now is what you plan here. So why don't you dictate me a list of the trinkets, and I'll call our twittering cleric from his bed.' He was speaking more calmly now. Smiling at his father. Motioning him to be seated and reaching to pour him wine.

So it startled Ranulf when the warlord roared in his face.

'*You* be seated! *You*, who can't even pronounce the name of – This

18

nobleman comes hundreds, thousands of miles on his mission, and *you* –' then turned away, swinging back as Ranulf's buttocks stretched the leather of his chair.

'Young Baynard here – yes, that's true, he's out of it. And also true I'll soon be gone, pray God, to that scented Heaven you suppose. But until the last should happen – are you listening, Sir Ranulf? – Until I die I'm the Lord of Tremellion. Suzerain of the castle. Master of the surrounding villages. Overseer of all the lands and rivers for a damn fair stretch. And not only that – *sweet son* – but I'm guardian of Tremellion's treasures; its jewels and coins and plate. Bury me when you can, my dear Ranulf, but until that happy day greets you it is *I* who control the fortunes of this distant, Cornish domain. And as such,' he measured slowly, 'decide.'

Unmoving in the candlelight, Baynard felt himself distanced from the table, hidden and ignored in the smoke. He could not even guess what his father would say, though he supposed it would bring a squawk of anger from Ranulf.

'You ask me what trinkets I plan to give to the Cause? What proportion of our wealth? You tell me I'll soon be gone, and that's likely true. So I'd better hurry things on.'

He turned then to Baynard, Sir Geoffrey's good eye glaring bright as a beacon, his clouded twin closed by his eyelid. 'As for you,' he said, 'you know what you've been given.' Then turned to Ranulf to tell him it was not a question of trinkets. Nor a proportion of Tremellion's treasure. Apart from the castle itself – and its grounds – it was everything, each chest of coins, box of jewellery, sack or container of plate.

With a bitter, victorious grin, Tremellion spelt it out for Tremellion.

'Don't concern yourself with proportion, my dear Ranulf. I intend to give it all.'

In the extended silence that followed, all one could hear was the spit and crackle of logs. Then the wind, scudding through the arrow-loops. Then the creaks and whispers of the castle. Water dripped. A guard shouted, far away in the bailey. The painted leather curtains billowed against the walls.

Then Ranulf wrapped his muscular hands around the carved-wood arms of his chair. Pushed himself slowly, ominously to his feet. Passed his gaze like a sword-swipe across Baynard and inflicted the full hatred of his expression upon his father.

'Did I *hear* you aright? *All* of it?'

'Except for the castle itself, and –'

'But the rest? The money and –?'

'Such as it is.'

'You'd dare – you'd dare give away the things that have belonged to this family –'

'And now to me – oh, yes, most certainly I would. All the moveable wealth. It goes this very week to Plymouth. Lord Vaulmier informs me there's a fleet assembled in port, its destination the Holy Land. I intend to see the treasure sails with those ships.'

Ranulf Falkan's right hand rose in the hammer of a fist. Baynard lurched forward, reaching to intercept it, caught it in time to deflect the blow from Sir Geoffrey's impassive face. By way of recompense, Ranulf used the point of his left elbow as a bludgeon, slamming it high against the side of his brother's skull. Baynard staggered from the blow, lost his balance and went down in an unseemly heap on the floor. Ranulf snarled something unintelligible at Sir Geoffrey, strode from the table, swept his way from the Hall. The Lord of Tremellion was not to know it, but he would never again set eyes upon his firstborn son.

They would however, one final time, come close . . .

THREE

DAZED AND groaning, Baynard climbed unsteadily to his feet. He thought it typical of Ranulf to hit him in such a way that the ache in his head had magically fired the pain in his lower jaw. Avaricious in everything else, brother Ranulf was generous enough when it came to violence.

He groped for a chair, then obediently drained the goblet his father passed him.

Sir Geoffrey waited, gazing at the pain-drawn features of the younger Falkan. From the day of Baynard's birth – more realistically from the time the boy had outlived the sicknesses of infancy – the Lord of Tremellion had been aware his second son could not, under the law, inherit the castle. It would go to Ranulf, who would probably give Baynard a palfrey and a pack-horse, and half a morning in which to quit his lands.

Yet the warlord had realised there *were* things he could offer the child, the youth, the boy growing to manhood – opportunities that would be spurned by the dull-witted Ranulf.

At the age of ten, Baynard had been sent to serve as a squire in a nobleman's household near Winchester. Two summers later and he'd sailed with the fishermen off the Irish coast. The following year he was in Paris, studying architecture under the renowned Monsieur le Bey. Then back to England for a term of military strategy, six months of mind-goading theory, back-breaking practice in the Norfolk fens.

Finally, Sir Geoffrey had summoned his son to Tremellion. Not to remain there, but to hear what his father had in mind.

'I have discussed things at length with the Lady Elena. Nothing would gladden us so much as to have you here, though it would be for our own selfish pleasure. The truth of the matter – and I'll say it bluntly – is that Tremellion has no need of another official, an administrator, for that's the role you would play. I have a fair grasp of the problems here, and I can count on Guthric, to a lesser degree on Ranulf. But more than that, Tremellion would . . . stifle you . . . curtail your education . . . In plain, it would bring your mind to its knees.' He smiled at the odd imagery of the remark, then issued a challenge he himself had devised.

'Two months ago you entered your seventeenth year. From what I've heard you're quick to sponge up knowledge – and a sight too quick when it comes to clever ripostes. Keep a guard on your tongue, young Baynard. Impudence is best left to jesters and silly girls.' He paused to let the lesson sink home, then went on, 'You look fit enough, if a mite too skinny, and I'm told you do well at the quintain, equally so with a sword. So here's what I suggest. Leave England again and spend the next twelve months where you will. I'll equip you with a single outfit of clothes, helmet and hauberk, a pair of well-fitting boots. You may choose whichever horse you like from the stables, and I'll see your passage paid from one of the Channel ports. But after that, you tread your own path. You speak *only* the language of the country you are in, and you do not leave that country owing so much as a groat. Or whatever in hell their equivalent coins might be!' A brief smile, quickly gone, and Sir Geoffrey Falkan had waited for Baynard's response.

'In the matter of the horse,' the young man had murmured. 'Will you allow me Abaris, my lord?'

'The one *I'd* have chosen, were I as wiry as you. Ask Guthric for one of those saddles that come from Spain.'

But all that had happened three-turning-four years back. The man who now slumped wearily in his chair, head aching, tooth raging, had run the gamut of education, tasted the fruits of adventure, haltingly spoken the languages of his travels. He was here tonight to witness, it seemed, the decline in Tremellion's fortunes.

He had not expected it to be like this. Nor, in truth, had Sir Geoffrey. As for Ranulf, he had probably stormed from the castle and would soon be visiting his fury on one of his whores, down there in the village.

Growling low, the Lord of Tremellion said, 'Rather than let you retire . . . I can see you have had your fill of this day, but can you find the strength to answer me? Am I right to give those courteous beggars what they ask?'

Before he spoke, Baynard Falkan took a moment to search his soul. The easy answer was yes. It was a cause Sir Geoffrey had fought for, the Greatest Cause in Christendom, the Crusade that came near to unifying the West. And yes, because it was so satisfyingly *right* to see the lumpen, self-centred Ranulf denied the fortune he'd thought to inherit.

The obvious answer, quick and correct, was yes. The Lady Elena had been dead these past three years, so the warlord was free to do as he wished with what was his. See it from any vantage, and the answer *had* to be yes.

Yet Baynard believed he owed his father more than simply accord. It was Sir Geoffrey's decision, this desire to impoverish Tremellion and, by doing so, help enrich the Cause. A man who was courageous enough to part with all but the stones of his castle did not need to be reminded that one son would bellow 'No!', the other murmur 'Yes'.

'You will do what you will, my lord. Why else be the master of the house?'

The ageing Sir Geoffrey let his breath sigh out in agreement. Then he refilled Baynard's goblet, ignored his son's gesture of refusal, told the young Falkan he'd already sneaked a glance at Ardelet's letter. 'It seems you were somewhat plagued by his pretty daughters. Yet behaved with – what's the phrase he used? – a certain circumspection?'

'You'll forgive me, father. I've a tooth that's rotting in my jaw. Ranulf appears to have loosened whatever is inside my skull. I'm really no longer worthy of your time.'

'Don't make such a fuss, boy. Guthric will pull the tooth for you tomorrow. Your head will heal, you'll be prancing around by noon. You've given me the answer I wanted, and now I've some news to warm you. It's true I sent you to Ardelet with a message, and I'm pleased by his reply. But it's not the only reason I dispatched you to that Godforsaken island. He asked me to do so. Asked me to send my younger son . . . so he . . . and his girls . . .'

Baynard's eyes brightened in alarm. Then the mists of discomfort closed in again, and he groaned with freshening pain.

Unfeeling, Sir Geoffrey lumbered on. 'The thing of it is, he'd have you for a son-in-law. Grant you half his properties on the mainland. Thinks rather well of you, does Ardelet. Even goes so far as to say – wait, let me find it – "Of no great importance which of them he chooses, since they seem equal in their endeavour to be his bride." You're well liked up there, Sir Baynard.'

The young man floundered for an expression that would somehow convey his feelings. How to show that he'd willingly have bedded those nubile girls, dreamed of bedding them *both*, but hadn't done so, honour forbidding. Though that wasn't what worried him now. It

23

was nothing to do with Ardelet's daughters, quickly forgotten in the light of –

'Christiane de Magnat-Vaulmier?'

'What? I beg your pardon, my lord, but – what?'

'Here's a promise,' Sir Geoffrey measured. 'The moment I've finished speaking, you and your head and your tooth may clamber off to bed. But it's rare we get the chance to mull things over, and I've a feeling that with Ranulf's departure tonight . . .

'Well, be that as it may . . . I want you to know that if *this* eye of mine is chalky, the other's clear as day. You've been snared, my son, gutted and filleted and hung up to smoke by Vaulmier's young offspring. You'll be up betimes tomorrow, lurking about, thinking to come across her by carefully managed chance. The ache in your tooth will have gone. You'll strive to amuse her, howl at her humour where the merest smile would have done, brush invisible cobwebs from her path. And then, my boy, my dear Sir Baynard, do you know what you will do?'

'The way you tell it, my lord, I'll come to you for direction.'

Sir Geoffrey's scarred and life-worn face turned young there, for an instant, his lips stretched in a smile of pure good nature. 'I'll keep the door open for you! I'll even, if you like, hiss you some lines!' He filled his chair, loving the scene he knew would be enacted in the morning. 'What you'll do,' he predicted, 'is make a vow to your sweet Christiane. To see her again. To travel as far as love might require. In short, my young whippet, you will set out on Crusade to the Kingdom of Jerusalem, if not for the sake of Christendom, then certainly in pursuit of Christiane.'

Next morning, the young Tremellion was up betimes, the pain in his tooth forgotten. Shaved in such haste – and insufficient candlelight – that the blade had nicked his chin, he lurked for a while near the spiral stairs that led up to the guest rooms and the solar.

Aware he'd look foolish if Lord Vaulmier was the first to descend, he wandered down to the kitchens, helped himself to a mug of hot, spiced ale, chewed on a piece of stale black bread. Chewed on it! And his tooth didn't hurt at all!

Then he trudged upstairs again, taking care not to sweep the damp stones of the staircase with his best – though summer-wear – mantle. No matter that he was near to freezing, a spiteful mid-March wind scouring the castle.

He stood around – lurked *was* the word – in the Great Hall as the

24

servants raked the ashes from the fire-pit, laid the kindling, arranged fresh logs in place. He told them to bring mulled ale to the table – 'And mulled wine, and some decent cuts of beef and – well, everything Tremellion's guests might enjoy.'

One of the servants was brave enough to tell him the guests were still asleep, no sound from their chambers, so if the heated drinks were served now –

'Bring them anyway! What's the matter, you can't *keep* them heated?'

He told them to change the straw around the table.

He kicked impatiently at one of Tremellion's scavenging dogs.

And was watching the animal yelp away as Christiane de Magnat-Vaulmier asked if he had a special dislike of animals, or in particular the ribby English hound?

The shadows of fatigue had disappeared. Her gown was a mixture of green and cinnamon and white. His favourite colours, he decided, though he hadn't given much thought to it before. Nor had he liked plaits too well, yet liked them well enough now.

He invited her to be seated, then bawled at the servants to serve.

She asked about Ranulf and he scowled abruptly, telling her he thought, indeed he was sure, Ranulf had left the castle and wouldn't be back for days.

She fanned at the smoke as the wind blew it low across the Hall. Reaching forward, he flapped it away.

God, she is beautiful . . .

Less bored than before, she seemed content to be with him. Thanked him for saving her from the smoke, told him an amusing story about how once, in a castle in Palestine, the weather squashing the clouds . . .

He howled with laughter, remembered what he'd heard, trimmed his amusement to a smile.

And so it went on, this dawn-in-springtime courtship, this wooing of Christiane de Magnat-Vaulmier by Baynard Falkan, younger son of Tremellion.

'But to understand the true situation,' the woman murmured, 'one has really to visit the seat of Christ's Great Kingdom.'

Sweet Heaven, she is beautiful . . .

'My own description, and dare I say even my father's, are inadequate to convey to you –'

Her voice is nothing less, not a chime below the carillon of bells . . .

'It's a shame your duties tie you to Tremellion, my Lord Baynard.

A fine young knight, less imprisoned by a sense of servitude than yourself –'

'You misunderstand, Lady Christiane. Tremellion is not mine, nor ever will be. I'm free to travel wherever I –'

'Free to see the Kingdom of Jerusalem, my lord?'

'Free and willing to do so, my lady. And encouraged by the hopes of – of finding you again.'

Christiane shrugged the edges of her cloak away from her arms. With a lissome movement she twisted from her chair, gestured to Baynard to stay seated, then leaned forward, dipping down to kiss him lightly on the lips. 'It is not just some journey, you know,' she whispered. 'You'd be a fine young knight on Crusade . . . And . . . If you wished it, Sir Baynard . . . I could attend your arrival . . .'

Across the Hall, beyond the high, arched entrance and closeted in Sir Geoffrey's chamber, the warlord sat in quiet consultation with Magnat-Vaulmier, Duc de Querinard, Comte d'Almé. It took them some time to work out the details of Tremellion's bequest, and exactly how the treasure would be delivered to the Cause. Then the men sat back in their unyielding leather chairs, raised crudely-fashioned glasses of *eau de vie* in a toast, and glanced toward the door, looking beyond it, back through the entrance to the Hall.

Sir Geoffrey said, 'He's a firm old friend of mine, Ardelet. He'll suffer some disappointment 'cause of this.'

And Lord Vaulmier lifted his shoulders in a shrug of polite regret. 'She caught his glance the instant he arrived, your weary young Baynard. It's a trick of my daughter's, to yawn and look bored when something – or someone – takes her attention. Not that it's her only trick. She's also very good at making a fellow feel wanted. I should know. She's skinned *me* for enough bracelets and brooches in the past.'

'But never yet requested you find her a husband,' Sir Geoffrey murmured.

And thoughtfully, his visitor said, 'No . . . Never quite that.'

Yet neither love nor money prevented the aristocrats of Outremer from leaving the fortress of Tremellion. They had other places to visit, among them the island of Ardelet, and the mid-March storm was still scudding when Magnat-Vaulmier, his daughter, his scribe, and Christiane's chaperone – who'd stayed awake all night, fallen asleep at dawn, and so failed to witness the meeting in the Hall –

26

collected their escort of men-at-arms and zig-zagged between the walls of the narrow ravine.

Sir Geoffrey Falkan spent the rest of the day taking inventory of his wealth.

He was helped in this by his cleric, by Guthric, by a somewhat inattentive Baynard.

A search had been made for Ranulf, his name called from the inner bailey, the eastern bailey, the towers and walls and gatehouse of the castle. No one was surprised to find him gone; it was something he did whenever he was angry, and Ranulf Falkan was angry much of the time.

He'd gone to one of his whores, most likely. Used her as some kind of devil's confessional. Then attacked her for his pleasure, and paid her for her pains.

They could only guess at the value of the coin and plate and jewellery, though it would not be much less than three thousand marks. Enough to equip a sizeable force of knights – and with money left over for the archers, their portable shields, the services of farriers, blacksmiths, fletchers, cooks and laundrymaids they'd employ along the way. More than enough to finance a miniature army; a knuckle-bone at least for England's Crusading fist.

Baynard believed now what he'd believed when his father had asked his opinion of this extensive gift to the beggars. It was Sir Geoffrey's decision to part with the money, and his prerogative to deliver it to the fleet at anchor in Plymouth. Too old to set out for the distant shores of Outremer, he could at least undertake his own personal Crusade and see Tremellion's fortune placed safely aboard the ships.

Baynard would have accompanied his father to the port, save for Guthric's ministrations with the serrated, long-nosed pincers. But twenty minutes of that and not even the bullish King Richard of England would have managed a swipe against the Saracens, those dark-eyed disciples of the devil . . .

FOUR

THE DULLING mixture of oil, vinegar and sulphur had failed to work. Soaked into a sponge, the drug had been placed in Baynard's mouth while the self-styled *dentator* set out the cloth, the needle-point knife, the long, claw-headed pincers. He had then told the patient to stretch out on the bench, a small leather cushion under his head. 'There's straps if you want them. Otherwise, take a good tight hold on the bench.'

Baynard chose to grip the wood, spat out the sponge, then gazed at the vaulted roof of the constable's cell.

Having established which tooth it was – and Guthric remembered an occasion in the past when one of the guards had come to him . . . and he'd omitted to ask – he held Baynard's mouth open with the spring of his powerful fingers and inserted the long iron pincers.

Endless moments of searching, fumbling reaching for a grip on the infected molar. Baynard groaned, wordlessly cursing the ineffectual drug. The clumsy Guthric might as well have packed his mouth with honeycomb, for all the good –

He gurgled a moan of pure agony as the constable forced his mouth wider, tightened his hold on the pincers, pulled sharply upward, jerked the offending tooth free.

A gust of fetid air blew from young Baynard's mouth. Blood streamed from the socket, washing around his tongue. His hands rose from the bench – *he was choking! Drowning in his own blood!* – and he twisted violently, spewing the poisoned fluid on the floor. *Dear Christ, that hurt!* What else had the monster torn from his mouth? A piece of his very jaw?

Guthric gave him wine to swill out the wound, a hefty measure of *eau de vie* to kill off the worms it was believed burrowed into the teeth. He pronounced himself satisfied with his work and asked if Baynard had any other aches or twinges – 'Seeing as you're here.'

Racked with pain, his head hanging low over the bench, the young Baynard Falkan prayed God to give him the strength to turn and rise up and murder the massive, unschooled *dentator* of Tremellion.

*

Within less than an hour one side of the patient's face had swollen, tight as a bladder. Sir Geoffrey came to see him, to learn if his son would be well enough to accompany him to Plymouth the following morning. But a glance was enough to show that Baynard would not get further than the latrine, not for a few days yet. For all the constable's heavy-handed ways, he knew what he was doing, though he'd need to be attentive, if the patient was to be cured.

'I'm sorry you'll not be with me, my boy. I'd take Ranulf, if only that furious man could be found. I imagine he's sought solace with one of his – ladies. It's the pattern he usually paints.' He lifted his heavy shoulders in a shrug. 'No matter. I intend to have most of the garrison around me on the journey. It's less than fifty miles to Plymouth, but I'll take no risks with Tremellion's treasure. Meantime, you get yourself well. When I'm back we'll talk at length about your future, this desire of yours to take the Cross.' Reaching to lay a hand on Baynard's shoulder, he added, 'And the *real* reason for your seeking to go on Crusade.' Then he smiled at his son, heard Baynard mouth gibberish through his lop-sided lips and guessed correctly the young Falkan was telling him to take care; God speed you, father, on this, your own Crusade.

It cheered Baynard to see that even now, at fifty, Sir Geoffrey filled the doorway as he made his way from the chamber.

Guthric was placed in command of the Cornish fortress. Of course, when Ranulf returned, the constable would take orders from Sir Geoffrey's elder son. If, on the other hand, Ranulf did *not* re-enter Tremellion before Sir Geoffrey, Guthric would assume responsibility until Baynard Falkan recovered.

'We've known each other long enough, God witness,' the warlord growled. 'And even with the castle stripped of its garrison, I'm content that you'll be around, padding the yards. You may be a damned old charlatan in the matter of teeth, my friend, but I know I can leave my house without concern.'

The Saxon grunted the compliment aside. He owed everything in life to Sir Geoffrey, for it was this cloudy-eyed Falkan who'd admitted him to Tremellion, engineered his rise from common gate-guard, tested his competence, found abilities in him Guthric had never supposed. He was poorly paid, but what need of money when the Lord of Tremellion housed him, clothed him, asked his opinion, listened as he gave it? Who would be a plump-bellied merchant, tinkling with coin, when one could sit at table with Sir Geoffrey

Falkan, Lord of Tremellion, and be asked what to do for the best?

Now, however, without being asked, Guthric said, 'It's wrong there's no one with you, my lord. Sir Ranulf . . . Young Baynard . . . For the lack of them, myself . . .'

'Worried someone'll pinch my purse, eh, Guthric? Scarcely so, when I'll be escorted there by my soldiers. You'd do better to think how you'll keep my house safe, you and your bladder-faced patient. Manage *that* for the few short days I'm away, and I'll be well enough pleased.' Then he clapped the leathery constable on the arm, turned to growl at the dismal sky and went off to see if his cleric had finished copying out the list of Tremellion's wealth.

With the priest in tow, Sir Geoffrey led sixteen armed riders and two of his household servants out of the gatehouse and down through the long ravine maze. The baggage train – for so it was with its five laden pack-horses – would travel toward Launceston, turn south around the edge of the desolate Bodmin Moor, then follow the paths and cart-tracks down to Plymouth.

If there was any vanity in the fifty-year-old Falkan of Tremellion, it lay in his reasonable desire to be greeted by the would-be Crusaders who were gathering at the port. They'd respect him as a veteran of earlier wars in the East . . . Remark that he seemed fit as a boar for his age (all the while ignoring his clouded left eye) . . . Admire him for coming in person, this doughty old warlord . . . Who would then insist upon opening the chests and satchels right there on the dock . . .

He'd growl at this new generation of Crusaders, 'There, messires. *That's* for your war against the enemies of Christ! Guard it well. Buy only the best with it. And remember, if you've a mind to, that your victories were in some small part won with the help of Tremellion.'

Jogging through the forest that filled the valley, a few miles south of Launceston, the Cornish warrior muttered under his breath. Would that be vanity? And if so, what of it? Can't a weary old fool purchase readmission to his youth?

And then the arrows came flittering from the trees . . .

It was a murderous, well-planned ambush, laid and executed to perfection. The first flight of shafts killed the cleric, killed one of the servants, killed three of the armed riders. Five of the horses were brought down, others plunging, the damp air filled with yells of surprise, screams of the animals, angry howls of the wounded.

All of those who were hit were struck from behind, the effect being to goad the riders onward, make them turn in alarm, struggle to free their shields from the pommels of their saddles. Arrows continued to swish and flit from the briars that floored the forest, an angled cross-fire that brought down three more horses, cut the second servant clear through the spine, reduced the sixteen-strong guard to eleven.

But the number of deaths was as nothing compared with the arrows that lodged in the link-mail hauberks, flapped from cloaks, embedded themselves in boots, satchels, the small, iron-bound chests that carried the treasure.

Sir Geoffrey was hit twice, the arrows failing to pierce the annealed links of his armour. Past experience of battle had already saved his life, for a shaft had thudded against his helmet, caromed away, buried its triangular tip in the ground. Unshipping his sword, he dipped his head, chin pressed hard to his collar-bone. The sneaking, come-from-nowhere bastards might get him yet, but it wouldn't be with an arrow in the throat.

Then he roared at his company to spur their animals, out-run the ambush, get a half-mile along and regroup. These treacherous archers were good if they stayed hidden, but see how they'd run if a cavalry charge sliced among the briars!

So he called his riders onward, the broad nasal bar of his helmet touching his chest, and urged his mount along the shallow forest path.

Then felt the animal go from under him as a second wave of arrows hissed to meet him. He went down heavily, lost his helmet, felt a horrible sear of pain as his left arm cracked. Progress had turned to astonishment, order to chaos. All around him horses were floundering, men and animals screaming, someone running to pause in front of him, the man's forehead drilled by a shaft.

As the man flopped dead, the Lord of Tremellion hauled himself erect. His left arm hung useless, the limb below the elbow swinging, the shock of the ambush damming all sense of pain. It was broken – he could see it was broken – but all he could do was accept it, ignore it, trust the sword to his right.

The moans and shouts continued, chaos still seizing the throne. Then suddenly the confusion cleared and the hardened Falkan found himself in a group of six, eight, it was hard to tell how many of his escort. They were unhorsed now, braced around him on the mossy track, some with shields, all with swords, a bristling bush that sprouted from the path . . .

But their assailants did not give the men the chance for honourable combat. Crouched where they were among the trees, they loosed a steady, merciless stream of arrows, watching as Tremellion's soldiers sank to their knees . . . doubled over . . . spun to die on their backs . . .

Sir Geoffrey was not the last to die, though almost the last, and the one to take more arrows than the rest. No one would bother to count, but the elmwood shafts snapped as he fell, splinters of feathered wood tossed around him, the flowers of violence that marked the warlord's one and final defeat.

Cautiously, with the true hesitation of the coward, the ambushers crept from cover. They'd done what they'd been paid to do – massacre the riders – but they weren't quite sure if they should slit the throats of the wounded, or leave them be.

In the hope of pleasing their employer, they stooped down and began to kill the survivors. Then halted as they heard the drumming of hoofbeats and posed with their bows, grinning to show a difficult job done well.

The riders who came to meet them were armed from head to heel. Their identities were concealed by heavy, riveted helmets, their features hidden behind eye-slits and breathing holes. Their hands were engloved in link-mail mittens, their surcoats a uniform grey.

They went among the ambushers, hacking them to death, trampling them into the soft loam of the forest track, using heavy swords that cut the hirelings to pieces. The anonymous horsemen never uttered a word, too busy killing to crow.

Then they wheeled aside, dividing into two separate ranks, and waited as their commander urged his mount close to Sir Geoffrey's punctured corpse.

His head tipped forward, he gazed through the eye-slits of the helmet. When he spoke, his voice echoed within the confines of the mask. 'You foolish old man. I'd bet half the treasure you supposed me to be with a whore.' Then he lifted his head and turned to his companions. 'Two days easy. Deal with the Levantine, and we'll have the women brought in by the wagon-load, down there at the linn.'

A final glance at the man he'd paid to have murdered, though not even the blink of an eye for those who'd achieved it. What were they, after all, these hirelings, but worthless creatures who knew nothing beyond the fletching and loosing of a shaft? No loss to anyone. And what had they expected – to be allowed to blabber their tale?

Jerking the reins, the commander turned his horse back the way he'd come. His companions fell in behind him, guttural comments mingling with the occasional bark of laughter. The treasure was collected, the dying of men and animals ignored. The anonymous riders picked their way through the carnage, gathered speed as they cleared the scene of the ambush, spurred their horses to a canter.

None of them troubled to swivel his all-enclosing helmet and look back.

FIVE

NEWS OF the ambush took time to reach Tremellion. It was brought by a verderer, riding in advance of a line of farm carts, conveyances for the dead. Stammering with fear, he asked to speak with the custodian of the castle, and was led along the ravine and through the gatehouse.

Taking him at his word, the guards escorted him into the presence of the constable who listened in silence to the verderer's halting account of what he'd discovered, there in the Launceston forest. Telling the man to wait, Guthric climbed with heavy steps to Baynard's chamber. All the while, the Saxon's scarred lips moved in silent malediction, the bitterest curses levelled against himself. He should have ridden with Sir Geoffrey. He was the warlord's man. No matter how sensible it had seemed, how necessary he'd stayed to guard the castle, *he should have been with Sir Geoffrey*. Nothing would alter that simple, graven fact. He should have been there at the warlord's shoulder, should have died with him in the forest.

The young Falkan was asleep, the side of his face once again reduced to its leanness, though the cavity not yet healed, blood still weeping, pain webbing out from his jaw.

For an instant, gazing down at him, Guthric wanted to jar him awake, shake him from his sanctuary of sleep. If it hadn't been for his blasted, festering tooth –

But that was stupid, a purblind reaction to the news. The massacre of the riders had nothing to do with Baynard. Indeed, if he'd been well enough, *he* would have accompanied Sir Geoffrey. Then Tremellion would have lost its past and future, both. Better that the younger Falkan had survived. If anyone should have been slain on that forest path it was the Saxon. Or so Guthric would for ever believe.

But there was no time to spare for senseless recriminations. Justice and vengeance were hammering to be heard.

He woke the young knight, waited as Baynard spat blood into a basin, then told him to prepare for bad news. 'Worse than bad. Such as has cut my heart, and may well snap yours. Lord Geoffrey and his escort . . . They were ambushed somewhere beyond Launceston . . .

I do not yet know the how of it, but one thing seems assured. Your father is among those who died. There's a messenger waiting below . . . A forest keeper . . . He says there are carts and wagons bringing us the dead . . . Ah, yes, and a sole survivor, one of the escort, though he thinks it likely the man will die before he gets here.'

Staring at Guthric as if waiting for him suddenly to roar with laughter and admit to some ghoulish joke, Baynard Falkan reached blindly for his boots, his belt and scabbard. But no, the ugly Saxon wasn't given to humour, neither gay nor grotesque. What he'd said was the truth – insofar as he'd heard it. Falkan let it slowly sink in, dinning ever louder in his head, gouging at his heart. *My father has been killed. Murdered. Also the escort. The treasure presumably taken. Sir Geoffrey is dead. I shall soon be shown his corpse.*

Uncertain of what he was saying, Baynard reached for words like pegs on the wall. 'I am grateful to you, Constable. I hope the messenger – Did someone give him ale? We'd best go and talk to him. So he's the sole survivor, eh? Lucky fellow. I wonder how –'

'No, my lord. He was not in the ambush. He came across the –'

'But you *did* say there was an ambush? Excuse me, the blood still leaks.' He reached for the basin, spat in it again, listened as Guthric told him yes, there *had* been an ambush, but the verderer –

'I'm confused,' Baynard admitted. 'Quite honestly, Constable, this story of yours –' Then he suddenly jerked forward, clapped a hand to his eyes, stood shaking as the tears exuded between his fingers. Guthric thought to leave the chamber, allow young Falkan the privacy of anguish. Instead he stepped forward, curled his great paw of a hand around the back of Baynard's neck, then gently kneaded the tautened, quivering muscles. In all his forty years, it was the closest the Saxon had come to a show of affection. It surprised him, though he realised later he'd been comforting them both.

When they questioned the terrified verderer, Falkan's lean, dark-skinned face was as impassive as Guthric's. He had wept for his father, but would not weep again. Nor would he show much gentleness of character, his dreams of Christiane de Magnat-Vaulmier abandoned, his desire to take the Crusading Cross forgotten. Perhaps later, at some future time . . . But all that concerned him was to learn about the ambush, discover who'd been responsible, track them down and kill them and reclaim Tremellion's treasure. In this, as in most things now, Falkan was at one with Guthric. It was time to listen to the reasoning of Justice, the blood-flecked demands of Vengeance.

They heard little of advantage from the verderer. He'd come late on the scene, peered with horror at the long trail of corpses, noted that some were in link-mail hauberks, others in leather jerkins. 'All those in mail had been brought down by arrows, my Lord Falkan, whilst the rest, the archers, it seemed to us they'd been trampled, or cut by swords. God will it, my lord, the survivor'll still be alive when the carts bring him in. We made him as comfortable as we could . . . But the path around the moor . . .' He twitched defensively, praying he'd not be held responsible if the man-at-arms died on the way.

'How long will it take them to get here?' Falkan demanded. 'Before nightfall?'

'Oh, well before nightfall, sire. My own mount cast a shoe when I was still some way from Tremellion, which slowed me down. I'd say the carts will be here an hour before dark.'

Guthric made the man repeat his story. All of it. From the moment he'd come along the track and heard the whinny of wounded horses. He badgered the verderer for details, snarled at him to cudgel his memory, bullied the unfortunate keeper until the man began to contradict what he'd said.

Falkan then beckoned the constable aside. 'There's nothing more to be learned from him; we've squeezed the creature dry. Easy enough to pretend he'd never set eyes on that grisly scene. The thing to do now is feed him, give him a jar of ale and decent recompense for his trouble. See to it his horse is shod. Then saddle two others, so we can meet the wagons on the road. I want to hear what that survivor has to tell us. If he dies before we get there – well, I have my own suspicions, but I'd rather hear him recount what really happened.'

Guthric turned to see the orders carried out. Then he swung back, started to speak, contented himself with a guttural, 'What Lord Geoffrey would have expected, I daresay.' As a compliment, it lacked limbs, yet the constable's approval struck the core of Baynard's being.

Two important truths had already emerged in the wake of the massacre. Baynard Falkan wanted Guthric to stay on at Tremellion. More than that, stay with Falkan himself. And more even than that, be his man, as the Saxon had been Sir Geoffrey's.

But that could only happen if the ugly, humourless bear respected his new master. It was one thing for the literate Falkan to admire the grizzled Constable of Tremellion; quite another for Guthric to serve the younger son of his lord.

There were fifty, maybe a hundred nobles who'd snatch at the chance to employ this broad-shouldered monster. They'd pay him better than Sir Geoffrey ever had; lodge him in more comfortable quarters; see his bed was warmed by frisky women. As soon as they learned that Sir Geoffrey Falkan was dead, they'd make their overtures to the Saxon.

So Baynard flinched with agreeable surprise when Guthric remarked that Sir Geoffrey would have done things much the same.

It was not to say the constable would resist those other offers. But approval from Guthric – well, no man on earth would ever buy his approval. It would be given and, timely growled today, it helped stiffen young Falkan's spine.

By the time the men were ready to leave the castle, the guards in the gatehouse were tolling the alarm. As the bell clanged, men trampled down the narrow spiral staircase, hurrying to announce the arrival of the train.

A long, lumbering procession of farm carts and wagons, each of them bearing victims of the ambush.

By rights the young Falkan should have sought out his father's bier, knelt beside it and offered a prayer to Heaven. He should have allowed the drizzling rain to soak through his tunic, drip from the narrow blade of his nose, soften the mud that would cling to his knees, half-burying his boots. Obedient to custom, he should have stayed there until a priest could be found – some unhappy cleric hauled from Launceston.

But Baynard did none of this, ignoring the men who bowed to him, striding past as they indicated the wagon in which Sir Geoffrey's body lay.

He asked instead, 'There's a man who survived the attack. One of our riders. I'll thank you to say where he is.'

Masking their surprise at his cold-blooded manner, carters and foresters led him to a tented, two-wheeled vehicle that stank of its everyday use, a dung cart.

Not that its dying occupant cared about the smell.

Nor that Baynard cared, clambering in to crouch beside the victim, then wave the foresters away. He looked up sharply as Guthric appeared, gestured to the constable to keep silent, then leaned close to the soldier.

He was horribly wounded, the snapped-off shafts of at least three arrows protruding from his flesh. One behind the left ear, another in the thigh, a third that had somehow drilled its way between the links of his hauberk, an inch below his right shoulder-blade.

He was hunched on his side, and a glance could tell he would die within the hour.

So Baynard went to work on him, couching the man's head, lifting it to hear what had happened in the forest.

For the first time in his life he said, 'I am the commander of Tremellion. Baynard Falkan. You will know me.'

And the dying man whispered, 'Am I near home?'

'You *are* home, soldier, and merit in store, once we've rid you of these arrows.' Time spent in cheering him, though Falkan would not have had it otherwise. You do not address a dying man as you'd speak to a rheumy cur.

'We've chatted before, my Lord Falkan,' it pleased the soldier to remind him. 'We talked of that easy post I had . . . Guarding the north wall of the castle . . . You were making the rounds . . . And you came up to stand beside me . . .'

'So I did,' Falkan agreed, no longer remembering that brief conversation, whenever it might have been. He could feel the man slipping, no doubt willing to die in friendly arms, and hastened to ask him what had happened – who had commanded the ambushers? – what had the soldier heard beyond the screams and groans that are the dialogue of combat?

With extreme tenacity, the thrice-wounded soldier struggled to show his loyalty to Tremellion, obedience to Falkan. It wasn't easy, for the broad tips of the arrows were buried deep . . . But he'd do what he could . . . Hurry things along . . . Fight against the dimming of his eyes . . .

'We were riding through the forest, my lord. Suddenly this waspish buzz of shafts. Some of us injured. Many. Hard to tell. Then onward. And into another swarm. Horses dying. And men. I was one moment mounted, the next on the ground. I have to say, my lord, it was nice and cool, the moss . . .'

It was then that Baynard snatched the man by the shoulder, urging him to get on with it, tell what he had to tell!

The dying soldier reared from the skins the verderers had laid in the bed of the cart. Falkan braced him, knew his life was edging away, spoke urgently to him – 'After the ambush, what?'

'What, my lord? Why, the archers came out and the riders arrived and hacked them to shreds . . . And someone said, "Foolish old man. I'd bet half the treasure you supposed me to be with a whore." ' And then the soldier shouted – 'Oh, God, the arrows have found me! *I've been such a bad man, so evil in my ways. Don't let me burn, sweet Jesus, don't let me be flayed!*'

A priest would then have blessed him.

As for Baynard, he sank away, regretting the man would die with so little said.

But Guthric saw things differently. Heaved himself over the tail-board of the cart. Wrenched the victim from his bed and bellowed in his face. 'There must have been more! What else?'

The near-dead soldier reacted in terror, mouthing the words they needed to hear. 'Two days easy . . . Deal with the Levantine . . . Wagon-load of women, down there at – down there – at the linn . . .' Then, with the calmness of finality, he announced, 'Sara, you must always close the gate when –' and rolled his head, a pinkish froth bubbling from his lips.

Gazing at the Saxon with a mixture of awe and horror, Falkan asked, 'What did you hear of that?'

'Heard everything, my lord. It'll need piecing together. But from what this man's told us, I'd say we've enough to get started.'

Baynard nodded, then found it important to voice his thoughts. 'I've just watched you hurry a loyal man to his death. I've a deep respect for you, bloody Guthric, but I need to know – I need to be certain there are limits to what you would do. It may well be that my brother laid this ambush, and that I am now the justified Lord of Tremellion, at least in the eyes of the angels. I am therefore in a position to seek your support. I want it, and I'd demand it of you, but surely there are limits –'

'You repeat yourself,' Guthric growled. 'I'm as sweet or sour as events direct me to be. Stay out there in the rain, and what would this man have told us? *Nothing.* Shake him a bit and he speaks. There's always a sip of wine left in the flagon.' Twisting on his knees in the dung cart, the Saxon leaned toward Baynard. 'As for you, my lord, the sweet days are done with. Take my word for it, and acquire the taste for vinegar. Anything else is just fruit we nudge from the trees.'

Falkan spent an hour in the mud, kneeling in prayer beside Sir Geoffrey's bier. He remembered scenes he'd long thought forgotten. The first time his father had set him up high on a horse. The only time Sir Geoffrey had whipped him – for offering a pension to his tutor, if the man agreed to mark him high in Greek. It was a silly offer, in retrospect, for the ten-year-old second son of Tremellion was scarcely in a position to keep such a promise. And how that strap had hurt . . .

He remembered a walk by the Hexel River – he was fifteen then – and hearing voices in a grove of trees ahead of him – and softening his tread to see who was there – and espying Sir Geoffrey and Lady Elena, the two of them seated on a rush mat on the bank, his father fishing – the line snagged in the weeds – his mother brought to tears by laughter as he wrenched at the line, blaming the current, blaming the rod, blaming the cunning of the trout. What a genuine laugh she'd possessed, the Lady Elena. And how willingly she'd shared it with Sir Geoffrey. All in all, they'd been as well-matched a couple as marriage might ever have united . . .

As death must eventually ease apart . . .

There were other fond remembrances – recollected fruit from the trees. Then his private vision was scarred at the edges by the sound of restless horses, the coughing of men, and he pushed himself slowly to his feet.

He told the carters to conduct his father's body to the chapel. Alone, he climbed the zig-zag path through the ravine, intent on rejoining his one remaining ally, the humourless, ursine Constable of Tremellion.

Their decision to conjoin was not celebrated with the chinking of goblets, a trading of mutual compliments, nor the formal embrace that seals historic accord.

Baynard had made it clear he wanted Guthric as his man.

And the Saxon had told him the sweet days were done with, acquire a taste for vinegar – not exactly a willing response. But he'd also said, 'Anything else is just fruit we nudge from the trees.' Fruit a man might garner in his lifetime? Or orchards the two men might jostle through together?

Still spitting blood, though less often now, Baynard Falkan entered the gatehouse, his spirits clawed to shreds by the loss of Sir Geoffrey. He followed the path that traversed the inner bailey, crossed the wooden bridge that spanned the lake. Then he paused for a moment, raising his eyes to the ramp that led to the keep. It seemed longer than before. Steeper than he remembered. A dizzying lift of cobblestones that winked in the rain-washed evening. *You*, my Lord Baynard? *You* dare set your imprint here as master?

Watching the drizzle flash and run from the stones, Baynard Falkan trudged the slope of the ramp. He was in mourning for his father, blood on his mind for the killers, shards of memory piercing him as he thought of Lady Elena, felt the whispered lips of Christiane de Magnat-Vaulmier. He hated the suspected Ranulf, stumbled as he reached the head of the ramp and turned, indecisive, to enter his empty house.

Then saw the same, leather-tented figure he'd met on his return from the island. Blocking the entrance. Daring to bar his way.

'Is that you, bloody Guthric?'

Silence for a while, and then, 'It is. And you?'

'What the hell do you mean – *and you?* I'm drenched and I'm drained and I'm in no damned mood –'

'And you?'

'Christ's bones, you great hulk, who do you suppose –?'

'And you?'

Deep within him, Baynard Falkan sensed he was changing now; not only in rank and station, but in his grasp of responsibility, his personal stature, his desire for sweetness spat aside with the blood. It did not prevent him leaning against the outer wall of the ramp, staying a moment to suck the damp night air. But the repeated question gave him the pause he needed, told him what he knew he had to hear.

Knowing the Saxon would help him, he repeated the important, the essential formality of their greeting. 'Is that you Constable Guthric?'

'It is. And you?'

'I am Baynard Falkan – I'm Baynard Falkan, commander for the while of this castle.'

Then he waited; only going forward, only lengthening his stride, as Guthric acknowledged from the shadows, 'My Lord Tremellion.'

SIX

KNIGHT AND constable considered what they'd heard. *Foolish old man. I'd bet half the treasure you supposed me to be with a whore.* A glance between them, expressionless, the very lack of movement signifying agreement. They'd no need to discuss *that* derisive remark. Only Ranulf could have known of the treasure. And it was only Ranulf who had, throughout the years, stormed from the castle, made his way to the nearby village, purchased the solace of a whore. Never the same one twice – not twice with a devil like that – but nevertheless girls who were willing to suffer for the sake of his coins.

Baynard and Guthric were convinced. It was Ranulf Falkan who'd set and sprung the ambush, paid the hirelings to carry it out, then sent the riders to murder the bowmen. Assassinate the assassins and he'd hoped to cover his tracks. And yet, as with so many other things in life, he'd failed to complete the carnage. Failed to resist the chance to insult the dead or dying Sir Geoffrey. Seized the opportunity to boast – *Two days easy . . . Deal with the Levantine . . . Wagon-load of women, down there at the linn.*

A reasonable guess that Ranulf meant two days easy ride from the forest south of Launceston. But in which direction? And what did he mean by deal with the Levantine? Trade with him? Exchanging Tremellion's jewels and plate for coin? Or kill the man who was owner of the hideout, leaving the murderers free to settle in? And where in God's name was it, this unidentified linn?

Nodding at Guthric, Baynard said, 'You are better acquainted with these parts, even than I. We know that a linn's a waterfall, a cascade, something of the like. But where would we find one that's so well known to Ranulf and his friends he didn't need to name it?'

Hunching forward, his scarred face plunged into candlelight, Guthric muttered, 'I agree, my lord. I *am* better acquainted, and there are people I can ask. Give me a day –'

'Sweet Christ, another day lost?'

'These people – I shall need time to find them. They're river poachers, the ones I have in mind. They'll know every stream and pool in the region. And every linn.'

'I want them brought here,' Baynard said. 'Find them for me, assure them they'll be safe, offer them – I don't care what. A lifetime's fishing in the Hexel. I don't wish to know their names, nor where they live. Just find me a man who can point us to the linn that's two days easy from where my father died.'

The constable dipped his head. Left the room. Prowled from the keep, the courtyard, the castle. His plan was simple. He'd find the river poachers, relay his master's offer, then judge for himself if the thief had aught to say. If the man was willing to come forward, well and good. If not – then Guthric would take the reluctant creature somewhere quiet. And cuff the timidity clear out of his soul.

In spite of the Saxon's efforts, it was a day and a half before Baynard got his answer.

All who climbed to Tremellion – a few of them bruised, as if from some bad fall – were admitted to the Great Hall, given a mug of ale, then questioned until they clung to the edge of the bench. True to his word, the young Falkan ignored their names, chose to forget they were robbers on his lands. It was hard for them to live, these snare-setters, but equally hard for the castellan of a fortress, obliged to feed his household, his garrison. Sir Geoffrey had been lenient with those convicted of poaching, preferring to cut off their thumbs than see them hanged. Of course, if they continued to steal . . .

The first four men who volunteered information were forced to admit that, no, the cascades they knew of were far less, and on one occasion more, than two days easy ride from the forest of Launceston.

Guthric told them to collect a sack of grain, a quarter-side of salted beef from the gate-guards, then helped them on their way with a hefty nudge.

'Robbers to the last,' he grunted, 'though I believe they told you what they knew.'

With a humourless smile, Baynard said, 'I've no reason to doubt you, old Guthric. Their first being encouraged in the verities by you.'

But then things turned for the better.

The fifth man to be questioned was unlike the others. A whippy young creature, with a mane of cinnamon hair, he'd come of his own accord to the Hall of Tremellion. He was acquainted with the Saxon, though had only this morning returned from what he vaguely described as 'an errand for some friends'. Now, seated in his chair, he gazed boldly, almost insolently at Falkan.

43

'You ask me about this linn of yours, m'lord? Well, I don't know what the rest of 'em had to say, but two days easy from the woods down there? Then it's the mill I was sent to once to pick up flour. Be worth your while to visit it. See the water that spills off the rocks. Sixty feet high, they say. Comes down in a regular torrent, it does, the linn that feeds the mill.'

'And where might this be?'

The young man linked his fingers together, cracked his knuckles, helped himself to ale from the pewter jug. Then he grinned at Guthric, wiped it away and looked straight at Baynard Falkan. 'Heard there was talk of freedom to fish in the Hexel, for the man what could name the linn.'

The constable moved toward him, then halted as Baynard extended the barrier of his arm. 'You heard right,' he acknowledged. 'And I'll give written licence to prove it. But before you tax my patience, master –'

'Quillon,' Guthric announced with grim satisfaction. 'Known him for years. A cocksure fellow, our handsome Master Quillon. Quite a one for the women. And netting Tremellion's fish.' He glared at the lion-haired Quillon, the muscular young man grinning back.

'You ain't never seen me *near* your precious river, Constable Guthric. Wouldn't know a lamprey from a loach, if I saw 'em together. So you ain't got no call –'

Baynard's fist slammed the table. 'By God!' he shouted. 'Do you think I have time for *this*? I'll know the name of the mill, Master Quillon, and hear it from you *now*! Where is it? What's it called?'

The impudent villager had the sense to watch his step. One might seek to aggravate the Saxon, but not the present Lord of Tremellion.

'It's the Linn of Tresset, sire. Named after the village. Two days riding due west of the forest. 'Bout the same south-west from here.'

'I shall need you to guide us.'

'I never heard talk of –'

'Well, you've heard it now,' Guthric snarled. 'You'll lead us there, or I'll march you back to that hovel you live in –'

'Hovel? It's neat and clean as –'

'The one you share with your roundelay of women –'

'Faithful to one, I am. How can you –'

'Where I'm bound to find a basket of stolen fish . . . Just bound to . . . The moment I set foot inside the door . . .' Then, enjoying the moment, it was Guthric's turn to grin.

Quillon couched his hands below the table, imagining how it would

44

be without his thumbs. Avoiding Guthric's gaze he said, 'Be it as you wish, m'lord. Ain't averse to showing you where it is, the Linn of Tresset.'

A few hours later, daring to leave the fortress almost deserted, Falkan and Guthric led the remnants of the garrison in search of the murderers' hideout, following the storm-worried mane of Quillon's cinnamon hair.

The next day he'd recovered his spirits, revelling in his important, new-found role. He guided the horsemen through a string of scattered hamlets, winking at the girls who watched as the riders trampled by. From time to time he reined in, waited for Baynard and Guthric to draw level, then volunteered some comment, offered a quip.

Later, when the insolent young man had spurred ahead to check the route, Guthric mused, 'You'd have no need to issue a licence, my lord . . . If by hazard that joskin went and got himself drowned in the mill-race . . .'

Falkan felt a surge of warmth for the clumsy, loyal Saxon. 'He may not be to your taste, old Guthric, and I'm not yet convinced he's to mine. But before we watch him sink beneath the bubbles we should ask ourselves – how much does our dislike of Master Quillon stem from envy? Whatever his faults, he's a damned singular fellow.'

Then he heard his companion give a snort of disgust and they rode on in silence, south by west, across the bleak Cornish moors.

Assuming Ranulf and his henchmen had gone directly to the mill, they'd have reached it some forty hours before their pursuers. Time enough in which to deal with the Levantine, enjoy the wagon-load of women – and move on. It was this that most concerned Baynard Falkan; the fear that his brother would have traded Sir Geoffrey's treasure, paid off his henchmen, then fled. If so, where on earth would Ranulf have gone? To one of his friends' castles? To a fortified manor? North, south or west, all of which would bring him to the coast. Or had the murderous riders stayed together, circled back from their hideout, set their sights on what was, under the law, Ranulf Falkan's domain? In other words, *were they, even at this moment, ensconced in the fortress of Tremellion?*

With an imperious gesture, Quillon flagged the company to a halt. They were among gorse and scrubland now, the rocky ground giving sustenance to stunted oak trees, the morning's progress slowed by rifts and fissures in the earth. Away to the right, a series of natural shelves terraced an escarpment, and Quillon was pointing toward it, telling the group to listen.

'You hear that? Beyond the cliff over there? The toss and tumble of water? It's the head of the fall, seventy feet if it's –'

'Sixty, the last time,' Guthric told him, 'and we confirmed you as a liar even then.'

The young man shrugged, unabashed. 'The thing of it is, it's high. But knowing what you're about, that you plan to snare your father's murderers, m'lord, I'd offer it's the best way to the mill. Not the *easy* way, I ain't saying it is, for the easy way's to go left, down the slope and out on to the track. Leads around to the. mill itself, that track. But if anyone's there they'd spot us half a mile off.'

But now it was Falkan's turn to flag his hand. 'You've served us well, Master Quillon. And I agree with you. The approach must be made from the linn.' Then he signalled to his men-at-arms, the residue of the garrison, and the five men dismounted, four of them lifting sacks and satchels from their horses. The fifth man took charge of the animals, tethering them near the base of the terraced cliff.

Baynard swung down from his palfrey and the eight men grouped together below the escarpment. They were well away from the track that led to the mill; hidden from the path by the gorse and oaks, the jagged slabs of rock that reared from the ground. The sky was overcast, evening closing in. Rainclouds threatened to shorten the day.

It would suit the men to attack under cover of dusk, though not with the sky so dark they'd grope their way blindly, water below them, water hissing from above. If the thing was to be done with any likelihood of success, it would have to be started now.

'You,' Falkan said. 'Master Quillon. You've guided us correctly, at least to the sound of a torrent. You've earned your licence, and shall now stay here with the horses. But before we leave you – is there anything more we should know about the mill? Anything to prevent us descending the falls?'

Quillon shrugged. 'So long as your ropes'll reach to the pool. Eighty feet down, from where it tumbles over.'

'Grows by the hour,' Guthric muttered. 'Or anyway in the telling.'

'We've rope enough,' Falkan answered. 'Three tested lengths of it. A hundred feet in each. And belts that hold a half-dozen daggers, balanced to be thrown. Oh, yes, and –' nodding to one of the soldiers – 'these.' The man stood ready with a broad-mouthed sack. Baynard told him to open it, then invited Quillon to look.

Serpents squirmed and wriggled within a lining of damp green moss.

'Them!' Quillon exclaimed. 'They're just eels! Find 'em anywhere about. They're only what I fish from the Hex—' Then he clamped his mouth tight, turned aside, looked for a way of escape. He was aware of Guthric approaching. Aware that any court in the land would see him mutilated or hanged for what he'd said. *So, Master Quillon. You fish eels from the Hexel River, the property of Tremellion. Steal them, in a word. Poach from the lord who protects you. Such an admission as yours, Master Quillon, and this court has no choice –*

'Listen,' the young man hurried. 'Hear me out. Maybe I *could* be of use to you, helping you get to the mill. I ain't afeared of swimming, my lord, an' I'm sturdy enough, see it for yourself.'

'He's a self-admitted liar and a thief,' Guthric said. 'I'd no more trust him than –'

'Trust comes second,' Baynard Falkan told him. 'It's this man's knowledge of the mill we need tonight.'

'And you'll have it,' Quillon assured him. 'I've been there before. Told you I went to get flour. Think of me as you will, my Lord Falkan, I never had a bad word for Sir Geoffrey. He went easy with us. Gave the village work, and paid for it fair. An' that joke you just heard me make about the eels –'

'Give this man some knives,' Falkan said. 'He is sharing in the attack.'

Even with the long-haired conscript, Falkan's force was slight. They'd leave the horses tethered but unwatched. If the approaching storm made the animals restless – well, perhaps the rumblings of thunder would drown their distress. Then again, if they were discovered, a single Tremellion guard would be quickly overwhelmed. The only thing to do was check their tethers, and pray they didn't break away and stampede across the moors.

With the light closing fast, the eight men climbed the shelves of rock, heaved themselves over the rim of the escarpment. Guided by the sound of the falls, they struggled through the tangle of briars and weeds. By the time they reached the head of the linn they were ripped by the thorns, one of the soldiers whitened with the pain of a splintered ankle, another nursing a flap of skin on his eyelid.

These two would be left to make sure the ropes held firm; to lower the weapons; swing the sack of eels clear of the fall. The other six would descend to the pool, swim to the mill-bank, then seek a way in to the building.

If anyone lost his grip on the rope, he'd risk being swept down-stream, away from the pool and into the mill-race where, Quillon assured them, the victim would be churned and chopped by the massive, iron-rimmed wheel.

Surprised by the spout of water that gushed from the forest, Baynard and Guthric crouched at the head of the falls. They peered at the scene below them, sensing the sweep of darkness overhead.

The mill-house of Tresset bordered the far bank of the stream, some fifty yards west of the pool. Its roof tiles were speckled with lichen, its visible walls green with ascending damp. The yard to the east of the house was empty, outbuildings locked tight.

Falkan decided the stables were elsewhere, and waved to the poacher to join them.

Meanwhile, the knight and constable studied the rear wall of the building.

By the set of its tiny windows, the mill supported three separate levels. And it seemed to the watchers that all of them were dark.

Quillon sank beside them. The roar of water dinned in their ears, and Falkan had to yell at the poacher – 'Where do they stable the horses?'

'The other side! Beyond the millwheel! Where the track comes in!'

'So what are we seeing here?'

'The back of it! That yard below us, it's –'

Then Guthric clutched Baynard's shoulder. 'Over by the corner! That last window along! There's a light moving behind it!'

The thunder of water was matched by the thunder of the storm. Water sprayed from the river, sluiced from the clouds, the men now shielding their eyes to see below, hauling each other close in an effort to be heard.

'That light!' Falkan shouted. 'What is it, the room –'

'A food store! It's joined to a sort of gallery! There's others beside it, all along that wall! What he'll do, whoever's in there –'

'What?'

'Whoever's in there,' Quillon gestured. 'What he'll do, he'll cross to the middle of the gallery! Then he'll go down some steps to the main room of the mill! *To the main room of the mill!*' Ignoring his self-confessed crime, the muscular Quillon caught at Baynard's sleeve. For an instant their rain-swept faces came close, the poacher surprised as the wiry Falkan twisted from his grip. *Well now, he ain't so underfed as he looks . . .*

'And the way to get in?' Falkan shouted. 'What do you know of the way to get in from here?'

Guthric nudged his master, dropped his arm to point. 'There's a bar – you see it, my lord? – protruding from the wall. Half way up. Below the ridge of the roof.'

'I see it.'

'And the opening beneath? Seems to me –' his voice then dashed by the water and the wind '– seems to me it's where they heft the grain. Get in there and we'd climb on down to the gallery Quillon described – then the steps –'

'We'll do it,' Falkan rapped. 'Whoever's in the place, they're likely inattentive.' Then he paused to let the rain spill from his face, remembering what the arrow-shot soldier had told him. *A wagon-load of women, down there at the linn.*

Oh, yes . . .

It would suit Ranulf nicely to murder his father, steal away with Tremellion's wealth, and anticipate the pleasures brought by a wagon-load of women . . .

He wiped at the spray, at the storm. Then he motioned Guthric and Quillon to make ready, calling to them again, though the words intended for himself. 'We'll do it! We'll do it now!'

SEVEN

AT FALKAN'S signal, two of the ropes were sent snaking from the head of the fall. One end looped around outcrops of stone, the coils of rope shivered downward, snatched by the torrent, vanishing in the mist. The young knight seized one of the lines and began his descent. Guthric took hold of the other.

They spiralled and swung in the exploding clouds of spray. The force of the water slapped them aside, sucked them back into the fall. The men gasped for breath; skidded lower; felt their backs and shoulders slammed against the smooth sides of the linn.

Quillon followed, and one of the soldiers. Then the other two uninjured men-at-arms, leaving the final pair to lower the sack and the weapons. Each rope now bore the weight of three sodden men, though Falkan had forbidden the wearing of hauberks. Attempt to swim in a suit that contained upward of fifty thousand links of pincered iron, and a man would be already encased in his shroud . . .

Judging the distance as best he could, Baynard Falkan dropped into the pool. He kicked away from the rope, swam to the bank, then turned to see how Guthric and the others were faring. But rainclouds were already overhead, the ceaseless eruptions of spray drawn like a drab linen curtain around the fall.

Guthric released his grip on the rope, twisting clumsily as he fell. He hit the water, sank below the surface, felt a sudden jarring pain at the base of his neck. He'd struck the submerged branch of a tree, the impact stunning him, driving the air from his mouth. His body rolled as he swallowed water, his limbs made sluggish by the blow.

At the far side of the pool Falkan waited, peering into the mist.

But if the Lord of Tremellion was too far away to see, the poacher was not. He'd glimpsed the flinty old Saxon lower himself down the rope, and grinned as Guthric dropped sprawling into the pool. About as much use in water as a cat, Quillon decided. If God made cats that big.

Descending easily, he'd waited for Guthric to thrash his way to the surface. But he hadn't. He'd gone under and stayed there, and Quillon no longer found it droll.

He let go of the rope, arched his body, managed to turn his fall into the semblance of a dive. Then he was under the water, thrusting forward, clawing at weeds, at the tangle of branches, his long arms reaching – groping blindly – *You damned old rock, where are you?*

His fingers scrabbled at leather, caught hold of a woollen-clad arm. Even now the constable proved stubborn, and Quillon was forced to swim underneath him, urge the waterlogged body upward, his own chest hammering for air.

They surfaced near the edge of the spray-sewn curtain. Now Falkan could see them, Quillon gesturing urgently for help. The young knight went in from the bank, he and the poacher hauling the Saxon to the shallows of the reed-fringed pool. They dragged him ashore, rolled the man on his side, then watched with horror as water gushed from his mouth, ran from his nose. Remembering something he'd witnessed when Sir Geoffrey had sent him to serve aboard the fishing boats off Ireland, the warlord's son doubled his hands into fists and pounded at the spread of Guthric's back. There was no finesse to it; just a desperate attempt to make the victim fight for breath. A dozen blows and a further gout of water poured from the constable's mouth. Quillon wiped a matting of weeds from Guthric's face. There was still no movement – then suddenly a twitch, a heave of his shoulders, a raucous, spewing cough. 'He ain't no robber after all,' Quillon observed. 'Seein' as he's given back the river.' Then he reached across and with blissful disrespect, awarded the Lord of Tremellion a congratulatory slap on the arm.

The others arrived without incident. The weapons and moistened sack were lowered, collected by the attackers, the swords and knives handed out. There were no shields or helmets or armour; no grenades of Greek Fire; nothing bulky, for Ranulf's pursuers would rely upon the element of surprise. The speed of attack. And the eels.

It was all but dark now, wind drifting spray across the pool, a fine rain falling from the sky. It willed the men to action, all of them soaked to the skin. But Falkan knew the cold, inclement weather worked in their favour. Ranulf's watchguards would be huddled in doorways, hunched under trees, none of them anxious to patrol the rear of the mill. Why in the devil's name would they need to do so? The pool was walled in on three sides by a cliff, and the only approach,

51

unless from the well-guarded track, was down the fall. Fish might come down. And driftwood. But on a night like this, such a dirty night as this . . .

Even so, he would see to it that the men moved quickly, quietly, edging around the yard. He would give them their orders now, make sure they understood the layout of the mill, warn them that Ranulf Falkan was not to be killed. 'I want him arrested. Disarmed if he resists. Wounded if your own lives are threatened. But on no account shall anyone slay my brother. There's things I have to say to him – things he must recount to me – first.'

The men were nodding obedience when Constable Guthric spoke.

'Which of you was it? Got myself rapped by something under the water. Knocked the air from me. Likely I'd have drowned if –' He lumbered to his feet, swayed for a moment, then glared at the soldiers, the spade of his right hand offered to his saviour.

'So who was it fished me out? Earned yourself a friend. All the days I might live.' Then he watched as the three men-at-arms let their gaze slide across to where Quillon crouched on the bank.

Taking his time, the Saxon dug a deep grave for his voice. 'It was you, joskin? You?'

'All but fell on you,' Quillon shrugged. 'A tangle of limbs like that. Must have caught you as I surfaced.'

'And towed me unwitting to the bank?'

'As for that. It was Sir Baynard came to fish you. Left to me, we'd likely both have drowned.' Then he parted the wet, luxuriant mane of his hair, grinning at Guthric's discomfort.

But the constable's sense of honour ran as deep as the pitch of his voice. 'Get to your feet,' he threatened. 'Take this hand and count me as a friend. Or know what you risk if you spurn me.'

Quillon found much to scoff at in the world. But his impudence fell short of rejecting the Saxon. It wouldn't be so bad to have the flinty old rock as an ally. Knew what he was about, did Guthric. And better to have him as a friend than an enemy. Make a fellow writhe in his dreams, it would, aware he'd crossed the Constable of Tremellion.

He twisted to his feet, bit back his grin, extended his own strong hand. With touching formality Guthric growled, 'The both of us might be dead by dawn, Master Quillon. But it's like I said. You shall count on me. All the days I live.'

'I'll yell if I'm cornered,' Quillon told him. 'And hard though it is to imagine, you do the same.'

*

They skirted the yard, Falkan and the constable, the poacher and the three men-at-arms. The rain was now drumming with dismal intensity, sluicing the ground to mud. Darkness concealed their stumbling progress, though they seemed to Baynard a vulnerably small force to set against Ranulf and his friends. He did not even know how many there were. Ten at least? Twenty at the most? And were women with them, or were the murderers in conference, ready to kick back their chairs and draw their recently bloodied swords?

The attackers pressed tight against the rear wall of the mill. One of the soldiers tossed a length of rope over the high, protruding bar. He looped and knotted the free end of the cord, slipped it in place, tested the water-soaked hemp.

'It should bear our weight,' he reported. 'Though we'd best go one at a time.'

Falkan drew the men close. 'Keep in mind what I told you. If my brother is there, he is only to be arrested. As for the others, his henchmen, they are no concern of mine. Now, pass me the sack, and pray God the bar holds firm.'

It was an odd, unpleasant feeling, the bag of squirming eels against his body. But it swung away as he hauled himself hand-over-hand to the loading doors of the grain store. Revolving dizzily, he jabbed a knife blade between the doors, held it there as he steadied himself, then eased the blade upward, feeling for the hook. Three attempts and the catch sprang free, the shutters prised apart.

Rats twittered and scurried as he scrambled into the loft.

Crouched in the entranceway, Baynard believed he could hear shouts and laughter from the main room of the mill. The squeals of women – *the wagon-load of women?* – and the roared exchanges of men who were drinking, men comparing their pleasures.

He leaned into the cold slant of rain, beckoning the others.

One by one they climbed to the grain store, smothered their gasps as they slumped against the sacks. Baynard allowed them a while to recover, time to check that their knives and swords would slip easy from their sheaths.

He left the store first, edging cautiously down the steps to the long railed gallery. Guthric followed; then Quillon; then the soldiers. All of them crouched low behind the rail, peering at the ill-lit scene the young Falkan had feared, expected, even hoped for. A ripped-out page from the Devil's calendar. An obscenity of amusement in this dank and distant place.

He recognised Ranulf, straddling a woman on a bench near the main door of the mill.

He saw other men, their grey uniform surcoats cast aside. He counted fourteen of them, half with undressed women splayed or sprawled, the others drinking, advising on the performance, bellowing at some indicated joke.

And away to the right, on a sturdy side table, Baynard Falkan saw a row of small, iron-strapped chests, the ones Sir Geoffrey had filled with the plate and coins and jewellery of Tremellion. The lids were tipped back and, so far as he could see, the chests were empty.

He tasted blood. Not merely the blood of vengeance, but the scarlet trickle that emerged from the bitten channel in his lip. Just for an instant, his mouth twitched in a humourless smile. It was once again typical of Ranulf, who could mount his woman and yet somehow cause his brother's blood to spill.

A glance at Guthric, another at Quillon and the soldiers, and the younger son of Tremellion reached for the neck of the sack. 'Not until you hear me,' he whispered. 'Not until I yell.' Then he peered again at the gloomy, candle-lit turmoil of the orgy. Heard the moans and giggles of the women. The grunts and offered humour of the men.

And rose silently to his feet.

His drawn-out howl slashed their throats to silence. Bodies twisted, heads turning, minds unwilling to comprehend what they'd heard. No mere threat. No name. Nothing they could believe was meant for them. Just a single, extended syllable, springing their eyes and mouths open in shock.

'Snaaaakes . . .'

He followed it quickly – *give those bastards no time to react!* – calling down to them, 'Snakes in the room! All about you! Everywhere! There's snakes!'

He loosed the cord of the sack, pulled the neck open, jerked half the imprisoned river eels from the rail. Then he swung the sack behind him, hurled it forward and watched as the moss and serpents sprayed from the bag.

He was rewarded by a scene of shrieking, screaming panic. He saw men withdrawing from their women, rearing back from the chairs and benches, snatching mindlessly at their clothes, a candle, here and there a sword. They recoiled from the spread of the serpents, the shadowed floor seeming to move.

Baynard pulled a dagger from his belt, drew his sword and plunged down the steps from the gallery. *They mustn't be given time, those bastards! Allow them to recollect their wits and they'd once again be fifteen hardened murderers, enraged to be had for fools. The thing to do now was – cut them to ribbons – overrun them –* then corner the gaping Ranulf!

A man dressed in a thick woollen undershirt slashed wildly at Falkan. Deflecting the blade, he jabbed his assailant in the belly with his knife. The man gave a blurt of surprise, then sank away, a hand in retarded surrender.

Guthric went amongst them like a scythe at harvest time, not caring one whit if the men he slew were unarmed, undressed, unfitted for the fight. They were here with Lord Ranulf, they and the chests the Saxon had helped to fill. Their very presence condemned them – as did their being unprepared. Call themselves knights? They weren't worthy of the name! Deceitful murderers, that's all they were, and Guthric had little time for murderers-cum-robbers-cum-whorehounds.

He cut two men so deep they were dead before they fell among the eels. Stabbed another in the throat, swept a fourth across the groin. Glancing around, he saw two of Tremellion's garrison brought low, one of the women gaping in disbelief at the shortened fingers of her hand.

Baynard fought his way toward Ranulf, the elder brother only now thinking to scrabble for a weapon.

Quillon saw one of the enemy lurch from the far end of a table, rearing to hack at Baynard's unhelmeted neck. There was no time to shout. Would it anyway be heard? So all he could do was wrench one of the balanced knives from his belt, flick it underhand, without style, and pray to God it skewered the man before his high-raised sword –

Baynard's attacker jerked forward, an inch of the blade in his spine. His cry of pain alerted Falkan to danger, the young knight stooping, slicing backward, cutting through the cage of his ribs. Quillon glimpsed it, decided to make much of it later, then turned to find himself trapped by two of Ranulf's men.

No one has much to say in the course of hand-to-hand conflict. But Quillon heard one of the men observe, 'Stuff a nice warm cushion, your hair, you pretty.' They came at him then, one from each quarter, giving themselves a decent space to swing.

Issued with both a sword and the belt of knives, the impudent young poacher was at a loss with the long-bladed weapon. Swords were for knights, constables, wardens and sergeants; not for the likes of soft-stepping fishermen, busy with rods and nets in the Hexel River.

So the first blow spun the sword from his grasp, the enemy whirling closer. He flicked one of his daggers, saw a fount of blood as it sliced along a jawbone, then reeled away, shocked as he came up hard against a wall.

I'll yell if I'm cornered.

A joke at the time. But now the joke had curdled, the two men closing in to finish him, each of them eager to claim his cinnamon hair.

'Mine,' one of them asserted. 'It's me that's dripping from his knife.'

His companion faltered, muttered with ill grace, then levelled his sword, hoping to stab the poacher as he sank.

The confrontation had taken less time than the flinting of a candle. The whirl of blades, the flick of the dagger, the thud of Quillon's head against the wall. Even so, it surprised him when Guthric chopped his way forward, cutting the first man's arm clean through at the elbow, catching his balance and driving forward again, left foot slapping the blood-spattered floor as he all but transfixed the second unarmoured knight.

The dismembered man lay dazed, his life flooding away. The other was already dead, Quillon staring vacantly at Guthric. 'How are you so quick?' he asked, as a child might ask a magician at a fair. 'Brawny as you are, *how are you so quick?*'

'Pick up your sword. Keep with me. There's a few of them left as'll fight.'

But in this the Saxon was wrong. Eight of the fifteen murderers had been slain or severely wounded. Two of Tremellion's garrison were dead, the third soldier unscathed. But Baynard had been cut on the thigh, struck a glancing blow on the head, a trickle of blood leaking from the bruise. Quillon was fine, save for the rap when he'd backed against the wall. But Guthric – the indestructible Guthric – was now seen to be bleeding from three separate slashes, all down the left side of his body.

'Bastards caught me from the shadows,' he growled. 'You'll find 'em there, if you look.'

Apart from Ranulf, the seven uninjured survivors had retreated to the north-west corner of the room. They'd been joined there by a number of the women, and it made Guthric snarl with disgust to see the whores fencing the whorehounds. A pity there were women here at all, he thought. Without them I'd as ready mop that corner.

But the lodestone of attention was now Ranulf. Fumbling for his weapon, he'd been late to defend himself, dropping his sword as Baynard had speared a knifeblade at his throat.

He'd already asked, 'Those snakes? Will you see they're swept clear? You know my aversion to them, brother. Anything else, but not snakes.'

'I've a mind to hand you one,' Baynard told him. 'How would it be if I picked one out of the gloom and –'

Then he watched Ranulf recoil, probed after him with the knife-blade, beckoned him to come into the light. 'Don't be concerned. You're more venomous than any creature in England. And I haven't tracked you here to discuss the serpents of the hedgerow. I'm here to exchange a word about our father. And how he was ambushed. And how his attackers were slashed by you and your friends. And why those chests over there – why they're empty.'

Ranulf lifted his broad, square-framed head from the prick of the knife. 'You've been hasty, young Baynard. Hasty and misled. Sir Geoffrey's death was accidental. A clumsy, ill-aimed shaft. Seeing he'd been killed, then yes, I'll admit the injustice of it enraged me, and I saw to it the bowmen were cut down. But should you ever think –'

'Hush,' Baynard told him, lifting the needle-point knife. 'A clumsy, ill-aimed shaft, is that what you'd say?'

'The man exceeded his orders. He was merely told to halt – they all were – halt the train and –'

'You miss my point, brother Ranulf. I asked you if it was a clumsy, ill-aimed shaft that killed Sir Geoffrey?'

'What else? The man loosing wide.'

'Then explain to me – in your own good time – how our father was *riddled* by arrows. In every part of his body. And the saddle. And the satchels. And the palfrey itself, pierced from every side. But before you insult me with lies, add this. Explain what you've done with Tremellion's treasure. Is that what you meant by deal with the Levantine? Sell it all off and pocket the proceeds? You and your scavenging friends?'

Edging back from the knifeblade, Ranulf Falkan managed a weary, long-suffering smile.

'You've misunderstood so much of it, brother. Caused undeserving deaths. I'll agree I stormed from the castle, thinking Sir Geoffrey quite mad. I'll agree I set his lunacy to be halted, but not to have him killed, no, never. Why would I, when I loved him as deeply as you? As for the treasure, he'd no sense of value, our father, and would as likely have exchanged each chest for a suit of armour. God's teeth, my dear Baynard, just look at the row of coffers assembled there on the table. You, too, Guthric – you hear what I'm saying – just look at those chests and ask yourselves what Sir Geoffrey might have done.'

It was a clever speech, this accelerated outpouring of words. It made the listeners pause to unravel it, query it for the nonsense it was, turn toward the heavy, iron-rimmed chests.

And allowed Ranulf Falkan to duck Baynard's blade, edge to one side, then hurl his weighty body through the weather-worn doors of the mill.

It was the survivor of the garrison who yelled, 'My lords! The prisoner! He's out!'

Guthric and Quillon spun in concert, the constable's sword already probing the air.

But by then it was too late, the mill doors swinging, Baynard lurching forward in pursuit. He howled in fury, his voice lost in the rainswept night, for all the world like a blinded brachet in search of a skittering fox.

EIGHT

GUTHRIC BECKONED the women from the corner. There were nine of them in all, three of whom had been injured in the brief but bloody fight. The constable did what he could for them, then asked who'd brought them to the mill. 'Come to that, where's the miller himself?'

Whimpering with fear, one of the whores pointed across the walled front yard of the building. 'Over there, may it please you, master. There's a room of sorts by the stables. The miller and 'im what brought us, they was told to keep company there.'

'How long have you been here, rutting with these pig-swills?'

Uncertain of time, the woman shrugged. 'We was brought 'ere, what'd it be, two nights past? Are we to be handed over, master? I swear we only came along to – what you said.'

Falkan had meanwhile garnered other information, and was now shaking his head at the irony of events. The climbing of the terraced escarpment had been for nothing; likewise the near-tragic descent of the linn. The attackers might as well have burst in through the main doors, why not? *For there were no guards posted around the mill.* Ranulf had been so sure of himself – *and* in the exclusive company of his peers – that he'd simply not troubled to hire men to ring the building.

'I swear it,' Baynard murmured. 'My brother must think he enjoys divine protection. Or more likely the shadow of Satan's scaly wings.' At a loss to understand Ranulf's immeasurable conceit, he conferred with Constable Guthric. Quillon was sent to collect the miller and the man who'd delivered the whores, while the unscathed member of the garrison kept watch over the seven cowed survivors.

Denied participation in the orgy, the miller and wagoner had drowned their disappointment in rough Cornish cider. When they entered the mill it was with Quillon's hands on the collarless necks of their jerkins, their faces suffused, eyes glazed, knees scraping the floor. 'Bit the worse for the apple,' Quillon reported. 'Wouldn't count on 'em threadin' a needle for a while.'

'Take them out,' Baynard snapped. 'Lower them down the well, if you must, but I want them sobered quickly.'

Guthric jabbed a thumb along the room. 'Some of your brother's men, my lord – you can hear them – they've been left this side of dying. You want me an' the man-at-arms to – well, sort of nudge them over the edge?'

'I'd sleep just as sweet if you did,' Falkan told him. 'But you'd best tie their wounds. We'll be rid of them soon enough. The moment our friends in the corner have said their piece.' He turned then, his sword in one hand, knife in the other, and went back to address the prisoners, these titled killers who'd been so readily deserted by their leader.

Baynard Falkan made no attempt to hide his disdain for the captives. Even so, he was aware the man they'd sided with was his own treacherous brother, the man with whom he shared the name of Tremellion.

They were also Baynard's equal in rank; some of them no doubt senior to a mere second son. No matter their crime, they deserved to be treated correctly; *though let just one of them try a fancy phrase, and he'd weigh lighter, by a tongue . . .*

'You have one moment in which to elect a spokesman. He, alone, will respond to my questions. If his answers are insufficient, or if I judge them to be untruthful, I shall have him thrown in the river, upstream of the mill wheel. His death will be as simple, as ignominious as that. It may suit you to think I'd hesitate at the end. But beware, my lords. Each of you murdered my father as surely as did the hirelings. And you most certainly murdered them. I've done my share of killing tonight – and wish it had been more – the smell of death is in the air. Doubt me, my lords, and you'll live to regret it. For as long as it takes the wheel to chew you up.'

He stared at them, searching for a sneer, a smirk that would tell him, *The things Ranulf recounted about you, Sir Baynard Falkan! Sensitive as blossom in frost! With a mouthful of languages, and a pilgrim's knowledge of Europe! My, my, but you must have hardened fast, to speak so rough tonight! Why, my lean young Baynard, I'd wager those blades of yours are even now pulling down at your wrists!*

But the men were not yet ready to chance their lives. It was true; Ranulf *had* recounted a few amusing tales about his brother. But he'd omitted to tell them Baynard was twice his worth in intelligence; clever enough to track them to their hideout, cunning enough to send them howling from a sackful of eels, courageous enough to hack his way the entire length of the room. And quick enough to pin seven of them in the corner . . .

A murmured consultation, then one of the knights took a single step forward, his hands half raised to show he was inoffensive. 'You will not know me, Sir Baynard, though your brother and I – well, I've a manor near Gilberdon. Sir Ranulf has been there on occasion. We've hunted together, though it has to be admitted –'

'Just admit your name.'

'As you wish. It's Justin de Vallen.'

'Where do you suppose my brother will make for, de Vallen? Your place? Some better defended hideout than this mill?'

Unaware of the compliment he was paying, de Vallen said, 'Knowing Ranulf as I do – and you, sire, as I find you – I'd say he'll most likely make for the far end of the earth. Short of that, he might go anywhere. Possibly to my manor, though I doubt it. Could be to any of thirty haunts around.' Then, his voice honeyed with innocence, he asked, 'Why, Sir Baynard? Have you men enough to track thirty different ways?'

Deflecting the probe from the weakness in his armour, Falkan snapped, 'Time will see, de Vallen. Meanwhile, we'll talk of something I've no doubt lies closer to your heart. Plate and jewels and coin. And a phrase I'd like explained to me – *Deal with the Levantine.*'

'I have little to do with them,' de Vallen spurned. 'Perfidious Easterners . . . Turks and Armenians . . . and the so-called Chosen Race, though they were never of *my* special choosing.'

Anxious to forestall a discussion – how the prisoners would love to mire him down with opinions – Baynard Falkan used the blade of his sword to cut the spokesman's reply. 'Sleep with your own damned attitudes, if you will. But I'll tell you this. You're starving my patience. Guthric! Master Quillon! Be ready to see this prisoner to the wheel!'

With an odd show of subtlety, the Saxon pretended to misunderstand the command. Shouldering forward, the left side of his body strapped with blood-stained strips of linen, he snatched at de Vallen, jerking the man toward him. Quillon reacted quickly, seizing the knight's free arm. 'Shortest way's out by the stables,' he offered. 'No more'n twenty steps from there to the stream.'

De Vallen yelled at Baynard. 'I never said I didn't know! Deal with the Levantine? It meant trade with him! Sell off Tremellion's – what was in the chests there – sell the contents to that hook-nosed buyer, the one who's known as the Levantine! Christ in Heaven, are you mad, Falkan? *I'm telling you all I know!*'

Baynard might have released him then; allowed the man to recover. But he sensed he had de Vallen on the run, and that now was the time to pursue him, breach his defences, destroy him in front of his friends. If it wasn't done now, the captive knights might see his threats as no more than gaseous eruptions in a swamp. *Rough talk from the wiry young Falkan, though just like Ranulf told us, blossom in frost.*

'I regret, de Vallen. But you've not said all you know. If the trading took place . . . Where the Levantine might have gone . . . The whereabouts of the money . . . I thought to find some vestige of common sense in you, sire, but I don't. Hurry him off, old Guthric. You too, Quillon. But stay to see he's properly chopped by the wheel.'

With horrible satisfaction, the constable winked at the captives. It was almost as if to tell them the blades would keep on turning; lots of room for seven mangled corpses.

De Vallen went weak at the knees. 'Listen,' he managed. 'Listen, Tremellion . . . Grant me a moment . . . Oh, Christ, grant me a moment and I'll tell you . . . Everything . . . Everything I know . . .'

'Less than a moment,' Falkan told him, 'for all the while I'm reminded you were party to the killing of my father. But let me add this, de Vallen. The very slightest hesitation, and not only you, but all these others, they'll go one by one, skull-first into the wheel.'

Then he waited as the spokesman gabbled, the stones of his story mortared by his peers.

The results of the ambush had exceeded all expectations. So far as they knew, the hirelings had killed Sir Geoffrey, his servants, his cleric and every member of the sixteen-strong escort. The idiot bowmen had then posed with pride as Ranulf and his riders thundered along the track, their stupid smiles pinned to their lips as the horsemen cut them down. For certain, not one of the archers had lived beyond the hour.

The close-helmed knights had caught up the reins of the treasure train, turned the animals round, then led them a half-mile northward toward Launceston. At which point they'd swerved west through the forest, emerging to cross the belly of Bodmin Moor.

A short night's rest in a tavern, then onward again, reaching the mill some twenty hours after the ambush. *Two days easy . . .*

The buyer was already waiting for them, and Ranulf took him alone into a side room of the mill. The miller was entrusted with a small purse of coins and sent the nine miles to Torbridge, with instructions to hire the services of the wagoner and whores. By the time they arrived, the Levantine had departed, taking with him the wealth of Tremellion, hidden in the body of a stinking, unobtrusive cart.

He had valued the treasure at somewhat less than two thousand six hundred marks.

Then explained to Ranulf how hard it would be to dispose of. How long it would take. The risks he would run. The markets he must investigate, abroad. The best he could offer – and was bound to say there'd be little enough profit in it for *him* – was twelve hundred marks. Though by all that was just, it should have been eleven.

According to de Vallen, Ranulf Falken had announced himself well satisfied with the deal. 'The man's a robber, but aren't they all? And at least the Levantine paid smartly, and in gold. You'll all get the shares we agreed before we leave.'

Six words queued for issue from Baynard's tongue. Where is it now, this money? But de Vallen was already pleading to be free of Guthric's grip. 'None of us have ever touched it, save Ranulf. It's still in that side room, where he and the Levantine –'

Falkan nodded to the soldier. 'Break your way in. See if you can find it. And on the life of our helpful de Vallen, I hope you can.'

Silence then, as they watched the man-at-arms club at the door with a heavy stool. Silence at he kicked his way inside. Silence as Guthric squeezed tighter, hoping to hurt. Then a yell of discovery – 'Three sacks of coin, my lord! Don't know what they'd amount to, but they've a weight to 'em, God knows!'

Quillon was sent to collect the wagoner and miller. He'd dunked them in a horse trough till they'd choked, then dragged them to the stables and tied them to a tethering bar. When he brought them again into the presence of Baynard Falkan they were sober and shivering and scared.

Indicating the wagoner, Baynard said, 'Take him to hitch up the horses. Cut two dozen lengths of cord, each a yard or so long. Then wait near the wagon; I've passengers to be boarded.'

As Quillon propelled the unfortunate man from the room, Baynard stared down at the terrified owner of Tresset's Mill. 'You've a name?'

'Gwilym, my lord. It's all I've been known as since –'

'It's name enough,' Falkan told him, 'to be hanged by. And you will be hanged, Master Gwilym, unless I hear the ring of truth in your words. Now, tell me this. How does it come about you offer refuge to these knights? Have they used this place before, Master Gwilym? Are you extravagantly paid to harbour such high-born thieves?'

The miller fell promptly to his knees, shaking his head in frantic denial, words spilling from fear-dry lips. 'I was never allowed a say in it, my lord. 'Twas Sir Ramelar's wish, he's the master of these lands, an' the mill, Master of Tresset an' all the country around. He just sent word to me, told me he'd 'ave need of the place, an' I should be here alone. Normal times there's a lad who assists me –'

'Look over there. Get to your feet and tell me if Sir Ramelar is among those in the corner.'

The miller wiped his eyes, wiped his mouth, peered at the captive knights. Then he turned in misery, as if he knew his case was lost. 'Forgive me, my lord. I wish I could say he was there, but –'

'Examine the wounded. Investigate the dead. You'll find them scattered all about the room. Well, get on with it, damn you!'

Gwilym veered from body to body, whimpered with fright as he stooped to check one of the corpses. Then he called plaintively to Falkan. 'He's found, my lord. Though you've – what I mean is, someone's killed him.'

'How much did he pay you, Master Gwilym?'

'Never paid me at all, my lord. I swear it, sire! It weren't Lord Ramelar's way.'

Falkan gazed at him, believed him, then nodded curtly, allowing the man to see he'd been spared the noose. Gwilym fumbled behind him and sank slowly on to a bench. He was no longer part of the bloody events that had splashed the dull normality of his life.

The women were guided, the prisoners herded from the mill. They mingled in a sorry group in the yard, the knights employed to load their dead and wounded in the wagon. Quillon and the man-at-arms then pinioned the passengers' wrists, using the two dozen lengths of cord. Meanwhile, Guthric growled quietly to the wagoner. Whatever it was he said, it left the man gibbering, and the horses were lashed into the night, taking with them the cargo of whores and whorehounds . . .

One hour more, and the attackers had withdrawn from the Tresset Mill. They carried with them the three sacks of coin – *how pitiably small, compared with the wealth of Tremellion*. Skirting the linn, they called to the two injured soldiers at the head of the falls, then waited for the storm-soaked men to rejoin them.

Ignoring his companions, Falkan turned his thoughts inward. Assuming Ranulf had escaped, avoided the pitfalls of the night and would soon recover his malevolent spirits, the elder son of Tremellion would also remember the Cornish domain was his. Impoverished now

– the treasure bound for the distant markets of Europe, the coins guarded close by Baynard – but nevertheless, the castle belonged to Ranulf, and to him would accrue the income from the lands.

He would recruit again, then ride to claim what was his.

So what to do for the best, Baynard mulled. Conceal the money? Return to the fortress, raise what help he could, then defy his brother?

Or accept the law as it stood; allow Ranulf to govern Tremellion – *and meantime fulfil Sir Geoffrey Falkan's promise*. Take the money across the world to Palestine, why not? Deliver it to the Crusader overlords in the Kingdom of Jerusalem. And by doing so, if God and Magnat-Vaulmier were willing, meet again with the girl who'd touched her lips to his, the comely Christiane.

He announced his intended plan to Constable Guthric. 'I'd have you with me, my friend, though we'll not see England again for a while, if ever.'

'My place has been here at Tremellion,' Guthric said flatly. 'But that because of Sir Geoffrey. Now that he's gone – well, what else would I do, but honour that good man's wishes? Besides, if I stayed at the castle, it'd only be in the hopes of killing your brother. Let's get the money to Palestine first. Like the swine he is, Ranulf'll keep.'

Later, Baynard spoke privately to Quillon. 'The licence I promised you – it will not, I think, be acknowledged by Lord Ranulf. In lieu of it I'll give you sufficient coin with which to purchase a half-mile stretch, on both sides of a river. I suspect you're quite a fisherman, Master Quillon. Both by day *and* night.'

'Never go out at night,' the poacher told him. 'Lose myself in the village, I would, at night. Terrible sense of direction.'

'Well, now, that's a skill we might . . . Tell me, Master Quillon, have you ever been to sea?'

'Nor wouldn't want to.'

'Dreamed of lands more exotic than our own?'

'Can't say I 'ave, m'lord. Though I've a mind to visit London.'

'Heard the stories travellers relate about the women on the sunny isle of – of Cyprus?'

And Quillon leaned forward, saying no, but he wouldn't be averse to hearing.

With a gold mark worth some eighteen times its equivalent in silver, the three sacks of coin weighed close on sixty pounds. Leaving the Tremellion money untouched, Baynard used his own paltry resources

65

to pay for a six-man garrison and two household servants, retaining them until August of that year. If Ranulf appeared by then, claiming possession of the castle, the soldiers and servants were to offer him their allegiance. Otherwise, they were free to choose for themselves; wait unpaid beyond August, or lock up the castle, leave it to God's own will and the weather.

Reassuring them, he said, 'It is my belief you'll not go unemployed. If I know my brother at all, he burns to be Lord of Tremellion.'

He then sent Guthric to recruit a score of able-bodied men from the fields and farms that dotted the domain. They were a motley band, but they came uncomplaining, knowing they owed ten days' free work a year to their overlord.

Baynard issued the men with horses and weapons, told them what he required of them, then bade a silent farewell to the ghosts of Sir William Falkan, the Lady Elena, the cloudy-eyed warrior Sir Geoffrey. He could not promise the ghosts he would ever return to their haunt, though he vowed to deliver the traded wealth of what had once been theirs. Or surrender his life in the attempt . . .

Five days later, with as yet no sign of Ranulf, the young Tremellion led Guthric and Quillon south to the port of Plymouth. The sixty pounds weight of gold was distributed equally between Baynard, the constable, and the newly entitled *sauvegarde*, each man responsible for a strapped pair of saddlebags, with ten pounds of gold in each boiled-leather satchel.

Mishearing, Quillon had asked, 'I'll be what, m'lord, your safeguard?'

It was close enough, and Baynard Falkan had nodded. 'That's what you'll be, Master Quillon, though not just mine. You'll offer whatever protection you can to the constable and, more important than either of us, to the money. You'll obey me in everything, is that understood? *And* show equal obedience to Guthric. In all other things I shall see to your welfare, and respect the title you earned back there at the mill.'

Quillon had thought about it, juggled it in his mind, decided he could see himself as – yes, a springy form of address it'd be, Lord Falkan announcing, 'I must first consult with my constable, and my safeguard.'

On the ride from Tremellion – following the same path on which Sir Geoffrey had died; the only well-travelled route southward to Plymouth – the twenty recruits were sorry Lord Falkan had been murdered. Yet, all things being equal, they were lucky this year, for Sir Baynard would only need them as far as the port. After that they'd be free to go home, get back to their cattle and crops. As for the young knight, the burly Saxon, and the poacher who'd somehow squirmed into Falkan's favour, they were welcome to their future, whatever it might be. Lunatics, all three of 'em, daring to step off the edge of England's coast!

PART TWO

The Peninsula

NINE

It was said that King Richard had summoned more than one hundred ships to meet him in July, in the Mediterranean seaport of Marseilles. It was rumoured that the shipyards of England were crying out for carpenters, offering as much as fourpence a day to men who knew their trade. Word had it that entire forests had been levelled, all the southern ports dinning with the noise of preparation. The shriek of handsaws, clubbing of hammers, rattle of wagons as they delivered the casks of nails, barrels of pitch, lengths of sailcloth, oiled against the rigours of the sea.

Plymouth showed the reports and rumours to be true. There were nineteen vessels ready to leave with the tide, another three under construction in the yards. Swarming with activity, the atmosphere of the docks might well have been described as one of patriotic pandemonium.

With the onset of evening, lanterns were lighted all along the quay. Wooden cranes lifted foodstuffs aboard, then huge strapped bundles, each containing a thousand, two thousand arrows. Pack-horses and palfreys were led up the gangplanks, another crane swinging to load barrels of salted fish, kegs of fresh water, personal baggage and lances and wine and baskets of hard black bread. Crates of chickens were tossed from hand to hand. Squealing pigs were herded into pens on the crowded decks. Courier pigeons huddled in their coops. Knights snarled at their sergeants, who roared in turn at the common soldiers, the men now less afraid of their commanders than of what lay in wait for them beyond the harbour mouth. To risk their lives in battle with the dark-skinned Saracen – the infidel – was one thing. But to go out there on the surging swell of the sea, the foam of rage on its lips, oh, that was different. It'd take some getting used to, that vast expanse of water, with nothing on the horizon to mark its end . . .

The safeguard asked, 'Which ship d'you 'ave in mind, m'lord?' Then he watched as Falkan indicated a double-castle, clinker-built vessel at the far end of the quay. The fore and stern castles resembled the crenellated towers of a fortress, the deck between tented with canvas, a single mast rearing amidships, its square sail furled to the trees.

Without further ado, Quillon strode forward, shouldering others aside. They protested angrily, saw the cleaver he chose to carry, then muttered as Falkan and Guthric widened the wedge. Each of the three led a pack-horse. The animals were laden with hauberks and helmets, swords and lances, the boiled-leather saddlebags, cloaks that would double as blankets, sacks containing a change of undershift, linen surcoat, oil and blades for their faces. The belt at Falkan's waist held a purse of coins, a two-edged dagger. Quillon wore a scabbard for his cleaver, Guthric a pair of flat, empty pouches, carefully fashioned triangles of leather.

The safeguard leading, they made their way to the distant, broad-bellied vessel.

One hand curled to shade the light of the lanterns from his eyes, Captain Gregorius Bigorre watched the men approach his ship. Gazing down from the stern-castle, he waited for them to come level with the carrack, the bulky transport he'd sardonically named the *Gossamer*.

'You've wandered off-course, messires, or come 'ere with a purpose?'

Falkan handed the reins of his horse to Guthric. Then he moved a step forward, stared up at the captain and told him most certainly they'd a purpose – 'To take passage aboard this ship.'

'You'd best find one of the others. Ain't got no room for passengers this time out.' Landsmen, he decided. Eager to find glory in Palestine. The lean one anyway. As for his companions, the long-haired barley stook was in it for the mischief he could make, while the ugly one was probably wanted for murder. They'd likely be trouble, this trio, wherever they went.

Glancing the length of the *Gossamer*, Falkan said, 'I'll admit you're well laden, master, but you've room and to spare for three men and their mounts.'

His broad jaw hedged with a salt-and-pepper beard, Gregorius Bigorre leaned on the wooden battlements of his castle. 'You heard what I just said, messire. She's the very bitch of a vessel, the *Gossamer*, and I shan't have the time to nurse you when you go green. For all I know the three of you are marvels on horseback, but the sea has a way of turning a man's belly inside out. Go and find a steadier vessel, that's Captain Bigorre's advice.'

He was turning away when Falkan snapped, 'I'd have another moment of your time, Captain Bigorre.'

'Oh, you would? To tell me what?'

'Quite simply, that appearances deceive. You, for example. You *look* like a sailor, yet are guilty of wide misjudgement. It saps my confidence, Captain. I'm forced to ask – Is Captain Bigorre the sailor he appears to be, or did he nurture that beard in the safety of Plymouth Sound?'

The master of the carrack wheeled in fury. 'You dare to question Gregorius Simeon Bigorre? Thirty-six times crossed the Channel! Five times sailed to Bordeaux! Been as far north as Trondhjem, as far south as Oporto! And you, you would-be adventurer, who's never set foot on the deck of a ship –'

'Save to fish with the Irish trawlers. And sail to the Norman port of Cherbourg. And return – like you, Captain Bigorre – from Oporto.'

The men annealed their gaze.

Quillon stroked the muzzle of his horse.

Guthric studied the clumsy-looking carrack.

Then Gregorius Simeon Bigorre moved to the steps that led down from the stern-castle, peered the length of his ship and gave a series of low, permissive grunts. 'Well, possibly . . . If we moved some of the stores about . . . Damned extra work . . . But possibly . . .'

'You'd be fairly paid for your trouble, Captain Bigorre.'

'And expect to be,' he grumbled, jerking his head in ungracious invitation.

In the grey of the dawn, beckoned by the tide, seventeen of the nineteen Crusader vessels slipped from their moorings in Plymouth. Of the two ships they left behind, one was burning fiercely, the result of a lantern toppling on to a pitch-coated cask. The other ship had cleared the quay, swung around as her steer-board jammed, then gouged a hole in the overlapped planks of her hull. She was settling fast, listing to port, men struggling to release the palfreys from their stalls, or rid themselves of their link-mail tunics, the mishap already donning the cloak of disaster.

Small boats were rowed to the aid of the sinking vessel, her blazing sister, though none of the other ships dared shorten sail or turn about. The tide was ebbing, calling them to sea. If they were ever to leave as a fleet, they must stay together, abandoning those who'd fallen by the way.

Yet from all the seventeen ships that cleared the harbour, men looked back at the flames and smoke, at the angled mast. It was a bad omen, and some believed they heard the desert-dry laughter of Satan's most cunning disciple, the Sultan Saladin.

Accepted aboard the *Gossamer* by Captain Gregorius Bigorre, the constable and safeguard prayed that Heaven would take their souls. Clinging to the rail amidships, they were violently sea-sick, their eyes streaming with tears and the sting of the spray. Groaning in agony, the Saxon huddled on deck, Quillon sprawled a few feet astern, the younger man cursing with each lift and plummet of the clumsy, barrel-like transport.

So far unaffected, Falkan took the opportunity to crouch beside Guthric, a hand on the victim's shoulder. Shouting with the wind that scoured the Channel, the young knight said, 'My sympathies, old Guthric . . . Not unlike having a tooth pulled . . . Wouldn't you say . . ?'

Then he went away grinning, happily revenged, to join Captain Bigorre at the steer-board, and share with him a gulp of good French cognac.

'Your men seem unwell, my Lord Falkan.'

'Nothing they won't outlive, Captain Bigorre.'

'Like this, was it, when you sailed with the Irish trawlers?'

'One time, in February, I remember – But that story will keep. I'd be better pleased to hear of your own escapades, Captain Bigorre. In the north, say, up near Trondhjem?'

Liking the young knight more by the minute, the master of the *Gossamer* wiped water from the grizzled sponge of his beard. 'Trondhjem,' he recollected. 'Now *there* was a voyage. A vessel the size of a bucket, an' we were half a day out of port, when . . .'

This small part of King Richard's Crusader fleet was headed for Bordeaux. After that they would skirt the Iberian peninsula, docking at Oporto or Lisbon. From there they would pass through the Straits of Gibraltar, sail wide of the Moorish dominated south, then turn north between the mainland and the Islamic-held islands of Majorca, Minorca, Ibiza and Formentera. Clear of the Balearics, the ships would plough north-east to reach Marseilles – and greet King Richard.

That was anyway the plan, good as far as Bordeaux, where the sailors aboard the *Gossamer* grinned in amusement, as Guthric and Quillon made their uncertain way ashore.

And good for some way beyond, the contingent of the Crusader fleet cutting the corner of the quick-tempered Bay of Biscay.

Then suddenly bad, an April squall dancing with reckless abandon across the gulf. A storm so severe, so childishly spiteful, that it kicked the vessels aside like unwanted toys. It sank two of them within moments, drove another two on the dune-edged coast of Les Landes, expelled a further twelve to the grey Atlantic. As for the clumsy *Gossamer*, the transport was blown southward, her sail shredded by the infantile fury of the storm. Falkan's three trusty palfreys were tossed to death in their stalls. Crates and casks were swept overboard, as were two of Bigorre's sailors. Another was crushed, his injuries so terrible that the captain crouched beside him, saw there was nothing to be done for the man, then split his skull with the unseen swing of a plumb. Unceremoniously, the sailor's body was toppled from the stern.

Obedient to the commands of Gregorius Bigorre, the passengers worked alongside his depleted crew. All of them bore the weals of rope burns, livid bruises, stinging lacerations. Another sailor was lost to the waves, one of his shipmates screaming as a cask broke free, rolling jauntily to crush him against the rail. For a day and a night the wind and waves pounded the *Gossamer*, mocking its imitation castles, smashing them to driftwood.

Then, with a final kick of its heels the storm abated, and the shattered nautical fortress drifted, listing, into the tiny Spanish port of Zarueza. The ship's mast was down, her steer-board splintered, planks sprung along both sides of the hull. Carried by the current, the transport collided with the single wooden pier, blundered onward and embedded her bows in the sandy beach of the port. Listing more acutely, the carrack came to rest.

Baynard Falkan looked astern at Gregorius Bigorre. Then slowly, in the fashion of the time, the young knight hammered with his fist in rhythmic recognition of the man's courageous efforts. Guthric joined in. Then Quillon and the crew. Then the fishermen and villagers, Spaniards and English alike beating acknowledgement of Captain Bigorre's achievements aboard the barrel he'd named the *Gossamer*.

The injured were taken to a Cluniac hospice a few miles west of the village. That done, Falkan and the captain returned to Zarueza to review the situation.

A careful inspection of his vessel, and Gregorius Bigorre splashed ashore, shaking his head in weary acceptance of the damage.

'A full month's work, maybe more,' he reported. 'I'll have to send to Bilbao for masting wood, cordage, carpenters skilled in the patching of a carrack. I'd advise you to wait for another Crusader vessel, my friend, except that we're far off their route. You could travel up the coast to Bordeaux, I suppose. What'd it be, close on two hundred miles?'

'No less,' Falkan nodded, though in truth he'd already dismissed the idea of retracing his steps to the north. Likewise, he rejected the thought of crossing the Kingdoms of Castile and Leon, then the width of Portugal to Oporto. He could only guess at the distance – maybe five hundred miles – yet all of it leading away from his destination, the Kingdom of Jerusalem. And Christiane.

The obvious thing to do was ride east, skirting the southern edge of the Pyrenees. He knew the range of mountains guarded Iberia's northern frontier; knew too, of the city-port of Barcelona. From there, the three travellers could take passage for Marseilles, offer Tremellion's money to the Cause, then sail with the bulk of King Richard's Crusader fleet. Reach Marseilles, and maybe Richard would be there in person to greet them . . . thank them for Sir Geoffrey's contribution, safely delivered . . . smile as the knight, the constable, the safeguard knelt before him . . .

But first they must survive the crossing of Spain.

A brief dispute with Gregorius Simeon Bigorre.

'I intend to see your courage rewarded,' Falkan told him. 'In the manner of which, I'll finance the repairs to your ship.'

'You will not!' the captain retorted. 'You paid your passage before we left Plymouth, and it's no concern of yours if I let the old bucket get caught in some springtime squall.'

'You're a good enough sailor,' Falkan snapped, 'but damned ungracious ashore. Take the money and be glad of it. Think of your injured sailors, in the hospice. Think of the stores and weapons you still carry. They're needed in the East, Captain Bigorre. You've a duty to see they get there.' Then, knowing what he said next would win the day, Baynard Falkan shrugged and murmured, 'Perhaps you're right. That leaky old bucket. Hard to imagine she'd get back to England, never mind around Spain and out to the East. Tell you straight, Captain Bigorre, she always did seem unbalanced in the water.'

'I can't even write my name,' Bigorre thundered, 'but suppose a gentleman like you's not unskilled with the pen. So we'll draw up a paper, a copy for you an' for me. A loan against the next – let's see – the next five years earnings of the *Gossamer*. Write it like that, my Lord Falkan, an' in five years time you come to me in Plymouth. Leaky old bucket? She'll earn you half again what you lend her! Unbalanced in the water? By God, but she'll be plyin' her trade when you an' me are gone!'

Then he watched Falkan smile and extend his rope-wealed hand. 'The first thing you do with the money, Captain Bigorre – not to tell you your business – is have someone here in the village sew a flag. A red cross on white. Something your crew can hoist on a pole. Just to show the world what that tub of yours is about.'

Leaving the captain to busy himself with the myriad problems of his beached and battered ship, Falkan strode into the village, drawn by the sights and sounds of the weekly market. He'd already sent Quillon to reserve a night's stay in one of the waterfront taverns; Guthric to purchase three reliable horses and saddlery. Ignoring their whereabouts for the moment, the young Tremellion gave thought to the dangerous road that lay ahead.

He offered a portion of his purse to a slate-eyed merchant, saw what the man would give him in exchange and snatched back his English coins. *'Yo lla estube en esta region,'* Falkan lied. I have been in these parts before.

The merchant offered half again as much, by way of exchange.

Remembering his earlier travels in the Peninsula, away to the west, and the promise he'd made to his father to speak only the language of the country, Falkan said, *'No es bastante. No es nada bastante.'* Not nearly enough.

The merchant decided to be prudent, wary now of the dark-skinned foreigner who spoke his tongue. He added another handful of coins, bowing as he said, *Perdóneme, señor. Pensé que usted era un pelegrino.'*

Did you indeed, Falkan thought with disgust. So you supposed me to be a pilgrim? Someone you could cheat with impunity . . . Then he strode ahead, forcing the merchant to retreat, setting the man's stall of trinkets swaying perilously as he passed.

Gazing hard at the marketeers who took his money, Falkan purchased three brass cow-bells, a length of bleached linen, then three S-shaped cauldron hooks, hanging them from his belt. Along with these he bought shapeless woven hats, water flasks and stiffened panniers in which the riders would store their food.

He then returned to the port to find the Saxon and the safe-guard sprawled comfortably on a tavern bench beneath a canopy of vines.

Ridding themselves of their wine mugs, they came to their feet, Guthric jabbing a thumb toward a narrow alley that led beside the *taberna*. 'You ask me, my lord, I'd say the saddles are better than the horses. The best mounts they had, you can trust me for that, though you'd win 'em at a fair, back home.'

Falkan nodded, aware that Guthric had purchased the best he could. 'And you, my young safeguard? Have you found us a lodging for the night?'

Quillon delayed his reply, brushing aside the salt-stiffened mane of his hair. 'I done what I could, m'lord. Even had to, what you might say, get forceful with the landlord. But it seems – is there a market around here?'

'There is, back in the village.'

'Thought that's what he said. Well, bein' as it's market-time, he ain't got no rooms to spare. So what he's done – he's put us up on the roof.' He waited for Falkan's reaction, then frowned with disbelief as the knight said, 'You've done well, Master Quillon. It's the best place to be, in summer, on the roof.'

'He thought we'd slide off,' Guthric muttered. 'I told him to raise his eyes from the gutter. Told him the roofs were flat.'

'Never troubled to look,' Quillon said. 'Funny sort of a place, to go without thatch.'

They shared their meal of *sopa gallega, chorizos* and local wine with Gregorius Simeon Bigorre. The captain ate hungrily, as did Falkan and the constable, while Quillon poked suspiciously at the rough-cut lumps of fat that surfaced in his soup. He was no happier with the spicy stew that followed, finally restricting himself to bread and the *vino del pais*. 'Flat roofs, a language I can't understand, an' stew as sets fire to your mouth. We going to be here long, m'lord, in Spain?'

Falkan ignored him, leaving Guthric to mutter, 'Fuss with your food, an' you'll be too weak to travel. You know what then, joskin? You'll get left, that's what, left to die in the hills somewhere, or down on some dusty plain. An' the animals they got here ain't half as picky as you.'

The captain assured Falkan he'd do everything in his power to see the *Gossamer* repaired. 'You say she's a leaky old bucket –'

'A remark to provoke some sense in you, Captain.'

'Maybe it was, my lord, but you've my word on it, she'll one day be anchored in Tyre.'

'I have no serious doubts,' Falkan smiled. 'And who knows? I might risk a homeward voyage in the barrel, time and the tides coinciding.'

A while after midnight, Quillon asleep, the constable lay with his eyes half open, watching his master cut the length of bleached linen into three equal squares. Then, taking one square at a time, Baynard pinched the fabric, using the blade of his dagger to slice a number of shallow crescents in the cloth.

Satisfied, he walked to a corner of the low-walled roof of the *taberna*, gazing for a time across the moonlit port of Zarueza . . .

Guthric was lulled toward sleep by the buzz of insects, the lapping of waves on the shore. Then came suddenly awake, peering to see Falkan with one of the cow-bells suspended from a cauldron hook, his dagger reversed, the young knight tapping the rim of the bell with the pommel. Unaware the Saxon was watching, Baynard Falkan murmured to himself, 'Should we ever need them . . . As we might . . .'

TEN

THERE WERE rules.

The men would travel unencumbered by hauberks, wearing nothing more than an undershift and a full-length surcoat, strong boots and a soft, broad-brim hat. If the way became too rocky, they'd dismount and lead the horses. The thick leather boots would offer protection against snakes, spiders, the venomous dull yellow scorpions.

However uncomfortable, they were to wear their shapeless woven hats in the heat of the day. It was a lesson learned by earlier Crusaders from the north. Scorn the power of the sun and a man would collapse trembling on the ground. A few hours later and the skin of his neck would blister, his face peeling, fluid running from his nose. As often as not his mind would wander, his resistance weaken and he'd die. Hundreds had already done so, much to the amusement and advantage of the Saracens.

Here, in Northern Spain, the heat would be less intense, though strong enough to bring down the riders.

There were rules concerning the money. Knight and constable and safeguard alike, each was responsible for his twenty-pound weight of coins. He would keep his linked saddlebags with him at all times, unless he'd clearly entrusted them to his companions. At night, they would take it in turns to stand watch, two hours awake, four asleep, the duties in strict rotation.

They would take advantage of a *taberna* if they found one – so long as they could bar the door to their room. If not, they'd sleep in a deserted shepherd's hut, at the upper edge of a dry-walled field, in an olive grove, in a shallow cave; but always with one of them on guard.

If they were forced to camp in the wilderness, as seemed likely, they would sleep close to the horses. Falkan would allow no fires, however cold the night. They would eat what they carried, or go hungry. They would not fill their water flasks from the rivers, nor permit the animals to drink from them. The vast majority of *arroyos* were polluted, and for a variety of reasons.

Some were tainted with the carcases of sheep and goats that had drowned and been trapped upstream. Others were fouled by the thousands of pilgrims who trudged westward to what was, after Jerusalem and Rome, Christianity's most treasured shrine; Santiago de Compostella. Regarded as the final resting place of Christ's apostle, James the Greater, the shrine of Compostella drew the faithful from the farthest corners of Europe.

But even the faithful needed to fulfil their bodily functions, wash themselves and their clothes, treat their cuts and sores in the turgid, evaporating streams. By doing so, they turned the *arroyos* into drains, numberless pilgrims brought low by the water, as the Frankish troops had been smitten by the sun.

There were other rules, though the single most important dictum was quick and unquestioning obedience to Baynard Falkan. Gazing at Quillon, he said, 'I address this most particularly to you, my young safeguard. Whatever you are told to do, you will do without hesitation. You pride yourself on being – what shall we say? – the black sheep in amongst the white. Well and good. But remember, Master Quillon, my constable here wears a darker coat than you. And as for me – you'd do well to see me as nothing if not a sharp-horned ram.'

'I'm your safeguard, ain't I?' Quillon said doggedly. 'But there's *one* thing I'd ask you, m'lord. That meal they served us, back there in the port. We likely to get it again?'

During the first few days, riding inland from the coast, it was easy. Then they swung toward the east, the tracks less travelled, the awesome wall of the Pyrenees nudging them from the north.

The taverns gave way to crude, slate-roofed huts, these in turn to sheep-pens, then the corner of some long forgotten field-wall. Then to nothing but the ridges and valleys that serrated the land below the mountains.

On the eleventh day of their journey from Zarueza, the riders were forced to skirt a jagged outcrop of rock, nudging their horses down to a stony *rambla*. A torrent in winter, the river bed was now dry, sandy cliffs hardening to a high, rocky ravine.

Lost in the depths of it, their infrequent exchanges echoing from the walls, the travellers were watched by eagles soaring above them, the broad-winged predators assessing the movement below.

Falkan lifted his head in admiration, glimpsed something as he raised his eyes, lowered his gaze to see – yes, a glint at the end of the ravine.

81

He reined in gently, dropped back between the others, then murmured, 'Be ready with your weapons. Draw them if I tell you. But otherwise, here's what you'll do.'

Guthric and Quillon obeyed their lord without question.

They drew the squares of bleached linen from their pouches. Soaked them with water from their flasks.

Hung the upper curl of the cauldron hooks over their wrists, suspending the domed brass bells from the lower curl.

Then they leaned forward, the broad-brim hats concealing them, and covered their faces with the damp, clinging fabric.

His own face masked, Falkan said, 'If God wills it, we'll get through without bloodshed. If not, then I pray He protects you, messires. If it comes to blood, we'll see this river runs high. But before it's spilled, just copy what I'm about.'

With that, he moved his horse onward, hat brim tipped forward, his right hand near the bell. Gazing through the eye-holes of the cloth, he led the way along the bed of the ravine.

Once more the glint of sunlight on metal. Then a faint churn of dust from the mouth of the *rambla*. The chink of pebbles dislodged from the opposite bank.

Starting low, Baynard Falkan moaned a warning to those ahead. '*Enfermos . . . Leprosos . . . Quedese lejos de nosotros . . . Somos enfermos . . . Somos leprosos . . .*' Keep your distance . . . We are lepers . . .

He slapped his hand against the bell, heard Quillon moan in wordless warning, heard both his companions toll their unhappy approach.

Ahead of them, a voice called out across the *rambla*. 'I would not believe it. They sit too well. I would not believe those riders have the disease.'

Another voice answered. 'Do you not see their colour? How palsied they are? And why would they then have the bells?'

Pressing at their doubts, Falkan called, 'No miracle for us at Compostella! We have what we have, and are cursed to spread it like pollen.'

Pebbles fell, dust spurting as the brigands backed away. Turning to Guthric, the same message for Quillon, the knight said, 'The instant we emerge from the cliffs, set in your heels and we'll run. Now ring your bells again. Ring them! Keep up with me – and run!'

The horsemen charged into sunlight, masks snatched away, their shoulders hunched as they risked the gauntlet of the ambush. There were eight scrawny men scrabbling backward – then forward – to their right. Ten or a dozen to their left, the brigands seeing it now, aware they'd been hoodwinked, screaming and cursing and mindlessly hurling blades in the wake of the riders. 'All this time!' they howled. 'Three days and nights we have nested! And now we are greeted by this! We are taken for fools!'

Fools, maybe, but dangerous fools. So Falkan made his men ride hard along the river bed before guiding his mount up a natural sandy ramp and into the foothills. Most of the way Quillon was laughing, delighted by the grotesque trick. 'If you weren't the Lord of Tremellion, nobility an' that, we could go 'round the villages, showin' 'em bits of magic! How'd it be, eh? The three of us, with a bright painted cart –'

The scarred flesh of his face suffused with anger, Guthric swung close to clamp the safeguard around the neck. Biting deep with his fingers, he pulled the one-time poacher sideways in the saddle. 'You ain't got it right yet, 'ave you, joskin? No one addresses Lord Falkan like they was equal, 'less he's a knight of the Christian realm. Which you're not, and never likely to be. Now tell me, joskin. Am I clear to you?'

Quillon gabbled no, then yes, then no again, before wrenching himself from Guthric's bruising grip. Lurching back in his saddle, he massaged his neck, aware there were stairs in life a fellow was never meant to climb. All he could do was get sea-sick, come near to drowning, then be half-strangled when he dared to make a joke.

It was a world away from netting fish in the Hexel.

But more exciting. He'd have to say that. Face an' arse an' whichever way about, it was a good deal more exciting.

They rode deeper into the countryside of Navarre. For three days they followed an eastward tributary of the Rio Yesa, passing between the Pyrenees and the Sierra de la Pena. Several times they abruptly altered direction, swinging wide of their intended route. Notwithstanding their escape in the *rambla*, Falkan was in no mind to court disaster. He would not again risk their being hemmed in by the walls of a ravine, or trapped on some innocent riverside track. If they were forced to fight, they would do so, killing without hesitation. On the other hand, if a snare could be side-stepped, an ambush avoided, they would take the more prudent path. Their crusade was not against the brigands of Northern Spain, but the armies of Sultan Saladin, in the

East. And only that, when the coins were safe in the Christian coffers.

Seventeen days after leaving the coast, they approached an unnamed hilltop village in the region of Maladeta. The upper slopes of the hill were terraced and tangled with vines, the fields below planted with maize or fruit trees, other vineyards, an occasional olive grove. Their progress was watched in silence from the orchards, the stony, sun-scorched plantations. Men straightened from their work, pressed a hand to the ache in their spines; then gazed with shadowed eyes at the passing horsemen.

Airing phrases he'd learned from Baynard, the safeguard called, *'Buenos dias, señores. Que trabajen con gracia,'* but none of the peasants responded to his greeting. Quillon shrugged. *God rot 'em then, the surly bastards. Last time I waste my breath on the likes of them.*

The horsemen continued up the steep, winding track. Guthric was frowning now, worried by something, but unable to say what it was. Not just their lack of response to the joskin's greeting . . . But the absence of – what?

Then it came to him, and he glanced around sharply, glimpsing the peasants halt where they were. But away from the fields. Closer to the track. That was the difference! The sweep of their scythes, thud of their pruning knives was gone. They were no longer working, *but advancing stealthily to bar the riders' retreat . . .*

The Saxon growled at Baynard. 'Seems it's an ill-chosen place to get supplies. Those men back there in the orchards, they're closing in on us. And bringing their blades.'

Gazing ahead, Falkan answered, 'We must hope for another way out. If they mean to harm us, they've doubtless practised their plan. Master Quillon? Are you close enough to hear me?'

'Hear you well enough, m'lord. *And* the padding of feet.'

Without turning his head, Falkan looked down from the track to where the lower slopes levelled to a rock and scrub dotted plain. Some two miles away to the south a more significant formation reared from the *mesa.* 'You see that jumble of rocks? Looks like a child's puppet on its knees. If we need to separate, get yourselves to the far side of it, along by its heel. I trust we won't, but –'

Twenty yards back a man yelled in the dialect of the region. The riders could not understand what he shouted, though the sense was translated by his tone. He was warning those in the village. Spring the trap!

No longer feigning ignorance, Falkan unsheathed his sword.

Quillon drew a wicked long-knife from its scabbard, reaching to loose another in his boot. The Saxon was the last to make ready, for it took him a moment to unbuckle the straps that secured the flat, triangular pouches on his belt. Then he grunted, slipped a loop over each wrist and cupped his hands to catch the shafts of two crescent-shaped axes.

None of them had time to don hauberks or helmets, each vulnerable to arrows, lances, sling-shots. Their horses were untrained and would rear in the face of flame, baulk at a barricade. If the villagers were as practised in murder as Baynard Falkan suspected, then the place was indeed ill-chosen.

Five hundred yards and they'd know.

ELEVEN

HIS VOICE roughened by dust and the fear of death, the young Tremellion yelled to spur his companions. 'At all speed! At all speed!' Then he dug in with his boot heels, prayed the others would keep pace with him, and charged at the unwalled entrance to the village.

The layout of the streets confused them. There was no central thoroughfare, only a narrow circlet that divided, containing the ring of hovels. Faced with a blank wall of yellow baked brick, the riders were at the mercy of their mounts. Falkan's ran to the left, Guthric's to the right, Quillon's stampeding in pursuit of the constable.

Fine yellow earth was churned from the street, swirling around them. Blind to each other's position, they had no choice but to separate, Falkan riding hard and alone around the lefthand crown of the hill.

In response to the shouted warning from the fields, two men were already waiting for the knight. These two alone, so far as he could judge, though one of them armed with a long-reaching scythe, the other with a murderous, olive-wood club.

If he stayed in the saddle, the sweep of the scythe would gout blood from his horse, spilling animal and rider alike. Caught in the stirrups, or crushed by the fall, he'd be easy prey for the whirling, knob-headed club. This was no place for cavalry, even less for a chevalier whose armour was packed and out of reach.

Wrenching the horse's neck, Falkan hauled in on the reins. More dust spurted, obscuring the enemy, the palfrey trampling close to the outer edge of the street. A few more steps and they'd have pitched from the unwalled brink, falling twenty feet to the vines.

But if ignorance and mischance had brought them to this village, the balance was tipped – at least for the instant – in their favour. His feet free of the stirrups, Baynard threw his weight to the side, felt the animal stagger, steady itself, then back away from the edge. Aware that his mind was hammering his thanks to God, the young knight swung from the saddle, slapped the palfrey away, then crouched in the fresh explosion of dirt and dust.

Last seen, the enemy were ahead of him, to the right . . . The one with the club closer to the house walls . . . Yet the man he most feared, the one with the scythe, maybe less than ten feet away . . .

He sensed the air clearing in the wind. A leaking of time. The moment had come to emerge from cover. To go forward and kill, or be killed.

Quillon would remember the scene all his days. Four men barred the righthand curve of the street, two of them armed with scythes, another with an iron-pronged pitchfork, the last with a heavy wooden flail. The swingle of the flail spun in the air.

Like their separated master, Guthric and Quillon had reined in hard, dismounted in the dust cloud, then gone forward ahead of the horses. Whatever they did, they'd have to do it fast, for the peasants were even now pounding up the track from the fields and orchards. A few moments more and the constable and safeguard would be trapped, the treasure-laden horses seized and looted.

So, blinded by the dust-storm, Quillon turned in astonishment as Guthric said, 'You got your water flask with you?'

'What? No, it's –'

'Take mine then. Here. *Here!*'

'For the love of God, Guthric, there's men –'

'Wash your eyes with it, joskin. Do it, boy! *Do it to clear your sight!*' He thrust the flask at Quillon, the carved wooden stopper already knocked aside. The young man lifted it, splashing his face, then hurriedly rinsed the yellow dust from his eyes. Discarding the flask, he heard Guthric snarl at him. 'That one, the one with the flail. Fish him, joskin. Fish him with your knife. Then him, with the pitchfork. Throw at both of 'em. Poach 'em for me, the way you've done for years.'

His face now smeared with rivulets of mud, Quillon no longer defended his crimes. He'd been accepted by both Falkan and Guthric, offered adventure, entrusted with a third part of the treasure. He was now regarded as someone worthy of more than mutilation or the noose.

Apart from which, the moments were worn to a ravel.

His long-knife took the man with the flail in the chest, the laden air seeming to stir with the shriek of pain. He reached into his boot, hurled a different, wider blade, then cursed as it did no more than slice skin from the one with the pitchfork.

Unarmed now, he turned helplessly to Guthric. But the Saxon was no longer beside him.

*

Memories tumbled like fragments of glass in Baynard Falkan's mind. Sir Geoffrey, dying in ambush . . . His younger son being trained to fight in the mud and rain of the fens . . . The attack on the mill, Ranulf escaping so easily . . . The need to see Tremellion's money delivered . . . Live to see it done . . . Once again to see Christiane . . .

He came low and fast from the dust cloud, his sword arm bent, elbow couched tight to his body. Going first for the man with the scythe, he managed to slip beneath the sweep of the blade. Then he thrust upward, hearing the man gasp, seeing him glare with dying disapproval. The man's eyes seemed to say, you should have been upright; I've been killed unfairly.

But this was no summer joust, with pennants flying, silken favours tied to a blunted lance. This was just another form of ambush, with no quarter offered, *sauve qui peut*.

The second villager came at Falkan, swirling the olive-wood club. Caught off-balance, the young knight rolled sideways, abandoning his sword.

The bludgeon swung down, Baynard scrambling wildly, unsure of his direction. Please God, he thought, my father can't see me from the station he's earned in Heaven. A son of Tremellion rolling in the dirt, squirming like a weasel to avoid some peasant's club.

He glimpsed the man come after him again, the weapon hefted for its final, shattering blow. No chance now to weasel away. All that was left was to roll in tight at his attacker, frantically clawing at the man's sore-pocked legs.

He felt the wind of the bludgeon on his skull, heard a roar of surprise, then winced as the man tipped over him, over the edge of the unwalled street and down to the terrace of thick, corded vines . . .

Ignoring his enemy's moans, Baynard tugged twice to free his sword from the bone and muscle that claimed it. Then he stumbled in search of his horse, caught at the reins and swung shaking into the saddle.

Only now did he spare time for his friends, praying they too had escaped from this unnamed hilltop snare.

They hadn't, not yet, though Quillon was standing in slack-jawed witness of events.

His own efforts expended, he'd peered to see Guthric lumbering forward, the Saxon's crescent-shaped axes cutting the tangible flesh of the air. And all the while he advanced, he bellowed from the depths of his body, the words without meaning, the sound of them enough to scatter wolves.

But the men who faced him with scythes were less than lupine, already backing away from the monster, tripping in retreat. The call from the fields had come late, they told themselves. They'd had little time to prepare, they told themselves. They should have been warned these weren't ordinary travellers. God knows it, not ordinary at all.

Dropping their weapons, they fled. Guthric swerved to murder the man who'd carried the flail – *Go into battle, you must expect to die* – then yelled at Quillon to run the horses along.

Two from the right, Falkan alone from the left, the riders fled down the side tracks from the village. As companions, they'd come close to death, killed at least three of the enemy, failed in their innocent search for food and shelter.

Yet they'd once again protected the treasure. And, in their own terms at least, kept faith with the wishes of Tremellion.

It may well be that the taint of blood lingers, or that past aggression is reflected in the eye. What is certain is that each man has an aura about him; this one gullible, that one a weakling, the third untouched, emanating danger.

Whether rank with the blood of the unlamented villagers, or annealed by their escape, the travellers rode unchallenged through the sun-bleached Kingdom of Aragon.

Better yet, they reached a village near Escardille, found a tavern in the square and were told they'd timed things nicely; tonight would be the *Fiesta de la Fuente*, a celebration to which no priest had ever been invited.

Impressed that Baynard could – with some effort – understand him, the inn-keeper took his young guest aside, to explain how it would be, this Festival of the Fountain.

'The country you come from, I cannot say it's the same, Señor Halcón. But here, in our village – May I ask it, are you married?'

'Not – No, señor, I am not yet in that state.'

'Excellent. Then it's safe I continue. About the fiesta. And why we prefer our priests to be absent tonight. It is, how to say it, somewhat free, Señor Halcón. Much to the liking of the young. And lovers. And those who have always, if you wish, admired some certain lady from afar. Our only rule, and this we uphold with a hanging, is that at no time should violence prowl the streets. If a husband feels his wife has been, how did I say it, somewhat free, it's for him to settle accounts when the festival is ended. But from dusk tonight . . .' Then he opened his hands, stretched his fingers like starfish, and expressed an eloquent mixture of worldliness and happy resignation. *'Señor Halcón, la vida es la vida, no?'*

Baynard relayed the news to Guthric and Quillon. Whatever their views of morality – probably none – he wanted them to know the dangers of violence.

'Any brawls, skirmishes or the like, and they'll haul you away to be hanged. I'd regret that, messires, for I count on your company, at least as far as the Christian port of Tyre. But we have to understand; the rules are not of our making, though must be obeyed. So, if someone insults you, you'll – What, Master Quillon? What will you do then?'

'Take him aside for a quiet word, where it's dark?'

'Then start pushing? An exchange of fisticuffs? A roundelay with knives? No, my young safeguard, you'll do nothing of the kind. If it happens you're insulted, you'll wear it like an honourable scar. If you're struck, you'll withdraw with dignity, carrying the mark. If not – then here's the choice. You'll enjoy no girls in this pagan *Fiesta de la Fuente*, because the villagers will have hanged you. Or I'll have you reported tonight, to save your life, and see you locked away till the festival's over.'

Quillon looked at Baynard Falkan. 'Get insulted, an' wear it? Be struck, an' back away? I 'ave to say, m'lord, it ain't in my nature –'

'The girls, so I'm told, come from miles around, to see who's who at the fair. And you, with your lion's mane . . .'

'Well,' the safeguard murmured. 'So long as it's honourable. An' dignitied – that the word?'

'It comes close enough,' Falkan told him. 'It fits with what I ask.'

As for the seamed and hard-eyed Saxon, he was already raking women from the square with his gaze.

The village blossomed with torches and tapers, candles and sulphurous smoke. Within an hour of the eruption, the once Cornish poacher was known as *el léon*. Pretty young women paraded across his view, glanced to see if he'd noticed them, fought with calm determination to be close when he swivelled his feet. *Santo Dios*, but he was tall and well built. *Un hombre hermoso*. And see his hair, how it swung in the breeze of the night . . .

The ugly Saxon was not a man to be seduced. He'd already seen

90

the woman he fancied, barged a path through the crowd toward her, then simply caught her by the naked slope of her shoulders. 'I don't know a word of your language,' he told her. 'Don't even care to learn it. My name – me – it's Guthric. I'm Lord Falkan's man. And you? Who are you?'

Scared of him, yet fascinated, the dark-eyed woman seemed to spark her gaze in response. *'Guthric? Tu nombre es Guthric? Yo, mi nombre es Juana.'*

'If I'm knocked again by these dancers,' the Saxon told her, 'I'll give 'em a dance they never thought to see. Take me somewhere quiet, Juana. Just you an' me an' some wine. You understand?'

Then he nudged her from the crowd, handed her money and pointed at a wine stall, grunting as she bought a fine, fat-bellied flagon.

After that it was Juana who led the Constable of Tremellion along a series of alleyways and up unlit stairs, the strains of the fiesta fading behind them.

Falkan was meanwhile stretched out on his bed, determined to let the festival pass him by. God knows, they were attractive; these promised hours without violence; a rainbow of pretty women; and how much he wanted them, the thought alone disturbing him.

But more than some girl from Escardille, he wanted Magnat-Vaulmier's daughter. Wanted her with an urgency that made him toss and turn on the rope-webbed bed.

He rolled on his side, stared at the wall, then twisted on to his back again, laughing harshly at his pious pretence.

For the sake of all that's natural – You are twenty years old, Tremellion, and as lusty as the rest! What do you think to gain by sprawling here? Christiane's respect for your discipline? For your new-found celibacy? And all this for a woman you dream of marrying, yet may never see again?

Almighty Christ, you're not betrothed to Vaulmier's daughter! For all you know she has a dozen suitors more eligible than you! Why should she wait for you, Tremellion, when all you'll be is a penniless knight – and unskilled in the arts of love?

Oh, yes, you've enjoyed a few women in your time. Fumbled with girls in the grass. Been in and out of love on occasion, and each in the space of a week. But now you sprawl here, a man who's killed men, writhing with unwilling fidelity for someone who'll probably greet you and ask, 'Did we ever meet before, my Lord Falkan?'

He flung himself from the bed, washed his face, buckled his weapon-less belt. All the while he struggled to translate the things he might say. 'A pleasure to meet you, señorita. You must tell me the name of this village. And forgive my accent. I'm from King Richard's Realm of England. I call myself Falkan – Halcón, if you prefer.'

Then, with a scathing glance at the ghost of his own piety, he made his way downstairs. The coins safely hidden, Baynard alone knowing where, he emerged at the edge of the *plaza*, hoping to find a woman who, in reality, would help him forget the woman of his dreams.

An hour of music, the flaring of candles, cavorting of clowns, the sleight of hand of *ilusionistas*.

Pretty young girls tempted him with their glances, and he twice joined the swirling spectrum of the crowd. But it wasn't until an hour before midnight, that he saw the one he wanted. Saw her and lost her again. Carelessly tipped a table in his efforts to see where she'd gone.

By accident or design, she led him a desperate dance. One moment she was there in the throng; the next departed. The lean young knight edged his way in pursuit, his natural advantage of height denied him by the hats and ribbons, the mists of coloured smoke.

He saw her near one of the stalls and sprang to follow.

A man caught at his arm and demanded, 'Who would you be, señor, to nudge my wife?'

Anger rising, Baynard fought to suppress it. 'Forgive me, señor, I am clumsy. I have no wife as beautiful as yours, so must hunt the best I can.'

The man grinned at him then, pounded his shoulder, told him to continue with his chase. 'You have the eyes of a hunter, señor. I am sure you will corner your prey.'

Falkan bowed himself from the couple, glimpsed the girl again and moved to intercept her. Unfortunately, she was now hemmed in by three eager young men, one of whom presented her with a sprig of dried spring blossom, another with a gaudy ribbon keepsake.

Falkan's next move might well have seen him arrested, or worse. But it mattered to him to meet this girl, and he shouldered aside her cluster of admirers.

Aware his Spanish was not good enough for the task, he snarled at them in English, sensing them step back in confusion, scowling at this outlandish interruption. Then he took the girl by the hand, led her firmly away, and prayed to God his knowledge of her language would somehow see him through.

'My senses have been set alight, señorita, since my eyes were brightened by your passing. In my own country – far from here – your beauty would be as the summer sun, melting winter.' Then he grinned and said, 'I must ask myself, which offends you most? My behaviour, or my accent?'

The girl moved away from him – but not, he noticed, to seek the protection of the crowd . . . Her reaction was cautious, her dark eyes wide, the set of her lips not yet moulded, neither hardening to anger, nor filling to a smile.

'How do you know our language?' she murmured. 'This is not a place to which foreigners –'

'I have visited this country before. Not here, but away to the west. I'm from King Richard's Realm of England. You must tell me the name of this village, señorita. I call myself Falkan – Halcón if you prefer. And you? Or shall it just be the summer sun?'

'You chose well,' she said. 'All the way from wherever it is, to be here for the *Fiesta de la Fuente*.' Then she took his hand and led him to a shadowed corner of the square, colour and flame and scented smoke closing behind them.

Her name was Inés.

Fifty paces from the *plaza* and they were in her small, private chamber, half a flight up from her married sister's rooms.

Taxing Baynard's knowledge of her language, Inés said, 'You should know, Halcón, I have only chosen you tonight because . . . Because it pleases me to compare our different ways. The Spanish style of love, you understand me? And yours, the far from here.'

'Knowledge is fruit on the trees,' Falkan nodded, 'though I think we'll find no great difference, strolling the orchards.'

He made his way through the high-walled garden at dawn. Gently closing the gates, he looked back at the house, heard the creak of an upstairs shutter, then nodded in the direction of the sound.

Christiane remembered again, Inés would never be forgotten. For that is the thing about it, when love goes well. Memories remain, as fresh in the mind as if the body had never aged.

TWELVE

HUNCHED AND weeping in the heavy military saddle, Doña Amata, Condesa de Monzón surrendered to the nightmares of midday. Her mind assailed by the demons of guilt and regret, she dared not even glance at those who shared her suffering. What had happened was none of her doing, but, had she honoured her vows, it might never have happened at all.

Some four months earlier, the young condesa had set out from the Catalonian *señoria* of Monzón, accompanied by her *compañera*, Doña Rosalía, ten devout members of the household and twenty-three from the village below the castle.

It had started well, the pilgrims escorted by a detail of the Knights of Santiago, a military order also known as the Knights of St James of the Sword. Strong, arrogant young men, they wore white surcoats, overstitched with a red cross on the shoulder. The cross was designed in the shape of a downpointed sword, a stab at the heart of the enemy, the Almohad Moors. These had swept up from Africa centuries before, seizing all but the north of the Iberian Peninsula. Since then, little by little, the Spaniards had driven the Almohades back. Though even now, almost five hundred years after their first invasion, the Moors had not yet been hurled into the sea.

Not that the Knights of Santiago were concerned by events in the south. *Their* task – and one they guarded with the utmost jealousy – was to protect the pilgrims who made the arduous journey to the shrine of St James of Compostella.

Offering a handsome contribution to their Order, the Condesa de Monzón had been granted the protection of six young knights, dramatic in their white surcoats, black helmets, black link-mail tunics, black scabbards and gloves and boots. With these élite defenders of the Christian Way at her side, the thirty-year-old Doña Amata had led her fellow-pilgrims to the burial place of St James the Greater, out there near the western tip of Spain.

She had never asked – in truth never cared to know – why the others had chosen to visit Santiago de Compostella. We each have

94

our reasons, she supposed, content that she would pray for the soul of her husband, Don Alejandro, killed in a skirmish with the Moors. Two years he'd been dead, and her pilgrimage late, God drumming His fingers with impatience. But she'd been there now, she and Doña Rosalía, those from the household, those from the village, the black-and-white *freyles* riding attendance . . .

The journey to Compostella had been long and tiring, yet as God might have wished it.

Prayers had been said, votive candles lighted, offertory boxes filled. The vivacious Amata had recanted her sins and been assured Don Alejandro was with the Spanish nobility in Heaven. She had then turned away, her duty done, albeit later than she'd promised, and started back toward the security and comforts of Monzón.

And then, with all but a week of the return journey completed, a powerful force of brigands had surprised the pilgrims, tearing the band apart.

Outnumbered five-to-one, the knights had acquitted themselves with honour, cutting down some twelve of the brigands for the loss of two of their brethren. But the villagers had panicked, scattering across the sun-seared plain. The members of the household had likewise fled in disarray, the brigands swooping to murder or maim them, then strip them of whatever they possessed. The cart in which Amata and Rosalía were travelling was overturned. Mules and pack-horses stampeded, the ground littered with souvenirs purchased by the pilgrims.

When it was over, two of the knights were dead, another two wounded and unhorsed. Seven of the villagers had been killed, another three dying before dark. Of those from the household of Monzón, four had been slain, as many injured, though these last were able to limp and stumble from the scene.

In short, of the forty-one pilgrims and knights who had set out on the homeward journey from Compostella, fewer than a dozen had escaped the knives and bludgeons of the attack.

Tragedy enough that so many lives had been lost. But a tragedy that had not yet finished with the travellers, for the cart was wrecked, its horse's neck broken in the fall. The pack-animals had been driven off by the brigands, along with all but two of the palfreys, leaving the pilgrim band at the mercy of any sharp-eyed *bandidos*.

Doña Amata wept again, her slender legs spread wide on a saddle that wasn't hers, her fingers curled around reins too thick to control.

*Sweet God, if I had only enacted my promise sooner than this . . . But
I chose to keep You waiting . . . And gave the devil time to recruit his
filthy . . .*

A hand raised to her face, hiding her shame, the desolate young
condesa was unaware the weary mount had strayed from the
path.

The three Crusaders had camped below the skyline, the night spent
in comfort on the slope of a sandy hill. It had taken them a while to
climb the escarpment, but the effort had been worth it. A steep fall
on the other side of the ridge offered protection at their backs. In
front and below them the slope ran down to a plateau, beyond which
lay a series of arid hills, diminishing to a bare expanse of desert. Not
that they'd need to cross it. They'd ride eastward now, reaching the
coast in less than two weeks.

For once, Baynard Falkan had relaxed his rule, permitting a fire
after dusk. Guthric had dug a pit in the sand, Quillon skinning a wild
dog he'd snared, the carcase cooked on a spit. The men had chewed
the stringy meat, shared a flagon of wine, talked with something akin
to respect of the *Fiesta de la Fuente*. Then, with one of them always
on watch, they'd slept peacefully on the fast-cooling sand . . .

Awake at dawn, they'd followed the ridge of the hill, reaching a
stand of stunted oaks before noon. If travelling were as easy as this,
Quillon thought, I wouldn't hold it so hard against this foreign place.
All we need now is a fresh-water stream, bubbling out from the low
side of the trees.

He went to look for it, peered at something moving on the plain,
then turned to call the others. 'What d'you make of it? Think those
folks is alert to what they're doin'? Seems to me they're headin' out
toward the desert.'

Falkan took his time to study the scene. Heated by the midday sun,
the air seemed to shimmer and swirl above the plain. All colour
had been bleached from the ground, though he would afterwards
remember it as cheap-made parchment.

Squinting, then turning aside as if to cool his gaze, he noticed two
riders – children by the size of them, children on their fathers' horses
– and a string of twenty or so followers, all of them performing some
grotesque, slow-motion dance.

Were they arm-in-arm? It didn't seem possible –

He refreshed his eyes in the dimness of the trees, peered again at the column, realised now they were helping each other, not dancing at all, but staggering –

Guthric said, 'I count four of 'em dressed alike. Black and white. Two up near the horses, the others –'

'I see them now. I mark them as having swords. And you, safeguard, what do your keen eyes have to tell us it's about?'

'Those two on the horses. If they ain't children, then they're women. An' old – an' the constable's right. Four soldiers, armed an' they could be in armour. As for the rest, they're injured or dyin' of thirst. Look there! One of them's down. I tell you, m'lord, whoever they are, they're in the devil of a stew.'

Falkan nodded, muttered something to himself, then came to his feet. 'We'll pay them a visit. So far as I can tell they're just travellers, pilgrims maybe, though I'm wary of a trap. If you see me swing away, you do the same. Be ready with your weapons. Hold your mounts to a trot.' Then he strode through the stand of oaks, loosed the tether-rein of his horse and rode out into the blazing heat of the ridge.

Fifty yards on and the riders leaned back hard, their spines pressed to the cantles of their saddles, the animals plunging and slithering down the long shallow slope to the plain. Dust rose in a plume behind them, feathering their descent.

And alerting those below.

Of the six young knights who'd escorted the pilgrims, only two had retained their horses. These they had offered to the countess and her *compañera*, though on the strict understanding that if needed –

Enrique de Vaca saw the plume of dust to the north. His neck burned by the rim of his armour, his linen-covered helmet no more than a calyx of torture, he forced himself to the head of the column, blinking with pain as he told the condesa to dismount.

She turned away as though to refuse him, yet in fact to spare them both the shame of her tears. Then she slipped from the saddle, dropped to the ground, held out the thick leather reins. 'I have seen them, señor. By the dust they make, a force of –'

'We don't know,' he grunted. 'Maybe not so many. Keep close to your companion. And I pray you, Doña Amata, do not run.'

'Run?' she cried weakly. 'And to where?'

Enrique de Vaca's brother knight, Arias de Barragan, had already half-assisted, half-evicted Doña Rosalía from the saddle. 'You will forgive me, my lady, but we ride to save you both.'

97

Older than Amata de Monzón, the *compañera* was realistic, calm even now in the face of another attack. 'Save us or not, young Arias, you do credit to your Order. If we die, it's at God's behest. If it's you, I shall see your name remembered. If me, then the good Lord must have flicked back through the pages, catching up with those He overlooked.'

Arias managed the vestige of a smile, then jerked his horse to the left, to the north, to where the plume was now a crest across the plain.

The two remaining knights, those who'd been wounded and unhorsed, drew their swords and waved the women to stand behind them. If de Vaca and de Barragan died out there on the field, then honour and life might still somehow be saved. After all, a Knight of Santiago was as much a warrior afoot as ahorse, as ferocious when wounded as unscathed.

Two, Falkan remarked to himself, though drumming as if to have dealings.

He watched them come closer, admired the way they rode, parting now so their swords wouldn't touch by mistake. You would also have to spread your gaze, he noted, to keep them both in sight.

He allowed them to come within earshot, then caught a hand around the pommel of his saddle, rose in the stirrups and yelled at them, 'I am as you! Knight and traveller! And to help you, not to harm.'

In a single, unbroken manoeuvre, the Spaniards swerved away, Enrique de Vaca to the right, Arias de Barragan to the left. The knights seeming to flee – but no, only to turn and rejoin each other, this time approaching more slowly, but with swords still naked.

In the accent of Catalonia, Enrique said, 'Three foreigners? How could that ever match against us two?'

'I salute your confidence,' Falkan told him, 'though you must rope the bulls, before you call them yours.'

'Your Spanish is not good,' Arias told him. 'But I like the idea of the bulls. You are perhaps what you say, señor –?'

'Lord Falkan of Tremellion. From the island of England. These two my companions. Dressed though we are as travellers, we are bound for Marseilles, then the Christian Kingdom in Palestine, where we intend to serve the Cause. And you, my brothers? Do you also carry your blades in the name of Christ?'

Aware that Falkan's weapon was sheathed, the Spaniards buried their swords in their long black scabbards. Then with weary, sun-hammered ceremony, they announced their names, their station, their *encomienda*, near the port of Tarragona.

Each man taking his turn, they recounted the events of the pilgrimage, offering no apology for their defeat at the hands of the brigands. Halcón would accept it, or he wouldn't. Even as a foreigner, he surely had a mind of his own.

'Six shepherds,' Baynard murmured. 'Thirty sheep, and about the same number of wolves. I'd raise this shapeless hat to you, my brothers, if I wasn't so worried the sun would cook my head.' He'd wished to say fry the scalp, but the words were missing, not that it seemed to matter. Enrique said, 'We welcome your presence amongst us, the three of you, and as proof –'

Then with foolish determination, he jammed the heels of his hands under the linen-draped rim of his helmet, lifting the casque to reveal a circular welt of torn and blistered skin.

For the first time since their meeting, Falkan nudged his horse forward. 'Wear it,' he said gently. 'One never knows when the next attack might come.'

Enrique de Vaca blinked at him, found something to respect in Falkan's eyes, and lowered the blood-rimmed helmet back in place. 'There are women,' he announced. 'We must guide them to safety. Soldiers of the Cross . . . Together . . .'

The arrival of the English Crusaders was greeted with suspicion, then a sad display of relief. The pilgrims lurched toward them, swayed unsteadily, reached to grasp their hands. They believed themselves saved now; who wouldn't, with the ugly Guthric up there in the saddle, a pair of crescent-shaped axes pouched and buckled to his belt?

Baynard dispensed what little they could provide. A flask of water. A roll of linen strip. Three clean undershirts, these torn apart to make a crude form of headgear for those pilgrims who'd cast aside their robes in the panic of flight.

Arias de Barragan asked if they'd be willing to dismount, and let the injured ride.

The Englishman told him no. Under no circumstances would he be parted from his horse. Nor would the others. Not for the sake of the women, or even the wounded.

Arias retreated, eyes hard as dark-veined marble.

Then Enrique said, 'You saw from up there, from the trees . . .

Saw how we gave our horses to the condesa and Doña Rosalía. Yet de Barragan tells me –'

'What I will tell you, Señor de Vaca. If your last two animals were to die, then your ladies would walk with the rest. You'll not understand me, and I've no wish to explain, but without these mounts, and the special burden they carry, the Christian Cause will be weakened. Now, dampen that murderous glimmer, and have me presented to the countess. If it were not for her and these melancholy pilgrims, we'd be far ahead on our trail.'

Notwithstanding the heat of the day, the meeting was chilly. Doña Amata managed a formal murmur of gratitude to Falkan, accepting his offer of protection as far as Monzón. But she was still at the mercy of her own guilt-ridden thoughts, still casting around to find fault with the world in general. The pilgrims had spent too much time at Compostella. Wasted time on the homeward journey. Shown their weakness by fleeing from the brigands.

'I trust the pilgrims of England are better disciplined than these, Señor Halcón. *And*, I would add, that the knights of your military Orders fight with more determination than our own *freyles caballeros*.' She cast a dismissive, tear-stained glance at her escort, deciding they were the ones to bear the blame.

Enrique de Vaca stared up at her, muscles cording in his jaw. He said nothing, shocked and damned by her accusation, knowing that, yes, the Knights of St James of the Sword *had* failed to save the pilgrims, but not, in the name of God, through lack of courage.

Falkan looked around, saw that not only de Vaca, but Arias de Barragan and their wounded brethren had heard the condesa's words. He caught sight of Doña Rosalía, her fine-boned features soured with displeasure, the older woman glaring at her mistress.

Not caring that his Spanish was perhaps unequal to the task, Baynard Falkan said, 'A moment of your attention, Doña Amata. Sad events have overtaken your party, and I regret to hear of your losses. But your remarks concerning these knights are ill-founded, discourteous and – wanting a better word – quite simply untrue. I have seen these men ride, seen how they handle their swords, though do not need a display of either to be assured of their prowess as knights. They were, I believe, attacked without warning and out-numbered five-to-one. The brigands were mounted, the pilgrims scattering, and you choose to say your escort lacked determination in the fight? In my opinion, Doña Amata, you are fortunate to be served by these Knights of Santiago. You are even now riding de Vaca's horse. Hire me, and you'd be walking.'

Then he pulled his mount away, gestured to Guthric and Quillon and rode ahead to where the plain narrowed to a long, shallow valley. Another of the many places in which *bandidos* liked to lurk.

Quillon thought, I don't know what all *that* was about, but Lord Falkan can't 'alf snap it out in their language when he cares to. Last I saw, the woman was all set for another spray of tears.

As ignorant as the safeguard, Guthric was unconcerned by the exchange. His duties were simple. Show allegiance to Tremellion in the sinewy shape of Baynard Falkan. Defend him, protect the money, help see both delivered safe to Marseilles or the Holy Land. Arguments in a foreign tongue were just that to the constable. But the scouring of a valley for brigands was much more to his taste.

THIRTEEN

TWICE THEY spotted movement in the hills, the riders spurring to face an attack. But nothing came of it, the ragged band continuing on its way. During that last long week another pilgrim died, while a second disappeared, muttering madness, in the night.

And then it was over, the towers of Monzón sighted to the east, the survivors croaking their cheers, chanting their prayers. With swollen faces, festering wounds, parched and scabrous lips, the pathetic group stumbled toward the valley, the river that watered it, the shelter of their homes.

Horsemen galloped from the fortress to greet the condesa and Doña Rosalía; to demand a full accounting from the escorts and query the presence of the English on the *señoria* of Monzón. It took time before they were satisfied, though with their doubts dispelled they led Falkan and the others into the coolness of the castle.

Their hospitality would have surpassed many a royal court. Unstinting in their efforts, they saw the men of Tremellion want for nothing. It was now a question of honour, a debt to be fully and handsomely repaid.

Throughout three luxurious days, Quillon, Guthric and their master were offered salves for their skin, fresh-killed meat and the finest wines for their strength. Their possessions were placed under rigorous guard, their horses nursed like pets. Time and again, Baynard was assured the two wounded Knights of Santiago were on the mend, and that Enrique de Vaca and Arias de Barragan were as well treated as the *Inglés*.

'And the ladies, the condesa and her companion?'

A moment's hesitation, and then, 'As for Doña Rosalía, she has the fortitude one would suppose, Señor Halcón. But Doña Amata is not yet recovered. She rests without sleeping, heaping her mind with the ashes of remorse.'

'Ask her if she will receive me,' Falkan said. 'There is a certain remark she made that – well, there's a measure to these things. She perhaps needs to settle other minds before finding peace with herself.'

'I'm not sure I understand, Señor Halcón.'

'Maybe not,' Falkan told the man, 'but the request is yours to transmit, not comprehend.'

The servant flinched from the retort, though obediently delivered the message, word for word. And was surprised when the condesa said yes, she would receive Lord Falkan whenever he wished, suggesting that selfsame evening.

Dressed in undershift and surcoat, an unworn pair of boots, his sword and dagger looped to his belt, Baynard Falkan marked the condesa low on his list.

He first went to find his constable and safeguard, the two men in an extravagant painted chamber, the room furnished in imitation of the Moors.

A glance was enough to show him they were recovered from their sun-scorched journey from Zarueza. Quillon grinned at him, Guthric looking sheepish, both men out of place on the gaudy spread of cushions and gold-weave coverlets.

'You seem well mended, messires. And adopting this as your future way of life?'

'Awaiting your orders,' Guthric told him. 'The joskin appears to wallow in it. But for me, I'd wish us on our way.'

'There's one thing they're mean with,' Quillon remarked, 'an' that's women. Asked every way I know how, but they all turn deaf, these servants, an' blind when I try to show 'em –'

'Save yourself,' Falkan warned him. 'Remember what I told you back at Tremellion. How it is with the women of Cyprus. Keep *that* in mind, safeguard, and forget the girls of Monzón.' Then he suggested they made the best of their comforts now, for they'd be on their way soon enough. 'Hard riding, messires, to the coast. Then rough sailing to Marseilles. The next sprawl of cushions you come across will be quite a distance from here.'

He left them with their jugs of wine, jars of olives, bowls of sweet summer fruits. It pleased Baynard Falkan to see his companions well-treated, if only for a while, though he closed the door hard, to let them know how quickly they'd tire of their colourful, cosseting cell.

Impressed by the endless corridors of Monzón, he accosted one of the servants, demanding the whereabouts of the Knights of Santiago. The man led him back the way he'd come, up the sweep of a railed staircase, along another vaulted passageway, through a gallery that overlooked an inner courtyard, then finally to a series of long, windowed chambers.

As a son of Tremellion, with its weeping walls and a hall in which one could suffocate with smoke, Baynard let his hand rest on the dry stones of Monzón. He watched the servant bow and depart, allowed himself a brief sigh of envy, then went in search of the Spanish *freyles*.

He was met by Arias de Barragan, the young men standing for a moment, as if barring each other's path. Falkan reached for words with which to explain his earlier refusal to part with his horse, willing now to tell the man he was carrying money for the Cause. But before he could do so, Arias said, 'Your presence might well have saved us, these last few days, Señor Halcón. I had no right to ask a brother knight to dismount.'

'You had every right, Señor de Barragan, wishing it for the comfort of the wounded.'

'Even so.'

'Nevertheless.'

Hard to tell whose hand was offered first, though the rough jar of their skin was sufficient, all trace of animosity dissolved.

'You have spoken with the condesa, Señor Halcón?'

'Not before visiting you and your brethren, Señor de Barragan.'

A smile of approval, the offer of wine, and Arias gestured to Falkan to precede him – 'Along there, if it please you, and the door – just so, Señor Halcón – on the right.'

A gaunt, yet well-proportioned chamber, devoid of colour, furnished with a single, darkwood wardrobe, a row of clothes-pegs, a double row of narrow, leather-strapped beds.

Enrique de Vaca was standing near one of the windows, his wounded brethren sprawled asleep on their cots. Turning from the view, he smiled with pleasure at Falkan. A gesture then by Baynard, and Enrique dismissed the Englishman's concern. 'They've been drugged to dream sweet, Señor Halcón. A few days on and their wounds will be sealed, my brothers good as new. You are free to shout to the vaulting, if you wish.'

Arias said, 'You should know, Enrique, Señor Halcón has offered me his hand.'

'Meeting yours half-way,' Falkan interjected. 'How else could it be done . . .'

With an exactitude of courtesy, the knights shared a long-necked flask of wine, standing together to admire the view from this upper level of the castle of Monzón.

Then Baynard murmured, 'I'm invited into the presence of Doña Amata. She is apparently unsettled in her mind. There may be reasons for this I don't understand. But one thing she said, back there on the plain – this I believe adds to her present anguish.' Then he looked away at the long, water-fed valley, leaving the Knights of St James of the Sword to think the thing over, to give or withhold their assent.

Enrique refilled Falkan's glass. The Spaniard said nothing for a while, then quietly asked, 'In the matter of our defence of the pilgrims? And the lady's accusation? You would address her again about that, on our behalf?'

Falkan turned from the window, set his glass aside and gazed at his brother knights, his *hermanos*. 'It is my intention to do so,' he said, 'with your permission.'

'And if she still insists we failed her?' Arias queried. 'What can you do then?'

'Nothing at all,' Falkan told him. 'Doña Amata will believe what she believes. However, if you allow me to interfere in this matter – and she acknowledges her error – I shall demand an apology from her, to be announced in your presence. She at least seems willing to meet me. But beyond the meeting –' and he shrugged.

Enrique de Vaca said, 'A personal apology would suffice.'

Arias de Barragan said, 'Anything less, and our fraternity would be tainted.'

And Falkan nodded, understanding them both, for nothing was more important to a knight of the Kingdoms of the West than that his aims and honour be untarnished.

If he thought to meet the Condesa de Monzón alone, he was mistaken. Guided to her chambers by first one, then three, then an emerging flock of her servants, he found himself ushered into a breathtaking temple of a room. The painted ceiling was supported by columns, each of these perfectly plastered to resemble the trunk of a tree.

The windows were blinded with tapestries, the polished floor bright with carpets, the unreal trees sprouting bracketed flares and candles.

There were also a dozen more servants beyond and around the columns.

Suddenly angry at being shepherded, young Tremellion turned on his escort. 'I am safely delivered! Go about your business!' Not knowing what else to do, he let his hand swing to the pommel of his sword. The servants scuttled away.

Looking forward again, he strode between the decorated pillars, satisfied that the other servants withdrew, men and women shrinking from the weapon he'd loosed in its sheath.

He found Doña Amata at the far end of the plastered and painted forest, though the woman a younger sister of the one he'd escorted from the plain . . .

No longer tearful, her features now spared the ravages of the sun, she was a fine, arrogant creature, her chin tipped high as he approached. Her slim body lost in an ornate, broad-armed chair, she was flanked on the left by her companion, Doña Rosalía.

Even as he came into her presence, Baynard Falkan knew he must break every rule she made. Anything less, and he too would be regarded as a shadow among the trees.

'I trust you've been well-treated, my Lord Halcón.'

'Better than you treat my compeers, Countess Amata.'

'And have no complaints, you and your companions?'

'Speaking for those from England, none. Though the brethren we met on the plain –'

'A sad affair, those black-and-white soldiers being overrun by the brigands. I wish now I'd hired twice their number. Or sent my appeal to England.'

Falkan found himself grinding his teeth to the flat. He glanced at the handsome Doña Rosalía, silently begging the woman to come to his aid. But the *compañera* stayed where she was, her eyes on the dark-skinned foreigner, maybe wishing to help him but knowing he must do it for himself. But do it, she seemed to be saying. Do it for us all.

'The pilgrims who fled,' Falkan introduced, 'aren't they the ones for whom you should feel the greatest sorrow, Doña Amata? Or, failing them, the survivors? Or then the knights who died in your service? Or those you've lodged in your castle? Or us, the foreigners, who broke our journey to see you and your band safe home? Spill your tears where you will, Condesa, but don't pretend you were failed in this mission. It's you who stamped the date to it, am I wrong? You who decided how much you'd spend by way of escort, am I wrong? And you who sat in charge of this pilgrimage, riding back on a horse that belongs to the Knights of Santiago. Contradict, *but am I wrong?*'

Attracted by Amata's appearance, yet incensed by her behaviour

– and the two mixed together, inseparable now – the young knight jabbed a finger to indicate her sins, then strode forward across the bright-carpeted floor.

Doña Rosalía concealed her smile of comprehension. She moved calmly to defend her mistress, halted in the face of Falkan's anger. She waited to see Amata rise from her chair and say no, she'd no wish to contradict him, she regretted her outburst. But surely he could understand. A woman who'd gone to pray for the soul of her husband, surely a man like Falkan could understand . . .

And then she edged away, the *compañera*, leaving her mistress to plead with the Englishman . . . Agree she owed an apology to her escort . . . Catch at his hand and draw him through a shadowed door at the far side of the interior, imitation forest.

From the moment they were alone, they knew how things would be. Pliant and unresisting, Amata allowed Baynard Falkan to disrobe her, lead her to the canopied bed, then make love to her with a hunger that neared brutality. If she suffered, she did so willingly, moving against him, her fingers stretched wide on the broadness of his back. She cried aloud, though not as a woman in terror, their bodies pulsing to the rhythm of their needs . . .

When it was over they lay for a while, sprawled in languid embrace. Then came together again, their appetites reawakened, not caring that they were strangers in all but this.

The following morning Baynard sent word to Enrique de Vaca and, as witness, Arias de Barragan. The Knights of the Order of Santiago presented themselves before Doña Amata, Condesa de Monzón, to hear her voice her apologies for the accusation she'd levelled against them.

By way of recompense, she offered a valuable gold-wrought casket to the Military Order, a purse of coins to each of the four survivors, the same as a mark of respect for Baynard Falkan.

Arias de Barragan said, 'Should you ever have need of us, Condesa, we four whom God's seen fit to leave alive, you have only to send word to our *encomienda*.' Then he turned in surprise as Enrique murmured, 'For myself, it must be otherwise. I intend to seek my release, then follow the route these others are taking, Halcón and his friends. I've had time to think it over, brother Arias, and desire to see the sword of Santiago raised for the Cause in the East.'

He glanced then at Falkan, who said quietly, 'Follow us, Señor de

Vaca, and you'll be coughing in our dust. Better you should ride alongside. If you agree.'

The briefest pause, necessary in these matters, and then a nod of acceptance from the Spaniard. 'A courteous offer, Señor Halcón. Though you must remind me to slow my pace, lest my own dust sets you coughing.'

They stayed two more days at Monzón, time enough for the wounded Knights of St James of the Sword to gather their strength for the ride to the *encomienda* near Tarragona.

For reasons of her own, Doña Amata kept to her private chambers.

Yet on the final evening Falkan was making a leisurely circuit of the castle, his trained eye taking in details of the defences, when Doña Rosalía made her way along the skirting path toward him.

A word of greeting for the knight, a glance to parallel his own and then, 'Could it be held, in your opinion, Señor Halcón? If the Moors were to once again invade?'

Falkan shrugged. 'It's a well-designed fortress, Doña Rosalía – in my opinion. But grander places than this have been overwhelmed; lesser castles held against whole armies. Monzón is only a shell after all. A carapace. Much would depend on the animal inside.' Then he laughed aloud. 'By God, I sound pompous. But military architecture – I've an interest in it, and you hooked me with your question.'

'I intended to,' the *compañera* said calmly. She gazed away to the south before asking, 'Could you see yourself as that animal, Señor Halcón? Commanding the defence of Monzón?'

Mistaking the point of her question, he said, 'I'd be of little use if the Moors attacked tonight. But perhaps, if I had the time to study the place, probe its weaknesses, test the value of the garrison –'

'And given that time?'

'I don't know. I suppose –' Then, thinking he understood, he raised a hand, palm outward, pushing gently at the air. 'I'm offered the command of Monzón? Inexperienced as I am, and a foreigner? But Spain is renowned for its leaders. The condesa could find –'

'Yes,' the woman told him, her voice pitched for only the two of them to hear. 'But you'd not just be its commander, Señor Halcón. You'd have more intimate a station than that. More, how can I put it, all-embracing a position?'

'As her husband?'

'As her husband, nothing less. That's why you've been accosted on

108

this path. Why the condesa dare not face you again, fearing your response.'

He thought of telling the fine-boned *compañera* about the death of Sir Geoffrey, in ambush. About the vengeance he would one day visit upon Ranulf. About the woman who'd brushed her lips against his – no others counting, save for the moment – the one who had said they might meet again in the Holy Land. The woman whose image stayed in his mind, Ardelet's daughters forgotten, Inés a pretty memory, even Doña Amata no more than a sweet oasis in the desert of his desires. He thought to say, 'In so far as I command anything, I have already made my choice. Her name is –'

But no, it was not necessary to let Doña Amata hear the name Christiane . . .

'You will tell the condesa this, Doña Rosalía. That her willingness to have me as her husband all but blinds me to my resolve. Yet I've vowed to assist the Cause in the East, and do so in the name of Tremellion, and will seek no wife till it's done. If she cares to see me again, which I doubt, I will vow to remain in the unmarried state until I have honoured my obligations to Tremellion, to England and to Christ.'

Doña Rosalía let a wry smile shape her lips. 'She'll be impressed by that, Señor Halcón. It will go some way to softening the blow. You're too young for her anyway – in my opinion. I've a few men in mind who might prove themselves worthy of the condesa, and Monzón. Even so, I think it best if I tell her tomorrow. And you and your companions leave at dawn.'

FOURTEEN

THE EARLY departure came as no surprise to the riders. There were seven of them now, the English Crusaders and the Knights of St James of the Sword. Of the Spaniards, Arias de Barragan and his two scarred companions would accompany Enrique de Vaca as far as the *encomienda*, where Enrique would bid them farewell.

He foresaw few problems with the master of the garrison, the *comendador mayor*. Present him with the gold-wrought casket, and he'd surely release de Vaca from his duties. *It's not as if I'm reneging on my vows. I shall still fight for Santiago, be it on the islands of the Mediterranean Sea, or far away in the East.*

Convinced his request would be granted, he invited Falkan, as a brother knight, to visit the gaunt, unembellished stronghold of his Order near Tarragona.

Curious to see the workings of a true military household, the Englishman stripped off his shabby, traveller's clothes, and donned his hauberk, helmet and surcoat. He looped the sword-hangers to his belt, buckled the belt and scabbard, then pulled on a pair of studded, wrist-length gloves. He was still no match for a white-coated, black-armoured Knight of Santiago, but at least he wouldn't be mistaken for a leper.

Even as they reached the *encomienda*, Falkan was caught off guard. The time he'd spent abroad in his youth, the places he'd seen, the skills and knowledge he'd absorbed – none of them had prepared him for this.

From the very first, the stronghold broke the rules. There was no climb to the castle, no zig-zag path as at Tremellion, no moat or drawbridge or gatehouse. Instead, the path dipped *downward*, curving to a pair of ten-foot-high, ten-foot-wide lapped-iron doors, the entrance to a mine.

'Were I to dare attack your house,' Baynard volunteered, 'the first thing I'd do is flood it.'

'You would?' Enrique retorted. 'And with what? The rain falls infrequently here, my dear Halcón, and what does come is channelled there – and there – by those gullies. Flood the entrance and you'd need half the country, bearing buckets.'

Baynard glanced up at the squat, dominant walls. He thought fire might be the next thing to try, looked again at the massive iron doors and held his tongue. Even if an invading force could pile enough faggots near the entrance, and live to set them alight, the flames would probably anneal the overlapping plates into a single, rock-framed shield.

Already impressed by Monzón, he halted in silent respect before this stronghold of the Knights of Santiago.

Their approach remarked throughout the last five miles, the doors were opened, the riders greeted by no fewer than twenty armed defenders. Enrique addressed them and the men came forward, separating Guthric and Quillon from the rest.

The constable took it hard, being herded by foreigners, and waited for one of the men to slap his horse. Then he leaned down and with the flat of his hand cuffed the defender's helmet, growling as the Spaniard spun backward, dizzied by the blow.

Members of the garrison closed in on the Saxon. Enrique snapped at them, supported by Arias, and the watchguards of Santiago halted, glowering.

Falkan said, 'A welcome like this, de Vaca, and you'd suppose we had indeed brought buckets to flood you out.' Their new-wrought friendship was suddenly in peril, the Spaniard noticing Falkan tighten his reins, ready to pull his horse away.

'You must understand,' Enrique said quietly, 'this is not a castle like others.'

'Nor one that welcomes callers, so it seems.'

The young knights stared hard at each other, Enrique secretly pleased by the way his *freyles* had issued from the tunnel, Falkan content that the Saxon had cuffed the interfering watchguard. Then something flickered in their eyes, and they spoke in unison.

'The invitation –'

'So long as I'm assured –'

'– is still offered, Señor Halcón.'

'– my men are safe, Señor de Vaca.'

A nod from the Spaniard, a gesture of agreement from Baynard Falkan, and the men dismounted. Then, with Arias de Barragan and the two who'd been wounded by the brigands, Santiago and Tremellion strode into the underworks of the castle.

*

111

A series of wide, ill-lit tunnels. Thirty yards in and the rocky floor was replaced with tight-fitting boards. 'If the enemy were to get past the doors,' Enrique explained, 'they'd find these boards chopped through. There's a pit underneath, its sides smooth as marble. We have five like that. And see up there? The first of several grilled gates we can wind down from the roof. And further in – yes, you see them, Halcón? – another pair of iron-plate doors. We can also fill the tunnels with smoke if we need to.'

'As well protected as this,' Baynard grinned, 'a man would sleep well at night, Señor de Vaca.'

'We do,' Enrique said evenly. 'Why else build a castle, if not to be protected?'

His attempt at humour crushed by the Spaniard's logic, Baynard said, 'What's he like, the master of this *encomienda*?' And for an answer was told, 'He himself designed the defences.'

They climbed a long curving slope, turned a zig-zag of corners, then emerged without warning into a featureless inner courtyard, its sunlit floor covered with fine white sand. Falkan recoiled, all but blinded by the glare. He guessed it to be another example of the Master's defensive cunning. Penetrate this far into the castle – an unlikely event in itself – and the attackers would find themselves groping, sightless, in the yard.

Enrique de Vaca put a hand on Baynard's arm. 'This way, *amigo mio*. We have still some distance to go.' He guided the visitor to a corner of the courtyard, Arias and the other two following, the five men once again plunging into a maze of shadowy passageways.

Another hundred yards, maybe more, and they entered a long, vaulted hall in the heart of the *encomienda*. Part of it underground, Baynard supposed, for the lower edges of the windows were twelve feet above the level of the floor. No more than square apertures, they narrowed in the thickness of the stone.

Their eyes once again accustomed to the gloom, the knights were met by the Master's bodyguard, an expressionless group who came forward to bar their way.

'You know us,' Enrique said curtly. 'I would speak with the *comendador mayor*.' He waited as one of the guards made his way to the far end of the hall, rapping twice on the door of a small inner chamber. A murmur of words, the guard returning to say, 'In a while, Señor de Vaca. When he's ready.'

Enrique hefted Monzón's gift to the Order, the decorated casket.

He seemed anxious to speak to Falkan, though hesitated to do so with the bodyguards there to listen. Then, in a single, oblique remark, he said, 'There are more traps to be avoided than those in the tunnels.' Falkan looked at him, heard the slam of a door, turned to see the *comendador mayor* emerge from his chamber and make his way to a dais, the man seating himself in what would elsewhere have passed for a throne of princes, of kings.

An arid voice, devoid of warmth or welcome said, 'Approach and declare yourselves. And explain why your business cannot be dealt with by my servitors.'

Falkan heard Enrique clear his throat. Heard him scuff his feet on the darkened tiles. Heard him smother a cough, suck the smoked air of the hall into his chest. He's terrified, Falkan decided. What he said just now – he fears the Master might spring a trap to prevent his release.

The toneless voice arrested his thoughts. 'You are close enough. Stand where you are. And you, de Vaca. Speak out.'

'Grand Master . . . Diaz de Quintana . . . I'd report the events of our journey to Compostella . . .'

'It seems you have to be instructed more than once,' the Master grated. 'Reports are made to my servitors.'

'Yes . . . Yes, but there's more. Doña Amata, Condesa de Monzón has charged me to bring you this, a gift for the Order.'

'Generous, beyond doubt,' the voice droned. 'But it's not the first time Santiago's been thanked with jewels or – what is that, a casket? Give it to one of my guards, de Vaca. And now you may withdraw.'

'There's more. Two of the escort were killed in an ambush –'

'You press my patience, de Vaca. Prayers will be offered –'

Dogged now, convinced he had nothing to lose, the young Spaniard said again, 'There is more. The last few days of our journey to Monzón . . . We were aided by three Englishmen . . . This one here, Lord Baynard Falkan of Tremellion, he and his companions. He merits our gratitude, Master. And that is not a thing done by servitors.'

Diaz de Quintana hunched forward, peering through the smoke and shadows of the hall. Baynard could see him now; a cowled figure, cadaverous face, the skin of his jaw sunk against the bone, his all but fleshless nose pinched to a beak. More monastic than military, the *comendador mayor* extended a long-sleeved arm, a skeletal finger beckoning the foreigner to approach.

I know how de Vaca feels, Falkan acknowledged. This creature's enough to make a statue run in fright. He found that he, too, was clearing his throat, sucking air into his chest. But he went forward without hesitation, drawn by Diaz de Quintana's hooded gaze.

'I am conversant with your language, Tremellion, impure though it is. It is not to de Vaca's credit that you were allowed in here, nor that he should need the help of foreigners on his mission. He has chosen to embarrass me, demanding I thank you in person. Very well. You have the thanks of the Grand Master of the Catalonian stronghold of the Knights of St James of the Sword, known also as the Knights of Santiago. I trust that's enough to satisfy you, Tremellion.'

Falkan stared back at the man, aware the bodyguards had withdrawn to the edge of the dais. He sensed Enrique beside him, Arias and the other two knights close behind. Then he thought to himself, all this way in, be a shame to waste the visit, and let his voice ring low around the walls of the half-buried chamber.

'For myself, de Quintana, the grudging insincerity of your thanks is enough – to make me think I'd been stung by a scorpion. But before you dismiss us from this squat and colourless nest – there is more.'

The arrogance of his words sent the bodyguards' hands to their swords. Diaz de Quintana came silently to his feet, his monkish robes swirling, so it seemed, around a shadowed framework of bones.

'You seek me out, the two of you, disobedient to the running of this Order; dare to waste my time, insult my office, then tell me again – *there is more*?'

Falkan snapped back at him, drowning the Master's gravelled tone. 'Sunk in your chamber, even in this hall, this dismal mine of a fortress, you suppose yourself to be powerful, de Quintana –'

'You will call me Master! Grand Master! I am the –'

'What you are, de Quintana, is buried alive in the tunnels of your own design. But the world does not know or care what happens in this cleverly planned warren. Continue to defend the pilgrims on their way to Compostella, yes, that, but don't imagine the route from England to the East need ever pass the lapped sheets of your doorway, unless by choice. I said there's more, and it's this. I wish you to release the courageous and honourable Enrique de Vaca from his duties, so he may ride with us to the defence of the Holy Land, and in the name of Santiago.'

Tension pressed against the walls of the vaulted chamber. No one spoke, the bodyguards glaring at Falkan, listening for their Master's enraged command.

Yet when he spoke, his arid tone seemed reasonable, his words measured, weighted with thought. 'In view of this casket – valuable to the Order – I see nothing to prevent de Vaca employing his undoubted skills abroad. For the glory of Christendom, and Spain.' Then he added quickly – too quickly for the Englishman to unravel – 'But not in the name of Santiago, not that. If he goes, he goes naked. Strip him of his armour.'

The bodyguards moved to take him, Diaz de Quintana allowing his sickly teeth to show.

Falkan sensed movement around him, prayed he'd not mistaken Arias and the others, determined he'd not be skewered like some twitching rabbit. He drew his sword, heard the slide of metal on leather, glanced to see the Spaniards he'd been with out there on the plain – see them closing to protect Enrique, their weapons a match for the guards . . .

Enrique de Vaca used his free hand to snatch something from his belt. 'You have no call to see me stripped, *Comendador Mayor*. I've never run from conflict, nor ever will. But take this, as purchase of my release.' Then he tossed his purse of coins at the Master's feet.

As did Arias de Barragan – 'To see de Vaca safely on his way.'

As did the other two knights, their purses chinking, the coins trapped by the leather.

Then Falkan himself ripped Doña Amata's pouch from his waist, held it for the Master to see, and moved against the bristling blades of his guards. 'Attempt to have de Vaca stripped, and there'll be blood spilled in this chamber. We are all of us armoured here, de Quintana, so you know what a long and grisly fight it'll be. For my part, just a visitor. But for you, all of you, a skirmish between brothers. A disgrace to the name of Santiago. A stain that will spread for years across the name of Diaz de Quintana.

'So I ask you, *Comendador Mayor*. Ignoring the rest, will you allow me to purchase the release of Enrique de Vaca, tested Knight of the Order of Santiago? And be honoured by his company in pursuit of the Christian Cause?'

Aware that if the skeleton was to save his bony face, Falkan had no choice but to back his words. He extended his lean, gloved hand, offering his own purse of coins.

Diaz de Quintana plucked it from his grasp. He said nothing about the casket, the other four sacks of coins on the platform, the knights who had moved to defend Enrique de Vaca. His feelings barely

115

concealed, he told Falkan, 'Your generosity becomes you, Tremellion. I have always held de Vaca in high regard.'

'It was never doubted,' Baynard lied. 'You conduct yourself as a true Master of the Order, Señor Diaz de Quintana.'

'You will stay for some wine, Lord Falkan?'

'Kindness on kindness, *Comendador Mayor*. But the hour presses.'

'In truth,' the man told him, his mouth winched to a smile. 'And our time on earth so brief. Be it here, or in the deserts of the East.' Then he turned abruptly and, as if by accident, let Falkan's purse fall to the dais.

No one moved until the small side door was slammed shut. Then the bodyguards sheathed their swords and sighed with relief, desiring to be friends again with Arias de Barragan and the others. Enrique bade farewell to those who'd helped escort the pilgrims to Compostella. Falkan said, 'Perhaps one day in the future, señores,' and extended his hand to Enrique's loyal companions.

They retraced their steps, Santiago and Tremellion, through the passageways and across the blinding yard and down past the unsprung traps of the tunnels. Along and around and out through the entranceway, where Guthric and Quillon were tossing pebbles across the path, to see who could pitch his stone nearest the wall.

FIFTEEN

BY LATE afternoon the riders had reached the hills above Tarragona. The port spread below them, the bay to the south dotted with Crusader vessels, supply craft, a variety of fishing boats, a score of Spanish traders. They could see a heavily laden raft being towed sluggishly through the water by a fan of slender rowboats. Lines of men coiled down from the beach, passing kegs and bundles through the listless surf and out to the waiting dinghies. The beach itself was an ill-planted forest of tents and shelters, pennants flying like single leaves from an array of sun-parched saplings. England was there. And France. Germans from the Holy Roman Empire. Along with these were the gonfalons of Flanders and Scandinavia, other nations as far apart as the Kingdoms of Poland and Portugal.

A babel of languages drifted up from the camp. That, and the unifying feature of any military assembly – the stench.

Turning in his saddle, Falkan pointed to a stretch of dunes inland of the beach. 'Guthric. You and the safeguard find us a place along there. I'll go with Señor de Vaca and secure passage on one of the ships. Take charge of the horses, and for God's sake keep close to the money.'

The constable nodded, then scanned the dunes, waiting for the knights to dismount. Above that line of saw-grass, he decided. High enough so the wind might save us from the stink. It was a vain hope, but better than the noisome odour that arose from the shoreline.

Leaving Guthric and Quillon to lead the palfreys along the wind-piled ridge of sand, Baynard and Enrique descended the track, now surfaced with cobbles, to the overcrowded township of Tarragona.

They were directed to a crude plank shed at the landward end of the quay. Sailors, soldiers and civilians loitered in their path, backing away as they recognised the black-and-white garb of a Knight of St James of the Sword.

Nevertheless, it was Falkan who addressed the Passage Master, a truculent-sounding Englishman who was clearly half-drugged with power, half-drunk on the local wine.

117

He straightened somewhat in the presence of the knights, then gazed blearily as Falkan told him he had need of four berths aboard one of the Crusader ships bound for Marseilles. 'And with stalls for our horses. On a vessel that skips along.'

'Wish I could 'elp you, my lord, in truth I do. But the thing of it is, what with ships bein' wrecked all around the coast, the ones we've got 'ere are filled to the point of sinkin'. 'Mongst all those men on the beach – you seen 'em? – well, there's close on a 'undred what'll 'ave to bide their time till –'

'Check your lists again,' Falkan suggested. 'And here. Use these to stop the papers blowing away.'

The coins were snatched from the wide, barrel-propped counter. Valued at a glance – the man not so drunk after all, so it seemed – and he turned away, muttering that now he came to think of it . . . storing up trouble for himself . . . but maybe he *could* squeeze them aboard, there being just them and their mounts . . . a sturdy ship out of Romney . . . the *Gros Ventre*.

Falkan glanced at Enrique de Vaca, both men shrugging. The *Gros Ventre*? The Big Belly? Scarcely the name for a vessel that skipped along. But could it be any worse, Falkan thought, than Captain Gregorius Bigorre's bucket, the wryly-named *Gossamer*? And with a hundred men stranded on the beach, did the knights have much choice?

Aware he'd been cheated, and that he himself was guilty of bribery, Baynard snapped at the Passage Master, 'Spare us your moans.' The muttering stopped and the man returned, offering a handful of coloured wooden spills.

'The reds are for you, my lords, green for the horses. Passage an' food for everyone, far as Mares Eye. But I'll need the names. Regulations.' His furred tongue protruded as he added to his list in a faulty, unjoined hand. Baynard Falkan, of Tremellion; Guthric, Constable of Tremellion; Quillon, Safeguard of Tremellion . . .

At which point – though a moment too soon – one of the loitering crowd retreated through the throng, quickened his pace, broke into a trot and went running to tell what he'd heard.

They learned the *Gros Ventre* would sail with the morning tide. They should be at the far end of the quay by first light. Captain Burywell would see them snug aboard.

I very much doubt it, Falkan thought. We'll be lucky if there's space in which to stretch out. But at least we might get to Marseilles in time to join the main Crusader fleet. In time, God willing, to deliver my father's treasure to King Richard.

No matter the inconvenience or hardship, Baynard Falkan was determined to see the sixty pounds weight of gold coins tipped safe into the Christian coffers. That done, he believed, Sir Geoffrey would find eternal peace in the sanctity of Heaven.

Meanwhile, the knights had other, more mundane tasks to fulfil. With Guthric and Quillon encamped among the dunes at the far end of the beach, it was left to Enrique and Baynard to buy food and wine, nourishment for the horses, a four-gallon flagon of water, all of which they'd see carried back to the camp. But before they rejoined the Saxon and the safeguard, they settled themselves at a table in one of the *posadas*, each eager to learn all he could about the other.

They were more or less the same age, Baynard the taller, Enrique more muscular, and probably the stronger in a fight. In one other thing at least they were alike, for de Vaca's dark skin was matched by Tremellion's, the son of Spanish parents sharing the same pigmentation as the son of the Greek noblewoman Elena, found and wooed by Sir Geoffrey on the Aegean island of Khios.

In other things they were different, very different, the Spaniard quick to boil, the Englishman waiting longer, simmering slow. Courage meant much to both of them, everything to Enrique, for courage and honour were intertwined, inseparable, the breath and heartbeat of his being.

He would never, Baynard thought, rein in for fear of an ambush, or turn off the path and skirt wide of a would-be trap. I admire him for his touchy, brazen ways, this Knight of Santiago, and there may come the time when he'll have to push me on. Pray God he won't, but we'll see.

De Vaca's view of things was different, very different, thinking the Englishman calmer, more steady in a crisis, where he himself would have struck, and gone down striking. Courage was their mutual lodestone, though somehow Halcón balanced things better. Enrique could imagine being snatched by the hem of his hauberk, arrested against his will, Baynard hissing that now was not the time. He hoped it would never happen, though suspected it might.

The Spaniard then said, 'Indiscreet of me perhaps, *amigo mio*, but I sensed what you were saying to Señor Guthric, before we descended to the town. You never move far from those saddlebags, you and your companions.' He left the question unasked, the explanation to be offered if Halcón wished.

Drinking the good dark wine his friend had ordered, Falkan knew if there was to be openness between them he must answer fully, without hesitation.

He recounted the story of Tremellion. The ambush in the forest near Launceston; the death of his father, murdered by unseen archers; the culpability of Ranulf; the events at the mill of Tresset and then, concealing nothing, a description of the contents of the six leather bags.

'And you brought these all the way from England? Overland from Zarueza, Señor Halcón?'

'I hear things better as Falkan. Or Baynard, Señor de Vaca.'

'And I as Enrique.'

A shared expression, and the young men reached across the table, their hands clasped in a firm, dry grip. Then they eased back in their chairs, friendship confirmed, yet the bond far more real than just the casual amity of travellers.

The handshake assured the Spaniard of Guthric's loyalty. Quillon's too, even though the leonine poacher was a world away from the Knight of St James of the Sword. But he knew that, as he now trusted Falkan, he could rely upon the jaunty young safeguard and the scar-sealed Constable of Tremellion.

And they, in turn, upon Enrique de Vaca.

Some time later, the Spaniard caught sight of a friend of a distant cousin of his sister's husband – too complicated for Baynard to follow – and made his way from the table. As he crossed the *posada* its occupants saluted him, the men bowing in acknowledgement of his presence. It reassured them to see this guardian of Santiago, in town from the *encomienda*.

'You'll forgive me if I'm mistaken, but are you not Lord Falkan of Tremellion? I heard the name bruited about the port. Mine's Roger Grevel. Got a seigneurie in Suffolk. All these poxied foreigners about it's a pleasure to meet a fellow countryman.'

Falkan raised his eyes to see a face he recognised, *thought* he recognised, then told himself no, though he's not unlike – but who? The name Grevel meant nothing to him. He knew no one from the eastern county of Suffolk. Dismissing the imagined resemblance, he nodded at his compeer. 'I am who you say, Lord Grevel. But as for my name being bandied around the port –'

Grevel shrugged. 'Heard it out there on the quay. Assumed you'd just arrived in Tarragona, and thought to offer my greetings.' He glanced at the chair Enrique had vacated.

'I pray you be seated, Lord Grevel.' Clapping his hands sharply to summon the *posadero*, he ordered another squat stone jar of the local wine. The man brought it quickly, together with a fresh tray of salted fish, olives and sour pickled walnuts. It pleased him to have men of standing in his hostelry, no matter if they were foreign. They gave the place a certain attraction, and they paid their bills without protest. If the Crusader vessels continued to heave up the coast to Tarragona, he'd find a new name for the inn. Maybe the *Posada de los Cruzados*.

'Your health, Lord Falkan.'

'My Lord Grevel.'

'Tell me, are you camped along there on the beach? Damned cesspit of a place. But what else can one expect, with half the nations of Europe represented? Someone should have taken charge of things.'

'We'll survive it till tomorrow,' Falkan told him.

'Then you've passage aboard ship to Marseilles? Glad to hear it, my lord. I too, on the *Hawksbill*. And your craft?'

'The *Gros Ventre*. Comparing the names, Lord Grevel, I'd say you'll outstrip us before we're off Barcelona.' Gazing at the man, he thought, indeed he does remind me of someone. But not from Suffolk. Nearer by.

'I wonder,' Grevel murmured. 'It might not yet be too late to get you transferred. How many are you?'

Falkan was about to reply, when a second indistinct worry cudgelled his brain. Something about Roger Grevel's way of speaking? No, not really that. More his tone of voice, his – yes, of course! His accent.

'I asked how many there are in your party, Lord Falkan. Surely you're not so encumbered as to prevent us fitting you in aboard the *Hawksbill*?'

Ignoring the question, Baynard said, 'This seigneurie of yours, Lord Grevel. Is it a family holding, or an honour you were granted? I know little of Suffolk, though I'd have guessed you to be from my own part of the country.'

Roger Grevel smiled, his hands raised to his shoulders in surrender. 'I am so, Lord Falkan. A proud-born Cornishman, like you. Though more to the south, from the coast, from Mevagissey. Sent across to Suffolk when I was, what, twelve or thereabouts. But with an accent that sticks like a burr at the back of my throat.'

'Interesting,' Baynard said calmly, 'the things that stay with us.'

But far more interesting was that Roger Grevel should have agreed they were from the same part of England, pin-pointing the much-travelled Falkan – and Tremellion – as Cornish. As for his claim that he came from Mevagissey, he was citing a place far away from the castle. If the last was true, he would not have been aware of Tremellion's existence. One small fortress among many? Lost amid the forests and moorlands of the west? Yet its name and position known to a twelve-year-old child?

There were flaws in Grevel's story. He'd been too accurate in his placing of the castle. Too eager to learn where Baynard's companions were camped. Too willing to offer passage aboard the *Hawksbill*. Too pressing in his desire to know the extent of Falkan's party, the name of Tremellion's ship.

But it's more than that. More than just these inconclusive suspicions. Elusive though it is, he reminds me of someone, resembles a man with whom I've had dealings . . . But in God's name when? And as a friend, or an enemy?

Roger Grevel said, 'Your scowl would melt armour, Lord Falkan. Can your burden be as onerous as that?' Then he topped Baynard's glass, rested his arms on the table and said cheerfully, 'Tell me where you are on the beach and I'll send a man to bring your companions into town. I've paid the rent on a building here. Noisy, but clear of the stink. So why don't you lodge with us tonight, then we'll sail tomorrow on the *Hawksbill*. A damn good vessel, the *Hawksbill*. Be there in no time.'

Glancing beyond Grevel's shoulder, Baynard said idly, 'With your clear dislike of foreigners, my lord, I don't suppose you're cognisant of Spanish.'

'Speak their language? I'd let the devil damn me first!'

'A pity, because we're about to be joined by a much respected member of my band.' He reached to his left, dragged an empty chair to the table and signalled a brief greeting to Enrique, returning from family discourse.

'The devil notwithstanding,' Falkan said, 'you will allow me to introduce you to Señor Enrique de Vaca, Knight of the Order of Santiago, otherwise known as the Order of St James of the Sword.'

'A member of your band?' Grevel muttered. 'I thought we'd agreed there were three of you. No mention was made of a Spaniard.'

Indeed not, Baynard thought. *Though nor did I ever inform you we were three. So where did you learn that, I wonder, along with all the rest?*

Storing his suspicions, he introduced Roger Grevel, Knight of Suffolk. Enrique bowed in formal greeting, Grevel nodding from his chair.

'You should know,' Falkan said, 'the Knights of Santiago have been our shield in difficult times. I count on their protection, here in Spain.' Then he turned to Enrique, grinned as if to repeat what he'd said, and told his friend in Spanish, 'This man is of my country, yet not, I think, to be trusted. I suspect him, though without foundation.'

Enrique played the game perfectly, lifting his head and laughing at the unspoken pleasantry. 'Tell him you're protected by the brethren, here on the coast.'

Baynard slapped the table, as if in appreciation of de Vaca's rejoinder. 'I have already told him. And your presence confirms it.'

'You ignore me in this,' Grevel snapped. 'You leave me aside, my Lord Falkan.'

'Not at all, my Lord Grevel. I apologise if it seems so. A family joke on de Vaca's part. Really no more than that.'

'Maybe so, but enough for my tastes. I'd supposed to invite just the three of you aboard the *Hawksbill*, not this one and God knows how many others you use as your shield. Your knowledge of their dog-growl excludes me, Tremellion, so I'll wish you fair wind, and meet up with you again in Marseilles.'

He came to his feet, ignored Enrique, dipped his head at Baynard. Then he barged his way the length of the *posada*, leaving the Spaniard to gaze at his friend, curious to learn why they'd played their deceitful game.

But Baynard Falkan was unable to tell him. In truth, he was unable to explain to himself why this meeting with a fellow Crusader left him anxious, alert to a trap. If only he could piece it together . . . The man's accent . . . His probing questions . . . His knowledge of the whereabouts of Tremellion . . .

And his resemblance to someone who stalked the fringe of Falkan's mind.

The supplies delivered to the camp among the dunes, Baynard arranged for the men to take turns on watch. He himself stayed on guard until their sheltered candle had burned to mark an hour beyond midnight. Quillon relieved him and he attempted to sleep, though failed to do so, twisting on the single oiled sheet that served as his mattress.

Faces appeared to him, names that rapped to be heard. He saw his father alive, imagined the scene of his murder, ground his teeth as Ranulf came toward him, the child Baynard dodging to evade his brother's brutality. Other faces, some of them shadowed; names that wailed in echo from the past; figures and figments, phantoms that taunted his memory.

There was one brief moment when he *knew* it, knew for certain the link between Roger Grevel, claimant of a seigneurie in Suffolk and – and then fatigue suppressed him and he turned aside, recognition drifting beyond his grasp.

PART THREE

The Width of the Water

SIXTEEN

THEY DID not see the Englishman again in Tarragona. Trumpets were sounded an hour before dawn, smouldering braziers heaped with dry wood, torches lighted on the beach and along the length of the quay. One by one the Crusader vessels were towed into port, horses and men taken aboard, then their single square sails unfurled. By the time the *Gros Ventre* had been manoeuvred into place for the final loading, the other eight ships were already clear of the harbour. It seemed that Falkan's remark to Grevel had been right; the *Hawksbill*, along with the rest of the fleet, would quickly outstrip the lumbering transport, Big Belly.

The young knight presented the coloured spills to the captain, a worry-worn man named John Burywell. 'Once we're out there with the wind,' Baynard asked, 'what chance of our catching the fleet?'

'We might,' the captain told him, 'if they anchored from now till noon. If their boards sprang apart below the water, then we might. If they ran on the rocks –'

'You sound less than optimistic, Captain Burywell. What are you carrying to make you so mournful? Tombs for the dead?' He sensed none of Gregorius Bigorre's forceful manner in John Burywell. A man denied advancement, Baynard supposed. Ambitions thwarted, he'd first become bitter, exhausted his feelings of injustice and was now resigned to his place near the foot of the column. An error of navigation in the past? A lack of initiative? Even, perhaps, a display of timidity in the face of the elements?

Well, Falkan told himself, whatever the reasons, they're none of my affair. So long as Burywell gets his ship to Marseilles –

'Stuff for the blacksmiths and farriers, that's our cargo. Anvils, a thousand or more horseshoes, nails and hammer heads, crates of saddlery, iron that's been shaped, and bars of it that haven't. We were overloaded even before I was told to take you aboard. Anvils! I ask you. They don't have hammers and anvils in the East?' He moved away, a man of maybe forty, yet his shoulders already slumped in defeat of his days.

Falkan shrugged, praying the voyage to Marseilles would be

uneventful. With the best will in the world, he could not say Captain Burywell of Romney inspired much confidence. Nor, indeed, did his ironmongery of a ship.

Clear of the port, an even wind bellying the sail, the *Gros Ventre* pitched and wallowed. Badly designed, or badly loaded – and very likely both – she treated the low-running sea as a half-blind bull might react to the taunts of children, butting the waves, plunging clumsily at the merest flecks of spray.

Guthric and Quillon suffered as they'd suffered aboard the *Gossamer*, though Enrique de Vaca sought out his friend to tell him, 'Never in my life have I been further from dry land than halfway between the banks of a shallow river. Not once in a rowboat. And as for a craft like this! But you see how well I feel? Eating bread. Drinking wine. I am clearly not like your companions, eh, Halcón? Not for de Vaca the sickness of the sea!'

Pleased to find his friend so confident, Baynard told him he was one of the fortunate few. Then thoughtlessly he added, 'Anyone who's not seasick and can swim, widens the horizons of his world. And how much faster we can travel, in a direct line aboard ship to –'

'Swim? You say it's important to swim?'

Too late to make light of it, Baynard faltered, 'Well. You know. If the vessel should sink. Be wrecked in a storm. Or if, for example – it's unlikely – but suppose you were washed from the deck. You would then be forced to, as I mentioned, swim.'

Enrique thrust the half-eaten lump of bread, the half-empty flask of wine at his *confrère*, veered away, glanced apprehensively at the sea, then hurried to join the constable and safeguard at the rail.

Falkan settled himself against a pile of net-covered kegs. The *Gros Ventre* continued to lift and lurch beneath him. He gazed at the coastline to the west, chewing and sipping Enrique's unfinished meal.

When they reached Marseilles, he decided, he'd deliver Sir Geoffrey's money to King Richard. Then he'd see Guthric and Quillon enpursed for a few days of wine and women and whatever else they wished. And he'd take Enrique to a nearby part of the coast, encourage him to strip off his armour and venture out on the rocks. And there he'd teach him to swim. One way or another.

The storeship was some four hours north-east of Tarragona when the lookout on the foredeck struck the gong. Three resonant blows with the leather-wrapped stick, a pause, then three again. The general

128

alert. The crew to their stations. Captain John Burywell summoned to the bows.

Falkan went forward to join him, the men peering ahead at a plume of smoke, bent low by the wind, though clearly rising from the stern of a ship in distress. Her sail was furled, the smoke seeming to blanket the entire length of the craft.

'One of ours,' Burywell muttered. 'A fire in the hold. Maybe cooking oil caught alight. We'll go inshore of her. That way, if she sparks us too, we can steer unimpeded to the coast.'

Baynard glanced at him, approving his decision. A shame the man was so mournful, so beaten down. Whatever it was that had damned his career, it was surely not timidity.

Though they weren't there yet.

The *Gros Ventre* trudged closer to the stranded, smoke-strewn vessel. She was drifting with the current, though happily northward, parallel to the coast. With room enough for her rescuer to come alongside.

Whey-faced, and clutching at the ratlines, Quillon and Guthric struggled to join their master in the bows. Burywell yelled at his crew to hold their stations, then hurried aft to tell the steersman to angle to port, guiding the ship between the beleaguered craft and the shore.

Seen first from a long way off, the endangered vessel now loomed ahead of them, the transport seeming to accelerate as she bullied her way to help. A few moments more and they'd be up with their fellow Crusaders . . . Within hailing distance . . . Pitching and rolling alongside the stricken ship . . . Endeavouring to bring them together, fight the fire, or evacuate those aboard.

And yet there was something about it all that left Baynard Falkan uneasy. Something about the smoke that poured from the after-deck, to be tipped ahead by the wind.

It did not increase in intensity, this smoke. Nor did it diminish.

It was not flagged into gusts, into separate clouds.

It was not interfered with at all, this billowing smoke, though surely, if the fire was being fought –

The sturdy bow of the transport was within forty feet of the pluming vessel when the sharp-eyed Quillon said, 'Small world, eh, m'lord?'

Preoccupied with the progress of the *Gros Ventre*, Baynard thought to ignore Quillon's comment. All he allowed the safeguard was a grunt. Yet the wordless acknowledgement was enough to elicit, 'Small world, I said. De Vallen bein' 'ere.'

The Knight of Tremellion spun around. He saw the long-haired young Cornishman stabbing a finger; saw a face beyond him, there on the stern-deck of the smoke-wreathed ship. The face of Roger Grevel.

But no, not Grevel at all. Nor Justin de Vallen, the man Falkan had arrested in the millhouse of Tresset's linn. But close enough for Quillon to think so, bringing the name to the surface, explaining the resemblance – and the trap!

The so-called Roger Grevel was the image of de Vallen. His twin perhaps. At the very least his brother. And sent by Ranulf Falkan to waylay Baynard, snatch back the money, kill those who would see it safe to the coffers.

But for the presence of Enrique de Vaca, the attack would have taken place among the dunes above the beach of Tarragona. Or in the rented house in the town. But denied his chance, de Vallen's kin had sprung his trap out here, the Gros Ventre *lured to the aid of the* Hawksbill, *the fire no more than a fiction, the ship's crew crouched in hiding, ready to strike.*

Yelling at Guthric and Quillon to lie flat, Falkan ran as if fleeing from the bows. He shouldered his way past the sailors, used the swing of his forearm to brush Burywell aside, then lifted the steersman bodily, tossing him into the scuppers of the ship.

The craft were now less than twenty feet apart, the *Gros Ventre* slowing, her sturdy frame settling low in the water. There was little forward movement left in the ship, though maybe enough, God willing, enough for this . . .

He urged the tiller-bar of the steerboard to port, heaved on it, braced himself against it, cursed and strained as the iron-strapped rudder nudged the weight of the sea.

Ten feet now and the transport was turning, though with all the half-blind clumsiness of the bull.

Falkan called urgently to the man he'd brushed aside. 'It's not what you think! They're not in distress! They're laid here to seize us, storm aboard and kill everyone they find! Get here and help me, damn you, else I swear to you we're finished!'

Burywell blinked, swung his head in the direction of the smoking vessel, sensed at last that something was odd about it, the flattened cloud too regular for a fire.

130

'For Christ's sake, help me! We're on them! *Help me now!*'

Burywell made his decision, stumbled forward, added his weight to the knight's. The men heard their muscles crack as they pressed against the tiller-bar, the steerboard a shuddering spade below the waves.

Baynard gasped, 'The crew – alert them - tell them we're in danger of attack! Quick, or we're lost, I promise you! They must know we're hauling east!'

Burywell shouted, the vessels close to touching, the rest of it lost in a grinding extension of sound.

Obedient to their master, the crew of the *Gros Ventre* roared defiance at those aboard the *Hawksbill*. Crouched in the bows, Guthric drew an axe from the pouch on his belt. Quillon a knife. Enrique, dropping beside them, slid a thin iron bar from a sack he'd wrenched from the stores. Surprised by Burywell's shout, the men were uncertain what more they could do. But God help anyone who dared attack them. The first hand to grip the rail of the transport, and Guthric would cut it cleanly at the wrist. The first neck to appear and Quillon would skewer it. The first body, and Enrique de Vaca would transfix it with a raw-tipped iron bar.

Men were now visible on the stern deck of the *Hawksbill*, snarling bloody murder at those they'd intended to deceive. And all the while the *Gros Ventre* was turning, the distance well measured, the strengthened bow-strake ripping away the steerboard of de Vallen's ship, the transport then drifting to smash the tiller-bar to firewood with the weight of its overlapped hull.

Quillon whooped in triumph, his victorious yell cut short as grappling hooks tumbled on deck, then were jerked back, catching at the rail. Guthric chopped at the ropes with his axe, the safeguard slicing with his knife. Braced upright behind them, the Knight of Santiago hurled the untrimmed bars like javelins, adding to the chaos of noise with his full-throated bellow, '*Por Dios! Por Santiago! Por la Cruz!*'

Justin de Vallen's mirror-image had thought the smoke would be enough. Angry to learn that Baynard was a *confrère* of Enrique, he had nevertheless felt confident of trapping the *Gros Ventre* once the vessels were clear of Tarragona.

Instead, his ship had been crippled by the slowest member of the fleet, the grappling hooks cut away and lost, the cumbersome transport

131

now sailing due east from the coast. And taking with it, not only its cargo of iron, but Tremellion's treasure.

It would be several hours before a temporary steerboard could be rigged at the stern of the *Hawksbill*, by which time the *Gros Ventre* would be out of sight. The self-styled Roger Grevel supposed the transport to be circling wide – prayed so anyway – for other traps awaited her in Marseilles. His own failure enraged him, though he drew comfort from the knowledge that Baynard and his companions would be intercepted as soon as they stepped ashore. With the carriers killed and the gold recouped, the slab-faced Ranulf Falkan would be appeased.

So blunder on, he encouraged, glaring in the wake of Burywell's ship. Plough your furrow wide as you like to Marseilles. We've plenty more snares set out for you, my friends. More than you imagine.

Aboard the *Gros Ventre*, the morose John Burywell waited for Baynard's permission to swing the ship north. 'It's time we turned with the wind, my Lord Falkan. Stay on this course, and we'll pass Marseilles entirely. As it is, we're a hundred and fifty miles to the south.' Then in plaintive defence of his floating smithy, he added, 'She's only a coastal trader, the *Gros Ventre*. Laden like this, she'd never survive a storm. She's already further from shore than she's ever –'

'Two things I must tell you, Captain Burywell. Those men aboard the *Hawksbill*; they're not the only ones who'd do us mischief. I suspect there are others who await us in Marseilles. Enemies who dress as Crusaders, yet have no interest in the Cause. Enter that port, and it's likely we'll all be killed, you along with the rest.'

'Me? But why me? What part am I in this? You forced me to assist you back there –'

'So I did,' Baynard said gently. 'And by doing so made you a target for their wrath. Unfair, but unavoidable, Captain Burywell. As is my intention to hold this vessel due east.'

'But what if a storm –'

'Ah, yes. The second thing. We'll need to lighten the ship.'

His words half strangled with alarm, Burywell queried, 'Jettison the cargo? But I won't be paid if –'

'Yes, you will. You'll be paid.'

'You don't understand! How could you? It's only when I heard King Richard was raising a fleet –'

'You'll be paid.'

'– that I managed to secure – the *Gros Ventre* being old and –'

132

'I've told you,' Falkan snapped. 'Before I leave this ship, *you will be paid.* Now get your crew assembled. We'll leave enough ballast to keep her stable. Short of that I want everything dumped in the sea.' According Burywell a smile, he said, 'After all, it's as you yourself remarked. They must surely have hammers and anvils in the East.'

The unhappy sailor shrugged with resignation. He'd never wanted the four passengers aboard; never imagined the *Gros Ventre* involved in a fight; *never* supposed it would be with a Christian vessel.

All he'd wished from life, these past few months, was the chance to haul cargo from England. Show by his skills that the drowning of the drunken Hugh Marleigh had not – and it hadn't, God strike him – been his fault.

Marleigh's friends had claimed it so, and the authorities had accepted their account. But it had not been the way they told it; their stories distorted, embellished; their jewelled fingers extended in blame at the stammering John Burywell.

According to them, it was simply a case of clumsy navigation, Lord Marleigh's dinghy upset by the swing of the transport. Five voices to one, and Burywell was convicted, his licence to trade revoked, his livelihood cut from under him – until the day King Richard announced The Great Crusade.

His spirits extinguished, Burywell turned to the rail. His scarred hands gripped the smooth-worn oak as he gazed unseeing at the lift and fall of the sea. *Empty her belly, if you must. Throw the contents overboard. Make her as buoyant as you like. Then let me hear again, Falkan of Tremellion – Hugh Marleigh – how I'll be recompensed for the loss.*

The anvils ripped holes in the coverlet of the sea. Then the kegs of nails, the tools and horseshoes, chests of saddlery, boxes of leather, lumps of iron and cones of moulded lead.

The *Gros Ventre* rode higher in the water; ran faster now, scouring eastward through the Mediterranean Sea.

With the approach of dark the sail was furled, draglines lowered all around the ship. She was too far out for the anchors to touch bottom, but the draglines would slow her drift.

The crew and passengers ate salted meat, olives and dry Spanish bread. They washed the food down with wine and fresh water, then moved apart, the crew settling amidships, Falkan and his companions in the stern.

Nightfall acted as a drug on those aboard the *Gros Ventre*. They would sleep from now until the summer's early dawn, the rhythm of their minds and bodies attuned to the light. All except Baynard Falkan, who sat hunched near the tiller-bar, his spare frame wrapped in a cloak, hands folded on the pommel of his sword.

He doubted that John Burywell would attempt to turn the ship back toward Marseilles. The captain might distrust him, convinced the Crusader would cheat him at the last. But he was not the type to court trouble.

Nor was the vessel herself much at risk from pirate galleys, or the Moorish *dromonds* that probed north from the African coast. By day, perhaps, yes. But not at night, the lanterns doused, the *Gros Ventre* no more than a wallowing hulk in the dark.

Even so, Falkan remained watchful, hearing the slap of the waves, the night sounds of the sailors. Alone with his thoughts, he thanked God for delivering the transport from the iron-hooked clutches of the *Hawksbill*. Smiled briefly, and thanked Quillon for having identified the face of Roger Grevel.

The travellers must needs be more alert from now on. True to his nature, Ranulf would stay in the background, employing others to do his dirty work. He was most likely still in England, probably at Tremellion, though his presence would not be far off in the months to come.

He'd pay his henchmen well – if and when they snatched the treasure.

The payment doubled – if and when they murdered his brother. For by doing so they'd silence all talk of that other, earlier murder, the slaying of Sir Geoffrey.

Peering beneath the cloud-skeined moon, Baynard affirmed that the crew were sprawled as before. Murmurs and snores sussurated the air, one of the men coughing violently, another drumming a fist in a dreamed tattoo. Then sleep beckoned them down again, the night given over to the creak of the vessel, the splash of unseen fish, the curl of the waves.

Baynard closed his mind to future dangers, inviting instead the image of the woman he remembered, feeling again the brush of her lips, her name on his own . . . Christiane . . . Christiane de Magnat-Vaulmier . . .

He was a Crusader now, voyaging east in the name of Christendom. In memory of his father. In honour of Tremellion.

He was also the guardian of gold, hunted by his brother and the devil alone knew how many greedy hirelings.

Yet, along with all that, he was a lean young suitor; worldly enough in some things, naïve in others; wiry though lacking in muscle; dark-complexioned for a Cornishman; courteous to the point of pomposity; sensitive toward others and, yes, he believed he could say this, a man of his word.

But the clay had not yet hardened, his character still in the kiln.

And how would that match, he wondered, with those leathery warriors in the Kingdom of Jerusalem? How will she view me out there, my once-seen Christiane?

SEVENTEEN

HER BELLY emptied, the store-ship continued east. She spent a second night at sea, the watch now shared by Enrique and Quillon, then made sail again at dawn.

An hour before noon and a shout from the look-out brought Burywell and Falkan to the bows. Ahead of them, though still a smudge on the horizon, lay the mountainous island of Corsica; her more fertile sister, Sardinia.

Steering toward the Straits of Bonifacio, the *Gros Ventre* passed the rock of Asinara, turning south into the wide scoop of a bay. The *Golfo dell' Asinara*; an open port in the midst of the Western Mediterranean.

Twenty miles wide, the bay served as a harbour and sanctuary for every kind of vessel. Frequented by corsairs, fishermen, traders, off-course Crusader ships, smuggling craft and spies from North Africa, the waters of Asinara were controlled by a single, unwritten law. No one attacks another, and everyone minds his own business.

This was not true of the spies, of course, though neither the Moors nor the common corsairs would board another vessel in the gulf. Once out of it, the merchant ships were fair game. But anchored here, off Sardinia's northern shore, galleys and carracks mingled with fishing smacks and *dromonds*, Italians nodding at Arabs, pirates assessing their future prey. And – on this mid-July afternoon – Baynard Falkan studying a narrow-beam, two-masted galley, a dark blade in the water.

He told Enrique de Vaca, 'I shall bid for her services. We've come as far as we dare aboard the store-ship. Burywell's discontented with us, as I am with his coffin-like craft. The further we venture east, the greater our need for mobility. And that ship there, whatever her calling, would give anyone a run.'

At Baynard's command, the Big Belly anchored some distance from the galley. Then, taking Burywell with him, he went ashore, where he paid a local fisherman to find out what he could about the narrow, dark-daubed vessel. 'Ask if her captain will take passengers aboard, conduct four of us to Palestine. Tell him we're – no, I'll tell him that myself.'

Whilst he waited for the fisherman to locate the master of the galley, Falkan walked the morose John Burywell toward the headland that shielded the bay. As Baynard had expected, Burywell said nothing, his ruined spirits anticipating the worst.

Away from the port, Baynard said, 'I told you once, there were two things you should hear. There are now two more.'

'Spare me your apologies, Lord Falkan. It's much as I supposed. You lack the funds and – Let me ask. Are you in any way acquainted with the story of Hugh Marleigh, the nobleman who drowned in Romney harbour?'

'I am not. Why? Should I be?'

'I just thought –'

'Thought *what*, you miseried man? Thought to link me with some mishap in your past?'

'Drunk to the gills,' Burywell murmured. 'He stumbled and went over whilst transferring from the *Gros Ventre* to a dinghy. Oh, you'd no doubt charge me as a liar, you being Lord of Tremellion, and Hugh Marleigh –'

'Christ, you're a maudlin fellow! So all cats scratch, is that it, Burywell? All grapes are sour, and all men of rank cast you down. Yet you, whom I've promised to recompense for your losses, choose to disbelieve me, suggesting I lack the funds. You ask if I've heard of Lord Marleigh? Then I'd ask *you* if you've ever met Captain Gregorius Simeon Bigorre, out of Plymouth? As fine a master of his ship –'

'I did once,' Burywell told him, his head dipped in respect, or bowed in defeat. 'But we're not all cut from the same weathered wood.'

Falkan moved away, his patience exhausted. Then gradually, gazing at the surf that washed the headland, he spared a thought for the unhappy John Burywell, twice met with knights of the realm, and each time worse for the meeting.

Turning to him again, Baynard said, 'The points I wish to make. You heard me enquire about that galley. If all goes well, you'll be rid of us by tomorrow. In any event, you're to prepare a list of your cargo, all the things your crew were forced to discard when we fled the *Hawksbill*. You are also to estimate the cost of repairs to the bow and portside quarters of your ship, damaged when we struck. And finally, my doubting countryman, make sure you've enough feed aboard for the horses. They'll be yours to do with as you wish, for the galley I'm after is far too narrow to house them.' Then he watched the man's slowly dawning belief, and told him, 'Contrary to what you may think, Captain Burywell, not all dogs bite, even if they *were* raised in a muddy castle yard.'

Returning to the port, they were met by the fisherman who informed Falkan that yes, the dark-daubed galley was for hire. The captain's name was Renato Moretti, and he'd discuss terms as soon as the passengers wished, aboard the *Lampreda*, the Eel.

'But I should warn you, signor. Renato Moretti is not a man to be trusted. It's said that he –' Then the fisherman changed his mind, decided he'd spent long enough with the strangers, and disappeared among the nets and spars and caulking fires of the beach. He'd been paid to arrange a meeting, not invite his own murder.

Back on the *Gros Ventre*, the captain made an inventory of the cargo he'd abandoned. Scrupulous in his honesty, he checked the figures till they blurred beneath his eyes. When it was done, he presented the lists to Baynard, who settled the bill without comment, ignoring Burywell's moan of bemused satisfaction.

Then Tremellion said, 'Even if terms are arranged with Captain Moretti, we shall lodge on your ship tonight. I'd like to have heard more from our fisherman friend, but his very unwillingness to talk was a warning in itself. Keep the *Gros Ventre* well guarded, Master Burywell, else we might all get bitten and scratched.'

Leaving the captain to warm his hands at the fire of his re-kindled future, Baynard held Enrique de Vaca, Constable Guthric and the safeguard Quillon in earnest conversation on the stern deck.

He told them who they would be, and what, if anything, they would say. For the moment however, the Spaniard and Quillon would remain aboard to protect the treasure, whilst Guthric rowed Falkan through the swell of the bay and alongside the *Lampreda*.

The two men exchanged a glance as they neared the galley, aware they were venturing unarmed, and with a well-rehearsed lie on their lips . . .

Seeing them approach, Renato Moretti guessed the lean one, huddled uncomfortably on the thwart, to be a petty official from some minor southern port. His face was too dark for a northerner – unless, of course, he'd been spawned in some casual coupling . . .

As for the other one, the burly lump who was rowing – well, all he'd be was the skinny one's protector – *bend to the oars and be sure you don't splash the young master.*

The captain of the *Lampreda* watched with interest. What was it the fisherman had told him? Four would-be passengers, eager to be conducted to the East? A pity they weren't nicely burnished Crusaders, equipped with arms and armour. A decent profit to be made from arms and armour. Sell it anywhere. A wide open market, the Mediterranean, especially for –

With a thud the dinghy swung clumsily against the hull. Moretti gave a start of anger, smothered it with a smile and hurried from his vantage point to greet the men whose throats he would happily slit – but only if they made it worth his while.

'Welcome aboard, signori. Have we a common language?'

Falkan reached for the rail, missed it on purpose, tried again and was hauled aboard by one of Moretti's crew. He gasped and grinned foolishly, attempted a bow, spluttered that French was his native tongue, but a smattering of Italian – then stumbled against the shrouds.

Renato Moretti's smile was as insincere as the workings of his mind. 'You are not a natural sailor, m'sieur. It takes practice to walk with the waves.'

'I am not practised in anything, Captain, unless it be with inks and paper, and the sand to dry my scribblings. Oh, yes, by the way, my name is Baynard, senior clerk in the household of Thomas Guidron, a wealthy and respected pillar of England. This man here, this Guthric, he's a soldier, not long ago returned from the East. If it was not for what he found out there, I'd be forced to mark him as a sweaty and noisome companion. Is this ship at anchor, Captain? The way it rocks –'

'I've been told there are four of you, Master Baynard. You and this lumpen creature, and who else?'

'Allow me to be seated, Captain. The motion of the ship . . . I fear I might disgrace myself . . .' In keeping with his plea, he grabbed at Guthric, the Saxon holding him firmly, turning him to the rail.

Renato Moretti studied the antics of his visitors. Saw Baynard for what he claimed to be. *As clownish a dupe as I could wish for. If the other two are as flimsy as this – But first, let's weigh him for value.*

He gestured toward a canvas sling, halfway between a hammock and a chair. Guidron's clerk settled himself gratefully, then watched as the *Lampreda*'s captain prowled the deck. The man was smiling,

smiling, all the while smiling as he told the scribbler it was no mere jaunt, running the length of the Mediterranean Sea.

'Busy at your desk, m'sieur, you'd be ignorant of the dangers we must face. The currents and whirlpools. Monsters that arise by night from the depths. Black-faced enemies who'd cut us to pieces, flay the living skin from our bodies.'

Baynard raised a hand to his mouth. He seemed unable to speak for a while, then swallowed his fears and said, 'The thing of it is – why we need to take passage – this ugly Guthric was out there in Palestine. Ambushed by the Saracens, he sought refuge in a cave in the hills of Judea. When it happened, what, five years back, he was with a young priest –'

'Dangerous and costly,' Renato Moretti elaborated, still smiling.

'Yes, yes, but you should hear, Captain, hear how they found a Holy Relic, started home to England –'

'In the matter of money, Master Baynard –'

'– and were almost there when the priest was drowned in a squall, leaving only this soldier, this illiterate Guthric, to bring back word of a chiselled stone tablet –'

A what? A slab of stone? No crowns or amulets, coins or coffers? They'd travel across the world for scratchings on rock?

Moretti's smile vanished on the wind. He strode toward Baynard, telling him now, 'The devil with your relics! If you wish to be taken aboard this ship, I'll be paid. And in advance!'

Feigning surprise at the outburst, Baynard hastily searched inside his tunic. Producing his purse, he allowed Renato Moretti to glimpse the deep dull shine of gold. Ingenuously he said, 'You must not suppose this is all of it, Captain. But until we bring our chest aboard, might it not suffice? If only as a token of good faith?'

The Italian's smile was in place again, thin and wide. Denied the chance to kill Crusaders for their armour, and aware the Holy Relic was beyond his comprehension, he'd at least seen the gleam of money. *And what was this about the chest they'd bring aboard?*

'I fear I may have startled you, Master Baynard. But be assured, the *Lampreda* will conduct you safely to Palestine, you and your worthy friends. And that joke I made earlier, about serpents and whirlpools; there's little to be afraid of, m'sieur. Take the word of Renato Moretti. They'll not trouble you at all.'

Baynard risked a none-too-subtle sigh. 'It's a relief to hear you say it, Captain. Simple travellers as we are.'

The predator took the purse he was offered, then invited his new-found passengers to join him in a toast. 'To our safe departure from these islands.'

'*And* our arrival in the East, eh, Captain?'

'Oh, yes,' Moretti laughed. 'That too.'

The sometimes murderer and rapist, ofttimes smuggler and corsair nodded in cordial salute as the clerk and his lumpen protector departed the galley. The day had gone well for him, he believed; his hand on the purse, his hopes on the undisclosed contents of the chest.

And tomorrow, why not, things would go even better.

Clear of the *Lampreda* Guthric growled, 'You'd trust that creature with money? What's to stop him slipping away in the night? Ask me what I think and –'

'You did well, old Guthric. But the play's not over yet. Until the moment seems right you're the mindless hulk Captain Moretti believes you to be. For my part I'll continue to twitch and ask palsied questions. Enrique will be stand-offish and arrogant, our scriptural scholar, caring only for the day when he can decipher our fabled tablet. As for Quillon, he might be the weak link in our chain. Weak in nothing, I hasten to say, but his apparent inability to deflect the shaft of an insult. You'll keep a close eye on him, Guthric, if you will.'

Approaching the *Gros Ventre*, the Saxon asked, 'And once we're out of the gulf?'

'Oh, he'll murder us then,' Baynard said equably. 'Strip us naked and throw us to the fish. He has every incentive to do so, especially since he knows about the chest. Which reminds me. I saw one on the store-ship. We'll load it tonight.'

'Looking about, I totted nine sailors on the galley. So ten with that pike-faced Moretti. Gutter-rats, the lot of 'em. Yet you still say the four of us –'

'We need that ship, Master Guthric. So all we can do, for now, is play along.'

They spent the night in muted preparation. Captain Burywell – a revived and even cheerful John Burywell – happily surrendered his personal, salt-pitted chest. He told Falkan he would sail the *Gros Ventre* to Genoa, refilling the ship's belly there.

Baynard reminded him to say nothing of the passengers he'd conveyed from Tarragona. 'And be on the alert for the *Hawksbill*, Master

141

Burywell. If those so-called Crusaders recognise your vessel, they'll be none too gentle with their questions.'

The grateful sailor vowed to keep silent, though both he and Tremellion knew that if Roger Grevel – de Vallen's kinsman – Ranulf Falkan's hireling – ever seized hold of him, Burywell's vow would be broken along with the snapping of his bones.

EIGHTEEN

As THE sun cleared the mountains of Gallura, to the east of the gulf, Enrique de Vaca and the leonine Quillon were introduced to the captain of the Eel.

The Spaniard acted his role to perfection, swirling the colourless garments he'd purchased from the crew of the *Gros Ventre*, yet wearing his tatters like robes. Renato Moretti mocked him in his mind – this translator of chippings, dressed like a scarecrow, who chose to ignore the proferred hand of greeting. Well, the devil with the Spanish *cognoscente*. His heels would drum, like the rest of them, when a knife was drawn across his throat . . .

Quillon's behaviour was less convincing, his part merely that of an ostler, a labourer, a muscular young sprig from Thomas Guidron's domain. He suffered in silence as Renato Moretti fingered the mane of his harvest hair. But when one of the crew came forward to smile at him, murmur blandishments in a liquid, foreign tongue, then fondle his arm –

Rearing back, he jarred his admirer with a solid blow of his hand. 'You been too long at sea, shipmate, that's the truth.'

Bruised and unrequited, the crewman snatched at the hook that hung from his belt. Falkan glanced quickly at Guthric, watching the constable barge between them. Then he hurried to placate the spurned sailor, as Guthric drove Quillon backward, rasping in his ear.

The awkward moment passed, Falkan diverting Moretti's attention by raising the timbre of his voice. 'You men of the *Lampreda*! Leave that chest where it is! There are important papers in there! Valuable and costly – Leave it be!'

The corsair affected not to hear what Baynard Falkan had intended him to hear. Gesturing the clerk to the sling-seat, he said, 'Settle yourself there, m'sieur, and we'll sail. The weather seems to favour us this morning. A fine, flat sea, and a wind to scud us along.'

His hands waving in a vague approximation of distance and direction, Guidron's clerk piped in the tone of his role. 'How long before your galley's clear of the gulf, Captain Moretti? Before we're fully at sea?'

'Be out of it by noon, Master Baynard. Then on through the Straits of Bonifacio, and into the wide Tyrrhenian Sea.'

Silently Falkan acknowledged, *so, by noon.*

'Always an uncertain experience,' he said timidly, 'being set at large upon the waves.'

Moretti expended another lip-sealed smile. He was already tired of his passengers, annoyed that the law of Asinara forbade him to kill them here and now, strip their bodies, throw them over the side and go straight to the contents of the chest – *Valuable and costly* –

But at midday, yes, he could do it. Stab first at Guthric . . . Then slice the arrogant Spaniard . . . Then offer the jaunty young lion to his crew . . .

After which he'd secure the clerk in the sling. Wrap the canvas around him. And lower him ever so gently beneath the waves . . .

He laid a hand on Falkan's shoulder. 'Make yourself at ease, Master Baynard. I promise you, m'sieur, the voyage won't worry you at all.'

I don't doubt it, Baynard thought, nodding in fictive obedience. Why should it, when we're all to be slaughtered at noon.

Time passed slowly, the tension growing, the actors playing their parts.

Wandering forward, Guidron's scribbler sat in conversation with the arrogant *cognoscente*. Enrique reached beneath the lid of the flat-topped chest, withdrew a sheaf of papers, spread them across the salt-pocked straps. Then they discussed the wording, disputed the meaning, disagreed with fretful, impatient gestures.

Renato Moretti watched their petty squabble, these cloaked and scowling figures, then clicked his tongue and went about the running of his galley.

Quillon sat slumped near the port rail of the bows, whittling a scrappet of wood with a silly, three-inch blade. One of the crew came to crouch beside him, telling him to ignore the one who'd smiled at him before. 'Massimo fondles everyone. But he is not sincere. He would never be a true friend, Massimo. But me – I could be, yes – Can you see it, lion-hair, you and Pino, as friends?'

The safeguard grinned without humour. 'Don't know a word you're saying,' he muttered. 'But you're acting sweeter than any girl I ever met back home. Seems to me you're as bad as your shipmate – too damned long at sea.'

'You've a fine set of teeth,' Pino responded. 'I shall ask the captain to spare you, so you and I can be friends.' Then he brushed Quillon's thigh and swerved away, looking back once to see the safeguard gazing bleakly in his direction.

As for Guthric, he was hunched against the starboard rail, ignoring Guidron's clerk, the Spanish translator, the yellow-haired factotum. His sole apparent interest was in the lift of the sea, the distant coastline to the east.

The *Lampreda* sliced through the water.

'Oh, so you question my reading of the phrase?' the Spaniard snapped. 'The petty *escribiente* thinks to challenge the scholar!'

'I offered an alternative, that's all, Señor de Vaca. Though of course, in the face of such all-embracing wisdom –'

'Your sarcasm betrays your lowly origins, Señor Baynard. Stick to copying letters is my advice, and leave me to interpret these papers!'

And so they continued, snappish and bickering, earning themselves a sneer of disgust from Moretti.

Bored by his attempts to fashion something recognisable from the wood, Quillon pocketed his whittling knife and threw the scrappet over the side. Then he pulled himself to his feet, stretched and yawned, and went to stand idly near the squabbling Baynard Falkan.

The crew busied themselves with the running of the ship, though from time to time they glanced toward the stern. Renato Moretti barked his commands, the *Lampreda* cutting her way across the *Golfo dell' Asinara*. It would not be long before the law ceased to apply.

Guthric rolled his bulk from the starboard rail. He called across to Quillon, the safeguard cupping his hand to his ear and frowning at the Saxon. 'What? What did you say?'

The constable shook his head, grabbed at the shrouds to steady himself, then moved to where Quillon was standing.

Moretti was pleased to see his passengers grouped around the chest. All his eggs in one basket.

Then the arrogant Spaniard shouted angrily at Guidron's clerk, swirling behind him to overlook his shoulder. 'If you *must* have further proof, *escribiente*, the documents are under your stupid fingers. There, in the chest! Let's have done with your questions! Open the lid and I'll show you, once and for all!'

*

Their attention no longer attracted by such peevish behaviour, the crew of the *Lampreda* ignored this latest squabble in the bows. Those who bothered to look might have wondered why Guthric and Quillon moved in close, reaching as if to volunteer their help.

But by then it was too late, for the Knights of Tremellion and Santiago had already snatched their swords from the chest, Quillon his knives, Guthric his short-handled axes. Expecting a flurry of parchment, the corsairs were left gaping, unable to comprehend how these men, these skittish or lumpen passengers, how it was they handled their weapons with such ease, almost as if they were warriors, rehearsed in their action, even now sweeping along the deck.

Renato Moretti howled with indignation. This was *his* trick, not theirs! Another mile through the water and the Eel would have bitten them, coiled around them, crushed their shells and sucked the life –

Obedient to what Falkan had told them aboard the *Gros Ventre*, the Crusaders used the flat of their blades, the prick of the knives, the sideswipe of an axe. It was not their intention to massacre the crew. They would need the men alive, if the *Lampreda* was to reach Palestine. The element of surprise might be enough. But if not – if the attack was resisted – then the corsairs were to be killed.

In the event, and with Moretti still howling, the crew of the galley were herded toward the stern. Most of them were bruised or bleeding, though none too wounded to work. They gazed at their enemy, turned their eyes to Moretti, then huddled to nurse their pains.

Addressing the captain, Falkan said, 'We are of a like mind, I believe. Given the chance, you'd have seized our property, as we've now commandeered yours. The difference being that you'd have murdered us out of hand, and were planning to do so at noon. You must tell me if I'm wrong, Captain Moretti, though I've already been warned not to trust you.'

The Italian thought to bluster, saw Guthric lift an oiled-skin cover from near the base of one of the masts, then smiled his predatory smile.

'All kinds of blades stacked here, my Lord Falkan. I'd say his idea was much the same as ours.'

'Get rid of them, old Guthric. Clear the ship of its weapons. We've a long way to go, and are not, I think, among friends.'

The Crusaders took Renato Moretti to the bows. Roped his wrists and ankles, then tied him with a strangling knot to the prow. 'I've no reason to think well of you,' Falkan told him. 'You're most likely a cordial murderer, with God knows what other crimes tucked in your scrip. But you've a fine enough galley, I'll say that for you, Captain. So we'll go on together as planned.'

His head and neck held tight to the bow-strake, Renato Moretti gazed at the oh, so clever clerk-in-truth-a-Crusader. 'The mistake,' he admitted, 'was in keeping to the law. I must be ageing, m'sieur, for I should really have drowned you midway in the gulf.'

'Get us to Palestine, Captain Moretti and, if the devil strokes you, he may one day grant your wish.'

Cowed by their new commander, the crew of the galley guided her through the Straits of Bonifacio, heeling the vessel south-east toward that sharp-edged stone, kicked by the foot of Italy – the violent and unstable island of Sicily.

During the four-day voyage, Renato Moretti was kept a prisoner in the bows. He was released for the needs of nature; the strangling knot loosened so he could eat; the rope removed at night, allowing him to stretch out on the deck.

Baynard came to see him from time to time. Deeply suspicious of the corsair, he was nevertheless intrigued by the man, amused by his unlikely stories, impressed by his shameless admissions. Certainly he'd killed travellers, but a man had to live, *n'est-ce pas*? And had taken his pleasure with unwilling, wide-eyed young women, but a man had to love, *n'est-ce pas*? The one with the other. The necessary hungers. *N'est-ce pas*?

A few hours north of Sicily, and the young Tremellion was turning away when Renato Moretti called him back. '*Uno momento*, Signor Baynard. I've a further admission to make.'

'If it's worse than your litany of rape and murder, I can well do without it.'

'It's neither of those. Well – based on them, maybe, but – listen to me, Crusader. You know what kind of a person I am, with my appetites and such. Unworthy of a place at your table –'

'At anyone's table, you bastard!'

'Perhaps – But listen. I've had dealings in the past with certain friends in Sicily. Dealings that went wrong. In truth, m'sieur –'

'Say that, and even the devil will laugh in your face, Moretti. In truth?'

'I mean it, Lord Baynard. I'm unloved on that island. Well, not all of it, but in the major ports of Palermo, Messina, the length of its northern coast. Take the *Lampreda* there and I'll be arrested –'

'And with any luck hanged.'

'– and the galley impounded. Held for months. And you and your companions questioned from now till the winter storms –'

'So what are you saying, Moretti? We should avoid the island entirely, ignoring the need for food and fresh water –?'

'Avoid the island, no, m'sieur. But slip around to the southern coast, to the port of Losara, yes. I've been there once, but the *Lampreda*'s unknown. We'd be in and out . . . Then on our way to Crete . . . To Cyprus . . . To where you wish to be, signor . . . Your Holy Land in the East . . .'

Distrustful of the man, Baynard could yet see sense in what he said. Avoid the major ports, and they could touch at Losara, re-stock the vessel, then slip away and brave the next five hundred miles of open sea.

'Would your crew know of this place, having been there only once?'

'Oh, I think they could find it, m'sieur. Tell them Losara and the tall white castle on the rocks.'

Driven by his desires, Falkan saw the *Lampreda* skirt the western edge of the island, the galley veering dangerously close to the arid, North African coast. He admired the way the ship cut through the water, heeling and tacking, as speedy a craft as any he'd been aboard.

If his knowledge of the world was accurate, he and his companions were now halfway along the Mediterranean Sea.

Spain was behind them.

And the pendulous islands of Corsica and Sardinia.

Sicily approaching.

Then Crete and Cyprus and, yes, as the murderous corsair had reminded him, the Holy Land awaiting him in the East.

The Holy Land and the Cause.

The Frankish nobility and the monarchs of the West.

And Christiane.

Her image reawakened in his mind, he studied the curve of the harbour of Losara, raised his eyes to the towering, sun-bleached castle that dominated the port.

Then heard a rattling of chains, a splash as something solid hit the water. He turned from his position near the bows, shouted at Enrique, at Guthric, then ran the length of the deck to see Quillon waving wildly. Beyond the safeguard – thirty feet beyond the stern of the galley – two great counterbalanced bars protruded from either side

148

of the entrance, a dozen chains suspended from each of the bars, the lower links attached to a pair of metal-sheathed beams.

Cleverly constructed, they formed a barrier, a net, a boom that sealed the entrance and exit from Losara.

His features pinched tight with anger at his own stupidity – 'Christ, I should have known!' – Falkan returned wearily to the bows.

The *Lampreda* slipped toward the quay, where armed soldiers were already waiting, more troops running from the side streets. A trumpet blared from the ramparts of the castle. Archers and crossbowmen stood ready. Other members of the garrison hefted spears or long-shafted axes, the port of Losara glittering with blades.

Renato Moretti smiled as Baynard approached. 'If you were really just a scribbler, m'sieur, I could understand it. But a Crusader knight? Tut, tut.' He enjoyed Baynard's defeat, waited to be freed from his bonds, then pulled himself upright, massaging his wrists and the rawness around his neck.

He extended a hand for Falkan's sword. 'A bitter moment, eh, Crusader, but resistance would be – unwise.' Glancing cheerfully at the port, he said, 'It's true what I told you before, how unloved I am in Palermo and Messina. But here, in Losara, I'm their very best of friends. One might say I have friends in high places.' Then he used Falkan's sword to indicate the castle. 'The *Governare* Atzeri has been a, how should I put it, a client of mine for years. He has a weakness for the Arabic opiate, hashish, and for pretty young Moorish girls, and well, almost anything I come across on my travels.'

'You mean plunder, don't you, Moretti? The profits from piracy, the objects of abduction?'

'Ask me how you were hoodwinked, Crusader. How we lured you into port. You won't? Well, I'll tell you anyway. Look up there at the mastheads.'

Falkan hesitated, then shrugged abruptly and turned to gaze at the tops. He'd been well and truly gulled by the corsair, the young knight a victim of his own success in the Gulf of Asinara. God alone knew what the governor would do with his unwanted visitors. Free them? Hold them for ransom? Lock them away to rot in some stinking dungeon? If he was so enamoured of Moorish women, so addicted to the drug hashish, he'd have little reason to love the Christian Cause. Even less when he discovered the contents of the salt-pitted chest.

'So what do you see, Crusader?'

'Nothing. There's nothing up there to see.'

149

'That's true. But there should be, don't you understand? A bright red pennant at the foremast. Yellow at the other. The one shows the *Lampreda*'s here to trade, the second to show there's no one in pursuit, no other corsair eager to gobble the Eel. Without them, the port's alerted. Atzeri too. And the boom, as you've just seen, m'sieur, is lowered.' Another wide, hard smile and the corsair added, 'Eels are slippery things, Crusader. You must never expect to tie a cord around their necks and think them caught.' Then he snapped at his crew, and they cheerfully, vengefully goaded Enrique and Guthric and Quillon to stand with Tremellion.

The *Lampreda* nudged the quay. Men from the *Rocca di Losara* swarmed aboard. Moretti spoke to their leader, nodded at something the Sicilian told him, then turned to relay the news to the men he'd outwitted.

'You should feel flattered, messieurs. Salvino Atzeri is on his way down to greet you. Though what happens to you after that –' And he allowed them an eloquent expression, wordlessly conveying his doubts and fears for their future.

NINETEEN

BUT THE game was not yet over, the dice still in play . . .

Closely guarded, Falkan and his men were made to stand like exhibits in the bows. Moretti was kept busy, explaining – and calmly distorting – the events that had taken place in the Gulf of Asinara. The garrison captain knew him for the liar and cheat he was. But it had to be admitted, Renato Moretti spun a story you could weave into a multi-coloured cloak. A blanket to keep you warm in winter. A tapestry for the walls.

Then a disturbance in the side-streets caught their attention. The garrison captain gestured urgently at his men, and even the corsair's smile lost its grip. The *governare* was descending to the quay.

Driven brutally from the ship, the Crusaders were run down the gangplank, stumbling as they reached the stippled, unyielding cobbles. Guthric snarled at one of his guards and was rewarded with the jab of a wicked, needlepoint dagger. Blood welled from his forearm, staining the sleeve of his woollen shift. He blinked with the shock of it, then settled his gaze, reminding himself that if ever – then this one –

Salvino Atzeri might, for all the world, have been mounted on a low, wheeled trolley. His jowled face dripping with a carefully razored moustache, he was fat and bald, his eyes too small, his lips cherubic, his pudgy fingers sparkling with rings. Swathed in satin, in gold-and-silver weave, he wore a floor-length robe so exaggerated in its decoration that the stitched flowers seemed to bloom as he advanced, the orchard fruits grow ripe.

His feet concealed – and Falkan realised now the man walked with tiny, tipping steps – Governor Atzeri progressed smoothly across the cobbles.

Halted to speak with his garrison captain and the corsair.

Then he tip-toed forward to peer at Baynard, swept upward with his arm and cut the young knight's face with a backhanded slap of his jewelled fist.

'Whatever Moretti may have told you, I have no love for him. But

151

he's of value to me. He brings me things I enjoy. So I will *not* – and he struck again – 'allow the likes of *you*!' – and struck – 'to *interfere*! – with the *running*! – of his *ship*!' His too-small eyes fixed on the lacerated Baynard, the governor heeled his way delicately back.

The corsair watched the punitive display, though no longer smiling. Until, suddenly, he remembered the sea-worn chest.

'I don't know what these men would be worth as ransom, *Governare*, but they're doubtless carrying something for their expenses. They brought a chest aboard the *Lampreda*. Half to me for luring it here, and half to you as usual?'

Turning to spit blood from his savaged lips, Baynard let his shoulders sag with the weariness of defeat. It was too late now to warn Moretti; too late now to let the corsair know the dice were still rolling . . . And that only the disgusting, decorated Salvino Atzeri could win.

'Produce it,' the governor commanded.

'And half to me, half to you –'

'We'll see, Moretti. I never was one to take women in the dark. And I always hold gem stones to the light.' Then he ignored the pirate, ignored the prisoners, and centred his porcine gaze on the leather chest.

With the discovery of the Tremellion treasure – the saddle-bags packed tight on the floor of the chest – the quayside of Losara erupted with a shriek of delight from Atzeri, a bellow of fury from Renato Moretti, shrills of command from the governor, and a low moan of anguish from Baynard, his eyes closed tight in disgrace, but the frowning displeasure of Sir Geoffrey Falkan burning in his brain.

Only as far as this, my son? Crossed by a pirate, then double-crossed by some fattened Sicilian official? I'd hoped better of you, boy. Counted on you for a greater achievement than that.

'Oh, but there's real wealth here!' Atzeri crowed. 'Enough to be rid of *you*, my sinister friend! Drown the lot of you! Sink your slippery ship!'

'But we agreed! Half and half!'

'Agreed *nothing*, Moretti! You and I were *never* agreed! All you've been to me is the cheapest supplier of girls and goods and – Hah! If I could remember the number of times I've fooled you, seeing you sell me emeralds as glass. The stories you've swallowed! The fictions

152

I've fed to you! You're as drab a man as the daubings of your ship, *caro mio*. When I needed you, I made use of you. But no more. Not with what the good Lord Falkan has brought me from the rainy isle of England.'

'So what do you –?'

'What do I plan to do with you, Moretti? Why, enter you in our contest, what else? Our jumping contest. The one in which you leap the fifty feet from the ramparts, hoping to clear those horrid rocks below.' Then the cruel, cherubic creature turned away, pretended to remember and swung back to add, 'Did I say to you fifty feet, *Capitano*? And with a forty-foot rope around your throat?'

Herded together, the Crusaders and corsairs were pricked and pummelled up the slope to the *Rocca di Losara*. Their individual fates not yet decided, they were taken to a bare, fourth-floor room in the castle, the prisoners left to nurse their cuts and bruises, the triple-hinged door slammed and bolted behind them.

The crew of the *Lampreda* sprawled in frightened disarray. Never well-disciplined, these scavengers of the sea were now out of their depth, ironically high above the waves.

They held life cheap in others, happy to rape or murder. But never imagined they too, could be taken, their own merciless careers brought to a sudden halt.

More proficient in his trade, Moretti left his crew to mew and murmur, sinking beside the ring-whipped Crusader.

'You should have told me about the contents of the chest, M'sieur Baynard. Had I known –'

'Had you known,' Falkan moaned, 'you'd have brought us all the quicker to Losara. Remember, Moretti, it was *we* who controlled the *Lampreda*, beyond the gulf. And *you*, you saddened creature, who placed your trust in Atzeri.'

'It was always half and half before.'

'No, it wasn't. Didn't you hear him say? How he valued your jewels as glass –'

'Well, maybe.'

'And deceived you with his stories, the fictions you swallowed like bread. Sweet Jesus, but he's right, that decorated devil. You'd fare better with your enemies, Moretti, than the friends you're fool enough to choose.'

At other times confident, Renato Moretti now crouched at the feet of his master. 'Tell me then – you who I've just seen repeatedly slashed by Salvino Atzeri – tell me, Crusader. How do you see us out of here, four storeys up above the rocks? And how will you reclaim your money? And escape this island –?'

'I don't yet know, but –'

'And me? Am I to regain command of my galley? Liberate my crew? Slip away and –'

'I've told you,' Falkan mumbled, his lips beaded with congealed blood. 'I do not yet know how we'll do it. But you'd be advised to join us in our efforts, Moretti, before the governor sends for his forty feet of rope.'

There was not one single stick of furniture in the prison.

No bedding, no candles, no picks or shovels left negligently in a corner.

Quillon produced the three-inch blade of his whittling knife. He was treated to a sneer of laughter, all he needed to throw the knife through the bars of the single window.

The single window . . .

At first glance an obvious escape route, for the window was no mere hole in the outer wall, but a caged balcony, floored with stone, projecting above the rocks that fringed the port.

Guthric and Quillon hauled a number of Moretti's crew to their feet. 'Time to work, friends. Time to loosen the grille.'

But nothing so easy, the bars holding firm, their ends mortared deep in the stone.

Quillon said, 'There was a time I got caught in a village near Tremellion. No need to name names, but it was me an' this girl, an' her hus— her brother came home an' I had to get out fast. Funny fellow, her brother. Anyway, what I thought to do was skinny up through the roof. See what I mean, Guthric? Shift the tiles and climb out *over* the bars.'

But nothing so simple, the slabs of slate too heavy to be moved.

Angry now – and aware that Atzeri might have them hauled from the room at any moment – Moretti and his crew joined the Crusaders as they slammed their heels against the flooring of the balcony.

But the single jutting stone would not be broken.

Intention gave way to fury, the men taking turns to wrestle with the bars, scrabble at the roofing, stamp until their feet were raw.

They were free to stand in the high, caged window, gaze out to sea, look downward at the surf that spumed from the rocks. But try as they might, they could not bend the metal, lift the slabs, or break the solid, buttressed platform.

Exhausted by his efforts, Falkan stumbled to a corner of the room. A few moments later Moretti joined him, the corsair snarling imprecations at the name of Silvano Atzeri.

'So! All these years he's cheated me, that tinselled pig! Swore he was paying me fairly, then afterward squealed with pleasure at –'

'Tell me about him, Renato. Whatever you know of *Governare* Atzeri. But spare me your flytings. I like him no better than you do.'

The corsair sank dispiritedly to the floor. Falkan turned away to wipe blood from his face, then hitched around to repeat, 'All you know about him. He and his family. Whatever comes to mind.'

It took a while to control Moretti's fulminations, but he finally recounted what he knew of their jewelled gaoler. 'The pig's not as important as he pretends. He's just one of a number of governors on the island. Palermo, Catania, Ragusa, Messina, maybe a dozen others. But it's true he controls the port of Losara. There's nothing you can do to prevent him stealing your money, Crusader; nothing any of us can do if the swine decides to hang me.'

'Does he live here in the castle?'

'Somewhere below us, though on the side away from the sea. He's got a garden there, well, more of a walled courtyard, filled with a mass of spiny, bright-flowered plants. He took me there once, laughing when I got scratched by the spines. Told me most of them were poisonous; I'd likely die in agony in the night.'

Gazing across the room at the solid, barred window, Baynard watched as Enrique de Vaca hurled himself at the grille, then sagged in bruised defeat. Turning toward Falkan, the Spaniard shook his head . . .

'Does he live alone, our Silvano Atzeri? That's to say, him and the young Moorish girls you supply?'

'Live with the girls? God, no. He's a respectable married man, *il porco*. His wife is the daughter of Don Flavio Abruzzo, Governor of Caltanissetta, one of the most prosperous towns in all of Sicily. It's how Atzeri came to be Governor of Losara. As for his girls, his private harem, he keeps them in a house up there in the hills.' With a snort of reluctant admiration, the corsair added, 'He chose well when he married Signorina Abruzzo, for rumour has it she never leaves her rooms, unless it's to walk the fifty or so paces to her private chapel. It seems everyone knows of Atzeri's pretty sows, except his wife. It'd suit us well, eh, Crusader? A genteel wife at home, and a storehouse of *puttani* –'

Ignoring Moretti's humour, Falkan asked, 'Have you ever met the Signora Atzeri?'

'Met her? I wouldn't say met her. *Seen* her, yes, with a cross in one hand, candles in the other. She was veiled, of course, though you could see she was as hard-faced a bitch –'

'Then not the type to overlook her husband's infidelities?'

His spirits somewhat recovered, Renato Moretti barked with amusement. 'Learn of his, what you so delicately call infidelities, Crusader, and she'd have him dragged around his garden till the flesh was ripped from his bones. Might even venture out and do it herself. But why do you ask? Are you planning to shout it, as we're led up to be noosed and thrown from the walls?'

'You exaggerate,' Falkan snapped. 'It's you who's been invited to the jumping contest. No one else.'

They tested the walls of the fourth-floor chamber, though without much hope of finding some convenient secret exit. Inspected the triple-hinged door, not really believing an unknown saviour had silently slipped the bolts. Flung themselves in fury at the bars of the buttressed window.

Spat their frustration. Retired to the latrine in the corner. Emerged to curse the high, vaulted roof, ladle brackish water from a twenty-gallon keg, glare around at their well-constructed prison, the room as austere as their hopes.

TWENTY

BAYNARD FALKAN gestured to the Knight of Santiago. 'I've a mind to visit the garderobe, *amigo mio*. Will you come?'

Seeing where the men were headed, Renato Moretti called after them. 'Is that how it is with the English, the Spaniards? The one goes, the other holds his hand? And me? What should I do for you? Dance to divert the crew?'

Once again Falkan ignored him, continuing to the south-east corner of the chamber, where a stone partition offered a semblance of privacy to whoever was in the alcove of the latrine.

Enrique waited as Baynard leaned into the narrow, doorless cell. What he saw was a single, rough stone slab laid two feet above the level of the floor, a chiselled hole in the centre.

And far beneath the hole, the dimness of light.

Moving back from the alcove, he said, 'Look.'

Enrique de Vaca frowned at him, pointed at the latrine and asked, 'There? You say I should look down there?'

'So I do. Study the sides of the shaft. Tell you what you see.'

Holding his breath to keep the unpleasant odours at bay, the Spaniard performed the task his friend had requested. Then he emerged from the cell, allowing himself the right to say, 'Had I known it would come to this, *amigo mio*, I might well have stayed in the *encomienda*.' But he said it without rancour, his thoughts already in tandem with those of Baynard.

'Worse is to come if we peck about here like mournful pigeons. So tell me. Do you think the slab can be lifted?'

'Lifted entirely? I don't know. But tipped back, perhaps.'

'And then?'

'Then below it there's a stinking shaft, cut all the way down to the rocks.'

'Is it wide enough, in your opinion, for a man to be lowered?'

'Oh, certainly it's wide enough. Even your constable – but it angles out at the base –'

'So I noticed. The thing we have to do is get one man down – a swimmer who can navigate the waters off the rocks – then trust him

157

to steal a dinghy, a sufficient length of cord, row the boat under the window after dark and toss the cord up to us –'

'Throw a rope forty feet upward?'

'No, you're right. We must tell him to find a weight and some fishing line. Catch it as it comes through the grille and we can pull the rope up after.'

'I admire your determination, Halcón. But there's something I must tell you. Before we even tip the slab. I don't know how it is at Tremellion, but a number of castles I've seen – the latrine shafts are barred at the outlet, to stop attackers clawing upward with picks and flexible ladders. The fortress of Punta Siderna was captured like that. And not the only one, I imagine.'

Remembering others he'd learned about during his months of military training in the muddy fens of Norfolk, Baynard said, 'Some are barred. Some aren't.' But he chose not to add that the outlets at Tremellion were grilled for that very reason . . .

Working fast now, time against them, the prisoners struggled to loosen and lift the slab of the latrine. Crusaders and corsairs alike were required to donate their longest garments, Guthric knotting the motley collection into a thick, knobbled rope. Striding three times the width of the chamber, he measured the hawser at fifty feet, long enough for a man to descend to the rocks.

But which man should it be?

Renato Moretti was the first to volunteer. 'Listen to me, Crusader. I know this port. And the fishing village on the other side of the headland. I can get you a boat, the line and cord and so forth, row it back to the window –'

'Or maybe reach the village and keep running? Or find a craft and hoist sail? Your offer's angelic, Moretti, but I think your memory of us might lapse.'

'You mean you wouldn't trust me to return?'

'No, my friend. I mean I wouldn't trust you below the first knot of Guthric's clothes-line. You're a liar and a trickster, Renato, with more crimes to your name, I'd guess, than there are dates on the calendar. If we ever get free of this place, my unlikely angel, the last two to leave will be me – and you.'

'You're making a bad mistake, Crusader.'

'It's possible. But no worse than allowing you to make good your escape.'

*

Enrique de Vaca volunteered, his loyalty unquestioned, though his offer rejected by the phrase he himself had once used.

'That time we were aboard the *Gros Ventre*,' Falkan murmured. 'Didn't you say to me then you'd never been further from land than midway between the banks of a shallow river? So when you find yourself pounded by the waves down there on the rocks? Will you really be able to breast them, *amigo mio*? Tell me you will and I'll credit it, but —'

'You could put me in the water keg and I'd drown,' Enrique admitted. 'Water's for a man to wash with when he's dirty. Drink when he's thirsty. But otherwise — well, to tell you the truth, I flounder when it rains.'

Guthric offered to test his own rope, but was gently dissuaded by Tremellion. There were many reasons for prohibiting the Saxon, Baynard imagining how it would be if Guthric ever reached the village. He wouldn't so much steal a boat on the sly, as commandeer it, fisting aside all those who'd dare prevent him. Oh, he'd get the cord and the fishing line, then bend the oars as he rowed beneath the window. But he'd also leave a score of men moaning on the beach, panic spreading, a trumpet once again blaring from the ramparts of the *Rocca di Losara*.

Ask Guthric for the galley itself, and somehow he'd secure it. But with Silvano Atzeri alerted, his soldiers tramping the stairways to the prison.

Sparing the man he so deeply admired, Baynard preferred to tell him, 'Your failings are those of Enrique de Vaca, old Guthric. You're not worth a damn in the water.'

Which left the crew of the *Lampreda* — none of whom could be trusted, not even by Renato Moretti — and the one-time poacher, the man who'd saved the Saxon at the foot of Tresset's linn; the so-called ostler, the jaunty young joskin who swam like a fish and owed his loyalties to Falkan.

'Me? You're singlin' *me*? Well what's wrong with some of them shipmates? I don't even know where we are 'ere! Why don't you lower one of them down the shaft? Bony little bastards. They'd be out an' back in no time!'

Enrique set his features in a cold, waxed frown.

Guthric gazed at the doorway, swivelled to stare at the joskin, the constable's granite hands lolling as fists.

The crew of the *Lampreda* held their breath, Pino and Massimo watching to see how their handsome hero would perform.

Then Falkan said calmly, 'Any moment now and the plump Atzeri will send for us – hang us with the dying of the sun, or shackle us to the walls of some seeping dungeon. The choice is yours, Master Quillon. It's that, or make use of your skills.'

He stepped back, leaving the safeguard to decide. And only moved forward again when Quillon snapped at Guthric, 'Well? What are you waiting for? Get your home-made clothes-line around me!'

Falkan and Enrique took the strain, assisted by Guthric and the corsair. They lowered Quillon as fast as they could, if only to spare him the noisome stench of the shaft.

A Phrygian cap pulled low to conceal his harvest hair, he slid the first twenty feet without trouble. Then snagged his belt, the knotted cord slackening above him. The safeguard hissed for the men to haul in, take up the slack, wait for him to work loose from the outcrops of stone.

Too quickly free, he dropped five feet further down the chute of the latrine. But by doing so he wrenched one of the knots, the separate fabrics slipping, the clothes-line coming apart . . .

Quillon fell. Jarred his spine on the angle of the shaft, then skidded to where the feared grille would bar his escape. Crash into a grille like that and . . .

But the base of the drop was open, the young man sprawling down a smoothed-out runnel of stone – out from the rocks – and flailing into the sea.

The waves lifted toward him, to throw him against the base of the *Rocca di Losara*. But the swell of the water had met its match in Quillon. He'd faced worse than this in the winter floods in Cornwall. Worse than this languid slap of the sea when he'd poached for fish, plunged below a mill-race, ploughed through the rapids to escape the verderers who'd have so much liked to collar him – then hurry him off to be hanged.

Apart from the numbing ache at the base of his spine, the safeguard was in good enough shape to swim wide of the rocks. He turned on his back and extended a hand in the direction of the high, buttressed window.

With darkness falling, he couldn't be sure if they'd seen him. Not that it mattered. It wasn't as if they'd be leaving. Acknowledge his departure or not, they'd still be in the prison when he returned.

Then it occurred to Quillon that maybe they wouldn't; maybe they'd have been dragged out by Atzeri's soldiers and taken up to the ramparts.

The thought of it made him twist in the water, dip toward the fishing village and stroke his way powerfully, urgently inshore.

It took him a while, the daylight now fading, to collect what he needed, skulking low as he searched the array of bright-painted craft hauled up on the beach.

An elderly watchman sat huddled over a brazier of glowing charcoal, his gaze on the embers, his lips around a straw-wrapped flagon of wine. He glanced up once as Quillon scooped a handful of small lead plumbs from the deck of a fishing boat, the safeguard crouching in silence until the watchman's attention was once again turned to the coals.

Encumbered by rope and line, and one of the heavier lead weights, Quillon edged cautiously to the far end of the beach. There, he stowed the stolen equipment in the bed of a rowboat. Then, hidden from the watchman's view by the assorted craft that littered the beach of Losara, he dragged the dinghy into the water.

An accomplished swimmer, he was nevertheless unpractised at the oars, and his progress was painfully slow as he drew the rowboat away from the shore. More time passed, the young man aware that time was also passing in the prison. Splash with the oars and he might be spotted from the beach. But dip them too gingerly, and he'd arrive beneath the window to see a yellow smudge of lanterns beyond the grille, the sign that Atzeri's guards had come for their captives.

Guided by moonlight, he rowed toward the base of the *Rocca di Losara*.

The weak Mediterranean tide was on the turn, allowing the boat to sit stationary in the water as Quillon attached the plumb to the fishing line, coiled the line on the thwarts, then sent the weight flying upward at the grille.

It struck wide of the window and fell back in the sea.

He hauled the lead aboard, dragged on the oars and repositioned the dinghy.

Then he tried again, cursing as the plumb hit one of the bars, the fish-shaped weight rebounding before a dozen outstretched hands could snatch at it.

He tried again – realigned the rowboat – tried five more times

161

before someone's fingers clawed at the plumb, dragging the line inward through the grille.

Remembering, but almost too late, he groped on the stern board, tying the end of the line to the stolen rope.

It was whisked as if by magic into the air.

A sibilant voice hissed down to him. 'Stay where you are . . . Stay off the rocks . . . Keep out to sea and wait . . .'

The first half-dozen to emerge from the shaft were members of Renato Moretti's crew.

Panicked by the stinking claustrophobia of the drop, they yelped with fear as they skidded down the runnel to the sea.

Heedless of their terrors, the safeguard dragged them aboard, shoved them to the ends of the dinghy, then signalled in the direction of the window. Seven was enough for the rowboat to hold. He'd take them to within a few hundred yards of the village, deposit them among the rocks, then return for the others.

But it worried him that the moon was now bathing the scene with her jaundiced gaze . . .

Twenty feet from a tangle of scrub and volcanic stone, Quillon shoved the men overboard, telling them to get ashore and wait. 'If you value your lives, you'll squat there and be silent.' Then he realised his language was not theirs, shrugged as they floundered to the rocks, and rowed back to collect the others.

Watching from the buttressed window, Falkan reported, 'He's landed them. It's our turn to slip down now.'

Three more sailors were sent, unwillingly, down the shaft.

Then Constable Guthric, his shoulders tight against the sides of the chute, a grunt of horror reaching those in the prison as he found himself wedged in the angle of the drop.

There was nothing they could do for him, though it occurred to them all – to Enrique de Vaca, the corsair and Baynard Falkan – that if the constable was blocked by his bulk, so were they.

They heard him growl and felt the rope tighten. Then slowly, painfully, the Saxon climbed upward again, hand over hand until he was ten feet clear of the bend.

Gripping the rope high above his head, he released his hold and plummeted downward, trusting his weight would compensate for his girth.

Peeling his scalp on the rim of the outlet, the Saxon slithered to the sea. Quillon reached for him, grinning with admiration at the flinty old warrior. 'You was never fashioned for this sort of thing, eh, Guthric? You're a man who stands better on his feet, ain't that so? Well, let's get you aboard, before I 'ave to dive for you again.'

Enrique de Vaca descended, biting his lips in horror of the water. All the way down the shaft he found himself silently reciting prayers he'd thought long forgotten.

Baynard Falkan glanced around the prison, crossed to the door, leaned against the single, studded plate. Then he strode toward the latrine, waving the corsair ahead of him.

Moretti said, 'Go first, and I'll guard your descent.'

'In a rat's eye you'd guard it,' Falkan dismissed. 'What you would do is hammer on the door and howl the alarm. *You* get down first, Moretti. It'll lessen your chances with Atzeri if he knows you joined the escape.'

Quillon ferried the second group to the hideout of scrub and rock that flanked the bay. He called to the sailors he'd already sent ashore, called again, then turned urgently to Baynard. 'They're supposed to be huddled there, m'lord. Waitin' to be joined.'

But they weren't. No sooner had Quillon rowed back to collect the others, than the six terrified crewmen from the *Lampreda* had fled, scuttling like rabbits from the slap of the surf, the already imagined pursuit of Silvano Atzeri.

Reduced to eight, the ill-assorted fugitives scrambled ashore. The *Rocca di Losara* loomed behind them, less than a quarter-of-a-mile away. At any moment they expected to hear the strident blast of a trumpet.

Peering upward, Baynard saw a small, thin cloud drift to veil the moon. He told his safeguard to release the dinghy, then watched as it was sucked out to sea, its slowly spinning departure concealed by the cloud. If one of Atzeri's watchguards saw it from the ramparts, he'd assume it had broken loose from its mooring near the beach. At least until the escape had been discovered.

Moving close to Moretti, Falkan said, 'You tell me you've friends in the village, is that so?'

'More than I could count, Crusader. Apart from the pig who governs it, I'm very well liked in this place.'

'Yes, yes, you're everyone's favourite, Renato. But could you get into the village and procure us some weapons? Anything we could fight with; gutting knives –'

'Rely on it,' the corsair assured him. 'Keep hidden here, and I'll be back with a clutter of blades.'

Baynard said, 'You're a liar in life, Renato, and you'll lie with your dying breath. But remember this, my angelic sounding friend. I intend to reclaim Tremellion's money. As for you, you doubtless hope to regain your ship. Play the traitor now, and we'll both be disappointed. But work together and – well, you must think it out for yourself. Now go and find those friends of yours, Moretti. But don't be so foolish as to tell yourself Silvano Atzeri's among them.'

Had the rough terrain permitted it, the captain of the Eel would have rubbed his hands with satisfaction as he scuttled between the rocks.

His first idea was to contact one of the fishermen, promise the man enough money to buy his own fleet if he'd call his crew together, hoist sail and carry Moretti south-west the two hundred miles to Tunisia. The pirate was very well liked in the ports of Tunisia. One of their favourites—

But no. For he'd then lose the *Lampreda*.

Very well. So I can't flee from Losara . . .

His second thought was to avoid the village, hurry instead to the castle and yell the alarm. If he told Atzeri the prisoners had escaped – *and* where they were – *and* that he'd been forced to go with them – well, surely the governor would see what a loyal ally he had in—

But no. For the sparkling swine would hang him anyway, the man who knew that Atzeri had seized Tremellion's chest.

Very well. So I'd best steer clear of the castle.

It was not in Moretti's nature to keep his word. What was a promise anyway, but sounds in the air? Yet, how to squirm out of this one, ignore what he'd told the Crusader, dodge Atzeri's forty-foot rope and sail away on the Eel?

It couldn't be done without the help of Baynard Falkan.

Very well. So I'll fetch them their blades. Then stand aside when it comes, the time for killing.

TWENTY-ONE

HIS EXAGGERATED boast no more than that – yes, sounds in the air –
the corsair returned to the rocky fringe of the bay with half-a-dozen
gutting knives and some light, cane-handled tridents, simple harpoons
used by the fishermen as they waded the shallows.

But it was better than nothing, and at least Moretti had come back,
and done so quickly.

'You're not exactly cluttered with blades, Renato –'

'Did I ever say –?'

'Yes, but no matter. It's more important we get away from here.
Now, tell me. What chance Silvano Atzeri's up there in his house,
with those girls you supply?'

'He's bound to be,' Moretti said shrewdly. 'If not, he'd have come
to gloat at us in prison. You should thank me, Crusader, that the pig
has those pretty young sows to distract him.'

'I should thank you with one of those knives for tricking us into
Losara! But you and I can show mutual gratitude later. The thing to
do now is make use of our fast evaporating freedom. Get up to that
house and – I assume you know where it is?'

'A mile or more back in the hills. Though I must warn you –'

'Lead the way.'

'– it's walled around, and with a gate –'

'Allons-y!'

'– that's closed against callers. And he doesn't go there alone to his
sty. There are four or five guards –'

'Tell me on the way, Moretti. Tell me anything you like. But keep
your shanks clear of this blade.'

Bruised and torn by their descent of the shaft, then further battered
by the grey, volcanic rocks, the eight men threaded their way around
the headland, through the deserted alleys of the fishing village, then
up a series of winding sheep-paths that led to the hills.

Goaded ahead by Falkan's threat, the Italian led them at a brisk
enough pace, Quillon herding the three remaining sailors. Guthrie
occasionally blundered as blood ran from his peeled forehead,

165

Enrique de Vaca assisting him, then turning to act as the rearguard. . .

Ashamed of the way he'd been lured into port by Moretti – and the corsair incensed by Atzeri's treachery – the men now shared a common fear; the tolling of a bell; the blare of a trumpet from the walls of the *Rocca di Losara*.

'How much further?'

'What do you think, that I bring the girls up this sheep-path?'

'The guards you spoke of . . . When we get there . . .'

'I told you . . . There's a gate that's kept locked . . . The guards are in a house inside it, to the left . . .'

'Move faster! We're borrowing time.'

The column struggled upward through the thorny, summer-dry brush. They halted once as a cloud trailed its cloak across the moon, the men stooping to gasp in the fast-chilling air of the island. Then Falkan grunted, jarring the corsair's spine with his fist. 'Get us there quick, damn you! I want that pig caught at his trough!'

The pirate opened his mouth to yelp at Falkan's blow. But the yelp came out as a snarl of achievement, the man stabbing a finger ahead of him, to the left. 'That's it, there, do you see? And that roseate light? It's leaking through the shutters of the house. And that other one, that glimmer below; it emits from the gatehouse. Now I tell you what, m'sieur; tell you what, Crusader. Leave me to keep watch from here and –'

'Lead the way, *mi angelo*. It's not just Tremellion's money we're after, but your own slippery ship.'

Some of them determined, others reluctant, the ill-matched group of Crusaders and corsairs descended in stealth to the walled-around property that housed Atzeri's harem.

Falkan leading one group, Enrique the other, they climbed the wall wide of the ornate, barred entrance, edging between the shrubberies of the garden, intent on catching the guards in their small, stone gatehouse.

It was then that one of the sailors stumbled, tearing the tendons of his ankle, the pain of the fall wrenching an instinctive shriek from his lips. The bloodied Guthric lurched toward him, intent on silencing his cry.

But too late.

Armed men emerged from the gatehouse, lanterns lifted, helmets pulled down to protect their skulls. Swords were apparent in the yellow of the lantern-light, the yellow of the moon.

The poorly-equipped invaders ran to overpower the *sentinelle*.

Brief in time, the skirmish seemed long, for although Atzeri's men were outnumbered, their armour deflected the bamboo spears and gutting knives, whilst their own swords cut terrible, unrestricted swathes.

Yet Baynard and Enrique knew their weak points, the Spaniard edging inside the swing of a sword, lifting the hem of a guard's link-mail cowl, then stabbing at the gullet with the blade of his fisherman's knife.

Falkan threw a second soldier off balance, chopped at his hand and, without hesitation, prised the weapon from his victim's unstrung grasp.

But by then one of the sailors had been killed.

And Quillon flung back with a sword thrust in his shoulder.

And the smiling liar whom Baynard would never trust, yet had come to accept as a fish who'd ever escape the hook – he too had been landed, the slice of a blade across his groin.

Guthric fought in the way he knew best, a knife in one hand, a thin handled trident in the other. Thrusting the spear ineffectually at one of the armoured guards, he snarled with disgust, and hurled his dagger at the man's face to disconcert him. Then he plunged irresistibly forward, the spear discarded, his massive hands reaching to lift the soldier and slam him against the rough stone wall of the gatehouse.

Protected though it was, the man's neck broke with a satisfying snap.

Pino and Massimo crowded the final *sentinella*, darting away from the slash of his sword, then slipping in close, teasing him to attack.

But the guard was less easily fooled than the sailors believed, advancing on Pino, then checking his stride, his arms extended, his double-edged weapon cutting clear through the top of Massimo's skull.

Over-reaching, he was met by Pino, who howled for the loss of his shipmate and drove his knife in so hard that the blade tore through the links of the armour, snapping at the hilt.

And then there were only the noises of dying, the moans of the wounded, the taint of murder that mingled with the scent of the summer trees.

Baynard Falkan crouched beside Quillon. 'I must teach you,' he said. 'When we get to Palestine; teach you to watch for the thrust.'

The Sicilian's sword had laid the safeguard low. It was a deep and agonising wound, but it had missed the main pipes that carried his blood, allowing him to say what Falkan wanted to hear.

'You told me once – a long time ago – how they were, those women of Cyprus. I'd like it well, m'lord – when you've sorted out your business here with Atzeri – if we could get along to that island . . .'

Then he fainted with pain, Baynard commanding Guthric to stay with him. 'Dress his wound as best you can. And see to Moretti. Meanwhile, I'll take Señor de Vaca with me to the house. Remain here till the alarm's raised – and God knows time's against us – then get this motley crew away to the hills. I want you to know, old Guthric; you've been as loyal –'

'Be on your way,' the Saxon told him. 'You and Sir Geoffrey, you both wasted time in talk.'

Each now armed with a sword, the Knights of Santiago and Tremellion hurried toward Silvano Atzeri's harem. Moving together, they ran up the steps, pounded across a wide, trellised porch and shouldered their way through the doors.

Once inside, they were halted by the opulence of the place; the complexity of the patterned carpets; the wealth of coloured fabrics that pleated the walls. Brilliant mosaics studded the tables; tasselled cushions scattered at random; all the colours turned to a deep, seductive haze by the candles that spilled their wax into odd-shaped receptacles – sculptured erotica, purchased by Atzeri.

A moment later, they were confronted by a severely dressed *siciliana*, the woman's eyes narrowed with fury, an arm extended in rigid accusation. 'What are you? *Demente?* You have no right! This house is private! You understand what I'm saying?'

Enrique de Vaca smiled grimly, propelled the woman to an ornate, satin-backed chair, then held his sword as a lateral barrier between them. His language foreign to her ears, the sense of his question was clear. 'Speak quiet and tell me. Where can he be found, your guest, Atzeri of Losara?'

Seemingly fearless, the woman matched his expression. 'I don't speak your tongue, signor, so I hope you – or your dark-skinned companion there – understand mine. Are you friends of Atzeri's, or would you wish him harm? To have got past the guards –'

Falkan came forward. 'Wish him harm, signora?' he measured. 'Oh, yes. We wish your favoured guest nothing but harm. You, no. But Silvano Atzeri. All the harm in the world.'

The woman let her gaze swing from Baynard to Enrique, then

back. Calmly she raised a hand to smooth the tight-combed gloss of her hair. 'His behaviour,' she murmured, 'it was always bestial. I have long prayed the monster would come to harm.' Then, ignoring them both, and as if to remind herself of some half-forgotten detail, the haughty *siciliana* mused, 'The Governor Atzeri . . . He's in rooms on the second floor this evening . . . Along where the passageway's carpeted with shells . . .'

Climbing quickly, quietly, they edged along the shell-patterned carpet, pausing briefly to listen at the doors that flanked the passage. Then Enrique nodded in silent indication; the door at the end; weren't those moans he could hear?

Now Falkan could also hear them, moved to within a yard of the panels, balanced himself and kicked out hard, the sole of his boot smashing the flimsy lock. Plunging forward, he swerved to let the Spaniard in beside him, the young knights traversing the chamber with their glare.

For a second time they were halted, though no longer by the opulence of the setting.

Totally naked, five young girls lay contorted and writhing on an extravagant, canopied bed. Startled by the splintering of the lock, they twisted around, their eyes wide with astonishment – wider still as they glimpsed the swords.

The plaited thread of a whip lay like a snake near the foot of the bed.

Two of the girls were marked by the welts of the whip.

Another bore beaded cuts on the side of her face – evidence of further bejewelled brutality.

Musing aloud, Baynard murmured, 'Harm's in the air, so it seems.'

Enrique snarled something in the dialect of his birthplace, then roared at the innocent, terrified victims, the sheer force of his bellow dispersing them from the bed.

To reveal the porcine Silvano Atzeri, Governor of Losara, respectable married man, son-in-law of the powerful and prosperous Don Flavio Abruzzo – who would surely see him suffer through the dictionary of pain, if he ever learned of this!

Atzeri caught at the hem of his discarded robe, hauling the gold-and-silver gown across the pinkness of his flesh. As he did so he babbled; the words without formation; the gluttony of his mind unable to comprehend what his veined eyes told him was the truth.

The prisoners were secure in the *Rocca di Losara* – but they weren't!

His *sentinelle* were on guard at the gate – but how could that be, if his enemies were here!

And their weapons – they didn't have any weapons – but just look at them! *They did!*

He pulled the robe to his chin, as if the flowered fabric was magicked and would save him from the agonies of a blade. Then he squirmed against the carvings of the headboard – further erotic designs to whet the voluptuous appetites of the governor. And all the while he babbled; his mind cowering, insensate.

Enrique recounted to his friend, 'In the village where I lived, it was the thing to do to keep pigs. They were well looked after. Oh, yes, Halcón, we always cared for our pigs. Then the time would come, as for all of us, and we'd hoist them upside-down from a frame in the yard, hold a basin under their snouts and slit their throats. And you know what would happen then, *amigo mio*? We would stand for a while and say how well it had died, that pig. With dignity. As befits all life at the end. And we'd nod in respect to the poor, suspended animal, for its flesh would keep an entire family alive throughout the winter.

'Now, I don't say we should string Atzeri to the frame of his cushioned bed. But it's not as if his flesh or blood are of value. All I ask is – Let me slice his throat anyway! *Allow me that single pleasure!*'

He moved as if to do it, striding toward Atzeri, and Baynard could only hope to stop him by shouting, 'Too costly, de Vaca! Kill the man now, and where's Tremellion's treasure? Believe me, my friend, we need this pulpy monster. For the moment at least, he's of value to us alive.' Alarmed by Enrique's insistence, he pulled firmly at the Spaniard's sword arm, then edged ahead to stare at the man who'd five times slashed his face with his pudgy, jewelled fist.

'Stop whimpering, Atzeri. Wet the bed if you must, but listen to me. I have only to urge my friend forward and your life will end with a smile – across your throat. If that's what you wish –'

'Oh, no! No, no! I'll – no – I mean yes! I'll –'

'What you'll do is what you're told, you overfed bastard. Decent men have been cut because of you. I fear your friend Moretti may die. *Your* friend . . . The one you chose to cross for the sake of the money . . . *My* money, or better yet, Tremellion's –'

His own anger building, he fought to control it, to somehow get his message across to Atzeri.

'Hear me on this. You could be killed for stealing the money. For striking me time and again down there at the port. For your abuse of these innocent girls. For the pleasure it would give de Vaca. But that's not all of it. There's your wife to be considered –'

'Oh, no. You've no call to – whatever you want – your money, well, of course you shall have your money – and extra – for the errors I've made. If it's simply a matter of money, Signor Falkan –'

'It isn't, *and I've not yet finished speaking!* I have yet to remind you of Don Flavio Abruzzo. And ask how he would greet the news of your frolickings here.'

The portly Sicilian collapsed against the tumescent carvings of the headboard. Then he gabbled at the men, begging them to spare his wife's feelings, and not only hers, but the elderly Don Abruzzo's. 'It'd be the death of him if he heard –'

'Oh, I doubt it,' Falkan rejected. 'He would surely not permit himself to die until he'd exacted his revenge upon *you*, the unfaithful husband of his daughter. I'm touched by your concern for the master of Caltanissetta, though aren't you confusing Don Abruzzo's death with your own?'

They allowed the man time to dress, dip his feet into his soft leather shoes, then buckle the jewelled belt around the protuberance of his belly. As they were leaving the chamber Enrique de Vaca said, 'One moment.' He reached forward to snatch a purse from the governor's belt. 'He's omitted to pay for his pleasures, I believe.'

Atzeri winced as the Spaniard scooped out half the coins; stared in horror as the Knight of Santiago called sharply to the girls, then tossed the gold and silver currency on to the bed.

They descended the stairs, Falkan nudging Atzeri ahead. With the governor unaware of it, he took the half-empty purse from Enrique.

Once again confronted by the fearless *siciliana*, the Crusader gave her no time to speak, but pushed her brutally aside, condemning her as quite the sort of sow who'd protect the swine.

'When we asked where he was, you lied to us, *signora*. Told us he'd departed the house. Whatever his troubles, and they've only just begun, he can at least count on *you* in time of need.'

The woman accepted his insults, knowing he'd lied to save her. Then she watched as Baynard urged the governor through the doorway, the young knight stooping quickly to let the purse drop on to one of the tasselled cushions.

Once again raising a hand to her glossy hair, she couldn't help but wish the foreigners well. And all the harm in hell to Silvano Atzeri.

*

They returned to the gatehouse to find the safeguard hunched in silence, Pino still mourning the loss of his shipmate, Renato Moretti attended by the Saxon, a line of congealed blood across Guthric's scalp.

The constable clambered to his feet, beckoned Baynard to the shadows. 'There ain't much time for 'im, the corsair. Belly wounds are the worst.'

'How's Quillon?'

'*That* tough young joskin? Don't you worry about him, Falkan. He'll live to bury us all.' The words were unfeeling, yet belied as Guthric glanced toward the safeguard.

'But not so Moretti? Will he live as far as the *Rocca di Losara*? We must go back there, with Atzeri as our hostage, if we're ever to reclaim the chest.' Then he turned away for a moment, Sir Geoffrey's second son fighting to cope with the mounting losses of this personal crusade. Speaking low, so only Guthric could hear him, Baynard murmured, 'All those men who died, alongside my father . . . The sailors who were swept from the *Gossamer* . . . The men we killed when we were accosted in Spain . . . And now this . . . Christ, is it worth it? How high a price must we set upon these coins?'

The Saxon leaned close to growl at him, the dismal mood shattered by the resonant tolling of a bell. Then the repeated blasts of a trumpet. Distant roars of anger and alarm, the sounds sweeping inland, upward from the fortress, all of them summoning Silvano Atzeri from the cushioned cruelty of his sty.

The young Tremellion discarded his doubts, casting aside the comforts of self-pity. *What else did you expect, you damned fool? That Ranulf would give you his blessing? That bandits and corsairs would bow you on your way? That creatures like Atzeri would recoil from the sight of money? God in Heaven, what you carry's a temptation to the world!*

What you carry? No . . .

What you've allowed to be taken from you!

Striding from the shadows, he told Guthric and Pino to take charge of the wounded Moretti. Enrique escorted the quivering governor, the safeguard assisted by his master.

Atzeri and the Spaniard led the way, Baynard and Quillon following, Renato carried by Guthric and the tear-stained sailor.

They left six corpses behind them – the entry fee to Silvano Atzeri's harem.

TWENTY-TWO

THEY REACHED the northern edge of the village without incident, once again following the sheep-paths, then rejoined the road that led behind the headland to the fortress. His wound bandaged tight by the constable, Quillon was able to move unaided, his main concern that he'd lost his fisherman's knife.

Peering across in the moonlight – and with cheering disrespect – he said, ' 'Ere. You got a blade I could use, m'lord? I'm as good with one 'and as the other.'

'Keep your voice down! The closer we get to the castle –'

Obedient at least in this, the safeguard whispered, 'Well, 'ave you?'

Content with the sword he'd taken from the *sentinella*, Baynard surrendered his knife. If attacked by armed guards, the weapon would be of little use to Quillon, though the mere possession of it seemed to raise the young man's spirits. 'You'll see,' he promised. 'Good with one as the other.'

They moved slowly, approaching the *Rocca di Losara*.

Renato Moretti suffered with a stoicism only Guthric could appreciate, for none but the Saxon had seen the extent of the corsair's wound. The man would die – a fact beyond question – and only his determination and resolve could prolong the moment.

He'd muttered once, as they'd reached the foot of the sheep-paths. 'Are we close to the *Lampreda* yet? Soon as we get to Tunisia . . . I'm very well liked in Tunisia . . . More friends down there than I could count . . .'

Ignorant of his language, Guthric had stayed silent, leaving the mournful young Pino to respond. 'Very near, my captain. And we'll soon be in Tunisia. Oh, yes, very soon.'

Then Renato sighed, and the menagerie of men made their slow, painful way toward the fortress.

Two hundred, maybe three hundred yards from the entrance, and the column was halted by the sudden appearance of soldiers, the *sentinelle* armed with crossbows, infantry spears and the weapons they'd employ in a bloody hand-to-hand fight.

Silvano Atzeri shrieked at them to stop.

'Stay back! This is your governor! I've been taken – they'll kill me – stay back!'

Lanterns were raised to identify Atzeri; to assess the chances of murdering his captors, then drag the governor free.

They were a sorry lot, these foreigners, two of them wounded, none of them protected. A well-loosed quarrel from one of the crossbows, and –

'Set those lanterns on the ground!' Falkan commanded. 'Let fly a single bolt and we'll send Atzeri's head rolling amongst you! No personal loss to you, perhaps, but try explaining to his wife how it happened. And then to Don Flavio Abruzzo of Caltanissetta!'

As a descending swarm of fire-flies, the lanterns were lowered to the track. No loss in itself, that was true, the beheading of the *Governare di Losara*. But afterward there'd be questions to be answered, tribunals to be faced, responsibilities apportioned, accusations levelled, punishments meted out – and hangings to be administered from the heights of the sun-bleached castle.

Allow Silvano Atzeri to die in a scuffle, and dozens would die in his wake.

The *sentinelle* retreated, not wishing to be recognised by their master.

'Get on through the gate. Lead the way to your chambers.' Then a sudden thought and he added, 'Wait!'

It occurred to Baynard that those outside the stronghold might attempt to bar their exit. Besiege the castle long enough for help to be summoned from Caltanissetta. Plead with Don Abruzzo to descend in force and save his daughter – and incidentally her husband.

'Tell your men – tell them this. If we see a single soldier near the gate, you'll be sent out to join him. From up there. The top of that tower.'

Atzeri babbled the warning, then was swung around by Enrique and sent skittering in his soft-soled shoes along a series of tapestried corridors to his quarters.

Impressed though they were by the magnificence of the colourful, over-furnished room, the Crusader knights gave priority to the wounded Renato Moretti. Expecting to be challenged by household guards, they were pleased to find the exotic chamber empty, save for two startled servants. A guttural threat from the Saxon and the men retreated against the wall, staring as the rapist and murderer was laid on a Moorish *diwan*, his pain-racked body comforted with cushions.

Guthric then moved toward Quillon, the safeguard swaying on his feet.

'What ails you, joskin? Jealous of the pirate? The prick of a sword, an' you think yourself worthy of a couch?'

The young man twitched, the movement intended as an arrogant toss of his head. But the pain of the stab flooded over him, and the retort he'd planned for the flinty old Saxon – the clever riposte – it wouldn't quite trip from his tongue . . .

Guthric caught the youngster as he fell, gesturing to Pino to set a few more cushions as a mattress on the floor. Then he knelt and lowered the joskin on his side, muttering a brief, unheard remark before rejoining the knights. *'I might just have to take it upon me – Teach you how to survive.'*

The wounded now settled, the Crusaders turned their justified anger on Atzeri, the governor watched in mute fascination by his servants.

'We are here for our belongings,' Falkan told him. 'Every scrap and item in the chest. And, as recompense for the men your guards laid low near the gatehouse of your brothel, we'll take the extra you offered. For the errors you made, you remember?'

Atzeri hastened yes. Things had been disturbed in the searching, but everything was safe in the *cofrano* – 'Your clothes and armour and weapons. And every last coin you brought to Losara! As for the extra – that desk over there – if you'll permit me to find the key and –'

Then he gaped in distress as Guthric ambled across to the delicate, inlaid piece, toppled the cabinet face down on the tiles and reached to tear away the polished cedar backing.

Lifting it upright again, he spun it on a single leg, slammed it back on its feet and extracted the drawers. His eyes fixed on Atzeri, he emptied the contents of the desk, holding the Sicilian's horrified gaze until the final compartment had been ransacked.

And then, uncaring of the contents, he looked across at Falkan and grunted, 'This one? This the desk he means?'

The knights, the wide-eyed Pino and the quaking servants, stared at the glittering heap he'd spilled from the drawers. It could only mean that Silvano Atzeri preferred to keep his accumulated riches where he could easily get at them; that the sparkling brooches and bracelets, the diadems and necklaces, the pins and buckles and heavy inset rings that now littered the tiles, were there to be admired at his convenience – *or that the cabinet contained but a particle of his wealth.*

'Were it not for the wounded,' Falkan told him, 'I'd stay longer and strip this castle to the bones. As it is, we'll collect our chest; and this, *the extra –*'

'No more than I deserve, signor. I was foolish to underestimate –'

'And one thing more than that.'

Silvano Atzeri waited, the Sicilian wondering what next he'd be forced to surrender. The chalices from that monastery chapel on Rhodes? The carpets shipped from that palace in Antioch?

'So what should I offer you, signor, as apology for our misunderstanding; as assurance of –'

'The Signora Atzeri. Don Abruzzo's daughter. I'll take your wife.'

The governor panicked and ran.

A ridiculous sight, his fleshy thighs slapping together beneath his robes as he struggled for purchase in his soft leather shoes.

Ten yards along the chamber and Guthric stepped in front of him, fisting the man hard in his corpulent belly. With an unpleasant belch of air, Atzeri fell back, yelping as his buttocks hit the tiles.

Winded and gasping, he stayed there while Enrique de Vaca checked the three doors that led from the far end of the chamber. The first opened on to a corridor, at the extremity of which was a small private chapel. The second revealed a spiral staircase. The third—

And a shriek of alarm as the Spaniard brought Signora Atzeri from a room containing a single bed, the bed of a nun; the walls of the cell as bare as those of a convent, adorned only by an olive-wood cross and a faded panel, depicting the Madonna and Child.

It seemed to hurt the woman's eyes as she was forced into the sensual glow of the chamber, urged into the presence of the still wheezing Silvano. Shielding her gaze, she took stock of the servants, the wounded, the Crusaders, then jerked her arm free from Enrique's grasp and stalked toward her husband.

'You've a reason for this, *mi marito*? An explanation as to why I've been dragged from communion with God? Who are these intruders? Are we now both to be murdered?'

Watching the woman, Falkan thought, I can almost understand why Atzeri seeks his perverse amusements with his girls. She's as bad as Renato suggested; a hard-faced bitch with a tone of voice to match. But she makes my task easier; no danger of feeling sympathy for the daughter of Don Flavio Abruzzo.

The bluish-black of her gown was unrelieved by ornament; her sharp features poking for knowledge; her bony fingers like thin, accusative blades. Moving closer to Atzeri, she snapped, 'I ask you again. Who are these armed and bloodied creatures, and why have you allowed them to wrest me from my silent communion –'

The Governor of Losara turned helplessly to Falkan. But the young knight ignored his unspoken pleas, addressing himself to the woman. 'We are all you say, signora. Creatures bloodied by your husband's soldiers. Intruders in this castle. But murderers? Not by choice.'

'Then what business –'

'Moderate your tone. The governor will explain things to you later. Meanwhile, prepare to keep us company. We're taking you to see the pretty boats in the harbour.'

Moments later, under the supervision of Enrique, the servants had produced Tremellion's salt-rimed chest. Its contents verified, the knights exchanged the Sicilian swords for their own. Atzeri's jewellery was thrown in with the saddlebags, the clothes and armour, the documents used to deceive Renato Moretti. The servants were ordered to carry the chest, Atzeri placed at the mercy of the Spaniard, the corsair once again entrusted to Pino and the Saxon.

Quillon was helped to his feet, insisting he was as fit as a cock on a midden. He staggered once, then grinned at his companions, challenging them to a duel. 'But I warn you, I'm as quick with the left as the right –'

Baynard Falkan escorted Signora Atzeri, the woman's lips pinched in a bloodless line, her body quivering with rage and apprehension. The rumours were true. She had not once left the *Rocca di Losara* in the past four years . . .

Impressed by Falkan's threat, the *sentinelle* had withdrawn from the entrance to the castle. But they lined the path that descended to the port, the terrible, square-headed quarrels of their crossbows levelled at the men who dared to abduct Atzeri.

And look! His wife!

They cringed from her glare, knowing that however it ended – unless in a massacre – her revenge would be awesome, her righteous fury unleashed. God help those who were chosen to face the wrath of Signora Atzeri!

The *Lampreda* lay waiting, her strakes rubbing gently at the quay. But between the Crusaders and the galley stretched a double line of soldiers, those in front kneeling to form a spiked wedge of blades, those behind with lances and tight-wound crossbows.

A voice from the centre of the ranks called them to a halt. 'You go no further than this! Throw aside your weapons and release the captives. Submit to the mercy –'

'You've missed your moment,' Falkan responded. 'It's no longer just Atzeri who'll die in the mêlée, but the daughter of Caltanissetta. Be sure of yourself before you tell your archers to let fly. It would take a dint of explaining, the death of the Lady of Losara.' Then he urged the woman forward, alongside her husband, murmurs of astonished recognition dissolving the ranks.

There were curses and threats and the swearings of revenge, but the Sicilian troops could see the Crusader swords laid close to the necks of Silvano Atzeri and his wife. A single, ill-aimed quarrel, and there'd be scarce enough branches on the trees to support the ropes. Better that Don Abruzzo's daughter was taken, than that all of Losara should be widowed . . .

Renato was carried gently aboard, then settled beside the tiller-bar. The servants hauled the heavy chest up the gangplank, resting it amidships. Atzeri tottered on the plank, turning on deck to half-raise his arms in mute appeal to the soldiers. Urged ahead by Falkan, the governor's wife elbowed her husband aside. In passing, she spoke for the first time since leaving the castle. Her words for Atzeri alone, they left him gibbering that it wasn't fair, it wasn't so, it wasn't true.

It was arduous work, releasing the *Lampreda*, though they managed it, Quillon jamming his knife in his belt to work with one hand, Pino scurrying from bow to stern, Guthric and Enrique obedient to the orders passed from the wounded Moretti to the anxious Baynard Falkan.

It took them an hour to clear the port. But the boom had been raised, navigation lights flickered at either side of the entrance. The oil-doused wood blazed in its cauldrons, each supported by the cage of a tall iron tripod.

And then, as the Eel slipped between the fires, the Governor of Losara seized his chance.

Abandoning his wife, uncaring of the future, he ran to the starboard rail, heaved his way over and toppled into the water. He surfaced behind the ship, splashing and squealing, then fumbled to rid himself

178

of his heavy jewelled belt. The weight of leather and gold and precious inset stones took it downward in a wide, swirling spiral, to be buried for ever in the dull basalt mud.

It was now mid-summer, the promise of day already conveyed from the east. Pino – the sole surviving member of the crew, other than the six who'd fled from the headland – took it upon himself to nurse Moretti.

But as Guthric had forecast, the corsair would die, and no amount of nursing would save his life. Though he was not yet ready, his knees drawn tight to help seal the gaping wound above his groin. He suffered agonies in silence, then emitted a brief groan of intolerable pain, Pino running to comfort him, or dab away the sweat that broke from his brow, the sailor who'd wooed young Quillon now showing the strength of his nature.

Guided by Moretti, the *Lampreda* skirted the coast, the pirate vessel sliding to meet the day.

And all the while, Signora Atzeri stood close to the port-side rail, her angular features fixed as in stone, her body immobile – an unappealing statue in transport across the sea.

Three hours' sail from Losara, and with the light now marking the glint of silver on the waves, Baynard conferred with Moretti.

'It was never my intention to take the Signora Atzeri from her home. To get us out of the port aboard your ship, well, yes, but it gives me no pleasure to abduct her –'

'Wouldn't give – wouldn't give anyone pleasure, an arid bitch like that, eh, Crusader?'

'Likely not,' Falkan murmured, 'though it has to be said, I do at last feel a stirring of pity for her. He's quite the fellow, Silvano Atzeri. Match him with my own brother Ranulf, and Satan himself would be dining at their table. But listen. Before I tire you –'

'Tire me all you wish, Crusader. I'd hate to die in silence.'

'Always the liar,' Falkan attributed. 'For once in your life you prove useful, Renato, so you threaten me with dying.'

They gazed at each other, the pirate with his knees strapped tight, the knight crouched beside him, both of them fearing that death would come with the day.

'You were about to ask? Something to do with the woman?'

'I want to put her ashore. And take on crew for the Eel. If there's a port –'

'Santadi,' the corsair told him. 'Less than an hour's sail ahead of us. I'm very well liked in Santadi. More friends there than I . . .' Then his voice faltered, his features twisted with pain.

Gripping the man's shoulder, Baynard said quietly, 'Yes, I know. More perhaps than the two of us could count.'

With Pino conning the galley, they entered the ramshackle harbour of Santadi.

The Knight of Tremellion rowed the Lady of Losara to the shore. Once on dry land, he said, 'Your husband has served me grievously, signora, though the cause of it must remain between the governor and I. However, I regret that you've been torn from your devotions, taken from your fortress and hauled away to sea. I've more important matters in mind than to see you safely home, but the least I can do is— Here, Signora Atzeri. Here's money enough to purchase a comfortable return to Losara.'

The woman took what he offered without a word. Then she stood for a moment, staring westward in the direction of the *Rocca di Losara.*

In her hard, saw-toothed tone she said, 'I have two things to tell you, you poor pretence at chivalry. I shall not travel in comfort to Losara. Nor shall I spend so much as a lira of your oh-so-generous consideration. It goes to the first church I see. But what I *shall* do is start inland from here and find my way to the town of Caltanissetta. I shall leave it to my father to judge what should next be done, and to whom.'

Baynard thought, she will do it. Be it fifty miles through the mountains, she will do it.

'And the second thing, signora?'

Her bleak gaze still directed to the west, she said, 'Oh, the second thing applies to my husband. You do not seem the type to be well-versed in the Bible, although you call yourself a crusader, so you are probably unaware of what the blessed Apostle Matthew wrote. "It had been good for that man if he had not been born".' She turned to Baynard, her smile stirring the hairs on the back of his neck. 'Now, don't you think that applies rather well to Silvano Atzeri?'

With three new crewmen questioned and approved by Moretti, the *Lampreda* continued east from the port of Santadi. But it was not until the galley had cleared the *Punto di Correnti* and was heading for the open sea that Baynard was able to forget the woman's final, horripilant smile.

TWENTY-THREE

THE ELDEST of the three hired Sicilians was named Domenico Balbo, his knowledge of navigation impressive, his breath raw with the stink of anchovy and garlic. When he'd come aboard in Santadi he'd brought with him a small wooden box of the salted fish, and a string of the bulbous plants. These he would chew with a sweeping disregard for anyone forced to stand near him.

But the odours of his breath were a small price to pay for the accuracy of his orders. He'd satisfied the dying Moretti, and that was good enough for Falkan.

'He admits to no more than a limited knowledge of the waters beyond Cyprus,' the corsair recounted. 'But he claims to have been to that island. And to where he's taking us now, the island of Crete. You've a long sail ahead of you, Crusader.'

'You say it as though you intend to quit the ship, Renato. How would you desert us? Steal the dinghy and –'

'No, no, I'll leave you the rowboat. But there *are* things I shall want from you, Crusader. Some good strong sacking, and a generous length of chain.'

Wish it as he might, Baynard could not pretend ignorance of the man's demands. It was apparent to all those aboard the Eel that Moretti's time was up. His periods of lucidity were brief now, the pain of his wound sapping what little strength remained. It was incredible that he'd lasted this long, his face cadaverous, his diet a few sips of water. He drifted into senselessness, awoke to boast of the hundreds, nay, the tens of thousands of women he'd enjoyed . . . His secret hoards of booty stored in hidden caves on Sardinia, or buried among the sand dunes of North Africa . . . Had he told them how loved he was, along that coast?

He asked Baynard to fetch the young Pino, then to stay and witness what was said.

'You're not very clever, are you, Pino?'

'Not very clever, captain, not at all.'

'Nor very much given to killing, or the stealing of goods?'

'In truth, my captain, I am not.'

181

'Then I wonder why I ever . . . A fellow like you . . . Aboard my slippery Eel . . .' He drifted away, jerked with a sudden spasm of pain, then hurried his words. All his life, time had been against him, justice and revenge in close pursuit. He'd been a hunted man, chased the length and breadth of the Mediterranean Sea, not really so well liked as he pretended.

But he'd never been caught – *slippery as an eel* – and here he was now, reclining on his ship, and never more safe from capture than in these, his final moments.

'I leave her to you, young Pino. The *Lampreda*. She is yours to run as you wish. A stronger fellow than you, and she'd be the scourge of the seas. Built for it. Slippery as . . . Slippery . . .'

Then he lifted his head, managed the semblance of a smile for Baynard and fell away, curling and shrinking, to be just another corpse.

No one but Pino was allowed to help with the stitching of the canvas, the winding around of the chain. When it was done the sails were lowered, the shrouded body laid on a plank, then tipped from the stern of the galley. The weighted bundle splashed into the water, Pino staring downward for a moment, before turning to Domenico Balbo.

'Understand this. Your task is to guide us to Crete. Signor Falkan and Signor de Vaca are our masters. But *I* am the captain of the *Lampreda*.'

Balbo gave a casual, affirmative shrug, then directed the raising of the sails. Baynard felt he should mark the passing of command with some formal gesture, however slight, though all he could think to do was extend his hand, the Knight of Tremellion offering his respects to the skinny, one-time sailor of this dull-daubed corsair ship.

'When we disembark in the Holy Land, Captain Pino, your vessel will be very much in demand by the Christian forces. I tell you this now, so you've time to reflect on the *Lampreda*'s future – and your own. What Renato Moretti told you may be true; become ruthless in your ways, and this blade of a boat could threaten half the traffic on the seas. But it could also be the scourge of the Saracen navy. Or a fast-moving messenger for the leaders of the West. It's for you to decide.'

'You mean well, Signor Falkan. I think you did, even when you deceived us in the Gulf of Asinara. So I'll promise you this. When we reach your precious Holy Land, I'll tell you straight what I intend to do with the Eel.' Then he grinned and said, 'But don't be surprised if I set her to hunt for innocent women and the illicit wealth of merchants.'

Favoured by the wind, they reached the island of Crete in the second week of August, restocking the ship in the port of Hierapetra. The slash across Guthric's scalp had healed to a long, narrow scar, while Quillon could now discard the sling that had held the weight of his arm, easing the wound in his shoulder. He still suffered the ache of the sword thrust, but his spirits were high, the safeguard indulging in fantasies of eager anticipation.

According to the foul-breathed Domenico Balbo, their next landfall would be Cyprus. And wasn't it there, so Lord Falkan had promised, that the women were special? And much to be enjoyed by a lusty fellow like Quillon?

His imagination stretched beyond its limits by the journey that had taken him from Tremellion to Plymouth, south to the Bay of Biscay, along the foothills of the Pyrenees, away from Tarragona to the island of Sardinia, then in a downward sweep to Sicily, and the prison in the *Rocca di Losara* – then eastward again to Crete and – not much longer now – toward the promises of Cyprus – all that, and he dreamed his dreams.

The girls would be waiting, near-naked, on the shore.

They would single him out from all those aboard the *Lampreda*, calling to him in some strange, enticing language that, as luck would have it, only Quillon could understand.

It was hard to envisage what Cyprus would be like. But mostly warm sand. Yet with sheltering trees. And rivers where he could show off his prowess as a poacher, the near-naked girls applauding as he scooped a trout from the rapids, their leonine hero raising his arms, a squirming fish in each hand, the smell of woodsmoke drifting from the fire they'd lighted, the strumming of guitars as—

' 'Ere! What's that? I just saw a bloody great fin, big as me arm.' Dreams dashed, a pallor to his skin, he gestured to where, ahead of the ship—

'There it is again! Hey, Guthric! M'lord de Vaca! Someone! Anyone! In the name of— What kind of fish is *that*?'

With Baynard as translator, Domenico Balbo told the foreigners of the flesh-tearing sharks that cruised the Eastern Mediterranean. More than half the length of the galley some of them. And with jaws that could chew through oak. Through mooring chains. Their teeth filed to points by the devil. Their mouths were fenced with not just one, but two and three and sometimes four razor-edged rows, a single bite enough to sever a grown man at the waist.

Quillon's spirits collapsed. His dreams became nightmares. He marked Baynard Falkan as a liar, realising now he'd been tricked from his homestead in Cornwall. All these promises of Cyprus, and what would he find? A blackened, grim-girt shore, the island swarming with lunatic hags – and the waters around it alive with the thrashing of sharks as big as the vessel, their fins cutting a greenish slice through the sea . . .

The safeguard now preferred to hunch amidships, wishing himself back beside the Hexel River, far away from the boiling, shark-infested waters; the basalt rock with its crazy, shrilling women . . .

With Quillon the victim of a terror-ridden sleep, the galley approached the sun-stroked island of Cyprus.

Guthric nudged the safeguard awake, saw him recoil from his remembered phantasms, then said, 'On your feet, joskin. Time to haul rope.'

The young man turned in alarm, pulled himself upright –

And gaped at the beauty of Pafos; the clear blue water devoid of monsters; whitewashed cottages clustered on the flowered slopes behind the port. And villagers watching from the quay. Bearded men and their straight-backed wives. And, yes, in spite of his fears and nightmares, all he could have hoped for in the way of fine young women.

Not near-naked of course. But attractive enough for Quillon to toss the mane of his harvest hair, then wave at them, his broad grin showing how pleased he was to be there; and Lord Falkan not a liar after all.

Pino and Domenico would stay aboard the ship. Baynard told them to find out all they could about the final passage; the two-hundred mile crossing from Cyprus to the Frankish ports of Tyre and Acre. Then he made his way into Pafos, where he paid rent for a cottage on the slopes above the village. The whitewashed house contained four small rooms, three of them little better than cubicles, the low-pitched roof sagging beneath the weight of Roman tiles. Uneven stone slabs formed a terrace in front of the cottage, the hill below wooded with olive trees, a narrow path winding from the port.

Pino's crewmen laboured the chest up the unkempt track.

A mule was used to bring food and wine, the owner of the cottage leading Baynard to a well at the side of the house. The man raised a hand to his lips, fingertips pressed together, then gestured to show the purity of the water. 'You will find none better on the island. See! I draw up this bucket! I drink the water! I smile at the sweetness of it! I look sixty years of age, not more! But do you know! You know? I am more than four-times-twenty!'

The deliveries completed, Baynard Falkan invited his companions to join him in the cottage. He volunteered a generous sum of money – an earthenware pot placed where only the four men would find it – then told them to use the coins as they wished. It was the first time since leaving Tremellion that Baynard and Guthric and Quillon, and with them now Enrique, could set aside the importance of their quest and relax beneath the caress of the summer sun.

But they had other forms of caress in mind; a single, identical reason for taking money from the jar . . .

The only inconvenience was the narrowness of the path, for the men found themselves passing *en route*, Enrique guiding a pretty young girl up from the village, Guthric returning his exhausted companion to the foot of the winding track.

Falkan preferred to wait till the path was clear, though the safeguard strutted his way cheerfully up and down, willing young women fondling his tangled, cinnamon hair. With coarse good humour, he told Baynard, 'You were right, m'lord, the way you said they'd be. An' they are!'

It suited them well, the tired Crusaders, this respite on the island. It gave them time to refresh their thoughts, their wounds now healing, the pain of their bruises lessened and forgotten. They ate fruit and fresh meat, hauled the stiff leather bucket from the well and yelped like deep-voiced children as they splashed their muscled bodies.

Eight days passed in the slow, sun-warmed spinning of sensual pleasure, the recounting of stories, the dreamless sleep of exhausted men, the knowledge that they'd come this far, and with not much further to go.

Another two hundred miles and they'd be there. In the Kingdom of Jerusalem. The Holy Land of Christ.

Spitting the bones from a strip of salted fish, Domenico Balbo climbed the path to the cottage. The exertion made him sweat, the stink of garlic and anchovy exuding from his pores. Not that he noticed, nor would have cared if he had. He'd more important things in mind than to worry about the odour that emanated from his skin.

It was Quillon who saw him first, the safeguard engaged in a desultory game with pebbles and sticks near the edge of the terrace. For once devoid of female companionship, the young lion was content to play about in the sun.

Seeing Domenico, he waved in greeting, stooped to collect a few pebbles from the stones and called through the open door of the cottage. 'We got a visitor, m'lord. 'Im what chews those roots.'

Falkan emerged to find the Sicilian level with the terrace.

'How goes it, Signor Balbo? You'll need something for the dryness in your throat. We've a good enough wine, though sweet to my taste, or water from –'

'I'll have them both, Crusader – but not now.'

Baynard glanced sharply at him, sensed the visit was important and gestured him to the shade beside the house.

Domenico paused to catch his breath, his hands pressed to his thighs as he leaned forward, the build of the man a perfect match with the Saxon. Set them together, Baynard decided, and they'd bar the way to anywhere.

His lungs again filled with air, Domenico muttered, 'I've been sent up here by Pino. He says I'm to tell you there's men down there at the port. Countrymen of yours by the look of their blistered faces. Not that I ever saw 'em. But it seems they came asking if there were Englishmen around. Crusaders set for the East.'

'And what did Captain Pino tell them?'

The question offended Balbo, and he barked his reply. 'Maybe he's young, that Pino, but he's careful with what he says. Told them to keep on searching, along the coast. But he thought you should know they're about.'

Falkan nodded, silent for a moment as he gazed across the olive trees that clung to the slopes of the hill. *Countrymen of mine, by the looks of their blistered faces . . . Demanding to know if there are Englishmen around . . . And more precise than that . . . Crusaders aimed at the East . . .*

Two names sprang to mind.

The first was Roger Grevel, whom recognition had shown to be a kinsman of Justin de Vallen. The master of the *Hawksbill*, sent from England to snare Baynard Falkan and recoup Sir Geoffrey's treasure.

And the second name – well, who else but Ranulf Falkan himself

– his henchmen scattered wide, scouring the ports of Spain and Italy, the islands of the Mediterranean and, yes – even this far to the east, even here to Pafos.

Addressing Domenico Balbo, Baynard told the man he'd be needed in the house. Then he called urgently to Quillon, beckoning him from his game.

A moment later and Falkan was rapping on the inner doors of the cottage, telling Guthric and Enrique to evict their women, hurry them down to the village, then assemble on the terrace. 'I fear the respite is over, my friends. If the news is to be believed, we're once again overtaken.'

TWENTY-FOUR

THE SHUTTERS of the two, main-room window apertures were closed, lantern oil dripped on their hinges, the shutters then swung open against the wall.

Domenico Balbo was told to light a fire in the hearth.

Meanwhile, Quillon and Baynard edged through the rear door of the room, stripping the straw-filled mattresses from two of the cubicle beds.

The Saxon and Spaniard were sent to tear planks from a mule pen near the house. Each returning with a stout length of wood, they left them propped beside the shutters.

The stiff leather bucket was hauled from the well, water poured on the palliasses. The bucket was then unhooked from its rope, the empty pail passed to Domenico, who stood it behind the entrance door to the house.

Guthric coiled the rope, looping it over his shoulder.

Falkan jammed the door key in his boot.

Then, their preparations made, the knights of Santiago and Tremellion abandoned the cottage, taking Guthric and Quillon with them. They left Domenico Balbo to tend the unseasonal midday fire, the Sicilian reaching in his pocket for a clove of stinking garlic.

Concealed on the rocky hillside above the house, the Crusaders settled to wait.

And long was the waiting as the August sun scorched the ground, its heat intensified by the bright, white rocks.

Insects droned in the air, their monotonous sound making the men drowsy . . .

Guthric would never admit it, but for a heat-drugged moment he dozed. Jerking awake, he applied the rough device of watchguards, pressing his thumbs hard into his eyes. The pain was intense, but it brought him alert and he once again squinted down at the olive grove.

And sensed movement.

Then *saw* movement, watching as cowled figures clambered cautiously up the tree-dotted slope from the village.

He looked away to the left, saw Falkan nod from the cover of rocks, then turned to the right to see Enrique de Vaca gesturing as if to pat some invisible dog. *Yes, yes, I have them in sight. Now we stay calm.*

A few yards below the constable, Quillon crouched behind a stack of winter wood, the dampened mattresses folded beside him. Guthric tossed a pebble in warning, the young man glancing up to acknowledge the chink and rattle of the stone.

And all the while the figures were advancing, the four, no, five, no, six men slinking quietly between the trees. Their long, hooded travelling cloaks disguised them, but from time to time they were forced to look upward – their faces reddened and blistered.

The Crusaders waited unmoving as the men reached the low, dry-stone wall that supported the front of the terrace. Spread out in a line, they studied the whitewashed cottage, saw the feather of smoke that rose from the squat, open chimney, scowled at the absence of voices.

Those at the end of the line gazed quizzically at their leaders.

How to be sure this was the place they were after? What if it was just some peasant's hovel? Or the bastards had left it already?

Maybe so. But what if Falkan and his band had grown sloppy, believing themselves safe, and were even now away from the house – *yet the money inside, unguarded?*

As so often happens, caution was banished by greed. The scent of victory was high in their nostrils, for these men had travelled far on behalf of Lord Ranulf of Tremellion. They imagined how it would be – storming the cottage – locating the treasure – then waiting with weapons drawn as Baynard Falkan and his friends came wearily back from, well, from wherever, to be silenced – the killings unwitnessed – in this commonplace cottage above an unfrequented port, on a foreign island far from the House of Tremellion.

Recover the money, and Ranulf would be pleased.

Add that his brother was no more, and he'd be overjoyed, generously rewarding his blistered peers, and the men they'd brought from England.

So – a murmured consultation between the leaders, a nod of agreement, then an urgent, onward wave to their flanking companions. Swords were drawn, the six men scrambling upward to the terrace, charging across it, converging on the doorway.

*

His eye to a crack in the boards, Domenico Balbo pulled the door open and met the charge.

Gusting a mixture of garlic and fish in their faces, he pretended to be unaware of their blades, addressing them in a language they could not know. But even as he spoke he was thrust back inside, a mailed fist stammed at his head, a knife point slashing the storm-hardened leather of his jerkin.

He stumbled back, lost and caught his balance, veering as if by accident to stand near the inner door of the room. The six intruders were pleased by the speed with which they'd invaded the cottage, though even with the light from the open windows it took them a moment to accustom their eyes to the gloom.

The leaders drew back their hoods – and were mimicked by their men.

They peered about for a trace of Falkan's presence, then saw the odoriferous Balbo pantomime the fetching and filling of glasses. Grinning in spite of the bruise above his eye, he concentrated his performance on the four men-at-arms, ignoring the leaders who were already dismissing his offer.

Wine, he signalled. A *barile* of wine. Big as this. I fetch it from the back. Then we drink it together, yes? You wait. You stay here. I bring it –

And he shuffled through the doorway in the corner, springing the trap.

Determined to see them all suffer for the way he'd been attacked, Domenico Balbo barred the inner door with a heavy lateral beam. It slipped into place with a satisfying thud, and he allowed himself the pleasure of hearing the intruders hammer and curse. *'He's in Falkan's employ, the stinking peasant! The money's through there!'*

Then the Sicilian lifted his head, opened his throat and roared as if to bring down the roof. 'Now! DO IT NOW!'

Listening only for this, Domenico's shout, the Crusaders sped to comply.

The stiff leather bucket had served its task, the container squashed by the entry of Ranulf's men . . . then expanding to its original shape . . . the door swinging almost shut on its lamp-oiled hinges . . .

Falkan slammed it, locking it with the key he'd extracted from his boot.

As for the shutters, they were banged together in a staccato of sound, Enrique de Vaca at one side of the house, Guthric at the other. And to hold them in place, the planks torn from the mule pen, the heavy boards jammed at an angle, as props would support the sagging of a wall.

Trapped, and in darkness, the six men howled in concert, furious to be fooled. They hurled themselves at the shutters; at the inner door; the outer door; collided with each other in a fiasco of frenzy, the scent of victory turned to woodsmoke and the lingering stench of garlic.

And then, to top things off, Quillon pulled himself on to the shallow pitch of the roof, tore one of the mattresses to shreds, and dropped the lumps of dampened straw down the open chimney.

The fabric and its filling smothered the flames, smoke belching into the room. But a dozen handfuls of the palliasse and he too was driven back from the mouth of the chimney. Dragging the second mattress toward him, he laid it over the shaft, forcing the smoke to stay, like Ranulf's henchmen, in the very room they'd invaded.

Within moments they were scratching at the shutters, begging to be spared. Death by suffocation is an unpleasant and agonising end, be it in water, a mineshaft, or a sealed room in a commonplace cottage above an unfrequented port, on a foreign island . . .

Enrique de Vaca stripped them of their weapons. Quillon had already removed the mattress from the roof, Domenico returning to stamp out the fire.

Guthric made use of the rope he'd coiled from the well, tying the men-at-arms ankle to ankle, wrist to wrist, their bonds looped together – 'Four little rabbits in a hutch.'

The soldiers glared at him with smoke-teared eyes. 'The loyal lump of Tremellion.'

Looking down at them – and always pleased to catch rabbits – the constable queried, 'Loyal? Well, yes, ask around if I ain't. And as for being a lump? It hurts me to say so, but there's truth in it. I'll admit I'm on the bulky side of thin. But you ask if I'm the loyal lump of Tremellion –' And he leaned down, his scarred face shoved toward theirs, the prisoners drawing back as he bellowed, 'It's a name, Tremellion! There's Lord Falkan's Tremellion, and there's Ranulf's Tremellion, *an' you an' I don't pronounce it quite the same!*'

The safeguard came up to him, touched the constable on the shoulder, then wisely retreated as Guthric swung round.

'And what are *you* after, joskin? Praise for disjointing a mattress?'

'No, Master Guthric. It's just that you're wanted. Your presence is, ah, requested by Lord Falkan. We've taken the leaders to the terrace.' Then he turned to the door, dropped an arm beside him and flicked a finger, as if to beckon a lumbering bear.

Improving with time, there was still a way to go before the erstwhile poacher would don the trappings of respect.

The leaders were not, in fact, subjected to the full glare of the terrace, but had been allowed to squat at the eastern side of the building. The high summer sun had baked the ground dry, though at this hour of the day the overhang of the roof gave some shelter to the prisoners.

Not that the two blistered and smoke-seared knights offered much by way of resistance.

Having chosen the one he judged the more truculent of the two – *break the shell, and you break the egg* – Baynard told him, 'I made a mistake, back there, in the port of Tarragona. Failed to identify my enemy, the self-styled Roger Grevel. Though subsequently discovered, and not before time, that he was the kinsman of Justin de Vallen. *You*, on the other hand, I recognise from the mill. The mill of Tresset.'

It was a lie, for the torrent of the linn, the drumming of rain, the climb to the loft and the hurling down of the eels-called-snakes – all of it had blinded Baynard Falkan to the identities of those who were sprawled with the women, or admiring the carnal display.

But out here on Cyprus, months away from the millhouse, the pin-point accusation was accepted as the truth. For the captive knew no better than his captor, and could well suppose his blistered face was recognised by Baynard.

'If it matters to you,' the man yawned, 'I'm Ansel Sauvery, Lord of Merril.'

'And your compeer?'

'Ask him yourself,' Ansel sneered. 'His tongue's as healthy as yours.'

Baynard moved away, nodding as if in agreement. He glanced back once at the other leader, then strode out of sight, crossing to the far side of the terrace.

With Enrique de Vaca and Domenico Balbo in the cool of the house, Guthric and Quillon glared angrily at Sauvery of Merril and his, so far, unnamed companion. The Saxon snarled, 'Tell him, damn you, an' get us out of the heat.'

Ansel's fellow knight shrugged, but said nothing.

They heard Baynard returning, the sound of his voice preceding his appearance. 'We'll do as we planned at Tresset. Not under the blades of a mill-wheel, but this time down the well. Keep a hold of Sauvery. Then tip the shy one down.'

The disembodied voice and calmness of tone both added weight to the threat. By the time Baynard Falkan had rounded the corner, the second knight was muttering, 'For all it'll mean to you – I'm Renier Bertin of Petrock – but none of you the wiser.'

His strategy planned, Falkan said, 'Oh, but I am. And allow me to tell you why.'

'You suggest your names mean nothing to me, messires. That's true. I remember you, vaguely, from the mill at Tresset, and know the approximate whereabouts of Merril and Petrock.

'There is, however, someone to whom the names Ansel Sauvery and Renier Bertin will be of considerable significance. I mean, of course, my brother, Ranulf Falkan. When he hears how you failed him – you and the so-called Roger Grevel – preferring to profit from your time out here in the East –'

'That's not true!' Sauvery shouted. 'We came here –'

'Not true!' Bertin echoed. 'We were sent –'

'Yes, yes, you were sent here to kill me. And, I imagine, my companions. Then to steal Sir Geoffrey's money. But I think you should know . . . I'm fast becoming as ruthless as you . . .

'So here's your last chance. Say nothing, or lie to me, and I shall see a message is sent back from this very port to my brother at Tremellion. In it you'll be accused of disloyalty, personal aggrandisement, ineptitude and – well, there's time enough to compile a pretty list.

'On the other hand, I might just view you as the murderers you are, stained with the killing of my father, and have you tipped down the well. I tell you truly, my lords, the latter course is the one I would rather pursue.'

He waited a moment, searching their faces for the merest sign of arrogance, the shading of a sneer. Then quietly, his voice nailed firm, he invited them to tell all they knew about brother Ranulf.

'And God help you if the carillon rings false.'

From time to time he prompted them with questions, though the story was theirs, Tremellion content to listen.

Fleeing from the mill of Tresset, Ranulf had survived the hiss of the rain, the chill of the night, trudging his way with the devil's own sense of direction to a fortified manor near Savening, twelve miles south of the mill.

A few days later, with Baynard preparing to leave from the port of Plymouth, Ranulf had rejoined his companions, survivors of the surprise attack at Tresset.

Dismissing the fact that he'd abandoned his friends, he once again exerted his dominant personality, alternately raging and cajoling, scattering blame like nails from a keg. Impoverished now, he asked – and Baynard could imagine the manner of asking – for financial assistance, all of it to be one day repaid with interest.

It was here that Baynard Falkan interrupted.

'Ever since we were lured by the *Hawksbill* and de Vallen's kinsman . . . Tell me, messires; I have long wanted to know . . . How exactly does my brother plan to repay these generous friends? Is Tremellion up for sale?'

Sauvery and Bertin told him no. Quite the opposite. The seigneurie of Tremellion was almost, by itself, the high card in Ranulf's hand. But not quite by itself, for what was a castle without its castellan?

'I sense you veering toward a lie,' Baynard warned. 'Step careful. You may yet tip down the well.'

The prisoners hurried to allay his suspicions. As God was their witness – the blasphemy ignored – they were telling him the truth. It was not the castle and holdings of Tremellion that were up for sale. It was Ranulf Falkan himself.

In short, he was entertaining marriage.

'Keep this up, and you bring yourselves to the very edge of the well. *Marriage?* To whom? Name me a single nobleman, apart from riff-raff like you, who'd sacrifice their daughter to a monster –'

Again the prisoners said no. The marriage-go-round had nothing to do with nobility. When Ranulf married – and the bids were pouring in – it would be to the daughter of some wealthy merchant, the woman entitled as Lady of Tremellion, her father elevated by association, whilst Ranulf himself – well, Ranulf Falkan, Lord of Tremellion would be enriched.

The news brought a humourless smile to Baynard's lips. But of course. How perfect. How fitting. Marry a rich man's daughter – pretty as spring, ugly as sin, what would it matter to Ranulf? – and everyone, father, mother, bride and slab-faced groom, they would all, in their way, be satisfied with the match. The exchange. The trade.

Then Ansel Sauvery took pleasure in saying, 'So you see how it is? You can never be allowed to return alive to Tremellion. The reclaiming of the money –'

'Call it theft,' Baynard snapped. 'Call it seizure. Call it plain, bloody robbery. But do *not* call it the reclaiming of what was never yours. Nor his.'

'As you will, Lord Falkan, as you will. It anyway makes no difference. With or without the money you remain a threat to your brother. Find your way home – Ranulf's home now – and you'll doubtless upset things by accusing him of murder.'

'Be certain of it,' Baynard measured. 'They'll be the very first words I utter.'

'So, you see? No matter what happened to Grevel and the *Hawksbill*; no matter what happens to *us*. There'll be others. Most likely there are already others, awaiting you in Palestine. You suppose yourself to be engaged on some honourable quest, eh, my Lord Baynard, sworn to keep your father's promise to the Cause? But the money's only part of it. The other part's your own skinny frame.' Leaning back in the scant shade of the wall, Sauvery glanced at Renier Bertin, then upward at Baynard, the prisoners' arrogant sneers again settled in place.

'It seems to me,' Sauvery told him, 'you should employ your gift for languages. Learn how they speak in the snowy lands of the north. Or maybe among the sands of the south. I can't see where else you'd go, since you'll surely be killed in the East. Or back home in the West.'

Ropes were found for Ansel Sauvery, Lord of Merril; for Renier Bertin, Lord of Petrock. The first was imprisoned in one of the cubicle rooms, the second in another, the four men-at-arms in the last.

The shutters were closed around the cottage, the main door locked, the key sent twirling to be lost in the olive grove.

Then Baynard, Enrique, Guthric and Quillon and the reliable, foul-breathing Domenico Balbo made their way down the path to the village, the men taking turns to bear the weight of the burdensome chest.

Having outwitted their enemies, they should by rights have been jubilant in victory.

But the taste of triumph lay sour on their tongues, for it is one thing to interrogate the foe for information; another to learn that all the news is bad.

PART FOUR

The Reward

TWENTY-FIVE

SOME THREE years earlier – to be precise on July the 4th, 1187 – the Frankish army, under the irresolute command of Guy of Lusignan, King of Jerusalem, had been annihilated by a superior Moslem force led by the Kurdish Sultan, *Salah ed-Din Yusuf, al-Malik un-Nasir*, on a waterless slope called the Horns of Hattin, a few miles west of the town of Tiberias and the Sea of Galilee.

Various reports put the Christian losses at 13,000 dead, 13,000 captured. Foremost among the prisoners was King Guy.

Whilst he and other members of the nobility were held for ransom, the common soldiers were marched away to the slave-markets of Egypt and Syria. The Christian captives were so numerous that a Moslem merchant could buy a healthy slave for the price of a pair of sandals.

Hattin was not merely a defeat, but a disaster. The castles and strongholds had been all but emptied; every available fighting man summoned to the service of the king. With their garrisons reduced, the Frankish outposts fell. Then the larger fortresses. The dominant castles. The inland towns. The coastal cities. All but Tyre in the south, Tripoli in the north. Three months after Hattin, the Saracens had entered Jerusalem.

In the spring of 1188, King Guy was released, having promised the triumphant Sultan Saladin that he would never again take arms against Islam. Yet no sooner was he free than he asked the Church to absolve him from his pledge, on the grounds that it had been made under duress, and anyway to a Moslem.

But Guy had other reasons for breaking his vow.

During his year-long imprisonment, a rival leader had established himself in the citadel of Tyre. This ambitious, lank-haired warlord, named Conrad of Montferrat, now claimed that King Guy had, by his irresolute leadership at Hattin, forfeited his right to rule. He levelled further accusations, then slammed the gates of Tyre in the monarch's face.

There was only one place left for Guy to go.

Thirty miles to the south lay the city-port of Acre, for more than eighty years the headquarters of the Frankish force in the East. Another victim of Saladin's victorious campaign, Acre was now in Moslem hands, though its ownership contested, its garrison besieged.

Swelled by ever-increasing reinforcements from the West, the Crusaders had encircled the city and blockaded the approaches to the port. So it was to Acre that King Guy and his supporters made their way, the king reasserting his command of the Christian troops.

Saladin retorted by besieging the besiegers, his Mamluks and Turcomans, Seljuks and Syrians, Sudanese archers and Bedouin tribesmen camped in the foothills, from where they could probe at the enemy, the Infidel.

A man would be safer in the citadel of Tyre than among the dirt and dust and disease of the camp at Acre.

But Guy of Lusignan, King of Jerusalem and rightful leader of the Cause, was even now, in the summer of 1190, at Acre.

And so it was agreed. The *Lampreda* would sail south-east from Pafos, risking the Saracen *dromonds* that lurked in the waters off Palestine. And, God willing, reach the biblical port of Ptolemais, the Arabic 'Akko, the Christian St Jean d'Acre.

'Who knows,' Falkan remarked. 'He might yet have beaten us to it. I mean the real king. Richard of England.'

Baynard and his companions gave no special thought to the men they'd left tied and shuttered in the cottage. They'd release themselves before long, force an exit from the house, then make their way down to the port.

He believed what Ansel Sauvery had told him – *Most likely there are already others awaiting you* . . . But he did not think Sauvery or Bertin would follow in the wake of the Eel. Impressed by Baynard's threats – as he was impressed by theirs – the lords of Merril and Petrock would probably hasten back to England, anxious to give their own, carefully crafted version of events to Ranulf.

Ignoring the enemy behind him, the young Tremellion prepared to face the sea-borne dangers ahead. He spent time with Captain Pino, pleased and yet disquieted by what the man had learned. With the ever present problems of language some of what Pino told him was uncertain, much of it confused. But of this he was adamant; King Guido – King Guy – was at Acre. The port was blockaded by Crusader ships. But outside the blockade were the *dromonds*.

'Shall I tell you what they're like, Lord Baynard? What the fisher-men of Pafos say they've seen?'

'Tell it, and in detail. Be a shame if we mistook one of theirs for a vessel of our own.'

'For a start then – they are three times as long as the *Lampreda*. Someone told me four. And how many are we here? Eight or nine of us? Well, a *dromond* can carry – and laugh if you will, Lord Baynard – as many as one hundred and fifty men!'

Falkan thought, it'd ease me to laugh, but it's possible. I've heard of Venetian ships as big as that, so why not the *dromonds*? Even so, Sweet Christ; one hundred and twenty feet long? One hundred and fifty men?

'They have as many as – if I understood it right – as many as sixteen sails. And as for the size of the crew, it's because the majority are rowers. That's the thing, you see, Lord Baynard. They need never be stilled in the water. They have a long bank of benches, so when the wind drops –'

'I understand the principles of rowing,' Baynard told him. 'If there's any more, get on with it –'

'There is. And here's the worst. They've a weapon aboard; it's called Greek Fire, or Wild Fire, or Wet Fire, or – well, anyway, according to the fishermen, it's a terrible thing to behold. Like a dragon's breath. A jet of flame they send vomiting from a tube. And once it catches hold, it can't be extinguished. *Do what you like, but –*'

Falkan interrupted him, snapping the man to silence. He'd heard of this too, this dreadful incendiary weapon, its ingredients known only to the East. But he'd also heard that it *could* be extinguished. With sand, or –

'When we restocked the ship at Hierapetra, or when you brought stuff aboard in Pafos. Did you think to buy vinegar?'

'We've a keg of it, yes. It's good for –'

'Then keep it by. And another thing. Place a bucket on deck. Empty a barrel – wine or water, I don't care which, but empty it over the side. We're about to refill it, Captain Pino, fast as we can. With our own little jets. With urine.'

'You mean we should –?'

'In the bucket. Then the contents into the barrel. By all means laugh if you will, my friend. But it's one of the ways, so I've been told, to extinguish Greek Fire.'

*

Weapons covered, metalwork daubed with the soot from lanterns, the *Lampreda* slithered south-east throughout the day.

Leather the wanted commodity now, the replacement sails and shelters were piled amidships. Then the men worked together, crew and Crusaders, stitching the sheets into a clumsy, weather-stained awning.

Helped by a wind that scudded from the coasts of Armenia, the corsair galley cut through the water at close to ten knots.

The keg of vinegar was broached, its contents ladled on to the leather.

With ribald comments, the men splashed into the bucket.

Falkan asked Domenico Balbo, 'Can you hold this course through the night? If we run on now, we should close with Acre at dawn.'

'If that's what you wish,' the Sicilian shrugged, garlic and salted fish gusting the air. 'It's for *you*, Signor Falkan, to tell *me*.'

Yes, Baynard admitted, that's what it's come to now. All these men – but more than these – the ghost of Sir Geoffrey – the promise of Christiane – the menace of Ranulf and his henchmen – the needs of the Christian army – the lurking presence of Islam – all these things will be influenced, if only in some small way, by what I now decide.

He looked at Pino, at Enrique de Vaca, at the Hand of Heaven, slowly closing the day. He thought to ask Guthric – *He's more often right than wrong, the old Saxon* – then even turned to see what Quillon was up to – *Why not? He must have sniffed the wind before poaching the Hexel River.*

But no. It was Baynard's decision. His alone to make. And he knew it.

'Reason's on your side, Signor Balbo. So here's what we'll do. We'll slip and slither through the night like the serpent we are. Captain Pino will be in overall command. *You* will navigate our course. *I* shall set the defences. The others aboard this blade will aid us in our endeavours. And come the dawn – *Deus Vult*, come the dawn, we'll be cheered from the shores around Acre!'

It was a pretty speech, and it encouraged them into the dark . . .

But it could not prevent the massive Saracen *dromond*, known as the *Siphon*, from cutting toward the Crusader galley in the early light of late August, seventy men straining at the oars, another twenty crouched near the bows; the mixture of naphtha, sulphur and quicklime ready to be bellowed through the long, bronze tube.

*

202

There might, after all, be something to be said for chewing anchovy and garlic. However unpleasant the smell of it, Domenico Balbo was the first to sight the *dromond*.

His roar of alarm seemed to skid the men from the stern.

Falkan, who'd been half-asleep, scrambled to his feet, stared at the helmsman, then followed his gaze to the south.

Dear God, but Pino had been right! They were set upon by a monster!

Running toward the bows, yelling and kicking as he went, Baynard struggled with the stitched mosaic of leather. Guthric came to help him, then Enrique, then Quillon and the sailors, the men cursing as the sheet was lifted by the wind and pulled from their grasp; cursing as they took hold of it again; cursing anew as they tore their ankles, their shins, their legs against impediments on the deck.

Domenico Balbo thrust the tiller-bar hard over, the galley veering away from the *dromond*.

But the massive and magnificent Saracen vessel matched her course, the half-mile lead reduced to a quarter, the slave-rowers flogged to a frenzy of effort, the Eel no more than a worm . . .

Bearing down on the Infidel, the nozzle of the *dromond* spouted fire. It bloomed hungrily across the sea, licking the air, slavering at the waves. Then it gulped and was silent, its engineers yelling as they refilled its voracious throat.

The Sicilian bellowed, 'We'll cut across their bows!'

Baynard howled in contradiction. 'No! They'll sear us as we pass!'

'So what do you –'

'Come around! Bring the Eel around! Pass beside her and— Why in Hell do you think the leather—'

But by then Domenico Balbo had understood. *A good chance of being burned alive by the liquid fire . . . Yet if the skinny young Englishman knew what he was doing . . .*

The *Lampreda* heeled about, clutching at the wind of morning as she turned toward the *Siphon*.

Its tanks refilled, its bellows pumped with air, the self-igniting fire was spewed at the galley.

Falling short, it burned the surface of the sea.

But not for long, for the *dromond* was also turning, the spouted flames sweeping across the water, nipping and biting at the Eel.

Close to panic, those aboard the *Lampreda* kicked at the hem of the leather curtain, the carefully stocked urine thrown on the awning, the shield then left to drape the bows as the crew and Crusaders fled toward the stern.

There was nothing more they could do; watching as the Saracens hosed fire from their high-riding prow.

The *Lampreda* began to burn.

Whatever Baynard had been told, the vinegar- and urine-soaked leather did little more than change the colour of the flames. The sulphurous fire spread quickly, splashing the deck, dripping against the hull, its corrosive heat consuming the ill-stitched shield.

The corsair galley passed alongside the *dromond*, dangerously close to the great Saracen warship. For a moment it seemed as if the Eel would collide with the long bank of oars, the smaller ship turning in as tight an arc as Pino and Domenico could manage. Meanwhile, enemy arrows came flittering from the *Siphon*.

And then the war-cries from those aboard the *dromond* turned to shouts of alarm.

As the liquid fire dripped from the leather awning it spread along the channel between the ships, not only burning the *Lampreda*, but clinging to the oars and hull of the *Siphon*. A babble of orders and the *dromond* sheered away . . .

Once astern of the warship, the Crusaders and crew scrambled to save the Eel. Tearing at their clothes, they bandaged their hands to protect them from the dreadful, adhesive fire, then dragged at the awning, tipping it to leeward of the bows. It fell into the sea, the elements of fire and water each eager to claim their victim.

Glancing back, Baynard could see men lowered from the stern of the *Siphon*, buckets of sand being hurled at the patches of flame. It was not too late for the warship to turn and bear down on them again, and the thought sent him hurrying to rejoin Domenico Balbo. 'Can you see the coast yet? Can you see the Christian camp around the city?'

The Sicilian peered ahead, but the smoke and flames from the bows obscured his view. Then Pino called to them, running back to say there were other ships – 'Twenty or more, all across the horizon! I can't be sure, but –'

Turning to Domenico, Falkan said, 'Your eyes are the keenest. Go forward and keep watch for us. I'll take the tiller. If they're enemy ships we'll make a run for it to the east.' He did not need to add that the *dromond* might pursue them, the flames fan back from the bows, or that their dash to the coast might take them blazing on to the rocks.

He wondered if God would allow such a thing to happen, here at the very portals of the Holy Land . . .

It was Quillon who yelled the loudest, punching gleefully at the Saxon, the Sicilian, at anyone he could reach. 'All with crosses! All with crosses! Every hulkin' one of 'em!'

Falkan heard him and understood. The safeguard was describing the vessels that lay ahead of them; Crusader ships; members of the Christian fleet blockading the entrance to Acre.

The young Tremellion kept the galley on course, flame and smoke still rising from the bows. Now, he thought, so long as we're not mistaken for a fire-ship. Then he laughed at the idea, knowing that Sir Geoffrey too would have laughed.

As, of course, in his own special way, would Ranulf.

TWENTY-SIX

THEY WERE now in a different world.

During the days and weeks to come, images and impressions would be thrust upon them; their preconceptions shattered; their attitudes altered; their daily life coarsened beyond belief.

They would see men clumsily hanged for petty crimes, the victims left to strangle, their feet but inches from the ground.

They would roam the camp, learning that the Frankish force numbered close to twenty thousand men, but that the leadership was contested, the English knights siding with King Guy, the French with the absent Conrad of Montferrat, the Germans leaning one way, the Danes another, each of the various nations in dispute.

They would witness the multiple rape of women who had chosen to sell their favours to the army.

They would be shouldered aside by the arrogant Knights of the Temple of Solomon – the Templars – and watch in astonishment as these military brethren squabbled and skirmished with the equally powerful Knights of the Hospital of St John of Jerusalem – the Hospitallers. Cast in the same religious mould, these warrior monks were now separated by enmity and ambition.

They would gaze at the mighty, double-walled defences of the city, glimpsing the helmets and turbans of the enemy as the Moslem guards patrolled the towers and ramparts of the one-time Christian stronghold. A rain of bone-tipped arrows would send the Crusaders diving for cover, though nothing could protect those who were unlucky enough to be doused with the ghastly Greek Fire. It was launched in leather bladders, or in stoppered earthenware jars, the grenades bursting on impact to fount their contents on the crowded plain. Every day scored fresh, searing channels in the Christian camp.

They would discover the rivers and estuaries that watered the coastal land around Acre. And be warned not to drink from them, for the Saracens in the foothills thought it amusing to tip poison in the streams. Or, if not poison, then the carcase of an animal. Or better yet, the mutilated body of an Infidel.

They would see the dust of late summer turn to the drizzle of autumn. They'd mature with experience, become hardened to the horrors of this all but stagnant siege, realising now that the twenty-thousand-strong army of the West was riddled with petty jealousies, fissured by a hundred different factions, the fist of Europe no more than an open-fingered claw . . .

Accorded the quarters due to a knight of the realm, Baynard had been directed to a limp grey tent, half a mile from King Guy's scarlet pavilion. Enrique de Vaca had been offered a similar shelter, their guide shrugging when Falkan asked what provision would be made for his constable and safeguard.

'Look around you,' the man had told him. 'There's half the army sleeping in ditches, or out on the plain. The only reason you and your compeer get housed is 'cause the knights who was here before deserted and went to Tyre.' Insolently, he added, 'In case you ain't noticed, we got them Moslems up our nose, *an'* up our arse!'

It was crudely put, but the man was right. The city of Acre was in Saracen hands; a mile-wide band around it controlled by the Crusaders; then the foothills – and Palestine – and all the Dominion of Islam poised to drive the Infidel into the sea.

Room was made for Guthric to sleep in the entrance to Falkan's tent. Enrique gave space to Quillon. They had come too far together for things to be otherwise.

Within hours of installing himself in his threadbare quarters, Baynard requested an audience with the king. His name was added to a list and he was told to await his turn. 'But be warned,' the clerk informed him. 'There's fifty men of higher rank than you, Tremellion. Go about your business. You'll be summoned in due course.'

Expecting better than this, Baynard said, 'And what do you suppose my business might be, if not to deliver –?'

But by then the clerk had dismissed him, the man beckoning irritably to an ill-tempered nobleman from Flanders.

Two days later, and Falkan tried again. But the response was the same – 'Await your turn; you'll be summoned in due time. The king is a busy man, Tremellion. Remark it or not, there's a war on for the city.'

True enough – Guy of Lusignan, King of Jerusalem was a busy man.

But not for the reasons Tremellion imagined.

*

207

Hard to believe, yet the uncertain, pale-haired monarch was a stranger to strategy, ignorant of any intended assault on the walls of Acre. Instead, he was plagued by complaints and bickerings, some of them trivial, most of them ludicrous, though all of them mouthed by the powerful warlords of the West.

'I would bring to your majesty's notice the fact that the flag of Montauban stands further away from the Royal Standard – oh, yes, by a good thirty yards – than the garish banner of Aalborg.'

'A word with you, sire. Where were the English, pray, when we launched our attack, yesterday morning? Are they here to do battle, or roll dice?'

'Fifteen fresh horses, or so I was promised! But to whom do they go? They go to those slouching Norsemen! And how many do I get? I who've served this Cause for –'

'A matter of some concern, my lord King. Whenever the scaling-ladders are assembled, the French retire to their tents. Can it possibly be that the entire nation is cursed with a horror of heights?'

'I'd seek your advice about the Danes . . .'

'With respect to our so-called allies, the Welsh . . .'

'Those strutting men of the Temple . . .'

'Those burned-out monks of the Hospital . . .'

And so it continued, hour beyond hour, the giants of Christendom growling like wolves and bleating like lambs in the presence of their undetermined monarch.

No easy task, therefore, for the second son of a minor Cornish seigneurie to gain audience with the harassed and irresolute King Guy. Immaterial that Baynard Falkan intended to offer him the wealth of Tremellion, embellished now with the jewels he'd taken from the *Rocca di Losara*.

The Christian army had adopted its own sense of priorities – a madness that much amused the Moslems.

Kicking his heels with impatience, Baynard sought the latch to other doors.

He returned to the *Lampreda* to be told by Captain Pino and Domenico Balbo that the galley was less badly damaged than they'd feared. 'That awning you made us rig across the bows, Signor Baynard; doused with vinegar and the contents of our bladders –'

Falkan smiled and said, 'About the easiest thing a fellow can contribute.' Then he asked what Pino would do with the Eel. 'You promised to let me know, do you remember? If we ever reached this port.'

'I've thought about it,' the handsome young sailor told him. 'Even went so far as to kneel in prayer and –'

'Spare me, Captain Pino. Smile and lie as Renato Moretti would have done, but don't ever pretend piety. It's not your way.'

As if cheered by Falkan's rejoinder, Pino shrugged aside his claim, grinning as he pointed at the odoriferous Sicilian. 'We talked things over, him and me, and agreed we wouldn't last long if we played at corsairs. Though neither are we in favour of getting an arrow through our necks on behalf of your Christian army –'

'I must hurry you, Pino. My name's on the list of those who would meet the king. So tell me quick; as you promised. Might we one day salute each other in passing, out there on the waves?'

'I pray we will, Signor Baynard. That is – piety aside – I hope so. And can you guess what the Eel will be doing! The very thing you yourself suggested! The fastest messenger in all the Mediterranean. Westward from here to Cyprus, to Crete, then up to the southern tip of Greece, and onward again to – *no, listen to me, don't go yet!* – onward to Italy, skirting the coast of Sicily and – *hey! there's still the islands of – hey!*'

But Baynard was satisfied. He'd heard enough. And it seemed to him that Pino and Balbo and the sleek *Lampreda* could make it work.

He would anyway pray so. Or hope.

He reached for the latch of another, more intimate door.

His attention never far from the walls of Acre – and twice sent running for cover by the arrows, the missiles, the flasks of glutinous flame – he questioned a number of his fellow knights. Had they heard, by chance, of a certain Gilles de Magnat-Vaulmier, Duc de Querinard, Comte d'Almé? Just an idle query. He'd met the nobleman before, that was all, and merely wondered if they knew of his whereabouts.

That's right, he was one of the Treasurers for the Cause.

With a haughty young daughter? Oh, really? And Baynard Falkan feigned ignorance, unwilling to declare his knowledge of Christiane.

But the answers were unhelpful. Nobody had seen Magnat-Vaulmier at Acre. Though perhaps he was up there at Tyre. Or wintering in Cyprus, awaiting the arrival of King Philip Augustus of France, King Richard of England.

'That's the question you *should* be asking, my Lord Tremellion.

The hell with Magnat-Vaulmier. What *we'd* like to know is where are our laggard monarchs?'

He made his way again to the faded scarlet pavilion of King Guy. And, as before, he was told to await his turn. He'd be summoned in the due course of time.

But Falkan had now had enough of waiting. It seemed that all of Christendom was waiting; the siege of Acre turned stagnant through indecision; the various warlords sulking in their tents. With the onset of winter they'd be mired by the mud, shoulders lifted in a ponderous shrug, the Frankish leaders asking what else they could do – but wait?

Sheltered from the October drizzle by a canvas awning, the clerk of lists was peering downward as he snapped at Tremellion to wait his turn. So it shocked him to feel a wiry hand reach beneath his chin and wrench his head upward, Baynard's wrist hoisting the scribbler's jaw.

'You and I,' Falkan measured. 'We should get a few things settled. I've heard the rumours, the stories of claims and complaints, but it's time you knew my interest lies elsewhere. You keep telling me there are men of greater rank ahead on the list. So be it. But what are they doing in there, save to moan and –'

Gargling in Baynard's grasp, the keeper of the lists said, 'And *you*? What makes *your* presence here so different? You're not so important that –'

'Not so important in myself? Well, that I'll grant you. But a weighty leather chest, half-filled with coins and jewels? Or would you rather I lifted the whole damned thing on my shoulders, made my way inland – then spilled it at the feet of the Sultan Saladin? Believe me, your behaviour tempts me to do it!'

'It seems,' the clerk said, 'though you never made this clear – seems your request for an audience – if you'd be good enough to release me – allows you to –'

'Keep it shorter, man. Much shorter. Do I get to see the Monarch of Jerusalem, or not?' His grip still firm, he allowed the clerk to peer at the list, invent some gap in the names and say, 'Fortune favours you, Tremellion. A space in the king's crowded day. Now, if you'll permit me –'

At last.

Finally it was to happen.

After the bloody attack on the mill – the storm aboard the Gossamer *– the ambushes in Spain – the escape from the* Hawksbill *– the*

210

imprisonment in the Rocca di Losara *and their further bloody skirmish in the grounds of Atzeri's harem – all that, and the attack at Pafos – the siphon of fire from the Saracen galley – and finally, at last, it was to happen.*

Baynard Falkan would be greeted in the doorway of the scarlet pavilion by Guy of Lusignan, King of Jerusalem, the young knight bowing in respect to his monarch, then the Christian leader bowing in acknowledgement of Sir Geoffrey's bequest and, if only in part, to his son.

Not before time, Baynard thought. He tugged at his rain-dampened surcoat, settled his sword comfortably at his hip and wiped the mist of drizzle from his face.

He had never in his life spoken to a king, and he tried to imagine what Sir Geoffrey would have said, the young Tremellion drawing knowledge from the old.

The clerk re-emerged from the extensive, dripping pavilion. Smirking at Falkan, he stepped aside, allowing the household guards of Lusignan to seize their caller, unsheath his sword, slip his dagger from his belt, pull down the tops of his boots and ferret at his spine.

'Treasure or not,' the clerk told him, 'no one carries arms into the presence of the king. Especially not those who tell us they'd be just as willing to offer it to Islam.'

Then he retreated under his open-sided tent, fastidiously brushing rain from the bench. And making a special show of massaging his throat.

Falkan had time to glance at him, then was hustled into the dismal, leaking headquarters of the king who was next to never seen at large in the Christian camp.

But it was not King Guy of Jerusalem who moved forward to face the caller. Guy was young – a well-known fact – though not so Baynard Falkan's immediate host. This was a warrior in his fifties – his face no longer handsome, though it might have been once, before life and its lines had channelled him with its marks. Taken unawares by the guards, Falkan yet thought it was a face he could trust. Not unlike Sir Geoffrey's. Nor as he himself would wish to be, thirty years from now.

The man said, 'We've been told to expect much from you, Tremellion. All kinds of promises relayed by our ill-humoured clerk. I hope to God they're true, for I'm filled to the gills with talk of banners and palfreys and who-gets-favoured-by-the-cooks. In short, my lord – Falkan, is it? – you stand to make a friend of me. Or a most uncharitable enemy.'

Some way behind the squat, grey-haired warlord, Baynard could see a group of knights clustered around a man who sat, as if imprisoned, in a wide, carved-oak chair. Pinched and sallow, his yellow hair receding, the man seemed further diminished by the outsize throne.

Yet who else could this be but the Commander of the Christian Army, monarch of the overwhelmed city and Kingdom of Jerusalem?

'You hear me, Tremellion? Which is it to be?'

Returning his gaze to the warrior, Baynard said, 'You have the advantage, my lord. I'm known to you now by both name and title, though you keep your own a secret.'

An expression, approximate to a smile, touched the man's lips. 'You must have reached us very recently, here at Acre.'

'Not so recently.'

'Indeed? Then my suspicions are confirmed. I'm fast becoming forgotten; spending too damned long in this tent, that's the trouble.' Then he shrugged and went on, 'I am Jobert de Blanchefort, Marshal of the Kingdom, heaped with more honours than you, or even I, could ever remember. It's a pity I'm forgotten, for I'm the next best thing out here to the king himself.'

The way he said it made Baynard also risk the vestige of a smile. A well-balanced man, he thought, Jobert de Blanchefort. Aware of his power, though not drugged with self-importance. And possessed of a sense of humour, as rare a thing in the camp as an untainted breeze.

Indicating the clerk, Falkan said, 'If this man relayed the truth, as I told it, you'll have no cause to unleash your uncharitable anger on me, my lord Marshal.'

'So you *are* bringing us money?'

'In obedience to my father's wishes.'

'And precious stones? The clerk made much of –'

'Those, too.'

'Well, now,' Jobert told him, 'I'm warming toward you already, Tremellion. But you're sure you've no moans or miseries up your sleeves?'

'None, my lord. Though two brief requests. The first – and with no disrespect intended – is that I be allowed to present my father's wealth in person to the king. It is what Sir Geoffrey Falkan would have wanted.'

'You speak of him as if –'

'He was murdered, sire.'

'I see.' He paused before asking, 'And the other request?'

And here the young knight faltered. I have gone too far, he thought. Yet I have to know. 'It is not strictly – That's to say – Well, there is a certain Gilles de Magnat-Vaulmier, Duc de Querinard –'

'I know of that man; he is much respected. Though he is not within the Kingdom –'

'No matter, my lord Marshal. It was only –'

'– and won't be until the tail-end of the year.' Then he turned with military precision, nodding the suddenly animated Baynard into the presence of their king.

TWENTY-SEVEN

REMEMBERING IT later, he prayed his deportment would have satisfied his father. Or that, anyway, Sir Geoffrey would have viewed the scene with sympathy, from above.

Jobert de Blanchefort had announced the young Tremellion as a caller who was worthy of the monarch's close attention. 'And that means, my lord King, that you set aside that pile of churlish petitions. Do we really care if the English claim their lines are overrun with vermin? There are rats throughout the camp. Or that the French continue to moan that they're unsupported whenever they move against Acre? God knows, it's the general cry. And has been from the first.'

Guy of Lusignan – a man not only uncertain within himself, but the victim of bullying noblemen, badgering priests – glanced up from the oak and leather prison of his throne.

'What? Worthy of what? Who did you say he was?'

The presentation was repeated, Baynard kneeling, the fretful monarch mouthing above his head. *He's here for what?*

It was left to Marshal Jobert to wave the household guards aside; approach the king and murmur to him; tip his heavy head as Guy responded; then finally turn to Baynard and say, 'My lord King will send a detachment of his knights to collect the chest. If you'd be good enough to wait over there, Tremellion –'

'They won't get it.'

The King of Jerusalem leaned forward, a hand moving as if to brush the strands of a web from his face. 'What's this you're telling me? You've brought money for the Cause, but my knights –? I don't understand this, de Blanchefort.'

The Marshal scowled at Baynard. 'No more, in truth, do I. Explain yourself, Tremellion.'

'Quite simply, my lord King, my lord Marshal, whoever you send will not be allowed to remove the chest from my tent. There's a man who protects it. The Constable of Tremellion. A Saxon named Guthric. It will not be enough for him that your knights lay claim to it. Too many others have tried.'

The troubled and balding monarch glared at Jobert. 'This is all I could have hoped for! To be told by this – this *parvenu* – what my own knights may and may not do! If the money's for the Cause, then it *belongs* to the Cause, and no shuffling ape of a Saxon –'

Stopping just short of discourtesy, Jobert de Blanchefort gestured at the king to wait, and be calm. Then he asked Tremellion, 'So what would you have us do? Are there some quaint terms to be met? Documents to be signed?'

'No, sire, there are not. I only ask that Guthric be permitted to deliver the chest himself. Escorted if you wish. But that it *not* be wrestled from him half a mile short of its proper destination.'

'Is that where you're quartered? Half a mile from the Royal pavilion? I'll see you're brought in closer. As for this constable of yours – Is he really a shuffling ape, as his majesty suggests?'

'He'd pass for one,' Baynard said calmly, 'if apes were as large and as loyal.'

King Guy of Jerusalem drummed his fingers on the terminals of his chair. 'Enthralling though it is, this talk of our simian Saxon, I fail to see –'

'Perhaps you do, your majesty,' Jobert told him. 'Very likely you do. But *I* now see what Tremellion is after. And I agree it.' Then he nodded at Falkan. 'Return to us in an hour. You and your constable and the wealth you've brought from – Devon?'

'A few miles further to the west, my lord Marshal. From Cornwall.'

'A good long way, with such baggage. Be annoying for a fellow to have strangers take it from him, when he was so close to the finish.' He nodded again, this time in part-dismissal, knowing his next task would be to explain to the king that even apes and *parvenus* were entitled to deliver their gifts to the door.

And so it was done; the leather chest lowered on to the carpeted floor of the faded and sagging pavilion; the balding Guy of Jerusalem coming forward from his chair to gaze at the glitter of jewellery, the glint of coin.

The wealth of Tremellion. Reduced in value by Ranulf's trade with the Levantine in the mill of Tresset. Then increased by the contents of Silvano Atzeri's cabinet in the *Rocca di Losara*.

In personal terms, a fortune.

In military terms, enough to prolong the siege of Acre by somewhat less than a month.

*

Guthric was thanked in person by the king, the two men keeping their opinions to themselves. Guy had no reason to alter his earlier pronouncement – *a shuffling ape.*

For his part, the constable concealed a deep, and almost childlike disappointment. Having never before set eyes on a monarch, he'd expected a man who was larger than life, encased in shimmering armour, an aura of light illuminating his presence. His voice – or so Guthric had imagined – would be deep and resonant; his gestures firm, his expression fierce, his gaze formidable; a creature worthy of the name of king.

But this sallow and shrunken backwater of a man? Without even a crown on his head? And no bright garments! No silvered armour! Meet him in the camp – meet him *anywhere!* – and he'd pass as the brother of that sour-faced clerk who sat outside the pavilion.

With the accurate simplicity of an infant, the scarred and illiterate Saxon told himself it was no damn wonder the army was in such a sorry mess. A king like that? He couldn't lift fresh-baked loaves from a cooling oven . . .

As promised by Jobert de Blanchefort, the Knight of Tremellion was brought closer to the Standard of Jerusalem. He asked his friend and companion, Enrique de Vaca, if he wished to come along, but the Spaniard gently declined.

'It pleases me to see, my dear Halcón, that it's not just the English and French and the Northerners who are here. There's a group of us from the warmer climes of the West; not many, I grant you, but enough to persuade us we're a force to be reckoned with. I'm welcomed there –'

'As you would be throughout the camp, Enrique. Most especially by me.'

The Knight of Santiago grinned, his expression combining gratitude with regret. 'We will not be so far apart, *amigo mio.* Though remember what I said to you once before. Take care you're not blinded by the dust of my horse –'

'Or in this case, the mud.'

'*Si, si.* Or in this case mud.'

The young men embraced, pointed out where they'd be in the camp, then quietly, unsmiling now, wished each other the protection of God and the Virgin Mary, of Jesus Christ and the feathered angels of Heaven.

It was no exaggeration to seek the blessing of all that was good, for they both knew how soon they might die.

' 'Ere,' Quillon said, 'you know what I found, m'lord? A bunch of English archers, an' more than a few of 'em from Cornwall! Now, I know as I should stay with you, bein' your safeguard an' all, but I thought I'd ask –'

'Is your shoulder healed?' Baynard queried. 'Are you well enough recovered to draw a bow?'

'Four out of six on the target,' Quillon boasted. 'I spend most of me time lettin' fly down there at the butts. Another week, an' I'll be tellin' 'em *all* what to do. That is, if –'

'Off you go and join them, Master Quillon. Though promise me this. When you loose your shafts at the Saracens, up on the walls, you'll have the sense to keep your own head down. They're the finest archers in the world, the bowmen of Islam. Get killed out here and the Hexel River will be overstocked with fish.'

The leonine Quillon roared at the joke – remembered that poachers could be hanged – strangled his laughter and said yes, he'd promise to be careful, Lord Falkan could rely on it.

Yet he couldn't quite resist telling Tremellion, 'After all. When it's over 'ere, we might go back via Cyprus, ain't that right? An' stay in one of them houses, up on the slope? An' get to see some of them girls again? Like we did before?'

The group now dispersed, they were each subjected to the harsh realities of life in the Christian camp. Enrique de Vaca and Baynard Falkan were offered the best of the poor, oversalted diet, Baynard ensuring that Guthric ate mouthful-for-mouthful in keeping with the knight himself.

But for Quillon things were harder, the archer forced to employ his special skills in the offshore waters, his popularity increasing as he speared the variety of spiny fish that lurked among the rocks. Without the poacher, his English companions would have been reduced to eating weeds, meat so rotten that it made them vomit, and the only edible part of the vermin that ran through the camp – the hind legs of long-haired rats.

As the Christian winter approached – the Mohammedan season of irrigation – the water-logged plain around Acre became a polluted mire. Disease was rife, the men's hair falling in tufts, swellings in their groins and armpits, their teeth loose in their sockets. This particular disease was known as *Arnoldia*, though dysentery and depression ran it close.

Baynard regularly summoned Quillon to his tent, enquired as to the safeguard's welfare, then forced the young man to eat from his own pewter plate.

He visited Enrique, the knights at first failing to recognise each other; then doing so and grinning as if they'd never been in doubt.

And all the while the siege machines continued to batter the city's double-walled defences. Assault towers, taller than the ramparts themselves, were dragged close to the battlements, planks thrown across, the Crusaders then lumbering forward in an effort to seize a section of the wall. But the towers were vulnerable, the wooden framework swaying unsteadily, easy prey to the all-consuming Greek Fire.

Position, vantage-point, cover; these all favoured the defenders. So long as they had food and fresh water, arrows for their bowmen, flasks of fire for their catapults; with these and the blessings of Allah, they could resist the Infidel for ever.

In November, Sultan Saladin achieved a master-stroke.

With a massive concentration of force, his troops poured down from the foothills south of the city, veering to within a few hundred yards of King Guy's scarlet pavilion. The Christian army swung around in fury, a dog teased from its bone.

The Saracens then appeared to falter, as if surprised by the extent of the enemy. The lightly-armed Seljuks and Syrians guided their horses southward again, back toward their lines.

Intent on overtaking them on the plain, the Frankish cavalry sent their destriers thundering in pursuit.

Lured from the city, the bulk of the Crusading army was unaware that a second Moslem force was riding directly at Acre – *and that the city gates were wide open.*

Saladin had been awaiting this moment for weeks. Messages had been sent by carrier pigeon between Acre and his outposts, the date and hour of the stratagem pre-arranged.

Now, with the Infidel drawn away, upward of four thousand Saracens rode or ran through the gates, bringing with them a convoy of vehicles, each cart laden with food, with bone-tipped arrows, with straw-protected flasks of their precious, immolating fire.

By the time the Frankish leaders learned of the deception, the garrison at Acre had been exchanged, its stocks of food and weapons replenished, imagined laughter echoing in the hills.

The insolence of Saladin's achievement turned depression to despair. Accusation was met by counter-charge, fault and blame the currency of the day. The king was held responsible. As was Jobert de Blanchefort. And the French. And the English. And the lookouts; the scouts; the sentinels.

It was as if the burned-down candle of the campaign had been replaced by another, its wick as yet unlighted. As if all the Christian efforts had gone for nothing, the men of the West now wallowing in mud, the garrison of the East safe and well-fed in the city.

It was, in short, as if Allah had slapped the face of God.

Yet there were some in the Christian army who ignored the internal squabblings, preferring instead to redress the balance by attacking those who haunted the heights.

Among them were Baynard Falkan and Enrique de Vaca, the two young knights riding with their own separate groups. Baynard under the banner of Marshal Jobert; Enrique supporting the pennant of Iberia.

They probed the rain-sluiced gullies, patrolled the treeless ridges, sheltered in the devastated villages of Galilee. It was hard to keep count of the hamlets and homesteads ruined by a war that had dragged on now for all but one hundred years.

Hard too, to keep track of history, though most literate men knew that the First Crusade had been proclaimed by Pope Urban II, and that this was now the third attempt to wrest the Holy Land from the cunning Devils of Islam.

But third, or thirty-third, the rain still swept across them, the Saracens as wily as before.

From time to time they'd skirmish, the wildcat and the boar. Throughout these engagements, the Moslems relied on their greater mobility, jabbing at the flanks of a Frankish patrol, then darting away to be lost in the drizzle – or in summertime cloaked by the dust.

Uncannily accurate, their bowmen could pick a rider from his horse at forty yards. They also knew the country, dashing from cover to hurl their reed lances, slash with their scimitars, brain a man with their terrible, lead-tipped flails.

If a Crusader group was caught unawares, it would likely be cut to pieces, the Saracen mounts not even breaking stride.

But the Christian boar was equally effective, given the terrain.

Deny the Moslem cavalry the room in which to manoeuvre, and they'd be hacked apart by the whirling swords and maces of their link-mailed foe. Or, if need be, crushed by the sheer weight of the attack.

A number of knights wore a necklace for good luck – no more than a cork on a leather thong. Bouncing against their hauberks it reminded them that the way to deal with the Saracen was to bottle him up; cork him tight; seal him in a corner.

Enrique de Vaca found his weary way to Baynard's tent. With the impertinence of friendship he said, 'You keep yourself busy, eh, Halcón, securing the pegs and brushing out the fleas?'

Wet and exhausted from a fruitless patrol, Falkan gestured the Spaniard to a section of log that served as his only chair.

'I'd have you know, *amigo mio* . . . I've been on some forty outings to the hills. We lost nobody today, thank God, though neither did we ever espy the foe.' Then he waved at a jar of wine in the corner, at the mugs beside it, and slowly lifted the link-mail tunic, bowing to let it slither to the ground.

'No more than forty?' de Vaca managed. 'Then you *have* been brushing at fleas. Me, now, I've come to tell you I've just topped fifty. I know for certain I've killed six of those skittering demons, and with not a mark upon me. Fifty sorties from the camp! A half dozen devils laid low! We should drink to this, my friend. To Santiago! To the honour of St James of the Sword!'

Stripping to dry himself with a linen cloth, Falkan donned a simple woollen shift. Then he buckled his sword belt, propped himself on the hard-edged rail of his bed, and raised the mug he was offered by the Spaniard. 'You know what *I* think, Enrique? I think you should climb down from the saddle for a while. Put your experience to use. Instruct the newcomers – and they're coming all the while – teach *them* how to deal with those frisky demons of Islam.'

'When I've killed ten of them,' Enrique told him. 'Ten would be a nice round figure. Send ten of them back to the hell they came from, and yes, I grant you, I might let my bruised buttocks heal.'

It relaxed them both to drink and talk, easing the shutters open on their friendship. They did it with good-natured gibes, with exaggerated stories, with occasional moments of truth such as they'd never have declared to someone else.

It didn't seem to matter, that night, that the rain spilled on the camp or dripped into the tent. Nor that the wine – if they'd cared to admit it – was sour to the taste. Nor that the walls of Acre loomed above the plain, its garrison refreshed, the Frankish army mired in the mud, and with Saracen laughter still echoing in the hills.

All that mattered was that Enrique de Vaca, Knight of Santiago, could trade stories with Baynard Falkan, Knight of Tremellion, each of them pleased the other was around.

Yet Baynard's thoughts and hopes, dreams and expectations – all of them kept returning to the magnetic name of Magnat-Vaulmier – to the remembered Christiane.

He stayed in contact with his safeguard, insisting that Quillon share the ever-diminishing ration of fresh food issued to the knights.

Guthric reported that Sultan Saladin had been sighted not far from the camp. 'Though our cross-bow bolts bounced off him! An' one of the knights – his sword just melted as it struck! They say axes shatter when they touch 'im. Wherever we go, he's out there ahead of us. An' laughin'. I heard it –'

'Nonsense,' Falkan told him. 'All he is – he's a clever commander. But don't ever suppose, my old Guthric, he's immortal. His time will come, as for all of us. And anyway, who hears laughter in the rain?'

TWENTY-EIGHT

IN LATE November Baynard Falkan sought an audience with Jobert de Blanchefort.

Baynard had now matched Enrique's earlier achievement; fifty sorties against the enemy; and believed he had the right to ask if the Marshal would give him command of a force of his own. An expedition that would not only scout and patrol, but would seek out Satan's representative on earth, the Sultan Saladin himself.

Permission granted by the Marshal of the Kingdom, Baynard went hunting for the Master of Islam, *Salah ed-Din Yusuf, al-Malik un-Nasir*.

He was absent for a month, his force of thirty riders reduced by events to twenty-three. They had five times skirmished with the Saracens. Twice been sliced by the fast-running enemy. Twice been forced to barge their way from a trap. But the last engagement had gone in their favour, the lightly-armed Moslems crushed by the disciplined weight of the Frankish knights.

Several times the Christian horsemen had shouted, 'There! You see him? Up there on the heights? It's him! It has to be! *It's him!*'

But it wasn't, and Baynard Falkan returned to the lines to tell Jobert de Blanchefort he was sorry; he'd failed to find the Sultan.

'Never mind,' the marshal said gently. 'We are after all playing in that man's own garden. The best thing you could do, my Lord Falkan, is retire to your tent. And await your loyal constable. He has, I believe, something of gravity to impart.'

He didn't come alone, the Saxon. He came with the safeguard, the two men standing shoulder-to-shoulder in the entranceway, as close in spirit as they'd ever been before.

An ill-matched couple, Falkan reminded himself; the lumpish Saxon and the taller, long-limbed poacher. Yet now drawn together like brothers – to tell him what?

To tell him that Enrique de Vaca, the Spaniard, the one in his black-and-white uniform, was dead.

Dead and already buried, since Lord Falkan had been out there in the hills.

Dead, but with four Saracens dead or dying around him, the Spaniard serving Christ and Santiago, even at the end.

Guthric growled, 'It must come harsh to you, Falkan,' and Quillon said, 'To us all. Comes harsh to us all.' Then they moved away from the flap of the tent, leaving Baynard to the privacy of his sorrow.

Ten days later and the balding King Guy was edged toward panic by the news that reached him from abroad. A short enough message, though sufficient to send the Commander of the Christian Army hurrying from his weather-worn pavilion.

'King Richard of England is involved in a personal feud with Sicily. He intends to conquer the island. Do not count on his leaving it before spring. He is far too busy with his enemies here to spare time for the enemies of Christ.'

The message was signed by one of King Guy's trusted observers; thus a report he could believe.

Yet worse was to follow, for rumours reached him that King Philip of France was pressing ahead, and would arrive in the Holy Land well in advance of his side-tracked fellow Crusader.

Evil tidings indeed, for where would the fumbling Guy of Lusignan be without the support of his English overlord?

But welcome news for Guy's lank-haired rival, Conrad of Montferrat, safe in the city of Tyre. After all, Philip and Conrad were cousins, and the moment the King of France set foot on the soil of Palestine, Guy of Jerusalem would be outranked, out-manoeuvred, easily outwitted by the combined cunning of the senior monarch and Montferrat. The Frankish army would acclaim Philip Augustus as their leader – and with him Conrad – pointing at Guy as a weakling and a failure.

Unless – and it was this that sent him striding from his tent – unless the city of Acre was recaptured. And soon.

Take back Acre, and Guy's reputation would be burnished by the victory. But fail to do so and Conrad would pounce.

Silently cursing the dilatory King Richard, his vassal monarch all but ran to command a fresh assault on the walls.

*

Meanwhile, away to the south-east, and far behind the Saracen front lines, the young Tremellion was facing problems of his own.

Leading a patrol of sixteen riders, he was unaware of King Guy's attempts to rouse the besiegers, having left the camp before the ominous news arrived.

This latest and deepest penetration of the hinterland was the result of a further request to Marshal Jobert. Though this time not so much a request as an urgent, angry plea. 'They have killed my friend! Had I been slain in de Vaca's place, he would already have ridden to avenge me. So I beg of you, sire; allow me every rider you can spare, then send me to settle accounts with the devils of Islam! Give me fifty horsemen and I swear to you I'll track that crowing Sultan –'

Jobert de Blanchefort had listened with sympathy, aware that Falkan's demand was excessive, yet touched by the young knight's willingness to risk his own life again, this time in the name of Santiago. With measured concern, the marshal said, 'If you were to take my advice, Tremellion – which we both know you will not – you'd allow your anger to abate. You're half dead on your feet as it is, so God knows how long you'd last, jounced in the saddle.'

'Long enough to –'

'Yes, you've told me. To square accounts with the Sultan. But I'm not just thinking of you, my friend. Everyone else is half dead on their feet. Even the horses have lost their wind. And where on earth do you imagine I could find fifty mounts, fifty riders –'

'Thirty then! Twenty! For the sake of Christ, my lord Marshal, spare me ten and I'll harrow the hills!'

No doubt you would, Jobert thought. Or do it alone.

Knowing Baynard Falkan would not be deterred, the rough-hewn de Blanchefort had granted him command of fifteen knights, the patrol to be guided by an Arab converted to Christianity, a Maronite named Zengi.

Reluctant to let the hollow-eyed Tremellion draw on the bitter nourishment of vengeance, Jobert sighed as he watched the men spur away. Then he once again turned his attention to the ever-mounting responsibilities of his office, overlooking the fact that among the riders was a certain Gaumar de Garin.

With Enrique dead, Guthric helping to work one of the siege machines, and Quillon teamed with the archers, the young Tremellion was friendless beyond the confines of the camp.

His problems began within hours of leaving Acre. The underlying reasons would not emerge till later, though it was clear from the start that the heavy set Gaumar de Garin did not take kindly to being commanded by the younger Baynard Falkan.

'You're a dark-skinned fellow for an Englishman, Tremellion. That mean your father –? Got took prisoner here, did he? Then decided to settle? And fell for the charms of one of those Allah-worshipping –'

'Your position's with the rearguard, de Garin. Get back there, if you will. Family chatter can hold till we're camped for the night.'

Gaumar lifted a link-mailed hand in sarcastic salute, then disturbed the line of riders as he trampled back to his station.

During that first day of their patrol they met no one, save for shepherds. An occasional farm cart was seen in the distance, though the Maronite guided them cleverly between the Saracen outposts.

At dusk, with the Crusaders sheltered amid the ruins of a burned-out farmhouse, Gaumar de Garin revealed more of his character. He chose as his target the youngest of the knights, taunting the man within earshot of their commander.

'Seems a shame you were summoned out here, *petit*, when you ain't got the need to shave. Be a waste if you were killed so soon, when you've not yet come close to a razor. Or a woman.'

The youngster blushed in the limited firelight, knew his companions could hear what Gaumar had said, and sought to save his pride. He started by laughing to show it was all a joke, then deepened his voice and said, 'Closer than you think, de Garin. Christ strike me dead, a whole damned sight closer than you'd bloody well believe!'

It was a nice attempt at unpractised invective, the older knights grinning in the shadows. But the youngster then spoiled it by doing what he'd seen men do before – and reached across to slap Gaumar on the thigh. *'A whole bloody an' damned sight closer –'*

He was hauled to his feet, de Garin's hand at his throat.

'You're quick with your fists, ain't you, *petit*? Can't take a fellow's humour? So you strike out to quell him, is that it?' Squeezing his victim tight, he looked around at his audience, waiting to see if they'd like the young man bobbed like a marionette.

Then movement from somewhere to his left. There was no formidable weight to it, but the speed outstripping his own reflexive defence – a wiry hand wrenching at his wrist – the bony slam of a fist below his heart.

The bulky Gaumar de Garin went down, bruised by the blow, stunned as he fell against a long ago burned-through beam.

Standing over him, Falkan said, 'Repeat your performance, de Garin, and I'll do my best to see you promoted by Marshal Jobert. But the next time you try it, let's be sure it's against the foe.'

They passed the second day as the first, the bearded Maronite guiding them deeper into the hinterland of Palestine. His sense of sight and hearing far exceeded those of the clumsy, armoured Crusaders, and Baynard came to rely on him, obedient to his courteous directions. Adhere to Zengi, he decided, and the Sultan Saladin might yet be in for a shock.

But the third day brought further trouble from Gaumar de Garin.

Dwelling on the fact that he'd been floored by Tremellion, he wanted it known that he – de Garin – had been here before any of them. 'And long before *you*, I dare say, Lord Falkan, foreign-faced though you are!'

Baynard looked away, clenching his teeth. He heard Gaumar exhaling with triumph at his shoulder, and could visualise how the destructive knight would be, nodding and grinning at his imagined half-caste leader.

Then he turned to repeat what he'd told the man before. 'Your place is at the end of the column, de Garin. If you're of any value at all to us, it's there.'

His command was met by another sarcastic salute, another jerk at the reins, another barging retreat to the rear of the line.

Dear God, Baynard thought, is it any wonder we're hemmed to the coast?

Four days south-east from the camp, and now deep among the hills of Moslem-held Galilee, the Crusaders reached an intersection of narrow, rain-channelled gullies.

The Maronite guide asked Baynard to hold the riders in check. 'With your permission, my lord –'

'Do as you wish,' Falkan told him. 'My trust in you is complete.' Then he raised a hand in the drizzle, dropped it to grasp the pommel of his sword and waited for Zengi to scout the gullies and return to direct them; south now; or onward, south-east.

An hour with the rain splashing from their helmets, and Zengi was back to tell them, 'There's an outpost to the south. If we continue south-east we can work our way behind them.'

'Oh, you'd like that, wouldn't you, you dirty little traitor!'

Shocked by this unexpected outburst, Baynard turned to see Gaumar de Garin once again at his shoulder.

'Follow you *there*,' the knight sneered at Zengi, 'and we'll all be killed! What do you think; we're as gullible as Falkan? Fool *him* if you wish, but don't try fooling the rest of us, you flea-riddled bastard!'

His warning issued, he goaded his horse close to the Maronite, then struck out with vindictive intent, ripping the convert's face with the welded links of his iron glove.

Baynard reached to stop him, but in vain.

Then stared in horror as the unarmed Arab rocked in his saddle, forced himself erect and blinked through tears of pain at the so-called Christians.

In the moments that followed, Falkan would respect the bearded Maronite for his dignity, the guide ignoring the blood that spilled from his nose and mouth, staining his beard with spurts and trickles of crimson.

'I am *not*,' the man said, 'a traitor. I would *not* – nor *ever* have – misled you. But beyond – beyond all that – you tell me I am dirty? You tell me I am riddled with fleas? *You tell me I am a bastard!*' He whirled his mount, driving it in a circle to set a certain distance between them. Wiped the blood from his face. Spat on the ground. Jabbed a finger in their direction. Then raised his voice to a manic, infuriated shrill.

'You believe yourselves of Christ? Yet think to strike your friends? Then I tell you this – the religion to which I've been drawn is no match for the one I was weak enough to deny.'

Dragging again at his horse, the appalled and injured Maronite let them see he'd abandoned all faith in the Christian teaching, his hand raised in a gesture of obscenity for the allies-turned-enemies, these mad and mismanaged disciples of the West.

Gaumar de Garin offered nothing by way of apology – though what use if he fell to his knees, with the treacherous Maronite turned against the Cross? So it suited him to shrug at Zengi's departure, insisting they were well rid of him.

'What we should do,' he told Falkan, 'is follow the gully to the south. Ignore the one that flea-riddled –'

'Don't say that again!' Baynard raged. 'You have destroyed this patrol as it is! All the way out here into the hills, and you choose today to strip us of our guide! You are a self-obsessed creature, de Garin; an evident danger to our troop. So don't ever again voice your opinions; neither of the Maronite, nor of my men!' Then he sucked in his breath and snarled at Gaumar, telling the man to show him he was all the things he'd claimed. 'Out here in the East before any of us, isn't that what you said? Then let's see you put your experience into practice, and lead us back home before –'

'Lead you home? But I thought we were –'

'Searching for Saladin? Yes, my stupid de Garin, so we were. But with the Maronite – with Zengi to guide us. Had we kept him as a friend we might have reached our goal. But the hunt is now over. Thanks to you he has lost all faith in our Cause. Been hurt and humiliated. Called a bastard and a traitor. All of it guaranteed to send him spurring to the nearest enemy encampment. We are no longer the hunters, my quick-fisted *confrère*, but the prey. They'll be on us within hours, so I look to you to fulfil your boast, and show this patrol how well you know the country.'

Gaumar de Garin attempted to hold Baynard's gaze, failed to do so and turned away to mutter. 'Well, listen . . . With all this rain . . . The night closing in . . . I couldn't be sure . . . How could anyone . . . You can hardly expect me . . .'

And Baynard Falkan nodded in weary comprehension, tipping water from the nasal bar of his helmet.

They were lost among the thousand humps of Galilee; each treeless ridge the same as the last, the same as the next. The intruders were now stranded in a maze of valleys, this one like that one, all of them washed to a height and width and size by the rains and winds that had gusted across the Holy Land since long before the founding of her faiths . . .

TWENTY-NINE

THEY SPENT the night huddled in a series of sandstone caves in the region of Shefar'am. The rain ceased, the sky pricked with stars. Falkan prohibited all fires, the Crusaders reduced to chewing strips of salted meat and lumps of black, husky bread.

Much as Tremellion had expected, Gaumar de Garin kept his distance, devoid of all initiative. Checking the position of the lookouts, Baynard passed close to Gaumar's cave, the men staring at each other before de Garin looked away. As well you might, Baynard thought, since you've proved yourself the effective traitor in our midst.

Fatigued beyond measure, Falkan nevertheless forced himself to stay awake throughout the night. Nodding with the accumulated weariness of months, he started as wild dogs howled in the distance, or as rocks shifted from the edges of the gully. Five – six – he could no longer remember how many times he'd heaved himself to his feet, brushed at the cloying sand that floored his shelter, then tramped the sides of the *wadi*, to make sure the lookouts were alert.

He wondered how best to make his report to the marshal, Jobert de Blanchefort . . . Wondered if those in Heaven could see in the dark, Sir Geoffrey watching this sad and stranded patrol . . .

A poor kind of vengeance for Enrique de Vaca . . . *What's this then, Halcón? Never once saw the enemy, and can't find your own way home? You should have stayed in the camp, amigo mio, securing the pegs and brushing out the fleas.*

Hunched on the ground, though not daring to stretch out for fear of falling asleep, the young knight turned his hollowed face to the sky. And made his wordless apologies to those who now lived in the Kingdom curtained by stars . . .

Clouds again in the morning. No stirring of wind, but a heavy, leaden overcast, the colours of the land turned to charcoal.

Groans and curses from the knights as they straightened up, past wounds aching, the damp of the caves in their bones. Their expressions spelled murder as Falkan told them they were once again to manage without fires. 'Light up in Acre, my lords, when we're back there.

229

Better yet, put the city itself to the torch. We could all do with a warming.'

He allowed them a while to get ready, in the meantime gauging their position by the reluctant glow of the sun. Then he saddled his horse, mounted with a grunt at the effort, and led the patrol around the edge of the *wadi* to the west.

By midday an eerie stillness had blanketed the land. A line of copper extended above the horizon, though the dome of the sky pressed down on them, the air of the hinterland as humid as a washerwoman's shed.

Baynard waved Gaumar de Garin alongside. Both men were tired, ill at ease, unwilling to ride together. But it mattered to Falkan to ask the man – 'All this time out here ahead of us; so what would you now advise?'

'This was never my part of the country,' de Garin dismissed. 'I garrisoned a castle to the north.'

'Yet thought to question Zengi?'

'Thought to challenge a traitor, that's what I –'

'Sweet Jesus!' Falkan rapped. 'I treasure your presence as I'd hug a desert spider! Get back to the end of the line, de Garin. I'd rather entrust ourselves to a blind and legless mute –'

But by then the bulky Crusader had wheeled away, once more jolting the formation of the troop.

Another hour and a half, maybe two, and Baynard brought the riders to a halt. Ahead of them lay a transverse ridge, the treeless hump barring their progress to the coast.

But it wasn't the formation of the hill that had stopped him. More the sound of – well, something, the chink and clatter of something he couldn't yet see.

He summoned a knight named Gerard Passerel, to ride with him, ordered the rest to stay quiet, then dismounted and led his horse to the base of the ridge.

Falkan and Passerel tethered their mounts, tipped water on to a sponge and pressed it to the muzzles of their horses. The animals sucked and snorted, lubricated their tongues and stood quiet, aware they'd not been forgotten.

Then the dull-eyed Crusaders crawled up the eastern ascent of the slope.

*

Reacting as most men will in the face of the unexpected, Baynard Falkan sought the simplest words he knew. 'Oh, Christ – Oh, Jesus – *Have we run against all this?*'

Beside him Passerel mouthed, 'Where in hell do they come from? So numerous? So complete?'

Ducking below the skyline, the commander and his ally turned to share the horror of what they'd seen. A triple column of horsemen. No less than a hundred riders. A brilliance of lightweight armour; of spear-tips, of arrow-heads; of decorated shields and high, conical helmets; a jaunty and arrogant force patrolling its garden.

Stay low, and the Saracens would pass.

Keep quiet and there'd yet be the chance to reach the coast and re-enter the camp.

So long as none of the Crusaders –

But sound travels below the overcast of clouds. Ricochets in the air. Skims the hills. Swoops along the gullies.

And reaches the ears of such as the impatient Gaumar de Garin

Slithering down the ridge, Falkan and Passerel were trying to find their feet when de Garin yelled.

'It's the enemy! I hear them! The devils of Islam, I hear them! It's our chance! *It's our chance!* In the name of God, we'll ride the bastards down!'

The well-intentioned Passerel waved in frantic silence to halt the charge. But the knights had been inflamed by de Garin's roar. Believing this the final moment in which to smite the enemy, they were jabbing the flanks of their weary horses, skin torn by the points of their spurs.

An instant later and Baynard was stamping for balance, flagging at the riders, yet knowing it was now too late. Gaumar had heard the enemy, as they themselves must have heard his insensate yell.

'Stand aside, Falkan! I say to you, stand aside!'

Then the vicious sweep of a long, double-edged sword, the outer blade slicing downward at Baynard's thigh. The power of the blow, helped by the weight of the downswing, tore into the links of Baynard's hauberk, driving the split and misshapen rings into the wound.

The young Tremellion could feel metal gouge at bone.

As for Gerard Passerel, he was slammed on the helmet by the spikes of a three-foot mace wielded by an unseen hand, the two knights flopping to the ground as the Crusaders spurred at the ridge.

*

With a howl of anticipated triumph, Gaumar de Garin led the riders to the spine of the hill, crossed it – and realised the truth.

Unable to turn aside, the horses floundering down the slope, the fourteen horrified Christians being jerked and jounced to a meeting with a hundred well-armed Saracens. And all of it beneath Allah's leaden gaze.

Stunned by the blow of the mace, Passerel lay senseless. Away to his right, beyond the churned up passage of the horses, Baynard Falkan writhed in agony, the embedded links drowned in the blood that welled from his bone-deep wound. Every twitch of movement dragged at the hauberk, skin and muscle hooked by the broken rings. Inarticulate sounds echoed in his throat, his eyes blinded by pain. His vision distorted, he reached for the hem of the hauberk . . . Clutched at it with his mittened hand . . . Prayed to God he could somehow quell his scream, *then tore the metal tunic from the bloody depths of the cut.*

In the event God was merciful, allowing the knight greater torment than his system could withstand. Even as the scream rose it was turned to a long, shuddering sigh, the young Tremellion robbed, like Passerel, of his senses.

The first to lose consciousness, Passerel was also the first to recover. Gaping about him, he saw the two horses tethered near the foot of the slope. Elements of memory returned. He scrambled to his feet, immediately succumbed to a wave of dizziness and went sprawling toward the *wadi*.

Moments passed, his head at last clearing, though his face a piteous mask of mud and sweat. *Those two mounts . . . Mine and . . .*

Wiping the dirt from his eyes, he peered across the steep, churned track, frowning with exaggerated concentration at the prostrate body of – *mine and* – Lord Jesus, yes, Commander Falkan!

Tenacious in his efforts, the young knight crawled to rejoin Tremellion, his face blanching beneath its mask as he saw the darkness of blood, the paleness of flesh and bone.

Flies were already exploring the deep, sweet wound.

Reaching beneath his own link-mail tunic, Gerard Passerel tugged at his linen shift, frantically ripping the garment from his body. It was clumsily done, his hands quivering and uncertain, but he managed to press fragments of cloth against the wound, then bind the wadding tight around Baynard's thigh.

He hoped no one would know his motives for saving Lord Falkan were mixed; in part because he respected the man, but also because he feared they were now alone.

No sounds at all from beyond the ridge . . .

Suppose it was true – the two of them alone – and Falkan allowed to die. Who then would help guide Passerel to Acre? *So, please God, let the man live; so we both might live.*

He felt Baynard stir, saw his eyes flicker open, flinched at the spasm of pain that seared his face.

'They have left us, my lord, all of them ridden ahead. I don't know how long – I was felled by the blow of a –'

'Help me stand. We must see for ourselves what's –Aah, but that hurts!' Afflicted by his own waves of nausea, he fought them down before trying again, an arm extended to the terrified Passerel. 'We'll do it as best we can, my friend. Hopping like sand-fleas, or crawling like beetles. But this time you must get us to the ridge. And let us both hope to God the valley lies deserted.'

It was true that the Saracens had gone. And the Frankish destriers. And the shields and helmets, swords and skirted armour.

But the fourteen Christian knights were still there, dead and stripped naked, crucified to the ground with arrows through their palms.

Gerard Passerel began to weep. 'I knew some of those men . . . They were friends of mine . . . And the youngster . . . The one de Garin kept taunting . . . We came out together from Marseilles . . .'

'We have both lost friends,' Baynard murmured. 'Though less to the credit of the enemy, it seems, than our own strange insanity.'

They made no attempt to bury the dead. It was as much as they could do to reclaim their mounts, Falkan all but yelling with pain as he was helped into the saddle, the two young knights then wending their way through Saladin's poisoned garden.

They would never know if it was any more than chance that brought them home. The hand of God, perhaps. Or the mercy of Allah.

They twice thought themselves sighted by Moslem scouts, the second time more likely than the first. Faint from loss of blood, Baynard told his companion to spur ahead. 'Follow the line we're taking. A few hours more and you'll be safe at the coast. You must risk it all, my friend, on this last run to the sea.'

But Gerard Passerel said no. He'd prefer to stay with Tremellion. And, once again, he hoped no one would know his motives for staying were mixed. In part to see things out with the man he respected, but no less because he would rather be with Falkan, than utterly alone.

His father had once locked the infant Gerard in a cupboard, leaving the child to hammer and scream for a night and most of a day.

From that moment on he'd decided to die in company, and not ever run for his life, if the fleeing meant being alone.

Spared by whichever god it might have been, the survivors of the patrol found their way to the King of Jerusalem's panic-stricken camp.

Learning that Tremellion had returned, Guthric and Quillon completed their tasks, then hurried to welcome him home. Both the constable and safeguard had clever phrases in mind, though they bit them back when they saw that Falkan was within easy reach of dying. Thin before, he now seemed bloodless and wizened, the skin of his face fallen in on its bones. Another few days and the cut in his thigh would fester – after which there was nothing anyone could do.

Leaving Quillon to stay with their master, Guthric scoured the camp to locate the exhausted Passerel. Then he took the young knight with him to the hornets' nest that was now the king's pavilion, barging aside the officials who tried to stop him, and growling insistence that Jobert de Blanchefort grant the callers a moment of his time.

Preoccupied with the desperate attack on Acre, the Marshal of the Kingdom was nevertheless appalled by what Passerel told him.

'I blame myself for much of this,' he said quietly. 'I should have known what trouble he might cause, our Gaumar de Garin. Rejected by the Templars; brushed aside by the Knights of the Hospital; he was ever unstable in his aims.'

'Well, I tell you,' Guthric said. 'With all respect – whatever is needed from a commoner of Cornwall – I couldn't care so much as a rabbit's droppings for de Garin. But the man you sent to command that patrol – he's been hacked to the bone by your bloody de Garin, and will die if he ain't given fast to the physicians! So here's where I stand, my lord Marshal. Me – an' this knight who rode home with Falkan. And it's here we'll stay until –'

'You must get him clear of this stinking, putrid camp. I've a house in Tyre. You will see him lodged there. As for doctors, there's one in particular I'd trust within that city. Though wouldn't you know it, he's an Arab.' Without further delay, de Blanchefort issued orders to his clerks, leaving them to pen a number of letters while he strode off to organise a cart for Baynard, an escort to protect him on the coastal road to Tyre.

He returned a few moments later, directed his gaze at Gerard Passerel and said, 'You have no special standing hereabouts, have you, Sir Gerard. Just one of our landless knights, isn't that so?'

'No, sire, I have not. I mean, yes, my lord Marshal, you are. I mean –'

'You mean well, I think,' Jobert smiled. 'So keep close to us here. The king himself will wish to show you that part of Aquitaine you will hold in his honour.'

His tired lips stretched as in the beaming of a clown, the promoted knight turned to share his pleasure with Guthric. But the Saxon had already departed, the letters of introduction snatched from the clerks, his only wish now to get Falkan to Tyre and into the knowing hands of the healers.

THIRTY

ONCE AN island, but now linked by a causeway to the mainland, the city and citadel of Tyre were defended by three moated walls, a dozen towers, a series of deep, dry ditches. Spared by Saladin – one of the sultan's few strategic mistakes – Tyre was all but impregnable, the sea around it patrolled by Crusader galleys, its food stocks plentiful, its garrison and inhabitants by-passed by the war.

Having missed the opportunity to strike when the city was weak, the Saracen spies reported that Tyre was now too formidable to be taken, not least because it was commanded by the ambitious and unyielding Conrad of Montferrat.

Reaching the first of the walls that barred the approach to the causeway, the cart and its escort were halted. The Tyrian guards questioned the riders, the leader of the escort turning to Guthric and Quillon.

'Surely Marshal de Blanchefort gave you his authority in writing. I hope to God he did, else Montferrat's guards will never admit us.'

Guthric remembered the letters, dug them from his pouch, then fanned them like oversized playing cards, staring blankly at the thick black script. The knight snorted irritably, reaching to take them from the hulking, illiterate Saxon.

'Not this one . . . Nor this . . . Nor – Yes, here's the one they'll want. He thrust the others back at the constable, gestured to one of the guards to lower the message-sack from the wall, then rode forward to deliver the sealed and folded parchment.

'And speed it to your master! We've a wounded man here who's well enough thought of by the Marshal of this Kingdom!'

Safe and smug within his heavily fortified stronghold, the Tyrian dismissed the knight's command with a jerk of his head. *Different rules apply, up here. We're Conrad's men, not Guy's.*

With insolent slowness, he hauled up the message-sack, extracted the letter, then moved along the wall-walk to the steps. Guthric and Quillon cursed him beneath their breath, the safeguard thinking how easy it would be, even now, to send an arrow through that bastard's piggish neck!

236

Guthric made his way to the straw-bedded cart, the Saxon appalled by the greyness of Baynard's skin. The young man seemed oddly stretched in length, though so thin, so hollowed and drained of life. He trickled water on Falkan's lips; gently sponged his face. Then muttered to himself – something about Sir Geoffrey using his influence with God . . .

As tall in health as Baynard seemed in sickness, the lank-haired Conrad of Montferrat read the letter from Marshal Jobert. Prowled the mosaic floor of the castle as he read it. Reminded himself that King Guy was his rival, and that Jobert de Blanchefort had chosen to side with Guy.

Reminded himself that King Guy was in trouble down at Acre, whereas he, the Marquis of Montferrat, was still the untarnished champion of the West.

So why admit this – who was it? – Baynard Falkan, Knight of Tremellion? Just so he could nurse his wounds, then canter back to the king? Come sunshine at midnight and Conrad would help the balding monarch. But until that time –

Then his long, artistic fingers – the only artistic thing about the Master of Tyre – touched the broken grey wax seal of de Blanchefort's letter.

Jobert de Blanchefort . . . Not someone who takes kindly to being denied. As for the king, well, to hell with the king . . . But spurn de Blanchefort and a man would store up trouble for himself . . . More than he might ever wish to bear . . .

His decision made, the cadaverous Montferrat spun on his heel, snarling at those who stood in attendance. 'I pray this was brought to me straight, this letter! He's a man I admire, our great Marshal! And I will thus befriend anyone he sends for safe-keeping! Well? What are you waiting for? Sunshine at midnight? Get those callers into the city, damn you, and the patient to his bed!'

The second letter was read by the keeper of Jobert's household, an immaculate, level-voiced man named Aubery – 'That alone will suffice, Master Guthric; it will please you to address me as Aubery.'

The constable nodded, then started to say 'The Lord of Tremellion –'

'He is already being carried from the cart, Master Guthric.'

'He's been sorely wounded. I think one of these letters –'

'For the physician no doubt. May I see? Yes, it is. I'll have it placed before him when he arrives. His presence has been requested.'

'It has? How did you –'

'A word from the castle, Master Guthric. The Marquis of Montferrat would have everything possible done for the Lord of Tremellion.' With neither the salt of a scowl, nor the sugar of a smile, the bland and unshakeable keeper told Guthric and Quillon they'd be quartered on the ground floor of the house; the escort thanked and fed and sent on their way back to Acre.

The constable said, 'I've another letter, though in truth I have to tell you –'

'That you're foreign to Tyre, is that it, Master Guthric? And lost for the address? And would have me deliver it?'

He knows, Guthric thought. Christ, you could slide on this man, he's so smooth; see your face reflected in his cheeks. But withal, he's saved me saying it; knows I can't read but has spared me admitting it. The joskin an' me, we could both learn a thing or two from Aubery.

The Arab physician counted slowly aloud as the sedative mandragora took effect. Baynard fought against the drug, writhed on the bed, muttered and mumbled as the opiate stole his senses.

And then, when the sharp-eyed physician was satisfied the pain would be dulled, he cut wider and deeper than Gaumar de Garin's original sword-hacked wound.

New blood spurted to wash away the old. The bone was scraped clean, the sides of the cut anointed with sulphur, the patient's leg lifted, the Arab threading horsehair through the eye of a curved bone needle.

Inserting the needle from side to side of the cut, he delicately drew the edges of skin together, twisting the last of the thread around a small wooden toggle. Then he bandaged the thigh, heaped pillows beneath it, and turned to ask Aubery – 'Likely though it is that he'll live, your God may wish to claim him. In which case – yet praying he's spared by both your god and mine – to whom should I send my bill?'

The final letter had now reached its destination, an elegant, Moorish-style house at the far side of Tyre. It was quoted aloud by its mystified recipient, the man's finely-modulated voice carrying across the chamber to a window-seat that overlooked the port.

238

' ". . . spoke of you, asking your whereabouts . . . I told him at the time you were not yet with us, though I sensed his interest extended somewhat beyond his inquiry . . . As one old friend to another, I would ask you . . . keep an eye on him and . . . came far to set the chest at our feet . . . months of courageous effort for the Cause . . ." '

The reader then looked up and asked, 'Should we know of him, this protégé of de Blanchefort's?'

'I'm sorry. I wasn't listening. There's too much going on down there in the port.'

'I said; this knight I've been asked to survey. This fellow who brought money out from England. This Baynard Falkan of – Remind me, were we ever at a place called Tremellion?'

Turning from the alcove of the window, Christiane de Magnat-Vaulmier left the ships to sink or sail. Well, now, she thought. So he's here. Kept his word and – 'Read me that last part again if you will, Father. Something about fighting for the Cause?'

Finding his place, Gilles de Magnat-Vaulmier, Duc de Querinard, Comte d'Almé, read the final line of the letter: ' "Tremellion's money donated, he has risked himself in months of courageous effort for the Cause." '

'And you say he's here, in Tyre?'

'So I gather. Seems he's been wounded and is lodged in Jobert's house, over by –'

'I know it,' she said quickly.

Magnat-Vaulmier watched his attractive, hard-to-please daughter smooth the creases from her gown. Twitch her head to settle the braids of her hair. Yawn as if bored, then make her way idly to a chair, its broad leather back draped with a fur-lined mantle.

The least of fools, the longtime widower Magnat-Vaulmier was alerted by Christiane's yawn. Where other girls might squeal with pleasure, his own would portray a marked lack of interest in the things – and the people – to which she was most attracted. The selfsame attitude, he thought fondly, that had drawn *him* to the Lady Isabel twenty years before.

But he still couldn't remember. 'This Tremellion place –'

'In England,' she told him. 'In Cornwall. We had to zig-zag around a series of walls to get there. The father, Sir Geoffrey Falkan, he's a fine old warrior, though as for his elder son, Ranulf –' and she twisted her full, wide lips in chilly distaste. 'But the other one, this Baynard you talk of, he's not nearly so bad. And it seems to me – since he's landed up in Tyre – I might as well see how he fares.'

Then, with a brief kiss for her father, she left him with Jobert de Blanchefort's letter in his hand.

Come to think of it, he mused, I *do* remember those tricky, zig-zag walls. And the grizzled Sir Geoffrey Falkan. And faintly the one called Ranulf. But with the best will in the world— Who on God's earth remembers the second sons of minor foreign families?

Accompanied by a female servant, Christiane made her way through the fresh drizzle of evening to the house of Jobert de Blanchefort, the lodgings of Baynard Falkan. She was met at the door by the silk-smooth Aubery, the two women installed in a downstairs chamber, the callers left in comfort, with wine and the warmth of a fire.

For a while the inquisitive servant worked on her question, then slyly asked, 'A friend of your father's, my lady, this Trewillman?'

'You've misheard the name,' Christiane teased. 'Its roots are from both the German and the French. Spoken fast it sounds otherwise, but it's really – and repeat after me – it's really Tremengewurtensteinen. And important we get it right, for you know how touchy they can be, these mispronounced lords from the North!'

It amused her to see the woman chew on the name she'd been fed. But the girl's smile faded when Guthric appeared in the doorway, bowed curtly to the visitors, then told Christiane she could not see Baynard Falkan.

'I regret, my lady, but Lord Falkan's in no fit state. He's been drugged and stitched, and would not – with all respect to you – recognise the difference 'twixt you an', well, anyone else.'

'How was he wounded? My father only mentioned –'

'He was cut in the thickness of the leg. It doesn't matter who did it. It's enough that he was out searching for the foe.'

'But he will –' she started. 'That's to say, he *will* recover with time.'

Not one to dissemble, Guthric thought how much better the keeper Aubery would have handled this exchange. For his part the constable could only shrug and say maybe. 'If the Arab's as good as de Blanchefort told us. And God looks Falkan's way.'

'Will you tell him I was here, Master Guthric? And that, should he wish it, I'll return when his strength is rebuilt?'

The Saxon nodded, saw distress tug at Christiane's features, and struggled for something to say. 'Yes, my lady, I'll – I'll make sure it's the first thing he hears.'

And with that she had no choice but to glance at her silly chaperone, incline her head toward Guthric, then allow herself to be escorted back from whence she'd come.

She awoke in the still, cold hours that precede the dawn.

For an instant she thought she'd been roused from a nightmare, her mind forcing her to cast aside the phantoms of her dream. Then she remembered – *He is here, in Tyre . . . Cut in the thickness of his leg . . . Drugged and stitched and unable to recognise – 'You from anyone else.'*

Her pretences abandoned – no longer yawning with feigned indifference – the eighteen-year-old daughter of the Treasurer of the Kingdom surrendered to her fears and feelings. She was aware that of all the young noblemen she'd met, all the stories they'd recounted to impress her, all the titles they'd unrolled and futures they'd mapped – the one she most clearly remembered was the lean and awkward Tremellion, his laughter too loud as she'd told him her not-very-witty tale of the smoke-filled castle.

Their time together had been brief, so *why* did she remember him? Why did she even *imagine* she remembered him?

And why was she now quietly weeping, and praying that of all of them, he especially wouldn't die?

The physician made regular calls to the house of de Blanchefort. Each time he came he offered the patient a draught of mandragora, warning him that further inspection of the wound was necessary, but that the probing would be painful.

No more courageous than others, Baynard nevertheless declined the drug, his plans extending far beyond the agony of the Arab's administrations.

He had heard from Guthric that Christiane de Magnat-Vaulmier had been to visit him – 'And she'll come again, when you want.'

'I doubt,' Baynard smiled, 'that those were exactly her words. She did not seem to me the kind who'd be summoned by the snapping of fingers, or the issuing of orders. Anyway, I've no wish for her to see me here, on these stained and unchanged blankets. It's the only reason I resist the good doctor's opiate; so I can learn to tolerate the barbs of de Garin's bequest. It's like – do you remember this, old Guthric? – like the time I had toothache? When it all became too much for me, I got you to draw the tooth. So be it with the wound. The pain will diminish, and *I'm* the one who'll go visiting. Or the Arab and you, you'll be either ends of a saw. Now, my loyal friend; let's get to working the leg again, for tomorrow I intend to touch the floor.'

Brave talk, though backed by a rare determination. Tomorrow left Falkan sweating in agony, the next day no better, the one that followed marked by a wave of excruciating pain. Yet the young Tremellion persisted, the Arab sufficiently impressed to bring him an odd-shaped bamboo cage, in which the foreigner could stand and sweat and recover.

Then a pair of crutches, bound with cloth . . .

Then just the single crutch . . .

Then a cane . . .

Baynard had already sent a note to Christiane, stiff and formal in its tone.

'It was both kind and generous of you, my lady, to visit the knight who now lodges in the house of Marshal de Blanchefort. You are ever remembered from the all-too-brief time we shared together in my late father's castle of Tremellion. Be assured, my Lady Christiane, I shall make the utmost effort to return your visit in person.'

Reading it over, he realised it was not at all what he'd wanted to express. It failed to give the merest flavour of his feelings – a dull-as-ditchwater message.

But that, after all, was why he'd spurned the mandragora. In order to live with the wound, come to terms with it, hop and hobble, then one day make his way to the house of Magnat-Vaulmier where he'd meet Christiane – and let them both learn what his heart would have him say.

Unwilling to call on him again, uninvited, she nevertheless replied to his note with one of her own. It was equally rigid, as colourless in tone as his, her imagination tethered by the disciplines imposed upon the daughter of Magnat-Vaulmier, Treasurer of the Kingdom.

'It pleases me to receive your missive. I remark the passing of your father, and add him to my prayers. May the Lord speed your own recovery, Sir Baynard, so that you might, before long, visit us here in person.'

It wasn't, she accepted, at all what she'd planned to tell him. But at least she'd been remembered – *the all-too-brief time we shared together* – and it encouraged her to wait.

THIRTY-ONE

ON FEBRUARY the 12th, 1191 – a date of no great significance in the calendar of the world – Quillon and Guthric accompanied their master through the narrow streets of Tyre. They made a point of ignoring his painful progress, knowing how he'd snap at them if they reached to catch his arm. Let him fall, and the thing to do then was stand back and wait till he climbed to his feet. But close in around him? Cosset Tremellion? Try that and they'd feel the sting of his cane, or more likely the lash of his tongue.

As it happened he *did* fall – once against the wall of a house, once as he slipped on the steps to Vaulmier's dwelling. The pain of the second misjudgement was terrible, though he'd only allow his companions to brush dirt from the hem of his cloak.

Gasping for breath, he approved as the Saxon turned away from his agony, the constable pounding – as always, too hard – on the door.

Greeted in silent query by one of the treasurer's servants, Guthric allowed himself a brief flight of fancy. 'We'd 'ave you tell your master – Lord Magnat-Vaulmier – 'ave you tell 'im that Lord Falkan of Tremellion is once again up and about – and would speak with his daughter – who he sweetly remembers from all that time ago.'

The man stared at him, saw the force of Guthric's slow, repeated nod, and found his own head bobbing in time.

'– would speak – with his daughter?'

'That's right.'

'– sweetly remembered – from all that – all that time ago?'

'Rain's still comin' down,' Quillon prompted. 'Ain't we ever goin' to get through the door?'

After that the safeguard and constable moved aside. Directed to the kitchens, they found themselves surrounded by the smell of fresh-cooked meat, the warmth of steam, the bustle of cooks and serving-maids. Guthric studied those who took his fancy, Quillon with a grin for them all.

'You fellows just arrived in the port?'

'Oh, tut, tut. Do we look like we've only just this minute landed? We've been pitched against the enemy, my sweet! 'And-to-'and with them Saracens! Terrible men, them Saracens. Let me tell you – but only if you want to 'ear it – 'ow the two of us got caught by, what was it, fifty of 'em –?'

'Too modest, joskin. Call it sixty.'

'That's right! Closer to sixty. And 'ow the two of us fought our way free. Though not to disturb you from the cookin'. Only if you want to 'ear it.'

The serving-girls nodded eagerly. The cooks made a show of disapproval, though not for long, the women soon crowding around to be told how desperate it had been out there – 'and-to-'and with the Saracens. Sixty or more of the demons pitched against the one who looked like an ugly bear, and the one who'd pass, if only in the imagination, for a lion.

Meanwhile, on the upper floor of the house, Baynard Falkan limped into the presence of the tall and aristocratic Gilles de Magnat-Vaulmier, Treasurer of the Kingdom.

Yet with no sign of his daughter.

Smiling politely at the man who might, if he threw away his cane and straightened his spine, match him in height, Vaulmier invited his visitor to be seated.

'It is good to see you recovered, or anyway progressing, my Lord Falkan. Your injury was mentioned by de Blanchefort. They can be the very devils, those riders of Islam, quicker with their scimitars –'

'No doubt, my Lord Vaulmier. I've respected them from the first. But the truth to tell, I was lowered by one of our own, so I cannot, with good grace, claim I ever sustained a cut at the hands of Islam.'

Vaulmier gestured to one of his servants to pour wine and distribute the sweetmeats. Then he settled himself against the carved-wood back of his chair and gazed at Falkan, holding the knight's attention with his eyes.

'You may find me odd, my young Tremellion – aren't we all? – but as a caller here, and no doubt on your best behaviour, you're bound to hear me out.'

'With pleasure, my Lord Vaulmier.'

'With anything but!' the man laughed. 'Or so I'd suppose. It's scarcely for me that you've limped your way half around the town. But you've done it, and here you are, and here you'll have to sit for a while, courteous and quiet in the face of my odd remarks.'

Baynard wondered if he was called upon to reply, decided he wasn't and stayed silent, obedient to his well-mannered host, both eager and anxious to hear what he had to say.

'No insult intended, my dear Falkan, yet it has to be announced that I cannot for the life of me see why it's you.'

'My Lord Vaulmier?'

'Where's your girth? Where's your wealth? Where are you from, but the distant side of some dank Cornish moor? And where's Cornwall in the world? Scarcely London! Scarcely Paris! Scarcely Rome, or the cities of Germany and Spain! I mean – my dear Sir Baynard – what in God's good name have you ever done to set my yawning and arrogant daughter plucking like a beggar at my sleeve?'

In the silence that followed they stared at each other, Vaulmier frowning with undisguised curiosity, Falkan suppressing the thrill of happiness that surged within him.

It took him a while to fashion his reply. But even then it wasn't – as with care and time he'd have planned it – properly delivered. Yet he blurted it with an honesty that widened the treasurer's eyes, the man no longer settled against his chair, but brought forward by the knight's response.

'Those things you ask? I'm deficient in them all. No girth, no wealth, nor even the right to be known as Lord of Tremellion. My father – and you'll remember him, I trust, that decent and honourable warlord? – well, my Lord Vaulmier, he was murdered at my brother's behest and the treasure he'd promised to the Cause was snatched away. It took time to reclaim it. Time to bring it out here. A damned long time to get it accepted by the king!

'But all that's apart. Let's ignore my father for the moment. You query your daughter's desires, and all I can tell you is this. She's worthy of more than a man with a limp. The landless and near-penniless son of a Cornish holding. As for you, my Lord Vaulmier, you've the power to see me barred from her presence –'

'No question of it.'

'– the power to stave me off. Very well. But supposing she continues to pluck at your sleeve! Might it not just mean – and tell me direct – might it not just mean she'd ignore the rap of a cane and the absence of riches?'

Magnat-Vaulmier leaned back again in his chair. He offered Tremellion the growing extension of a smile, the treasurer impressed by the young man's rejoinder. 'Indeed she might,' he murmured, 'for

246

that was always Christiane's style.' He dipped his head forward and remarked, 'An unlikely suitor though you are, it seems you're well enough started on your way.'

Rising to his feet, the nobleman directed one of the servants to refill Baynard's goblet. Motioning the knight to stay seated, he said, 'It's a scene I've played with others, both here and in the West. Ardent suitors, hoping to please me in the expectation of claiming my daughter. With due respect, Sir Baynard, I am bound to say, I never imagined *you* to be the one.' Then with an almost imperceptible shrug he added, 'Though when has a father ever gauged things right in matters of this kind?'

Saying nothing – risky to speak at this fragile moment – the young Tremellion preferred to straighten the set of his tunic, forcing himself to ignore the pain that throbbed from the depths of his sutured wound.

Then he watched as Magnat-Vaulmier strode to a curtained doorway at the eastern side of the chamber.

And listened as the treasurer called through – 'We have a visitor, *ma chère*. A certain Baynard Falkan of Tremellion. Returning the call you made to the house of Jobert de Blanchefort. Do I keep him here, or not?'

He wondered if she would be as he remembered. The image, or so he believed, was as sharp in his mind as the last time he'd seen her, all but a year ago. Yet were her eyes really as blue as the summer shallows, her hair the colour of corn, the texture of silk? She favoured gowns of white and silver, of cinnamon and green, her limbs slender as – well, slender as –

Thank God you're not a poet, he told himself. You'd starve within the week.

Then the curtain parted and she entered the chamber; and yes, her eyes *were* as blue as he'd remembered, her figure as slender, her carriage erect, her long, elegant fingers –

'My Lord Falkan.'

'My Lady Christiane.'

'I pray you, be seated, Sir Baynard. It can bring you no comfort, leaning on that cane.'

'I improve – I mean, the wound seals tighter every day.'

'You are being treated by the Arab, so I hear.'

'He's an excellent physician, my lady. Really a most – excellent physician.'

'Yes, so they tell me. One of the best.'

'For yourself, you look – permit me to say it – in the finest of good health.'

'As God would have it, sire, I am. Though I'm not much one for the rain.'

'It's the season for it, I suppose. Out here.'

'I regret to say it is. Ah, yes.'

Gilles de Magnat-Vaulmier tightened the muscles in his neck; forced himself not to shake his head and smile. *There's a fly in the ointment. And I am the one with wings.*

'You will excuse me, Sir Baynard, if I attend to other business. Should you care to stay and dine with us –'

'With pleasure, my Lord Vaulmier.'

'I was about to add, your injury permitting, though the alacrity of your answer calms my concern.'

With nothing to offer but the awkwardness of a bow, Baynard waited for the treasurer to leave. Christiane accompanied her father to the main door of the chamber, the girl murmuring something that sent the nobleman chuckling quietly from the room.

When she returned, it was to stand for a moment directly in front of Tremellion, her hands folded on the tie-knot of her girdle, her expression one of thoughtful curiosity.

'You look near wasted away, do you know that?'

'You don't. You look magnificent. As beautiful as you've been in all my dreams. What did you say that so amused your father?'

'Oh, that,' the girl said lightly. 'I told him to open his purse. Told him I don't like you being so skinny. Told him we might be married before long, and I wouldn't want the rattle of bones in my bed.'

'*You told him that?*'

'About the marriage?'

'No, no. The bones and – the bed.'

'Why not?' she shrugged. 'Don't we both intend the one should lead swiftly to the other?'

Though not yet lovers under the quilt, they were warmed and excited by the gifts they had to offer. Strong and independent in their ways, they were nevertheless magicked by the spell, each of them wishing to please, eager to be pleased, sometimes cautious, on occasion critical, but for the most part willing to share and agree and concede that it might be so. Their happiness deepened as they realised their opinions were not much different, their attitudes akin, their sense of humour so close that they thought themselves the only ones to appreciate what the world was missing.

It didn't matter at all that Christiane thought English food dull and cooked to a cinder, its vegetables boiled to a pap. If they ever went back there, as one day they might, she'd eat it without demur.

Nor that Baynard thought Moorish decoration somewhat garish, its brilliance enough to make a fellow squint. He was sure he could get used to it; might even come to enjoy the vivid and intricate workmanship of Islam. For Christiane's sake, he would most assuredly try.

It helped, of course, that the girl was the daughter of Gilles de Magnat-Vaulmier, Duc de Querinard, Comte d'Almé, Treasurer of the Kingdom of Jerusalem. Not for his titles or position – not those at all – but simply because the man himself was erudite and amusing, his mind as flexible as a freshly-peeled sapling, his knowledge of life extensive, his affection for Christiane leaving just enough room for a man like Tremellion to stand beside her.

It helped too, that Vaulmier had respected Sir Geoffrey Falkan, father and daughter listening in careful silence as Baynard recounted the story of his murder; the attack on the mill; the long and eventful journey out to Acre.

'Those knights you roped in Cyprus,' Vaulmier queried, 'Ansel Sauvery and his friend. Since they told you, what was it, that you'd surely be killed out here, aren't you therefore still hunted, my dear Baynard?'

'Your question speaks immediately of your daughter, Lord Vaulmier. And the answer is – yes, it's possible. But from Cyprus to Acre? From Acre to Tyre? It may happen they're still searching, though I doubt it. Tremellion's money is now in the hands of the king. For my part, I intend to stay here a while, so what threat could I possibly be to a brother lurking God knows how many thousand miles to the west?'

On the point of pursuing the question, Gilles de Magnat-Vaulmier thought of something else. It was no one's fault that he did so, for Christiane was leaning forward, her blue eyes aswim with excitement, her lips, as it seemed, swollen with the eagerness to encourage him to say it.

'If you truly intend to remain in the kingdom –'

'I see no reason why not, my Lord Vaulmier. With Christiane as my wife, she'll be safely lodged in your house, whilst I ride with de Blanchefort's –'

249

Then a wagging finger of negation from his father-in-law-to-be.

Misunderstanding, Baynard said, 'Perhaps you're right. Perhaps we should find somewhere of our own here in the city. Newlyweds, after all.'

But the treasurer was still denying them with his finger, smiling as he refused the couple the sanctuary of Tyre.

'Marry my daughter,' he announced, 'and the sooner the better, for you both look sorely taxed by your celibate state. Then get yourselves down to the coast to Yarash. It's an outpost of this city. No more than a grouping of towers on the shore. But safe enough from the Saracens, for the moment. And as good a place as any for Sir Geoffrey Falkan's son to show his skills.'

Christiane watched as Baynard limped toward her father. Already in favour of the marriage, the treasurer had now added his seal of approval by offering Falkan the wave-washed property of Yarash. To allow his daughter in marriage was one thing, though far less important than the giving away of stones.

'I will hold it,' the young knight affirmed, 'in the name of Magnat-Vaulmier.'

'No doubt you will, my dear Baynard. Though fooling with the defences to suit yourself.'

THIRTY-TWO

THE WEDDING took place in a side chapel of the over-sized Cathedral of Tyre; Gilles de Magnat-Vaulmier and a few invited guests in the narrow pews. Conrad of Montferrat had declined, sending a minor representative in his place. Jobert de Blanchefort had promised to get there if he could, but had not arrived. The service would be conducted by Engeram, bishop of the city.

A hundred candles guttered in their girandoles, the flames now and then recoiling from the draughts of cold, damp air.

The bride was arrayed in grey-and-white striped furs, the cloak held to her shoulders by Magnat-Vaulmier's gift of a heavy gold chain, his daughter's age reflected in its eighteen intricate links.

Compared to this, Falkan's gift had been small.

Weighed in a jeweller's balance, the bracelet was worth next to nothing, though the oddity of design drew Christiane's gaze to her wrist, time and time again. The more she studied it, the more she learned of her soon-to-be husband's past. The shape of a castle – a ship – an island. The profile of a helmet – the outline of a hill – the silvered flutter of a flag. A charm that depicted her father's house in Tyre – another that showed an Arab scimitar snapped by a Frankish sword – a dozen different symbols, circumscribing her wrist. Turning the bracelet, she smiled again to see that the clasp brought a pair of hands together, fitting in perfect unity. As she hoped and believed her life would soon fit with his.

Christiane's gift to Baynard had left him gaping. A decorated mantle, the hooded, triangular garment sewn with black and scarlet falcons – her affectionate play on his name – but also with eagles and peregrines, kites and merlins, sparrowhawks and kestrels and all the swooping predators of the sky.

'It seemed,' she'd told him, 'the natural way to paint you.'

They waited for Engeram, the cathedral looming dark and chilly behind them. Conrad's representative shifted with undisguised impatience. Guthric coughed, turned instinctively to spit, changed his mind and swallowed hard instead. Quillon stood quiet, awed by his surroundings.

It was a while before the bishop made his entrance, acolytes walking ahead of him, incense burners swinging in the air. He glanced at the congregation, emitted an audible sigh at the poor attendance, then stationed himself within the flickering ring of candles.

If the truth be known – and here was not the place to divulge it – the portly Bishop Engeram was reluctant to see Vaulmier's daughter married to a man of such scant importance as Baynard Falkan. A paltry turnout like this, and where was the profit? No sidesmen, no choir, no musicians, no wealthy relations weeping for joy, no drunken guests who'd apologise later with coin. But business was business, and the sooner it was over, the sooner he could return to the broad-hipped servant girl he'd left waiting in the bedroom of his palace.

Raising his hands, the prelate brought his jewelled fingers together in a steeple of prayer. 'We are here,' he started, 'in the sanctified house of the Lord –' Then got no further as the main doors of the cathedral banged open, boot-heels rapping the aisle.

Jobert de Blanchefort strode into the chapel, followed by Gerard Passerel and half a dozen others. 'Never rode so hard in all m'life,' the marshal bellowed. 'If I've missed it, you'll have to repeat it again!'

Engeram glared, his face suffused with displeasure. But not so his congregation, Vaulmier greeting de Blanchefort like the long-time friend he was, Falkan turning to embrace the young Passerel, the latecomers bowing to the treasurer, to the resplendent bride, to the groom in his predators' mantle. Cordial chaos filled the chapel, giving Engeram time to compose his features – *some profit to be gained after all, perhaps* – then slowly rebuild the steeple of his fingers.

Gilles de Magnat-Vaulmier hosted a banquet, the newlyweds side by side at the head of a long, refectory table, the treasurer opposite the marshal, the knights and nobility seated by order of rank, then Guthric across from Quillon. But it didn't end there, for Christiane had asked her father to find room for the members of their household, a request he'd granted without the flicker of an eye.

Even so, with the meal chewed to the bones, the servants took their leave of the family and friends, the talk then turning to the future of the Kingdom, the continued absence of King Philip and King Richard, the trouble King Guy was having down at Acre.

An hour of that and Jobert de Blanchefort heaved himself to his feet. A man who could take his drink, his words were none the less slurred as he wished Tremellion success as the castellan of Yarash. 'You brought credit to the Cause when you served the army at Acre, my Lord Baynard . . . My fault I sent that irres – irres – that hot-headed Gaumar de Garin . . . Glad to see you're walking next-to-normal . . . Prettiest lady this side of – this side of *anywhere*, you ask me . . .'

'I hope you will visit us at Yarash, my lord Marshal. And you, too, Gerard. And you others, who thought to ride hard and attend our wedding.'

'Fastest in all m'life,' Jobert repeated. 'Save for the one time – much younger then – when this German came home unexpected an' found me an' his wife . . .' Then he clutched at Passerel's shoulder, barked with laughter at his youthful indiscretion and weaved his way uncertainly from the chamber.

Turning to Christiane, her husband-of-hours asked quickly, 'Have *you* ever counted Germans among your friends?'

'I, my sweet Baynard? *Die Deutschen? Überhaupt niemals!* How could you think so!'

The banquet over, the celebration continued. Conrad de Montferrat's representative excused himself from the festivities, ducking away from the slow, unsteady procession that crossed town. But Vaulmier and his guests and their knights and Quillon and Guthric were still attentive, wending their way in noisy escort as the newlyweds were led to Jobert's dwelling.

It amused Christiane to see her own father somewhat unbalanced by the wine; the first time, so far as she knew, he had ever missed his step. She loved him all the more for letting it happen, then giggled aloud as she watched the men who meant most to her in the world, the limping Baynard – sober in expectation of the night – and the aristocratic Treasurer of the Kingdom, leaning and lurching together along the street.

Abandoned for the moment by her husband – *that didn't take him long!* – she watched the twitch and swirl of his mantle as he preceded her to the house. He wears it well, she thought; even now he wears it well. So imagine how it'll be when he's thrown away his cane. Falkan striding! The predator strutting the ground!

Another hour of drinks and sweetmeats; Guthric and Quillon gorging themselves on the sly. Magnat-Vaulmier abstained, once again the calm and courteous Comte d'Almé, friend and mentor of Tremellion.

'We have overstayed our welcome,' he told his daughter, then shrugged aside his apology to say, 'These past few weeks – I've been working on reams of advice – phrases I planned to slip in at a time like this. But all of a sudden – seeing you together – the advice seems old-fashioned, somehow out-of-style. I remember, when I married your mother, the Lady Isabel, how both her father and mine lambasted me with advice.'

'Did you take it?' Christiane murmured, the coolness of her hand on his.

'Take it?' Vaulmier smiled. 'A night with my wife, and I couldn't recollect a single thing they'd said. No, my dear, nor ever regretted not knowing.'

He leaned down to kiss her, crossed the room to break up a gathering around Baynard, then once again managed to leave the young man blinking in confusion. 'You were not what I'd expected, my Lord Tremellion – my Lord of Yarash. But I'm not so old that I can't admit my faults. Not what I'd expected when my daughter started yawning, but a sight better than I myself would have chosen. May God bless you both, and grant you His protection. And now – before you see this man turn maudlin – I'll attend your presence at dinner a week from today. Though I trust *not* to see you before.'

With a motion of authority, the treasurer cleared the room. The silk-smooth Aubery saw the guests on their way, locked and barred the door, jerked his head at Guthric and Quillon, sending them to the jovial warmth of the kitchen. Then he paused in the entrance to the ground floor chamber, bowed in silence and signified that henceforth the Lord and Lady of Tremellion would be alone.

Gazing about him, Falkan said, 'He's as fine a man, your father, as I –'

'But away from us for the week.'

'And good of de Blanchefort –'

'But now returned to Acre.'

'And seeing young Passerel! Decent of him to ride all this way –'

'But also departed. As everyone's departed. And aren't you a little cold?'

He seemed not to hear her, gesturing at the shuttered windows with his cane, moving to sweep the room with it, walking to poke at the doorway that led to the stairs. He'd covered the width of the chamber before she realised he was limping, though no longer leaning, the bride of Tremellion humming with pleasure as the Lord of Yarash propped his stick against the wall.

'Cold?' he retorted gently. 'Yes, it is, down here. But it needn't be – upstairs.'

They behaved with a fine and greedy disregard. Whatever the rules, they ignored them, far too enwrapped in each other to care what the world might think, what the world might say; Baynard moaning, Christiane gasping, the proximity of their bodies excluding all else. Their discoveries were too sensitive, too rewarding, their eyes blinded, their hearing deafened, their nakedness conveying the totality of their senses – their appetites fed, their hunger at last assuaged.

Though not for long, for newlyweds *are* greedy.

They made love again, this time starting gently, though with the urgency increasing, Christiane now moaning, Baynard gasping, this second disregard of the world even better than the first.

It was at Baynard's suggestion that she turned.

At Christiane's request that they tossed the coverlet aside.

With mutual agreement that the Master of Yarash padded naked to the window, opening the shutters to let the curiosity of moonlight seep into the room.

This way, they agreed, this time, then later slept.

A while beyond and one or the other came awake, excited the body that lay alongside and whispered in sweet temptation – the world forgotten, though the moon a remembrance of the candles in the chapel of the cold and vaulted cathedral . . .

In the morning, the daughter of Magnat-Vaulmier murmured her memories aloud. 'Those stories I heard in the past; from women who knew. They told me the good and bad of it, how rich or wretched it could be. But you know what *I* think, my husband? I think their stories were dismal in the telling!' Then she stretched in abandon on the tormented and love-stained sheets, her slender limbs made languorous by their eager comsummation.

Baynard Falkan busied himself with his clothes, turning away to conceal his glow of masculine satisfaction. That *she* should be pleased with *me*, he thought, when *I'm* the one who's drained by this lissome creature! Good God! Should we continue like this, we'd garrison Yarash with our own!

*

255

The grouping of towers that was Yarash.

Derelict now, it had once been governed by a neighbour of Magnat-Vaulmier, the force withdrawn when the Saracens swept onward from their victory at Hattin. Perched on the shoreline, it had evaded the troops of Islam, the outpost protected by the close proximity of Tyre.

Offered to Baynard Falkan, it would be the greatest test of his initiative and skills, for there was much about the place that needed improvement. The structure was really no more than a castle on the sand. Its turrets and wall-walks, gates and watch-towers, all of them were in need of someone who could unify their defence. Turn the abandoned face of Yarash into a strong and arrogant scowl.

Three days after their marriage – the newlyweds brimming with their hollow-eyed lack of sleep – they rode the short distance from Tyre to their future dwelling.

Baynard carried pens and charcoal and parchment in his saddlebag. He helped his wife ascend the ramp to the castle, then left her to explore the huddle of towers, whilst he wandered away to take measurements, sketch his designs, extend his gaze to the horizons of his future.

Christiane came to tell him the tower she thought they should live in was *that* one, over there.

He told her yes, why not, then crowded her into a sheltered corner, shamelessly lifting the pleated drape of her gown.

Not meaning it, she said no, the couple clutched tight together within sound of the sighing surf.

The hell with the world! The hell with Heaven! The hell with Hell itself! The pleasure he gave her – the thrill she offered in return – the driving, accepting excitement of their desire could do nothing but sharpen the ecstasy of their feelings. Vaulmier's only daughter and Tremellion's second son. Yet now allowed to do what they wanted – even this – in their turreted home of Yarash.

They returned to Tyre with Christiane repeating that the tower they should live in was *that* one. And with Baynard saying maybe, it would all depend, let's see how the plans work out.

Meanwhile, their master preoccupied with his bride and his building, Quillon and Guthric thought themselves in Paradise. The Saxon was much admired by one of the statuesque cooks, the safeguard favoured by a pair of dark-haired maids.

They were as well off here, they decided, as they'd ever been in

Spain, or the island of Cyprus. Maybe better, for the women were closer at hand.

Then Christiane told her husband there was a show to be witnessed in town. 'Conjurors and magic-men, performing tonight in the shelter near the square. Shall you come with me, my love? And spoil my enjoyment by explaining how it's done?'

He smiled at her, his lean face underlit by the candles he'd set at the corners of his desk. 'I tell you what. Busy as I am, why don't you go ahead with Guthric –?'

'I hate to say it, but your Guthric's already gone ahead with one of Jobert's cooks.'

'With Quillon then. Give *that* idle man a shout. He'll see you safe to the square.'

She did as he asked, the jaunty safeguard summoned to the room. He told his master he'd be happy to see the Lady Christiane to the shelter – 'Though you should know, m'lord, it's once again tippin' with rain.'

'So wear your warmest cloak,' Baynard told his wife. 'And as for you, young Quillon, take my own. Swing it about and who knows, it might get you both the best seats in the place.' Then he waved them off to the evening's diversion, his gaze returning to the detailed plans of Yarash. Lots of work to be done to improve the defences. To make the castle worthy of Vaulmier's confidence. And as a home to please Christiane.

On his way to the street, Quillon raised the hood of the borrowed cloak, grinning mischievously at Aubery. 'Conductin' the lady. Off to see the conjurors, an' that. Looks good on me, this garb, wouldn't you agree? All these birds; I might just take off an' fly!'

Unamused by the safeguard's manner, the keeper of de Blanchefort's household saw Christiane and Quillon from the building. He wished the Lady of Yarash a pleasant evening, then watched as they made their uneven way along the cobbles.

Turning to re-enter the house, a flicker of movement caught his eye. He glanced along the street again, blinking in disbelief as he saw Quillon sag, arrows sprouting from his back, kestrels and eagles transfixed by the shafts, others skittering crazily from the walls or bouncing up from the stones.

As if to be companionable, Christiane joined in the silly, sinking dance . . .

All but paralysed by the image – *unreal – impossible* – the keeper moved his head slowly, gazing bland and incurious at the group of archers who now broke and fled, jostling each other as they ran to be swallowed by the darkness of an alley.

Aubery looked again at the hooded couple, sprawled and unmoving in the street. Only then did he accept the truth of what he'd seen, the veneer of a lifetime splintering apart, the keeper cawing and flapping his arms in grotesque imitation of, yes, perhaps a falcon, as he stumbled across the rounded, glistening cobbles.

The two of them were dead. Scream for help and whoever came would know at a glance they were dead. Fetch the physician and the Arab would tell him there was nothing to be done but pray for their souls, for both of them were dead.

Not realising then why he did it, the civilised keeper of de Blanchefort's household leaned closer to the corpse of Christiane de Magnat-Vaulmier, Christiane of Yarash, Christiane of Tremellion, and jerked the three murderous arrows from her body. Later, he would know why he'd done it – offended by the obscenity of the shafts – but all he could do now was whirl to his feet, run howling to the house, in through the door, up the stairs and into the dim-lit chamber, his voice raised to a pitch of hysteria as he cried in dreadful witness to what he'd seen.

Jerked from his study of the architect's plans – and yes, the tower his wife had chosen *could* be the one they'd live in – Baynard Falkan asked, 'What? You're telling me *what*?'

THIRTY-THREE

HE SENT Aubery reeling hard against the wall. Saw the arrows fall like the spills of a children's game from the keeper's grasp. Mercifully failed to comprehend that the blood on the barbs was hers. But was anyway drawing his sword by then, a guttural sound in his throat as he stormed down the stairs, the blade clanging once as it struck the handle of the door.

He saw Tyrians in the street, grouped around the bodies.

Just in time, one of them sensed him approaching, gestured in alarm at the others and backed beyond reach of the blade.

Baynard knelt beside his wife. Laid his sword on the cobbles. Lifted her in his arms, turning her gently, then brushing at the smudges of dirt that marked her face. His lips moved, but the language was a sound only she and he could know. To the cringing spectators it was no more than a long and unbearable rending of the heart.

Removed by the mercy of God from all reality, he told her she was right; they'd furnish the tower she'd chosen, though he wanted her to know it would necessitate the building of a forty-foot length of wall to protect the outerworks. *Anyone else would have settled for the other tower! But not you, my love. With you it's the one with the kitchens already built-in – and what you said when we walked around the place – the contented sigh of the sea.*

Couching her body, limp in death, yet even lighter it seemed than in life, he bored her as a husband might with talk of the expenses, the time it would take to complete the extra wall, the dust that would fill the air. She wasn't to suppose it could all be done in the winking of an eye. So she'd better get used to weeks and months of discomfort. Cover her clothes. Protect the furniture. And for heaven's sake smile at the builders. *For you know what a damned touchy lot . . . what a touchy lot . . . what an awkward and touchy lot . . .*

A well-intentioned voice growled in the dark. 'Best get her in from the damp, my lord. Her an' her escort. Give you a hand with 'em, sire? Get 'em both in from the night?'

Falkan raised his eyes to the cautious citizens of Tyre. Saw them as a blur. Heard the well-meant voice as in the ending of a dream, the rope that hauled him for ever from communion with his young and vibrant wife.

She was dead. It was true. And she ought to be brought in from the damp. She and her escort. Both of them. Dead now and due to be sheltered from the night.

His future with Christiane banished for ever, Falkan reached for his sword. Then he came to his feet, his mind intent on murder, the weapon swinging ready in a grasp so tight it gouged blood from the palm of his hand.

Scattering against the sides of the street, the civilians watched as the knight cut his aimless way down the cobbled slope. The more intelligent among them went to find Jobert de Blanchefort's keeper, calming the stricken man as best they could.

It was a while before Aubery regained his self-control. Wiping the tears of shock and sorrow from his eyes, he thrust back his shoulders then pivoted to tell his neighbours what to do.

'You – and you – and you two over there – you'll bring the bodies. As for you women, you'll go to the head of the stairs, the door to your right, then strip the bed of its skins.' Calling again to the men, he said, 'Whichever of you can do it with decency will draw the arrows from the cloak. Lord Falkan's cloak.' Then he added in a voice that did him justice, 'And worn with a certain flair by his impudent safeguard.'

The neighbours hurried to Aubery's bidding. Citizens of Tyre, they were nevertheless villagers in their street, willing to assist, eager to see the interior of Jobert de Blanchefort's dwelling, pleased to be part of a drama that would shake the foundations of the town.

Soon busy within the house of the Marshal of the Kingdom of Jerusalem, they gave little thought to the Master of Yarash, the young man already lost in the mist of rain that dragged the hem of her gown from the sea to the inland hills.

Protected though it was by walls and towers and ditches and deep-cut dykes, the stronghold of Tyre was ever vigilant to a sudden attack by Islam. The slightest lapse of attention, and its guards were punished by death. An implacable rule of their commander, Conrad of Montferrat. A man who performs his duty is a man I might well promote. But a man who lolls or sleeps is a man I'll raise even higher – on a gibbet.

Determined to keep his Christian enclave free from the hands of Allah, Conrad instructed his soldiers to prowl the streets. They had done so for the past three years, scared to be thought inattentive, though never once threatened by the dark-skinned demons of the East.

So it jarred the patrol to a stumbling halt when Baynard Falkan rounded a corner ahead of them, his lean face dark as Mohammed's, his hair lank with the moisture of the night, his Frankish sword slicing the air.

The leader made his judgement. Not really a Saracen. More likely a drunkard from one of the ships that found their way into port. No foreign threat to the city, but why not arrest him anyway? Provide evidence that his patrol was on the alert.

'You!' he challenged. 'You from overseas! You stand arrested!'

Then flung himself back for his life as the young man swirled in his direction. Reversing the swing of his blade Falkan threatened the others, striding onward to disappear in the gloom beyond their flickering, high-held torches.

The disconcerted leader dredged for a joke. 'Now there's a fellow been locked up here too long! Eager to get at the enemy! Better not wear a turban, eh, else he really *might* use that sword!' He laughed to lead the laughter of his troops, though few of them joined in, for they'd all glimpsed the crimson glare in Falkan's eyes.

A short distance away, in a square below the southern walls of the castle, Guthric sat with an arm around the waist of one of de Blanchefort's cooks. They watched in amazement as the conjurors drew pure white doves from a drape of emerald silk; burning candles from a bowl of water; Saladin's head from a seemingly empty casket. A fine and extravagant show it had been, and with the promise of more to come.

So it annoyed the Saxon to feel Aubery clutch at his shoulder; he sealed his face to hear what the keeper had to say. Then he sent those around him spinning as he heaved himself to his feet, the Constable of Tremellion agonised to action. His progress from the square rocked families from their benches, parents yelling, children crying, the ugly Crusader tramping in search of his master, and oblivious to all else.

Falkan had meanwhile scoured the streets that descended to the port, his aimless fury now sunk to a grim belligerence. They'd be long gone now, the murderers, the rats run squealing to their holes.

261

Time to find one of his own, why not? Rest awhile and think the thing over. Settle the ache in his heart. Dull the pain of his leg. Drink deep enough and he'd wake to find it had all been a nightmare, the safeguard as insolent as ever, his beautiful wife pressing to know his plans for their tower at Yarash.

His sword as though fixed to his hand, the young man made his choice of the waterfront taverns. He barged inside, snarled at those who were slow to move from his path, and stalked to the far end of the room.

Within less than an hour, and as yet undiscovered, he'd swallowed his second flagon of strong red wine and was growling for a third. A bad night's business for the landlord of the inn, his customers clustered at the front of the tavern, unoccupied chairs and benches ringing the armed and dangerous drunkard.

Whispering to one of his friends, the landlord sent him to summon the patrol. Then smoothed the frown from his brow as Baynard slammed the table with the flat of his heavy sword. 'Do I get served, or would you have me come across there?'

'Stay where you are, sire. Keep your comfort. Here's the very best wine in the house.' He hurried toward the table, hoping it wouldn't be long before his friend returned with the soldiers.

With a fine drizzle of rain still misting the city, Guthric located his master. It was an easy enough task, the Saxon directed by those who'd been brushed aside. 'He went down those steps,' they told him. 'He was headed in the direction of the port . . . Fast, but with something of a limp . . . There, along the quay, you see those taverns?'

Checking them in turn, he reached the one that boasted a crudely-painted picture of a tent. Illiterate, the name meant nothing to him – 'The Camp Before Jerusalem'. All that mattered was that Baynard Falkan sat glowering within the hostelry, the flagons of wine his only companions at table.

Guthric shouldered his way between the apprehensive customers, slowing as he reached the scatter of empty benches. Then he stopped and stood silent, a yard from Falkan's lair.

'Oh, look,' Baynard said dully, his accusatory finger unsteady. 'My hideous deserter!'

To humour him, the Saxon ponderously agreed. 'That's right, my lord. So it is.'

'Couldn't get back in time to save Christiane! All too busy fondling the – fondling the generous buttocks of your cook! Tell me if I'm wrong! You just dare tell me –'

'That's right, my lord. So it is.'

'Much as I thought!' Baynard retorted. 'There we have it! Trust a man to be where he says he'll – Trust him to – Trust him at all and –'

'As you say, my lord. As you say.'

Then the Constable of Tremellion shrugged as if in apology, closed fast with the young Crusader, one hand slapped down to pin the blade of the sword, the other bunched in a fist that swung inward, his weight behind it, the force of the blow sending Falkan limp to the floor.

Aware his joke had failed, and that he must now regain the respect of his patrol, the leader came noisily through the door. 'Not the first time he's caused trouble! Knight or nobleman, it's a nice cool cell for this one. So let's have him. Let's be hauling him off.' Brisk and efficient, he advanced along the room.

To see Guthric shake his head and reach for his master's sword. 'You'd best stand away, for he ain't what he appears. By tomorrow you'll have learned the truth of things, but for now you can leave him to me. He's the son-in-law of the Treasurer Vaulmier –'

'I couldn't care less for his titles. He's a menace to the decent folk of this city, *that's* what he is!' A glance at his men and the rapped-out command, 'Haul him off.'

The soldiers moved forward, halting in confusion as the Saxon raised Baynard's sword.

'Now I ain't given much to speechin',' he admitted, 'so all I'll say is this. Lord Falkan has reason enough to be lowered by drink. But he's not what you claim, a menace to innocent people. An' nor is he to be locked in some stinking dungeon. At least, not before you've taken him from my charge. Which won't be easy, for I'd act just as ugly as I look. Tell the truth – I'd act worse.'

The soldiers regarded their leader. Watched as he made his second judgement of the night. Then sighed with soundless relief as he turned toward the counter, dismissing the problem with a gesture of disgust. 'Get him out of here, you oaf, and we'll let this stupidity pass. We've better things to do than splash through a drunkard's vomit.'

The men stood close together, Guthric now with Falkan slung across his shoulder, the patrol leader propped against the oakwood counter, beckoning to the landlord. Had the Saxon lurched or the Tyrian swung around, the tension would have erupted, blood in the air. But the constable kept his balance, the officer his back to the room, the soldiers only too happy to stand aside.

Customers sprang to hold the tavern door open, anxious to let the monster and his burden out and away along the quay.

News of the double assassination reached Conrad, Marquis of Montferrat, Governor of Tyre.

Aware that the murders touched Gilles de Magnat-Vaulmier – and indirectly the Marshal of the Kingdom, Jobert de Blanchefort – Conrad hastened to play his part in the hunt for the killers.

In a blameless display of loyalty to his peers, he sent riders in wild pursuit along the coast, convinced the assassins were, by the very nature of the word, the drug-addicted *Hashashin* of the East. He offered his riders extravagant rewards, dictated a message of condolence to Magnat-Vaulmier, another to Falkan of Yarash, then cursed in private to think it had happened here. The gate guards were clearly lax in their duties. As were those who patrolled the streets. Were they blind, that they couldn't see Moslem Assassins slinking about in the city? Sweet Christ, if they'd got in *this* close to the castle, the next time he himself might sag with arrows!

Furious at what he took to be the ineptitude of his troops, Conrad of Montferrat singled out names from a dozen different lists. As for the riders he'd sent north and south from the city, they found no one, the commanders of the coastal outposts lifting their armoured shoulders in a shrug.

Carried to Jobert's dwelling, Falkan was put to bed. Guthric and Aubery took it in turns to stand watch, each of them hearing the young knight moan and shout in his sleep. Some of it was too intimate ever to be repeated. Some of it too sad to be remembered. But all of it a reminder that death, in whatever fashion, by whatever form, snaps in a single instant the slow-made links of life – sundering the clasp.

Twelve hours beyond the killings in the street, and Gilles de Magnat-Vaulmier rapped wearily at the door of Jobert's house. He was met by Aubery, the keeper bidding him enter, the treasurer signifying no.

'I am here to inform you of events. No more than that. With Montferrat's riders sweeping the coast, I thought to send men of my own to check the port. It seems a vessel arrived from the west, maybe two or three days ago. She sailed again last night, empty except for three passengers who boarded her in haste.'

'Did your men – did they learn their names, my Lord Vaulmier? It might help young Falkan if –'

'No one remembers. Perhaps they were never announced. But the ship was the last to leave before the port was chained in for the night. Left in a hurry, so I'm told. And, yes, there's this about it . . .'

'My Lord Vaulmier?'

'Hmm?'

'You are weary, sire. Won't you come inside and rest?'

'Plenty of time to rest,' the treasurer murmured. 'With my wife and daughter both gone from the dish of the world . . . Plenty of time to rest . . .' Then he bowed his head in silence, grappled with the pain of his loss and drew himself upright, remembering what he'd come across here to say.

'When he's well enough, Tremellion, ask him this. Did he ever encounter the vessel that conveyed those men from Tyre? A galley my men found out was called the *Hawksbill*?'

PART FIVE

The Reckoning

THIRTY-FOUR

In the second week of April 1191, King Philip Augustus of France was greeted on the harbour wall of Tyre by his taller, cadaverous cousin. Towering over the Frenchman, it was nevertheless Conrad who knelt in allegiance, the men then embracing, Philip pale from the effects of a turbulent crossing from Cyprus, Conrad secretly amused to see his far more important kinsman weakened by the voyage.

That same evening, they discussed the state and future of the Kingdom.

His stomach hurting, one eye afflicted by a cataract, the monarch of France seemed a subdued and malleable ally. A powerful leader, but surely no more than warm wax in the artistic fingers of Montferrat.

Or so Conrad imagined, until the moment that Philip enquired, 'Amongst all these Tyrian nobles and their women you've paraded here tonight, my dear cousin, where's Vaulmier and his girl? A man I have much admired for his wit. And with a daughter – to keep it short and simple – I've very much admired. It's a good enough spread you've put on here, cousin, though I'll not feel the evening's complete till I've greeted them. Have them fetched, if you will. They're a couple I've thought on, all the way from the West.'

Searching for bolt-holes, it took Conrad time to admit that Christiane was dead. And even longer to explain the absence of Gilles de Magnat-Vaulmier, who had recently hanged himself from a beam in his house.

That second week of April saw Baynard and Guthric in the neutral state of Armenia, the young Tremellion goading his horse toward the Seljuk Kingdom of Roum, his right hand never far from the sword that swung on his opposite hip. All was clear to him now – the *Hawksbill* and Ranulf – and he only despaired that the nights were dark, his mount in need of sustenance and rest. Would to God it had been otherwise – *a badly managed world* – and Falkan would have scarred the face of Europe with the speed of his planned revenge.

Guthric found it hard to stay level with his master, sanity hooked by madness.

The eighth day of June 1191, and King Richard of England swaggered ashore from the raft that had brought him from his galley to the crowded beach below Acre. Visibly more than a monarch than Philip of France, the red-haired giant splashed through the surf, booming with pleasure at his own late arrival, hailing those who dug their knees in the sand.

'Well, now,' he bellowed, his gestures ever extreme. 'Is that the place we storm tomorrow? Is that the piddling town you'd have me regain?'

His confidence was as fresh, succulent meat to the baulked Crusaders. Forget Guy of Lusignan's hysteria; *here* was a man who'd get things done! A man as tall as any in the Kingdom, his shoulders broad, his voice no less than a clarion call to arms! With the Christian army now straining at the leash, he made the acquaintance of the stocky Jobert de Blanchefort.

'This whole bloody camp's full of unpronounceable names, my lord Marshal! Call them all to my tent and nothing'll happen this side of winter! So here's a list of the fifty I'd most like to see. The ones who brought us money. These Danes, for example. And this German. And him . . . and those . . . and this Englishman, what's his name, Tremellion? *They're* the ones for me, de Blanchefort. They're the ones I'll see preferred.'

The Marshal of the Kingdom of Jerusalem turned away, gazing beyond the tent flap toward the far distant mountains to the north. *You should have kept your place here, Baynard Falkan. With all you've done for the Cause; and the wound you sustained; and the wife you lost – You would surely have been rewarded to the hilt had you awaited the arrival of your king. Though that was never your intention, was it, my young friend. And no more, I hope, would it ever have been mine.*

Then he swung around slowly, returning to serve his monarch, the Crusader force determined that God should sweep Allah aside.

On the day that Richard of England reached the Holy Land, Falkan and Guthric crossed from the Greek shores of Byzantium to the boot-heel of Italy. Riding hard, they travelled north from Brindisi to the Alpine passes, the horsemen once fighting their way through an ambush, another time from the deceitful hospitality of a tavern, a third night cut short as bandits attempted to murder the pair they mistook for easy prey. The assailants were left to regret their error, two of them dead, two more moaning on the blood-stained ground.

It was a lesson to be learned by others in the weeks to come . . .

Meanwhile, the *Hawksbill* made her cheerful traverse of the sea. Convinced that Ranulf's inconvenient brother was dead, the assassins basked in the satisfaction of a job well done. Having scuttled so quickly from the scene, they were uncertain as to the identity of the cloaked Tremellion's companion. In the dark of the night and the drizzle of rain . . . His constable perhaps, or one of de Blanchefort's household, or even his wife? No loss if it was Guthric or a servant, though a pity if, by accident of course, they'd brought down an innocent woman.

The man who called himself Roger Grevel hastened to put the murderers' minds at rest. 'You should hope your hardest that it *was* Falkan's wife who died with him. Lower them both and you've wiped the slate clean. With those troublesome newlyweds gone, there'll be no one to lay claim to Tremellion. If you'll heed my advice, you'll assure Lord Ranulf it *was* his wife, and you saw her clear as day. Leave no doubts in the air, messires. Ranulf is not a man to countenance doubts.'

By the time the vessel turned south to start the skirting of Spain, the archers were convinced the couple had died together in the street. Who else could it have been, after all; him in his cloak and the smaller figure beside him?

Long before the *Hawksbill* hove in sight of Plymouth, the murderers had taken the phrase as their own. Obedient to Ranulf of Tremellion, they'd wiped the slate clean.

Neither those aboard ship, nor those in the saddle were to know that on July the 12th, the city-port of Acre fell to the Frankish army. It was from this time on that people spoke of King Richard as *Coeur-de-Lion* – the Lionheart.

The *Hawksbill* reached England some time before the riders. Roger Grevel – in reality the kinsman of Ranulf's friend, Justin de Vallen – led the assassins north to Launceston, then along the moorland track to Tremellion. They were welcomed by Ranulf, who assured them of glittering recompense for their efforts.

'Though not immediately, you understand. I'm not yet in a position to fish coins from a sack at my feet! But this much I can promise you – lean closer, my friends – there's a girl I have it in mind to marry. Less than a beauty, let me tell you – no more in fact than a bitch who sits on the shelf. But with a father who possesses more coins than he's hairs on his head! And how pathetically eager he is to have the Lord of Tremellion for his son-in-law; a title he can boast of to his neighbours.' He looked around the table, recruiting them with a wink. 'Marry the bitch is one thing, though lay with her is another. Plenty of other girls about. And plenty of hairs to be tugged, I'd say, from that pompous merchant's head!'

De Vallen's kinsman murmured, 'I'm glad to see things run well for you, my Lord Ranulf. But you'll understand if I say, I myself paid out good money to hire the *Hawksbill*. And devoted a year to the snaring of your brother.'

'Oh, and what's this? Sit at my table? Doubt my word? Hold Tremellion's promise up to question?'

'I didn't say –'

'And better for you if you don't! Good Christ, but I've told you what's going on! I'll be wed to the bitch in a matter of weeks. Then coins in the sack! Recompense for us all!' His spatulate finger close to Grevel's face, he asked if the knight would accept what he'd been told – or not?

Brimming with doubt and suspicion, the man who'd squandered a year of his life on behalf of the arrogant bully said yes, no question of it, yes and yes redoubled. What else could he say but yes?

It was part of Falkan's plan to stay unshaved. His lean face weathered by the time he'd spent in the Holy Land; by his four-month crossing of Europe; he was now, without even the benefit of disguise, unrecognisable as the callow young man who'd left England aboard Gregorius Simeon Bigorre's ill-named tub, the *Gossamer*.

Yet disguise was important.

A square yard of unbleached cotton. A circlet of plaited cord.

A flat-topped casque he'd purchased from a Frankish knight in Tyre, the helmet far too large for his head.

A loose long-sleeved garment that draped his body, the material embroidered with Arabic signs of prayer.

A shield he'd bought in Plymouth, then taken to a sign-painter, telling the man the design he wanted brushed on the thin iron plate. Eight or twelve gyrons, it doesn't much matter, so long as the alternate colours show bright. 'The important thing – I would have it seen from a distance.'

Drawing aside from the track that led to Launceston – *and close, I believe to where my father died* – Baynard rehearsed the Saxon in the part he'd have to play. It went badly, the men growling in disagreement, Guthric maintaining the role was beyond him, Baynard saying, 'Just do it, damn you! Now repeat it again, after me . . .'

Their anger exhausted, they slept that night in the forest, their dreams of tomorrow made ragged by the knowledge that their first mistake would most assuredly be their last.

They decided to catch Ranulf early.

In the bright July dawn, the guards on the southern wall and in the gatehouse above the zig-zag ascent to the castle saw an ill-matched pair of riders approach the gully. A knight in a flat-topped barrel helm, his shield bright with its widening segments of colour. Beside him rode a man some of the guards recognised as an Arab, a bearded creature whose head was swathed with a *kaffiyeh*, the covering held in place by its hoop of cord. The knight sat upright in the saddle, the foreigner conforming to the guards' impression of the sly and sinister Moslem, his shoulders hunched, a wary glance cast now and again at the castle.

The riders halted at the foot of the gully.

The sound of his voice made dull and resonant by the all-enclosing helmet, the knight demanded to know if this was the place called Tremellion.

Peering down from the gatehouse, the guard commander allowed that it was – 'Though we've no expectation of callers.'

Speaking slowly, careful of his words, Guthric announced himself as a knight of the county – 'Edwin Cerdas, and a damned sight off my route to favour your master. I've better things to do than trot up here, but this foxy creature approached me in Plymouth. Said he had news for Randolph of Tremellion.'

'It's Ranulf.'

'I'm not much concerned by *what* it is. But the Arab implored me to guide him. He's got some story about the death of your master's brother. Money that now accrues to Ranulf. God knows what else; his accent taxes the ear.'

Good, my old Guthric, you're playing it well. Now get us both inside!

'Wait where you are. Lord Ranulf might still be abed. I'll send to see if he's –'

'Try it, *mon ami*, and I'll be gone. I said it before; I'm far off my route as a favour to Tremellion. You either admit us now, or a curse on your blasted ingratitude!' With an irritable gesture – no bad actor after all, the Saxon pretender – he jerked at his mount, as if to nudge the Arab aside.

The guard commander shouted the length of the gully. 'Admit the callers! Lord Ranulf will be pleased to thank you in person, Sir Edwin! See you fed and on your way!'

Guthric grunted inside his prison of riveted iron. Then turned to Baynard Falkan, the eyes within the helmet gleaming in triumph at the eyes that were shadowed by the unbleached tent of cotton.

Forced to make their way upward through the maze of walls, they climbed toward the house they knew so well. Sure of Guthric's disguise – his head in a pot, who could ever guess he was not who he claimed to be? – Falkan was equally certain of his own. The guards stared hard at him as he passed, a number of them recognised by the Arab, but no one clutched at his embroidered robe or reached to snatch the *kaffiyeh* from his head. He remained stooped over, the way they'd rehearsed it in the forest, and was ready to sigh with relief as they passed through the gatehouse.

Where the Saxon unwittingly jeopardised the scheme.

Accepted and befriended by Sir Geoffrey, the Constable of Tremellion reverted to the role he knew best. He turned beyond the archway of the gatehouse, striding toward the gap in the curtain wall that would lead him through to the inner bailey and the lake and the bridge, then across it to the ramp and the keep that had for so long been his home.

But Edwin Cerdas would not have known these things!

Stumbling forward, the Arab barged violently at the knight. Grabbed at the man for balance, their heads close together as Baynard hissed, 'We are strangers here! We have never before –'

Quicker than he'd expected, the Saxon pushed him away, growled that if the fox would for Christ's sake stop trampling his heels – 'And now where? Or is all of it part of your maze?'

One of the men-at-arms went forward to guide them, the sun still sweeping clouds from the threshold of the day as the simulator from

274

the East followed the so-called knight of the county of Cornwall into the presence of their enemy . . .

'What the hell did you do, Cerdas, drag him along through the night?' His powerful hands rubbing the sleep from his eyes, Ranulf blinked at his visitors, then yelled for a flagon of ale.

He hasn't much changed, Baynard thought. An inch or two more round the belly, perhaps? A pudginess to his features? But still the bullying brother he ever was. And even more the man I intend to kill.

Remembering now that his question had gone unanswered, Ranulf moved closer to the knight. 'You hear what I said? A favour's all very well, but tell me the truth. You didn't haul Islam halfway across the moors as a pleasure to me. It's your intention to profit as well, eh, Cerdas? After all, what are *you* to the Arab? Or to me?'

'Nothing,' the man agreed. 'Not to you.' Then he struggled with the helmet, turning aside to lift it from his shoulders, turning back as he raised it from his head.

Drawn by the lodestone of dawning recognition, Ranulf Falkan leaned forward to stare at the scarred and impassive Saxon.

Then was called to attention by the second visitor, the hunched-over body uncoiling, the *kaffiyeh* discarded, the Moslem gown shrugged aside to settle on the straw.

'You're only half right, my Lord Ranulf. True what you say . . . Guthric is nothing to you. But as for me; oh, yes, my dear brother; as for me I'm all that's left to you. All you'll ever have to deal with from now on.'

Staggering from the shock, the elder Tremellion regained his balance. Howled at the dozen guards who lined the hall. Raised his howl to a shriek as he waved them toward him – then glared in disbelief as but three of them moved to his side.

The others remained as statues around the wall, the only sign of life the glint of the early morning light in their eyes. One side of their faces shadowed by the nasal bar of their helmets, they made their own silent assessment of their future.

'You are wearing a sword,' Baynard said. 'Use it in your defence.'

'Four against two? You really think –?'

'My quarrel is not with these men. If they move to protect you, I shall kill them.'

275

'Enough of these threats, brother! We've things to talk over, you and me. So let's have less of –'

But Baynard was moving now, his own sword slipped from its sheath, the blade glowing dull in the shadows, bright where the sunlight lanced through the windows. 'You are a wicked and murderous blotch on the name of Tremellion! Talk as fast as you will, my Lord Ranulf, for you've damned little time left to speak!'

A master of deception, Ranulf Falkan said their differences could be settled, edged his way past his three loyal guards, told his brother the killing of Christiane was all a mistake, the archers already hanged for it; and listen, he was sure there were prettier girls available here in England –

By which time he'd reached the entranceway to the spiral stairs that ascended to the south-west corner of the keep. And left the sound of his voice to echo around the long, vaulted hall as he fled the incandescence of Baynard's glare.

Guthric addressed the men-at-arms who'd moved to side with their master.

'It ain't too late to change. Get back to your posts against the wall, an' I shan't ever mark the difference. You've done what you supposed was right, an' that's the only choice a soldier can make. But do it quick, else I'll smack you up to the tower to join Lord Ranulf!' Then he looked away, honouring his word, as the trio rejoined their companions.

There was not much further to go, at least not in height or distance, and Falkan knew it. His brother would by now have reached the crenellated tower – the man still armed – and Baynard himself must now climb those spiral steps.

He spoke quietly to the constable, 'If by chance I'm cut down –'

'After Spain? The escape from Losara? The fight we had in the garden of that brothel?'

'Yes. But it could happen.'

'After all the patrols in the East? The brigands we rapped aside on our way back home? You dare tell *me* it could happen, my Lord Falkan, and I'll tell *you* it'd better bloody not!'

Then he raised a hard, leathery hand, brushed it affectionately against the beard of Baynard's disguise and nodded the young Tremellion through to the stairs, shutting the door behind him.

After that – if anyone wished to learn what was happening – they'd have no choice but to cut their way past Guthric.

Thank God the stairs opened to the sky. The lower steps were gloomy, though better lit as he made his cautious way around the spiral. Even so – the chance for Ranulf to attack, his booted feet kicking, sword probing downward, split-logs from the stack that fuelled the beacon, hurled at Baynard's head.

But nothing impeded his ascent.

Mistrusting his brother – *Who on God's earth would ever trust my brother; see what it did for Sir Geoffrey!* – the bearded knight held his weapon above him, its blade seeking the sky.

And then, as he emerged on the battlements, he was greeted – yes, even greeted – by a man who'd rested his sword against a merlon of the wall.

'We've things to talk about, young Baynard. It's why I brought you up here.'

'Why you –'

'Aspects of Tremellion to arrange. Think on it, why don't you? It's not as if –'

'Pick up your sword.'

'Oh really, brother, you tire me. We've surely no need –'

'Pick up your sword. Use it against me, or I'll kill you where you stand.'

'And all this on account of the aged Sir Geoffrey?'

'No, you excrescence, though that alone would be enough. There's Quillon as well.'

'Who? Never heard of him.'

'But above all else the woman I loved and married; the fine and beautiful woman your bowmen murdered, with Quillon dying alongside her, in my place. You were ever both clumsy and a coward, Ranulf Tremellion, the greater tragedy being that your hirelings were as inept as their skulking master.'

'And if they hadn't been? If they'd brought *you* down instead?'

'Oh, my God! *Don't you think I wish they had!*'

Concerned before, but now truly frightened, Ranulf changed his tack. Reaching for his sword he said, 'Just look at you. What *are* you but a skeleton that limps? You'd do well to settle for talk, my hirsute Baynard, or you risk being cut to a chittering pile of bones.' Then he gestured with his weapon, weight and power on his side.

*

Baynard drew back, his own blade tipped from the level of his waist. Remembering all he knew of his elder brother, he responded in toneless measure to the words. 'A skeleton that limps? Well, let's see. Let's both of us be sure what we are, you and I.

'You, who arranged the killing of our father. You, who abandoned your friends in the millhouse of Tresset. You, who sent your companions to trap me in Spain, in Cyprus, in the Holy Land itself. You, who crouch here like a spider, safe at the edge of its web. And you, most of all, who bear the guilt of Christiane's murder. If all the other sullied things you've done could be forgotten, I would anyway kill you for the killing of my wife.

'You doubt that this skeleton can deal with the likes of you? A man who's lost all he loved in the world, thanks to you? Well, I tell you what, my Lord Ranulf. *Why don't we put it to the test . . .*'

Ranulf flung his sword in Baynard's face.

Then he ran to the northern rim of the crenellated tower, squeezed his bulk through one of the embrasures, pushed himself free and dropped to the wall-walk that encircled the ramparts of the castle.

It was a distance of some twelve or fourteen feet; not too far for a man who'd measured his leap. But the bulky Ranulf had sprung in panic, eager to escape from the uppermost level; intent on evading the slash of Baynard's blade.

Even as he fell he turned to look upward, his arms milling in the air. His right leg crooked, his left was rigid, the impact shattering the limb. The weight of his body drove down hard on the splinters, his hands flailing, his mouth but a keening trumpet in his face as he toppled from the well-hewn defences, outward and downward to the rocks at the base of the wall, then outward and downward again in a shapeless sprawl of agony, all the sixty granite feet to the Hexel River . . .

Baynard watched the body float away. It occurred to him to call to the men who stood silent in the bailey, directing them to search for his brother's corpse. But it seemed more important to pick up Ranulf's sword, then hurl it from the tower, the blade spinning over and over as it arched toward the river.

After that – well, after that was the young man's future.